the DEAD ROOM

By

Luke Walker

A HellBound Books LLC
Publication

Cover and art design by HellBound Books Publishing LLC

www.hellboundbookspublishing.com

Printed in the United States of America

Also by Luke Walker

BOOKS:

Die Laughing: January 2015.
Hometown: July 2016.
Dead Sun: June 2018.
The Unredeemed: July 2018.
The Mirror Of The Nameless: August 201
Ascent: 2018.

SELECTED SHORT STORIES:

Serial Killers Tres Tria: Contains 'Bear': September 2013.
Postscripts To Darkness Vol 4: Contains 'Echidna': November 2013.
Wicked Words Quarterly: Contains '6/13': September 2014.
9Tales At the World's End 3: Contains 'Rapture': June 2016.
Creepy Campfire Quarterly #4: Contains 'All The Time In The World': October 2016.
9Chews (9Tales Dark): Contains 'Hungry': October 2016.
9Tales Told in the Dark #20: Contains 'The Sisters In The Green': December 2016.

WeirdBook Magazine: Contains 'The Mouth At The Edge Of The World': November 2018.

Luke Walker

ACKNOWLEDGEMENTS

Once again, a big thank you to James, Xtina, Savannah and everyone at Hellbound for their work on my story. This is book number three, and as always, it's a pleasure to work with people who really get what makes a novel work. As always, thanks to family and friends for their constant support. For reading through various drafts, offering advice and opinions (all of which helped shape The Dead Room into the book it is) and generally being great, I'm indebted to a few good women: Julia Knight, Jennifer Hillier, Laura Mauro, Diane Dooley, Scarlett Parrish, and my wife Rebecca.

This one is for Louise, Dave and Martha.

Luke Walker

the DEAD ROOM

Luke Walker

Chapter One

N icola stabbed a finger on her phone, the impact hard enough to split a nail. "Work, for Christ's sake. *Work*."

For the third time, Scott's voicemail answered her.

On the TV, the shot changed from Mishal Husain in the BBC studio to the scenes in Manchester, then to the shaky images from someone's phone as they panned across the rubble and the wafting threads of smoke. Offscreen, shouts broke out, the words meaningless. Away to the side, a couple held each other, both weeping as blood streamed from jagged cuts on their faces. A non-stop howl of sirens whooped through the smoke, the sound like a terrified child's screams in Nicola's head. She pressed on Scott's name again. The line refused to connect, let alone go to her husband's voicemail.

On the TV screen: **BREAKING NEWS: EXPLOSION IN MANCHESTER CITY CENTRE. HUNDREDS INJURED AND MISSING. EVACUATION UNDERWAY.**

"Julia," Nicola whispered. Her stomach clenched and her saliva became a thick, electric flood. Gagging, she ran to the kitchen and vomited into the sink. Spitting and attempting to breathe normally through the foul taste in her nose and mouth did no good.

"Julia," she croaked and spat again.

Words from the TV flowed from the living room. She caught one.

Bomb.

Nicola dashed back to the TV, socks skidding over the flooring. On the screen, Mishal checked her papers before gazing at the camera. Her words made no sense. They were simply a noise put over the images of the sobbing, people stumbling across rubble, of the overturned cars, of the blown-out windows in shop fronts, of the blood stains on the ground and the smoke staining everything an ugly black.

The paperwork Nicola had been going through until a few minutes before fell beside her discarded laptop as she collapsed to the sofa. Phone gripped tightly between both hands, she struggled to think through the panic and fear.

Her mobile rang.

Scott.

Through Nicola's terror, something hard and implacable in her head took over. Mouth bone dry, she answered the phone. "Scott? Can you hear me? Are you there?"

"Nicola?"

The line cut out for a moment, then cleared and he was there in her ear, in her mouth, in the fearful burning deep in her chest.

"Nicola? I'm here. We're here. Jesus Christ."

"Oh, my God, Scott. Julia? Is she—"

"She's fine. She's fine."

Tears exploded. Nicola bent double. She pressed the phone against her ear and had to fight for each boiling breath. Pain all over, pain in her head from the phone pressing into her ear, pain in her other hand as she dug her nails into her palm.

"Nicola? Are you there?"

The rock in Nicola's head grew, blocking the sting burning in her chest. "I'm here. I'm here. Are you okay? Please tell me you're okay."

"We're fine. We're all right. Calm down, okay? We're all fine. We're still with Nigel and Cate. We were going to drive into Manchester earlier but there was something wrong with the car. It wouldn't start." He broke off. The blustery breath of his sigh ran down the line. "Jesus, Nicola. This is unbelievable. They're saying more than five hundred dead. They're saying—"

The signal dropped again and Scott's voice fell in and out.

". . .Nicola?"

"Scott? Can you hear me?"

The line went dead.

"Shit." Nicola smacked the phone against her thigh and saw the images on the TV.

York. The city centre.

"Jesus Christ."

The historic city had become a bombed-out wreck. The camera, again amateur mobile phone footage, tracked over buildings and shops with missing windows and roofs, over blasted out chunks of brickwork, over the car wedged into the side of an overturned bus and the massive pieces of broken glass surrounding both vehicles.

Mishal spoke again, telling the viewers the facts were thin on the ground, that reports suggested the explosion was down to a bomb detonating a few minutes before which put it twenty minutes after the one in Manchester.

Gripping her phone with all of her strength, Nicola tried to speak, tried to find any words she could give herself.

Mishal went on. She told Nicola there could be hundreds of deaths in York and Manchester with countless injured. She told Nicola the authorities were evacuating the centre of the city and the surrounding areas. She told Nicola other cities across the country were on high alert.

Nicola managed a weak moan as the insanity of the scenes hit her. She could have been watching a report on Syria, not York on a Saturday afternoon. This wasn't York: the old buildings with jagged mounds of exposed metal and masonry poking upwards or pavements buried under tons of brick or wickedly sharp daggers of window glass scattered across the roads. York was people and cars and jobs and old streets and history. Christmas shoppers drenched in blood or staggering out of buildings and crying at each other belonged in images of foreign countries, not in the middle of York, for God's sake.

Julia.

The whisper rose from a deep place far below. It contained one basic command: to ensure her daughter was safe.

Nicola tried Scott's number again. No connection. Breathing fast, she stood and paced around the living room. On the TV, Mishal went through what little facts she had: massive explosions in Manchester and York about twenty minutes apart had killed an unknown number of people out for their Christmas shopping; hundreds of injured filled local hospitals while the police and the authorities were working to rescue those trapped under rubble, and the PM had boarded a plane back from Switzerland and—

The line connected. It rang once and Scott was right beside her.

"Nicola?"

"Jesus, the line went and I couldn't get through again."

"I know. All of our phones have got the same problem. Everyone's calling everyone else. The landline does nothing. Are you all right?"

"I'm fine. Are you all together?"

"Yeah. Keep thinking I should put the kettle on. Make us all a nice cup of tea. We're English and that's what we do, isn't it?" He laughed much too loudly.

Nicola did the same and her gusting laugh made her shake. She sat. Now that she had him back again, the rock inside sealing away panic seemed to be shrinking. Nicola focused on her breathing for few seconds.

"It's York, as well," Scott said. "Just seen it. Unbelievable."

"Me, too. It's bombs, isn't it? Terrorists?"

"I think so. I—" He broke off. "Someone wants to say hello, Nicola. Hold on. Jules is coming."

Nicola smiled and wiped at her tears, barely aware she'd been crying. On the TV, a burst of rumbling noise blew out of the speakers. There was a second, no longer, of Mishal turning to her side, of what could have been shock on her face.

Then static filled the screen.

Then the line died in Nicola's ear.

Chapter Two

Cate studied the thin grass of the slope, the ground growing darker as dusk closed in. Although the incline up to the bridge wasn't particularly steep, it still appeared huge.

"You can do this," she whispered and licked her dry lips.

Each step sent jagged slivers of pain running through her shins and calves. Clenching her jaw, Cate staggered up the slope to the bridge, leaned on the railings for a moment and took a few breaths.

"Nice."

The bridge crossed a river. All around, greenery rustled in the breeze and bare tree branches shook There was only a slight wind and she had to be grateful for that. The day had been cold enough without a wind blowing at her off the water.

"Day?"

Cate sniggered despite barely having the energy to do so. Sod *day*. Weeks had passed since she'd been anything close to warm. For some reason, the brighter days seemed even frostier than the mornings and short afternoons of low clouds and the fierce wind, not to mention the steady threat of a blizzard.

Cate tightened the straps of her backpack and checked behind again. Nothing there but the fields she'd crossed and the train tracks off in the distance. Night appeared to have already fallen out that way. The image of encroaching darkness chasing her while she stood on the bridge chilled the skin below her dirty clothes. Shaking it off, she crossed the bridge, followed a slope down to a cycleway and studied the pathway. Thorny branches hung over it and many of the bushes already grew out of control. Anything further than fifty feet away was lost in darkness. Shadows oozed down there and while she had no reason to think anyone lurked in the gloom, she still didn't want to walk in that direction.

Not for the first time, Cate wished for the map she'd been carrying until—

"God knows. I'm too tired for this."

There was a town ahead. She knew that much. Back on the train tracks, she'd seen the top of a cathedral in the distance and the roofs of other buildings surrounding it, all framed by the bloody red of a bleak sunset. The lack of food in her bag and her one remaining bottle of water had decided her path in seconds: get into the city, find some shelter and food, get out again. Exactly as she'd been doing since everything went to hell.

The grass to her side rose in a steep bank to trees. She took a second look behind to the river and the fields, telling herself there had to be another path close if not a road. Most of the fields and green were behind; the city lay ahead.

She smiled, aware it felt more like a grimace. A big risk. If she was wrong and the bank led to trees and nothing but trees, night would be on her by the time she got back down here to head along the cycleway.

"Yeah. So what?"

Moving with a determination she didn't come close to feeling, Cate crossed the grass to the bank and eyed it. Even without moving, she could imagine her leg muscles protesting.

"Up here, to the road and to a house. A real, solid house."

As silently as she could, Cate lurched upwards, legs and feet hellishly sore. One foot in front of the other. That's what it was all about. That's what kept her going. Kept her moving. Kept her running.

She wiped sweat out of her eyes and coughed. It burned in her throat and chest as it had been doing for the last day.

So what?

She made it to the top, fell against a tree and inhaled, tasting the winter and the smells of the trees. Through the brown of the trunks, a white line shone.

A road.

A road meant houses. And houses meant shelter.

Pushing twiggy branches aside, Cate strode through the little woodland, ignoring the pain in her legs and the urge to look back. She reached the middle of the trees and a black, smoke-like shape darted by her side to vanish from sight straight ahead.

She froze.

No. Not here.

A smell hit her nostrils. Something warm and cleansing. Something she knew.

Bath time.

Cate spoke aloud and her voice trembled in the gloom. "No."

The smell faded, leaving only the stink of her sweat.

Her feet. She had to move them. Now. Or she'd stay where she was as proper night fell.

Cold caressed her back and she shook at such a horrible thought. The road. She had to focus on that.

Cate walked on, treading carefully to avoid breaking any twigs, and reached the end of the woodland. Ahead, the road revealed itself to be a parkway. It headed in both directions, becoming little more than a dark slash further on before disappearing around a curve. There were no houses in sight. Not yet, anyway.

Cheered by the sight of the parkway, Cate left the trees and followed it. Within a few paces, her mind slipped into a neutral state. As much as she knew she should focus on her surroundings and route, doing so was too much of an effort. Keeping in a straight line was about as far as she could stretch.

Minutes passed. The shadows grew. And the first she knew of the figure stumbling over the field on the other side of the parkway was when they shouted in the dark.

Adrenaline dumped through her. Cate raised a hand, fingers tight against the handle of her knife. The figure drew closer, a shuffling shape heading to the opposite side of the road.

Cate relaxed although barely a fraction. They were drunk. She could outrun them if need be.

"Hey. . . you. . .hey. . ."

It was a kid. Some pissed up teenager probably not old enough to buy alcohol a month ago and now here they were, smashed out of their head.

Cate strode on, keeping the figure in sight for as long as she could. They called after her again but made no sign of following. She reached a curve and swore under her breath.

She'd walked right into a pile up. Vehicle upon vehicle had smashed together, forming a shadowy mound of broken glass and crumpled metal.

Behind, the drunk kid bawled something unintelligible.

"Shit," Cate said again. Forward or back? Neither was ideal. While she knew she could get away from the boy without much effort, she'd still be walking back in the dark; she'd still be no closer to the town, whatever it was called.

"Forward, then."

She remained as close to the hard shoulder as possible and kept her focus straight ahead. There was no need to see the bodies littering the road and cars. Imagining them was easy enough.

Blackened throats. Blood and snot coating their clothes. Burst buboes growing out of their skin. She'd seen enough since early December. No need to see it now.

Moonlight shone; the other end of the smash was directly ahead. All she had to do was keep in a straight line, keep her eyes off all the broken metal, keep her nose away from the stink of the bodies and keep walking.

The spinning movement at her side and the kid's scream seemed to happen at exactly the same time.

"Hey, what the fuck—" the boy yelled.

Cate whirled around, staring back the way she'd walked.

The boy screamed once more before falling silent.

Unbidden, the previous few seconds played over in her head.

A shifting by her side. Something terribly fast blurring as it raced back. The kid crying out a second later.

And she stood beside dozens of bodies in the dark while a freshly dead body lay somewhere behind, the blood doubtless already cooling around it in the January chill.

No. Cate tried to breathe slowly and failed. Her thoughts could have belonged to someone else. *Not here. Not now.*

A section of the air skittered away as if a gust of wind had pushed it.

Despite her aching legs, Cate found the strength to run.

Chapter Three

Nicola shifted the weight of the carrier bag in one hand and knocked on the door with the other. Three quick raps and she reached to her jeans pocket and her phone. She pulled it free, desperately hoping.

Nothing. Full battery. No signal.

She swore as quietly as she could although there was no surprise. It'd be a miracle if she had a signal now for no good reason. Thirty-six hours of nothing. Why the hell would it start working now?

Because I have to talk to them.

Her desperation changed nothing. Nor did the ever-present threat of frustrated tears.

A shadow approached the door on the other side, bobbing through the brightly lit hall. Nicola took a look back across the road. She'd left most of her lights on and made sure all the curtains were shut. While Stamford still seemed quiet, there was no need to make her house appear empty.

The door opened, held in place by a chain.

Nicola stepped forward so her face could be seen. "Jean? It's Nicola."

"Hello, my dear." Jean undid the chain and opened the door fully. "How are you?"

"Okay," Nicola said, amazed how easily the lie came to her lips. *Okay? Fucking okay?* "I've got your bread and milk."

"Thank you so much. Thank you." Jean, seemingly even smaller and frailer than she'd been when Nicola last saw her a few hours before, stood aside and gestured for Nicola to enter. Using all of her willpower, Nicola stopped herself from looking back at her house. She'd considered keeping a window open as if she'd be able to hear the landline ringing from across the road.

As if the phone *would* ring.

"I can't stay long," she said and entered Jean's bungalow.

"Of course. I understand. Any news?"

Jean gazed at Nicola and some of the older woman's confusion and fear broke through Nicola's own fears. Even though she couldn't get hold of her family, she at least *had* a family. Jean had nobody.

Nicola forced a smile. "Nothing yet. I'm sure Scott will call as soon as he can. Once the phones are working again."

"Of course. Come through, won't you?"

Jean led her to the little kitchen and Nicola held her queasy laugh inside. As with her house, almost all of the lights were on. Maybe there was something in the thinking of keeping the dark and the night outside.

She placed the bag on the table. Jean took two cups from a cupboard.

"Cup of tea, my love?"

"No, thank you. I can't stay."

From out of nowhere, tears fell. She gripped the side of the table, weeping, shaking, furious.

Jean took hold of her and eased her down to a chair, making comforting noises, holding her. The storm of tears died after a moment. Nicola wiped her nose and eyes.

"Sorry," she muttered.

"Not at all."

Jean fished in the sleeve of her cardigan and pulled a tissue free. Nicola took it, wiped at her face and took a few breaths.

"Sorry," she said again. "I keep doing that. It's the not knowing. Feeling like I can't do anything. Can't get through on the phone. No idea if my texts or emails are getting through." She looked at Jean. "And the anger. If we'd been five seconds quicker on the phone, I could have spoken to Julia. Just to tell her. . ."

"I know." Jean returned to the kettle. She flicked it on and dropped tea bags in the two cups. "I daresay there a lot of people in your position. Trying to get hold of family and friends."

She splashed milk into the cups. Nicola pictured herself standing, telling Jean she had to go, then running back to her house. Instead, she remained sitting. Other than her immediate neighbours and Jean, she hadn't been able to speak to anyone in over twenty-four hours. Human company was needed. Probably more than ever now.

"I've had the news on most of the day." Jean passed her a cup and another tissue from her cardigan. "Shocking. Absolutely shocking."

Queasy giggles threatened again. Nicola sipped her too hot tea to stop herself from laughing. Here she was in the middle of a nationwide nightmare and Jean sounded as if she belonged in some cosy, middle-class sitcom.

"The Prime Minister said earlier she hopes the roads are open again by tomorrow morning but she can't promise anything," Jean said, crossing to the living room door. Nicola took her tea and followed. "I must say, I never cared for that woman, but she seems to be doing a good job, considering."

Nicola tuned Jean out at the sight of the news on the TV. BBC Wales. She'd been watching the same broadcast for most of the day. Not enough left of the Beeb in London to broadcast from there.

For several moments, they watched without speaking. There was little change from the news Nicola had seen an hour before: Manchester, York, Edinburgh, Cambridge, London and Birmingham all bombed within minutes of each other; thousands dead in each city and thousands more injured. No rail travel. All roads closed to civilian traffic. Phone and internet down or jammed all over the place. People being told to stay in their homes and keep calm.

She could have been watching the news at any point since the previous morning.

The newsreader interviewed a couple of people; they talked about who could be responsible, about the assistance coming from Europe, America, Canada and further across the world, about the offers of medical supplies, of food and water. They talked about the government and the diplomats and Nicola knew she wasn't really listening. Instead, she tapped a light finger on her mobile as if that would give her a signal and access to her family.

She came back to herself and Jean as the news switched to a shot as close as the reporters could get to the mess of Trafalgar Square. The camera tracked over the rubble and glass, floodlights turning all of it into a ghostly white. Rescue workers shifted broken bricks aside; sniffer dogs led their handlers to possible pockets of air. A steady stream of hollering flowed from all sides as the reporter tried to make new facts out of the little news he had. All Nicola could focus on was his words—*"now close to two thousand confirmed dead from the London bomb—"*and she was up on her feet, shoving her phone deep into the pocket of her jacket.

"I have to go, Jean. I'm sorry. I have to get home."

"Of course. I'll see you out."

Jean eased herself off the sofa; frustration and the need to move turned Nicola's stomach into a tight ball. She dug her nails into her palms and waited for Jean to walk her to the front door and fumble with the lock and handle.

"You'll come over tomorrow?" Jean asked.

Nicola's understanding of the woman's fear returned. They were all going through this, but not everyone had to go through it alone.

"Of course. I'll be round about eleven."

Jean unlocked the door. Nicola stepped out to the small garden. Immediately, she hugged herself.

"Get inside," she told Jean. "Keep warm."

"I will. Take care crossing the road."

Jean shut her door. The hallway light remained on.

Nicola crossed to the pavement, hands deep in her pockets, gripping her silent phone. At the road, she checked for traffic although there were no cars in the dark. On the opposite pavement, she moved at not quite a jog towards her house, and a front door, five houses down from hers, flew open. A figure staggered out, lunged a few steps and dropped. As they smashed into the ground, three people followed, screaming. In the moonlight, one of them saw Nicola.

"Help. Jesus, help us."

From some ugly, primitive corner of her mind, a wish spoke to Nicola, whispering how she should have stayed with Jean or run to her front door.

"What is it?" Nicola shouted.

"John. He's. . ."

The woman's voice collapsed into coughing sobs. Seemingly without any instruction, Nicola's feet took her towards the figures. The woman managed to cry for help before her voice again fell apart into hacking, struggling breaths.

Nicola jogged towards them and realised the woman wasn't the only person fighting for air.

The man who'd fallen to the freezing ground was also coughing.

Chapter Four

Enough moonlight lit her silent surroundings for Cate to read the name of the road without moving too close to its curve. Middleton Gardens. She studied what little was visible beyond the turning, then made up her mind without any real conscious thought.

"Middleton Gardens it is."

Cate walked, eyes on the houses as she searched for any signs of life. All of the buildings were dark and appeared lifeless. She couldn't take any chances, though. More than possible for survivors to be hiding inside.

The road turned right in a bend. More houses lined both of its sides with what looked like a pathway cutting between two of them not far ahead. Cate walked to the path, already telling herself to stay on the road. The gap between the houses was no more than ten feet. Beyond it, dozens of bungalows faced a wide field. Cate strode to the end of the gap between the houses and made out a large, squat building beyond the grass.

A light passed by one of the windows.

Cate hissed and backed up fast.

A school. The building was a school. And someone was inside it.

She crouched beside one of the houses and watched the school's windows, watching for the light to reappear. After a few minutes, it shone in another window. Someone was wandering through the building. Her exposed flesh stung. Ignoring it as much as she could, Cate watched. Nothing moved or shone beyond the grass. For a moment, she considered the possibility she'd imagined the light, but that idea held no weight. She'd seen it. And that meant this town wasn't as empty as it appeared.

She headed back to the road and pavement to walk on. Her thoughts dropped away as they had on the parkway. Before the kid behind her. Before the scream.

Cate shook and kept her eyes straight ahead. She wouldn't look at the shadows living in the front gardens of these nice, middle-class houses. Wouldn't think about what other things might be inside those shadows.

Middleton Gardens reached another turning a few minutes later. Without much debate, she joined the next road, walked alongside a high wall of hedges and drew level with a second school. It covered much more ground than the first and was clearly a secondary school. What was left of it.

Fire had destroyed the majority of the main building. Several of the smaller buildings looked as if an explosion had demolished much of them. Roofs had caved in; windows were blown out, and scattered chunks of rubble lay all over the car park.

"Nice place," Cate whispered.

She followed the road around to the front of the school, walked on and reached a small shopping precinct. Although the dark made it hard to be sure, she thought she could make out a newsagents, a mini supermarket and a butchers in the row. Above, maisonettes were squat squares with all their windows sealed.

Trying to keep her breathing regular and her heartrate slow, Cate crossed to the newsagents and peered inside. Mess coated the floor. Magazines, newspapers and stock had been thrown to all sides but the building appeared structurally sound at least.

She pressed on the door, expecting it to be locked. It swung open, running over newspapers piled against the door and windows. At the abrupt whispering of door sliding over papers, Cate froze.

You need to get inside.

With as much care as she could, Cate eased the door open and slipped inside. The moonlight only made it a few inches inside. She fumbled with her bag and withdrew her small torch. Shielding the light, she shone it on the floor and walls. The place was a complete mess. It would do, though. And wonder of wonders, there were still chocolate bars and bags of crisps on the shelves. Ravenous, Cate grabbed as much as she could carry and ducked behind the counter. Her foot slipped on something soft and her light found it.

A sleeping bag.

At once, she listened for the slightest sound. A breath. A footstep. *Anything* that suggested she wasn't alone.

Long seconds passed before she decided the building was abandoned. Whoever had slept here in the last few weeks was gone. She had shelter for the night.

Cate pulled herself into the bag, shivering. Her stomach demanded food. Still fighting the cold, she ate a bag of crisps in seconds, then broke off a chunk of Mars

Bar. The mix of the sweet and savoury filled her mouth, coated her tongue and teeth. Grinning, she relished the tastes and bit off another chunk of chocolate.

Whispering slid over the floor from the front door.

Cate whipped her head around and stared into the dark.

The door had opened.

She found the knife and her mind shrieked words over and over.

No, you're not here.

A light step. Another.

Cate squeezed her eyes shut, still shrieking the negation inside.

Another step.

She lived in darkness. She lived in warmth beyond anything and she would be safe there.

Breath blew against her face. A whisper. A word.

And still her mind bellowed that she was alone.

Outside, a sound coughed into life. A sound Cate hadn't heard in two weeks.

A car. Another one. Then another.

People were coming.

Something pulled away. She felt it go like a wind blowing off her clothes and skin. And outside, the speeding cars skidded to a stop. In the pitch black, Cate listened to the noise of the car stereos, of the ugly laughter, of the men as they shouted at each other, and the hollow smash of all the breaking glass.

Looters. She was stuck a matter of feet away from dozens of men looting the suburbs. It could only be minutes before they found her, hiding behind the counter.

Cate held her knife, grateful that if nothing else, the arrival of the looters had scared away the whispering breath on her face.

Chapter Five

Groaning, Nicola pushed the bookcase along the carpet towards the front door. Sweat blinded her; she blinked it away, swearing. From outside, the chaos continued. Nicola muttered to herself in an attempt to block out the sounds. She'd taken a quick look through the curtains in the living room a moment before and seen dozens of people running along the road. Some held cricket bats or narrow planks of wood as makeshift weapons. Others carried shopping bags bulging with cans and bottles of water. And Nicola had forced herself to pretend that some people weren't chasing those with the bags.

She shoved the bookcase against the door, checked the locks and ran back to the living room. She'd left the TV on; the image of the newsreader kept cutting out and the sound went with it. Even so, Nicola could make out enough to know the reports were the same. Riots in East London last night. A lot of the areas unaffected by the bombing were going up in flames; the military were on the streets and countless people had been arrested. The bigger worry, unspoken by those in authority but brought up by the people in the studio, was the potential for the sickness to spread since so many were grouping together.

The Manc. That's what they were calling it already. Eight days after the explosions; eight days after it turned out the explosions all over the country were decoys for the real threat. The Manc. A new sort of flu. Or maybe just an old one.

Moving fast, Nicola shoved the sofa below the window and piled as much as she could on top of it to block the lower half of the glass. She knew the barrier didn't present much of a defence to anyone, but she had to do something.

"Things are bad."

Bad. No. That wasn't it. Things had gone mad. Every end of the world film, every potential disaster was here in her living room while she moved her furniture around and the voices from the TV faded in and out. Stay calm, they said. Stay indoors, they said. Avoid anyone showing any signs of the flu, they said. Things would improve soon. All everyone had to do was act sensibly and stay calm.

Tell that to the people outside.

The non-stop noise of their fleeing and panic made it through her closed windows and curtains and piled furniture. As much as she'd hoped it would stop, the noise had grown in the last half an hour. Given time and given enough fear, she'd be in the middle of a situation as bad it was in London.

"Riots in Stamford. Of course."

Her weak sarcasm helped nothing. She knew it was a shield.

In Nicola's pocket, her mobile vibrated and beeped.

Shrieking, Nicola yanked the phone free, dropped it and threw herself to the carpet to scoop it up. The text on the screen made her want to shriek her joy. Instead, she managed a single breath before tears blurred her vision.

Nicola i love u. Cant get thru on the phone. Nothings working. Pray you're ok. We are fine. All together. Roads shut. Nothing moving anywhere. Will keep trying to call u. J told me to tell u she loves u and sends a big hug. I love u. Will keep trying to get thru. Love u. S.

Nicola stabbed at her phone, scrolling through the text's details. Scott had sent it on the eighth. Tuesday night. Almost a week ago.

"Jesus Christ, let this work."

Nicola hit his picture and jammed her phone to her ear. In seconds, the voice spoke to her just as it had dozens, maybe hundreds of times since the previous Saturday.

"I'm sorry. The mobile number you are trying to call is unavailable. Please try later."

Nicola cut the voice off and dropped her mobile to the sofa. She stared at it as if she could force it to connect to Scott. From outside, someone bawled a woman's name; the woman screamed back, her voice full of fear and tears.

Nicola's heart felt as if it had exploded. *"Fuck."* She howled it again and again, doing so until her throat hurt and she ran out of breath. Weeping, she collapsed beside her phone and held herself.

Thuds hit her front door, a huge flurry of knocks.

Nicola rose and crept to the doorway. She peered around the corner into the hall and made out the shape on the other side of the door. Someone small. The panels of frosted glass gave nothing more away.

"Nicola? Are you home?"

A woman, the words weak and tired, almost lost behind the clamour out on the street.

"Nicola? It's Jean. Are you home?"

The letterbox rattled. Nicola slid backwards and pressed herself against the living room wall. In the hall, Jean's voice was clearer. Despite the bookcase against the door, Jean had managed to open the letterbox enough to let in the noise of the rampaging people. Nicola shook.

"Nicola? Please open the door. I need help. I'm not well, you see. Feel a bit under the weather."

Oh, Jesus Christ. She's got it. She's got the Manc.

Nicola put her forearm over her mouth as if the thought would emerge as a shout.

"Nicola?"

Jean was clearly weakening. Nicola closed her eyes, praying for the old woman to leave, to go back to her bungalow.

"Nicola?" Jean said, voice struggling with the one word.

The letterbox snapped back into place. She'd given up.

You can't let her go. You have to help her.

An emotionless voice spoke from a place inside Nicola had never been to.

You help her and you'll get it, too. You have to help yourself.

Horrified, Nicola ran to the front door, grabbed one end of the bookcase and tried to shift it. It moved less than an inch before her strength failed. Crying again, Nicola gripped the bookcase and pushed. Her breath fell out in a tremendous volley of coughing.

Nicola backed up, unable to take her eyes off the bookcase.

Just dust. Just dust in my throat.

Bending double and holding on to the doorframe for support, Nicola coughed hard enough for black spots to swim in front of her eyes.

Outside, the awful noise of chaos and fright and the pound of feet went on and on.

Chapter Six

Cate crouched between the trees lining the perimeter the field. Clouds blocked the moon, leaving her surroundings in almost complete darkness. Good on one hand in that she couldn't be seen. Bad on the other. She couldn't see *them.*

I would give anything for a decent night's sleep.

She grinned bitterly. Didn't look there was much chance of that happening here. Even if she'd stayed in the newsagents, the men outside were much too close to her. She'd run out the back, found a twisting side road, which fed back to the main road she'd come off earlier. Across that, along a cycleway and out to playing fields.

Straight towards the dark figures of two men.

She crept forward and reached a wide trail cut into the grass. The harsh air stabbed at her gloveless hands and slipped down the spaces in her scarf where it had come loose. She tightened it, shuffled forward and gazed at the line of the black river. The opposite bank was a wall of nothing. If the men she'd seen minutes before had gone across to the other side, they had no chance of seeing her just like she was unable to see them.

No comfort in the thought. Just a deep exhaustion and a steady throb of fear.

Cate rose into a crouch and ran alongside the river without making a sound. Shapes loomed up from the darkness ahead and terror filled her mouth for a moment before she snapped her teeth together.

Trees. Just trees.

She crept between them and cracked a twig. Wincing, she kept moving.

Thudding steps emerged from the trail behind her.

Cate shot forward, reaching for the night as she ran blindly. Skinny branches and twigs scratched at her, sending stinging lines across her fingers. Voices joined the thudding steps. Two men. Behind her.

Cate grabbed hold of a thick trunk, ducked and pressed herself against the old bark. Its rich smell filled her nose and the night sank talons into her flesh.

"I saw her. I'm telling you," one of the men said.

Cate strained to hear the other's reply but only caught a mutter that suggested the man didn't believe the first.

Go away. Leave me alone. Just fucking leave me alone. I've had enough. Just go away.

They crunched over dead leaves and twigs, the sounds too hard to place. They could be coming closer or walking around her. Either way, she'd make noise if she took a single step.

Cate eased the switchblade out of her jeans pocket. She rested a thumb over the release button and took slow breaths through her nose.

More words floated out of the dark—*another one. . . we need. . .tired. . . come on*—followed by heavy steps cracking twigs somewhere off to her left. Cate stared into the pitch black. Cooling sweat ran over her upper lip. She licked it away and raised the knife. Her fear, non-stop for the last days and weeks, had been replaced by a blankness. Rationally, she knew she couldn't kill both men before they'd be all over her but she could injure or kill one of them.

Just one. That's all I want.

Deeper into the trees, branches cracked. Swearing followed it. Cate squeezed her mouth shut and tried to make as little noise as possible.

"Stupid bastard. What the hell was that?"

"Christ knows. Can't see a thing. I think it was a branch."

They were a matter of feet away, two monsters in the night woods. Cate kept her eyes open. If they saw her, she wanted to see them. Wanted to watch as she swung her knife at them.

Again, the plea inside spoke, desperate to be left alone, to find somewhere to rest and be warm and be with others.

Cate opened her mouth, readying a bestial cry she could bellow at the two men when they saw her, readying herself to stab and kill and—

"Fuck this," the second man said. "I'm going."

A few of his steps shuffled through the fallen leaves. The first man sighed.

"Yeah. Okay. Let's go," he said.

More steps pushed through the leaves and twigs. Cate made no move to relax as she listened to the few words she caught of their conversation. . .*woman*. . .*cold*. . .*the house*. . .

After several seconds, the men sounded as if they were out of the trees and back to the trail of grass between river and woods. Cate rose, keeping her back off the trunk. The last of the men's voices reached her. One word.

Hospital.

Cate frowned.

Hospital. They'd definitely said something about a hospital. Their base, maybe? No. One of them mentioned a house. The hospital was something else.

Cate headed back in the direction she hoped she'd come. After twenty minutes, she found a gap between trees that opened to grass. She crept out of the woods and gazed at what she could in all directions. The trail and the river were somewhere off in the dark. The field she'd run across to get away from the two men was in front, and what were probably houses formed a silent line away to her right.

Hospital.

Something inside her welcomed the word. Something wanted more of the comfort and hope it implied. As much as Cate warned herself to calm down, it did no good. A hospital meant safety and maybe food. It definitely meant people. Here, in this town she didn't know, she might have a chance of some shelter.

Still gripping her switchblade, Cate jogged over the unkempt grass towards the dark houses.

Chapter Seven

The stink pushed through Nicola's confusion, shoving her up into consciousness even though the pain filling her body tried to keep her under.

Struggling, Nicola cracked an eye open to see gloomy light spreading on all sides. Her other eye was gummed shut. As much as she tried to lift a hand to wipe at it, her arm and fingers wouldn't obey.

The smell registered fully and she let out a weak groan of disgust. Nicola pushed herself up, stopping when her head hit the end of the bed. Even the little movement was exhausting. She could have dragged herself a hundred feet, not the length of her pillow.

Through her confusion, panic broke in. She fought it off, took a breath and groaned again. Steeling herself, Nicola glanced at the little she could make out of her bed and the room.

She'd kicked her covers off at some point. Her legs.

"Christ," she whispered and her throat cracked. She swallowed and did her best to ignore how dry her mouth and throat were.

She'd been lying in her own waste for days.

Nicola gripped the bedframe and eased her dirty legs to the carpet. The effort it would take to stand was unthinkable. But so was laying here in this stink and gloom.

Her mind shrieked for water, driving out almost all other thought. Using the wardrobe beside the bed as support, Nicola stood, leaned against it and took a few steps. She collapsed, hit her arm on the bed and sprawled on the carpet.

Below the almost overpowering need for water, Scott spoke to her. *You have to move, babe. You have to get out of here. Crawl. Move.*

"Scott?"

He wasn't there. Hadn't been there for days. Neither had Julia.

Nicola barked out a noise that wanted to be weeping. She couldn't let it. Not here in this horrible room.

She slid along the carpet to the door, pushed herself out to the hallway and crawled to the bathroom. The smell there was marginally better than her bedroom or her skin. She ignored the stench, dragged herself to the bath and twisted the hot tap. A few drops of water fell, then stopped. Nicola stared at the tap, unsure what had happened. Realisation was a murmur inside.

The water had been off for days.

"Shit," she whispered, and another murmur spoke to her.

What day was it? She could have been unconscious for twenty-four hours, forty-eight, or more. There was no way of knowing.

She left the bathroom and made her way back to the top of the stairs. The big t-shirt she wore, one of Scott's, stuck to her sweat-soaked body. Wincing,

Nicola pulled it over her head and threw it behind herself. At once, the chill of the house registered on her naked flesh. She needed warmth. She needed water. She needed to be clean.

Downstairs. Everything was downstairs.

Nicola remained on her bottom, knowing there was no point in attempting to stand. She'd be a broken mess at the bottom of the stairs if she tried it. Instead, she held the rail and slid down step by step.

After long, sore moments, she reached the ground floor, took a few breaths and made it upright by leaning against the wall.

"Scott?"

There was no point in saying his name. He was over a hundred miles away. So was Julia.

Nicola took faltering steps into the living room, drew level with the mirror over the fireplace and couldn't stop herself from looking.

As much as she wanted to say something, to give some flesh to her shock, all she managed was a weak sigh.

Dirt encrusted her legs; her hair was a sweaty mess of tangles; dark circles, thankfully fading, jutted under her armpits, and her ribs were defined lines against her too pale skin.

"Sexy bitch," she whispered and staggered to the kitchen. Sunlight filled the rear garden although it brought no warmth. A rich stink emerged from the fridge. Holding her breath, Nicola opened the door, grabbed a bottle of tepid water from the shelf and drank half of it in a single go. Her throat demanded more; her stomach protested, unsure if it would accept the liquid. She told herself she couldn't be sick, couldn't waste the water, and stared at the window until her stomach settled. She took two more large mouthfuls, then praying the taps would work, she twisted the hot one. Not a single drop fell. At the far end of the kitchen, the toilet door was visible beyond the utility room. No point.

That left the pond.

You need to get out of here. You need to find Scott and Julia.

Absolutely true, but Jesus Christ, the stink, the fucking stink.

She returned to the living room, grabbed a blanket from the sofa and wrapped it around her shoulders and chest. Lurching, Nicola crossed to the back door, fumbled with the key and unlocked it. As soon as she opened the door, cold air enveloped her. She staggered outside, freezing stone of the patio eating into her feet, and crossed to the fishpond. From what was visible through the scummy surface, most of the fish were dead.

"Sorry," she said to the pond and stuck her right leg into the water as far as it would go. The burning freeze made her want to weep; she kept her leg where it was, thrust her hands into it and washed her leg as best she could. Everything other than the howling from the muscles in her shin, calf and knee faded. She had to keep it away from her while she did this.

Moments passed. Then her leg, whiter than snow, broke free from the water. She shoved her other leg below the surface and washed it. Wind pushed against her. The sunlight broke apart as clouds drifted over her house, her street. On all sides, shadows danced back and forth. The cold sang with her. The cold forming Julia's face in the air.

Nicola jerked her leg free and pushed herself off the ground.

"Jules. My Jewel."

She hates being called that, Scott said.

"I know."

Nicola returned to the kitchen, shaking, hugging herself. She dried her legs on a hard towel resting on a radiator and made her way back upstairs. Unable to face the bedroom, she dressed from the airing cupboard and headed to the front door.

"What day is it, Scott? How long was I out?"

Scott didn't know. She could only guess it had been at least two. Three, maybe. Any longer and she'd probably be dead from dehydration.

Three days out of it. Three days while Scott and Julia were up near Manchester.

Nicola unlocked the bolts, readied herself and opened the door.

She managed a sad little word.

"God."

Chapter Eight

C ate reached the end of the cycleway, gazed left and right to both ends of the road and jogged across it.

She crouched beside the metal railings lining the path and listened. Nothing around her but the wind and her own breath. She resisted the urge to check any of the windows in the houses. No point in looking at the dark squares. She rose and ran on, moving lightly, the switchblade still in her hand. Overgrown bushes lined the cycleway on both sides. She kept to the middle of the path, drew level with an electricity substation and noted the torn barbed wire and the smashed fence around it, seeing all of it without stopping.

Further ahead, she passed a high hedge bordering a driveway. The moon had made it through the clouds in the last few minutes. White light shone on a detached house and its many windows and its one remaining car in the drive. Ordinarily, she would have considered sheltering there for the night. The owners were clearly long gone and probably long dead for that matter. Chances were they'd left all sorts of stuff behind.

Cate slowed, then told herself to keep going. There was a hospital somewhere. There were *people.*

She came out to a curving road and tried to get some sense of place. The field and river were a mile or so behind which meant the carriageway she'd followed to this town—wherever the hell it was—had to be about two miles to the east. She'd go further along here for a bit, see what was what and run back to the carriageway if she found nothing.

Cate jogged to the centre of the road and set out. The recently developed muscles in her legs protested. Despite being fitter than she had been in years, her body couldn't take much more. No proper food in over a day. No decent sleep in probably three. And the constant threat of someone coming across her and wanting to rape her, kill her or eat her.

"Or all three," she whispered and tried to smile. The smile failed to come out.

Constant threat. Right. Like the men in the trees. She'd not got a look at their faces and could only guess at their age from their voices. They'd both probably been no older than twenty-five. Two men who wouldn't normally have given much thought to her at ten years older than them. But what did *normally* matter now? Normal things were all dead. They'd gone in the first explosion, gone when the centre of Manchester fell into rubble and the disease had been released. And all that meant now was two men who would have saved her from attack a month ago were now two men who'd take whatever they wanted from her because they could, because there was nobody to stop them, because the world had gone to hell so what did it matter if they made it just a little worse?

"Cheer up, you miserable bitch."

The thing was she was right. The men could have beaten her, raped her and probably killed her there in the woods. As horrific as that idea was, she knew death was the best she could hope for if they'd found her. Either that or be taken back to wherever they lived now. Back to be kept alive and—

It flew from her left, a burst of silent speed. Cate tried to shriek. A hand slammed over her mouth, pulled back and punched her in the stomach. She collapsed, unable to even gasp, trying to see a face.

"Hello. What's your name?"

Strings controlled her head. Someone pulled it up. Had to be strings like a puppet. No way could she move. No way could she do anything but try to breathe through the burning in her mid-section.

The man's skinny legs, clad in dirty jeans, were inches away. She threw herself at them, fingers digging deep into the man's flesh through the thinning material. He swore, drew back a leg to kick her and she moved with him, still holding on to his legs.

"Fucking bitch." He yanked her hair, pulling her head, and punched her in the face.

Pain roared through Cate's skull, and somewhere beyond that pain, she lost her grip on his legs.

"That's better," he said and yanked her upright, pulling on the scant meat of her arm. She swayed, cheek bleeding from his punch.

"Have you got it?" the man asked.

Cate continued to sway. His fist rose and she cringed, hating herself, hating him.

"Got what?" she muttered.

"The Flu. The Manc."

She shook her head.

"You sure?"

"I think you'd know if I did," she said and spat at his feet. His attention didn't move from her face.

"Come on," the man whispered. "We're going for a walk."

He pulled her to the pavement and along the silent street for several minutes before stopping to tighten his hold on her.

"You're not going to be any trouble, are you?"

She shook her head.

The man pushed his face close to her. Knowing what he expected, Cate stepped back and he held her tight. "What's your name?" he asked.

She had to clear her throat before she could reply. "Cate."

He smiled and she caught a whiff of his breath. She refused to let herself gag. Her breath probably smelled the same as his.

"I like that," he told her. "Now, listen, Cate. I know you're scared. Everything's gone to shit, right?"

He leaned closer to her. There was nothing behind but the exterior wall of a small house, nothing around her but the night and the long road.

"I won't tell you not to be scared. I'm not stupid." His lips were an inch from hers. "Do you think I'm stupid?" he whispered.

"No."

"Good." He pulled away, still smiling. "And don't worry. I'm not going to rape you or anything. Come on. I want you to meet some friends of mine."

He pulled her again. Her scuffed boots dragged on the pavement and she had to pick up her feet to avoid stumbling and to match the man's quick pace.

A horrible tightness filled Cate's stomach. She swallowed a few times and it did little to ease the sensation.

Not going to rape her. Jesus. And the worst part of it was his tone. The bastard had said it as if doing her a big favour. He might as well have offered her a hot drink.

They crossed a turning into a pleasant, suburban street. Knowing to do so was pointless, Cate scanned the windows. While all of them were whole, none showed any candle or torch light. Even if they had, she couldn't expect help. Not here. Not now.

She stole a glance at the man. He didn't appear to be as big as her first impression had suggested. Layers of clothing gave him the impression of bulk. Underneath the thick coat, the scarf, the heavy sweater and the hat, she had the idea he was as lean as she'd become during the last few weeks. And while that didn't give her any particular edge over him, it did help. Especially if she was quick.

I'll kill you if I have to, Cate thought at the man who held her.

They walked along the black line of the road and Cate waited for her moment to come.

Chapter Nine

Nicola opened the garage door and wheeled her bike out to the driveway, making sure she kept her eyes down for as long as possible. Where her driveway met the square of grass in its centre, she stopped and lifted her head.

The road ahead and her neighbours' houses appeared just as they had three days before when she'd got her first look at what the town was now.

She wanted to call it a ghost town, but that didn't quite fit. The term brought to mind old Westerns, the sort of place Clint Eastwood would come to after riding through a desert. This, all around her, was still her town; she was still in Stamford, but it was a Stamford to the side of everything she knew. *This* Stamford was outside. That was the right term. *Outside.* Her neighbours' houses with their gardens untended for the last few weeks, with their open windows letting in the winter rain, and the road with its cars parked at mad angles. *Outside.*

"Shut up," she told herself and wheeled her bike to the road. On the pavement, she shifted the weight of her backpack and mounted her bike. Inside the bag, the cans of food she'd raided from the cupboards shifted together. She'd packed them in as firmly as she could with a blanket, then wedged two bottles of water in tight. Already, the bag felt as if it weighed twice as much as it had when she picked it up. Already, her body wanted rest. There was no way of overstating the seriousness of what she'd been through: close to death and now here she was, three days later and about to try biking halfway up the country.

"Shut up," Nicola said again. Too many thoughts. Too much noise in her head when all she wanted to think about was Julia and Scott.

She'd checked her watch a few minutes ago and checked it again as she stood outside her house. Five minutes past nine. If the date was correct, today was the twentieth. Just over two weeks since the bombs, since the Manc, since she'd spoken to her family.

"All of this in two weeks. Jesus Christ."

Across the road, Jean's bungalow showed no signs of life. While the windows were whole, the place could have been abandoned months before.

Not letting herself look back, Nicola got moving. She stuck to the pavement, keeping an eye out for broken glass. Most of it appeared to be in the road. Holes that had been car windows let the wind blow through the dead vehicles, and the jagged pieces of remaining glass made the sunlight glint and wink.

Nicola turned onto Station Road, followed it to Wothorpe Road and slowed to pass a tangled wreck of cars. There were no bodies although she couldn't help but see the splashes of red on the ground.

She told herself to think about the fall in the wind behind her. As she left the river behind, the chill blowing off the water eased. She loosened her scarf and came close to falling off her bike when the three figures stepped out from the turning in front of her.

"Christ."

Nicola yanked her handlebars, turned her front wheel to the side and slipped off the seat. The people ahead, all women, stared at her.

"Hello," one said.

Nicola licked her lips and found her voice. "Hello."

"Didn't mean to scare you."

"It's okay."

Abruptly, Nicola laughed. It shook in her stomach and throat. It felt nuts and it felt great.

She covered her mouth to stop the giggling. "Sorry. Nerves."

The woman smiled. "Christine." She pointed to the other women, both younger than her. "Jenny and Laura."

"Nicola."

"By yourself?" Jenny asked.

"Yes," Nicola replied. "Sorry about laughing. It's just I haven't seen anyone in a few days." Despair closed in as it had done often since that first morning. "My neighbours are gone. . . I thought. . .I thought I might be the only person left here."

The fear she'd been struggling with for three days threatened to suffocate her. She fought it off and managed a smile.

"Where are you going?" Christine asked.

"Out of town."

She'd pushed her fear away but failed to do the same with her disquiet. Christine was smiling; the two other women weren't.

"We were heading to the train station," Christine said. "We heard the police left some food there before they left a couple of days ago. Worth a look."

"Right." Nicola shifted on her bike, bringing a foot up to a pedal. "Have you been out of town? To the roads?"

"The roads?" Laura laughed. "They're blocked solid." She gazed at Nicola's bike. "Is that your plan? Head up the roads?"

"Probably." The disquiet kept poking at her. Momentarily, she wished she'd put a knife somewhere in her coat instead of in her bag.

"Do you want to come with us? Safety in numbers," Christine said.

"You think it's dangerous here?" Nicola asked, fully aware she was avoiding the question.

Christine pursed her lips. "We haven't seen anyone in a few days, but, you know. We're women. It could be dangerous. Especially to be alone."

The word remained unspoken and Nicola wanted it more than spoken. She wanted to bellow *rape* and have the sheer insanity of the word in their town and in their lives made flesh.

Except there was nothing insane about it. Christine was right. They were women. They were alone apart from each other. And anyone could do whatever they wanted now without any punishment or justice.

Julia's face swam in front of her and she held onto the image.

"It'll be okay. People are. . .they're not that bad."

"If you're sure," Christine said, and now her eyes joined Laura's to wander over Nicola's bag.

"It's fine. Thanks." Nicola spoke as firmly as she could. Christine blinked and took a couple of steps back.

"Good luck," she said. Any warmth there might have been had faded to cool.

"Thanks."

Nicola steered her bike around them, convinced three sets of hands would yank her bag from her at any second. Once past the women, she pedalled harder than she meant to and glanced back after a few seconds. The three women were walking away, Laura and Jenny in front of Christine. The older woman gazed at Nicola and gave an unmistakeably friendly wave. Through her guilt, Nicola waved back.

"Shit."

There'd been no danger or threat there. Just women who didn't want to be alone.

"Sorry," Nicola muttered.

The apology helped nothing. She considered cycling back to them, explaining herself and asking if they'd come with her if only to keep her going, to keep her on the move.

The women turned out of sight. Nicola waited a moment as if they'd reappear. All she had was the bright day and the quiet. She cycled on, trying to keep her route in mind. Ahead to the end of the road, then on towards the A43. If the road was as clear as she hoped, it wouldn't take too long to get to the A1.

They were just scared.

As true as that was, she had to put it out of her mind. She'd already lost time through being sick and having to wait until she was better to get moving. Her family were miles away. Nobody would get in the way of her making it to them.

"Nobody," Nicola whispered, pedalling faster. Aches ran up and down her body; she kept pedalling. The road curved; she went with it, pedalling fast, breath burning in her throat, and all of her weak muscles weeping for her to stop.

Then she saw the child's body sprawled on the road.

Everything stopped. Nicola was frozen to her handlebars while the wind felt as if it no longer landed on her sweaty skin.

No. I'm not seeing this.

But she was. All she saw was body in the road. The dead child between her town and the road leading out of it.

"It means nothing. Julia is fine. She's perfectly fine," Nicola whispered. At some point in the last few moments, the wind had kicked back into life. It rustled over the grass. Nicola closed her eyes and pretended she didn't hear the mocking mutter of her name in the whispering.

"I need to keep going. I need to move."

She spoke as loudly as she dared, and the solid feel of her words helped to calm her down.

Eyes open, Nicola steered past the body and kept her eyes fixed firmly on the A43 and the dead vehicles filling it.

Chapter Ten

"You're not from here, are you?" the man said, his words more of a statement than a question.

At first, Cate considered saying nothing, then dismissed the idea. The bastard would take any chance he could to say she'd pushed his buttons.

"No," she replied.

"Where you from?"

"Devon." The lie was an automatic one.

"Devon? You don't sound like you are."

Cate tried to shrug as if it was a non-issue.

"What are you doing in Dalry?"

The town had a name, then. Dalry. It rang a vague bell and that was unsurprising. After the last few weeks, she had no idea what county she was in let alone the name of many of the towns she'd run through.

"Looking for food."

The man laughed. "We've got food. Water. Some heat. Want to get warm?"

Jesus, she did. Cold had been her constant state for so long. How mad to think all that had kept it away in the old life was the push of a button or the turn of a thermostat.

"You'll have to work for it, though."

Cate's jaw clenched at that. Here it was—the bastard's justification. Give a little, get a little. Whether she liked it or not.

Fuck you. Fuck you.

He grinned as if he'd heard her thought. "This way."

He pulled her to the other side of the road and to a side street. The moon shone on a wide block of what appeared to be new flats on one side of the road, and a green on the other. The man marched her over the grass, the frozen earth rock solid beneath their steps, and to a cycleway. After a short time, they reached another street. Cate studied the area without moving her head, desperate to not alert the man.

The houses were all well to do detached homes. Plenty of money here in the old days. The road curved out of sight ahead. What appeared to be a small park was a silent square encircled by bushes. The man pointed to the park.

"We can cut through there, then we'll be with my friends. I've got a couple who'd like to meet you."

He stopped and gazed at her.

"What?" Cate said, cursing herself for speaking.

"This way," he said, voice thick.

Here it is.

He pushed her towards a house, and for a single glorious second, his fingers weren't on her arm. Cate threw herself forward, yanked her knife from her pocket and spun around. He came at her, a monster wearing a man's body.

Click.

The blade popped out and a glint of moonlight shone on the blade. Then the man's stomach was less than an inch from the tip of the knife.

Cate's voice was every bit as thick as the man's had been a moment before. "Get away from me."

He backed up, taking jerky movements. "It's not what you think. I wasn't going to hurt you. I wasn't—"

"Shut up."

Spots danced in front of Cate's eyes. She blinked. The spots flew to all corners of her vision.

"Turn around and walk away," she said.

"Look, you need help. Me and my mates, we can help you. But you have to pay your way now. Work for it. That's how it is."

Fury pulsed in her ears, thundering in time with her heartbeat. "How many times have you said that?" she whispered.

"Huh? What do you mean?"

"How many women have you said that to?"

He pulled a face. "It's not like that. I'm saying things have changed. We have to change with them. It's just how it is. Nothing's free. We all have to do our bit."

He moved closer to her, arms and hands up as if calming a frightened dog. Cate's rage faltered for a moment. Was he skirting around the threat and the suggestion she had to have her body used to be kept safe? Or was he simply talking some variation of the spirit of the Blitz—everyone mucking in?

Coming as if through a pitch-black tunnel, memory said: *it's not like every man is a threat.*

But this one was. The danger and threat registered in her neck and spine and bellowed for her to run. Somehow, she managed to speak although her voice didn't make it past a weak croak. "If I see you again, I'll kill you."

He sighed. "Okay. Fine. That's your choice."

He headed towards the silent park, a shadow inside shadows. Cate held herself together until his shadow merged with the others and the steady tread of his steps faded. Her tears dropped, she hugged herself and wept silently.

You bastard. You fucking piece of shit.

The rage was still with her, and that was great. That was welcome. Anything was better than fear. Anything was better than hearing him believe he was justifying his plans for rape as some kind of exchange—her body taken for shelter.

Cate took a few breaths, wiped at her eyes and headed back the way they'd come, moving fast. Sod this town. Sod Dalry. She'd get back to the carriageway and walk through the night. Had to be somewhere further ahead. A village. A few houses. Coming into a town had been a bad move. Too many people left in towns and cities. Too many people like the man behind her.

Pretending she felt better, Cate reached the side street and jogged until she returned to the main road. The silence streaming out of the lightless houses and in the pools hadn't changed in the last few minutes. She sniggered. The silence hadn't changed in weeks. Nobody here to make any noise.

She crossed to the opposite pavement, attempting to get her bearings while her breath fogged out of her mouth and nose. If she ran for a few minutes and found the pathway, she'd make it back to the field. The parkway was another fifteen minutes from there. She would be away from this town in less than half an hour.

And screw getting to the hospital. Screw finding people who'd be decent and welcome her. There was none of that here in this town. It seemed likely if she *did* find anyone in the hospital, they'd be the same as the guy who'd attacked her. No. Better off on her own. Better to go back the way she'd come, find the road and get the hell out of Dalry.

Pretending the plan made her feel better, Cate ran back the way she'd come.

She barely made it a few feet before the man loomed up at her in the dark.

Chapter Eleven

Nicola steered her bike to the side of the road and stopped. Her breath burned in her throat. She swallowed a few times, loosened the lid off her water bottle and drank. The bottle was half empty. Have to fill it up soon. Or find a new one.

She rubbed her chest, wishing her heart would slow. Not surprising it was beating so fast. She'd been cycling too fast for the last couple of miles, feeling that she wasn't getting anywhere on these long, straight roads.

"Almost dying probably hasn't helped," she said and forced a smile. The action felt much too affected, as if she was being ironic. She swallowed more water and studied the land on either side of the road.

Flat fields. A grey sky, thankfully free from snow. The wind blew steadily but thankfully weaker than it could have been. Dressed in her thick coat, hat, gloves and scarf, she sweated. If she remained still for too long, the sweat would cool and chill her in seconds.

Nicola set out. She'd been on the A1 for about half an hour. There weren't as many abandoned vehicles as she'd expected; the further she went, the less she encountered and that could only be a good thing. Less chance of coming across a rotting body slumped in the driver's seat. Less chance of seeing the dry splashes of blood and vomit coating the car doors. She kept her eyes focused straight ahead. There was no urge or need to look back towards Stamford just like there was no need to check for any signs of life in the fields. There'd been nobody in sight since Christine and the other women. While she'd felt as if she'd been watched a few times, that was probably down to imagination and the wish to not feel so alone. While she didn't think she could handle company or a conversation about her plans and her fears, she knew the worry over what lay ahead would cripple her if she let it. Sharing that worry with someone might help.

"Then again, at least there's nobody around to steal my food," Nicola said and wished she hadn't spoken aloud.

A drop of moisture hit her forehead. The sky had darkened a fraction in the last few minutes. Not cold enough for snow. Rain could be on its way although the grey cast to the sky might have been approaching dusk. She'd left her watch at the house so any idea of time had been a guess since setting out. Now it felt to be about three o'clock. Night would be on her within an hour and a half.

Need to find somewhere soon.

Nicola steered her away around an overturned van. Ahead, a figure rested on the road, an old bike beside them.

"Shit."

She slowed and did her best to control her breathing. Her front wheel crunched over gravel and the figure shifted. A man. Late middle age. Stocky. Short. Holding his leg close to his knee. He attempted a wave but couldn't lift his arm without spilling himself flat.

"Hello," he called. "Can you help me?"

He had a strong voice. Nicola didn't need the breeze to carry it to her in order to hear him.

"I came off my bike. Can you help me up?"

Nicola neared him. She stopped a few paces from him and took a quick look to either side. Nothing moved in the grass. She licked her upper lip and tasted sweat.

"Please," the man said. "Don't worry. I'm not dangerous. My name's Tom. Tom Lewis."

Nicola forced herself to speak. "Nicola."

"Nice to meet you."

He smiled. The genuine cast to it and the surreal situation made her laugh. It became a cough and she thumped herself in the chest to regain her breath. Still on the ground, Tom tried to shuffle backwards.

"You're not sick, are—" he began.

"No. I was. I got over it." She kept her eyes on the man and named it. "The Manc."

He nodded. "Yes. Same here. I didn't get out of bed for four days, I think. Might have been five. By that time, it was all over."

Nicola dismounted and laid her bike flat on the road. Her forearm, exposed between glove and coat, brushed the ground and she winced. Standing straight, she remained still, watching Tom and choosing her words.

"I've got a knife, Tom. I'll use it if I have to."

He eyed her, face still. Wind blew across the fields. "Understood. It can't be safe now. For a woman."

Nicola thought of Christine and the others back in Stamford. Safety in numbers. But how much would that safety be worth if five or six men came across the three women?

Not much.

She strode to Tom and squatted. "Let me see." She let no tremor into her voice and took his hand off his knee before he moved.

"Landed right on it," he said.

Silently, Nicola slid his trouser leg up his shin. An ugly graze wept just below his knee. The knee itself had swollen and would bruise before long. Tom would be limping for at least a week.

"Up," Nicola said. She gripped close to his armpits. He held her shoulders lightly. The weight of the knife taped to the inside of her coat pressed on her breasts. She pulled him. Grunting, he made it upright.

"Thank you," he said, face red. He eased his hands from her shoulders and stood carefully, clearly favouring his left leg. "Not too bad. Just don't ask me to run for a bus." He smiled. The black hair of his stubble stood out against the red of his face.

"Can you manage your bike?" Nicola said.

"I'll wheel it. Home's not far. Just a couple of minutes."

He bent, gripped his handlebars and pulled his bike up. He faced up the road. "Listen. I expect you to say no, but I can offer you food and a warm house. Even if you only want to stay for a few hours or overnight. No funny business. And I meant what I said. I'm not dangerous."

Nicola considered her options. Sour amusement filled her. She had no options.

"Food?" she asked.

"Nothing special. I've got a lot of cans. Bread. Been keeping it outside. It's getting tough but it's not stale. Got bottles of water, too."

Her tongue and teeth itched at the thought of fresh water. She'd found a bottle the day before. The water she'd been drinking since already tasted stale.

"Just for a couple of hours," she said and knew without verbalising it she was giving herself a problem. Night would be on them soon. If she left Tom's house at night with no idea where to find shelter, she'd be in trouble.

"Not a problem."

Tom faced ahead, tested his leg and walked with his bike by his side. Nicola followed, watching his limp. She kept a few paces behind him and watched his back.

"Are you from Stamford?" he asked.

"Yes."

"A lovely town."

"Yes."

He stopped and faced her. "Listen. I know this is going to be difficult. But you can trust me. You can."

"I will. Probably. Let's just walk for now."

The sweat on her back and head had dried since she'd come off her bike. The dampness made her want to tear off her coat and fleece and stand under a boiling shower. For an hour, maybe.

"Fair enough," Tom said and walked again. A minute passed before he spoke again. "The Manc." He glanced back at her. "Did it leave anyone in Stamford?"

"Not really. I tried a few of my neighbours when I woke up and could move, but nobody answered. I've only seen a couple of people since I left my house."

Nicola fell silent, remembering the stink of her body and the staleness filling the bedroom.

"Nobody left," she muttered, and Tom gave no sign he'd heard her.

Nicola drew level with Tom and shifted her arm. Inside her coat, the knife's weight was a comfort.

"The worst thing's not knowing what happened," Tom said abruptly. "The bombs. We know that. Manchester, York, Birmingham, Cambridge, Edinburgh and London. We know that, but that's about all we know, isn't it?"

"More or less," Nicola said. She forced herself to stare straight ahead. The images from the explosion in Manchester played in front of her again and Scott's voice was in her ear: *hold on. Someone wants to say hello.*

Then the dead line and the explosion in London. Then Scott in her ear again and again.

"I think I could handle this a little better if we knew who was behind it." Tom's voice hitched as if he was about to start crying. "Not that it would change anything. We're all still dead, aren't we?"

"Yeah," Nicola said and her eyes and ears were far away.

Hold on. Someone wants to say hello.

Chapter Twelve

Cate shoved her arm up. Moonlight flashed on her blade. The man smashed his fist into her wrist; she dropped the knife and he kicked it away into the dark. His hand over her mouth pressed hard and she screamed against his flesh.

"Quiet," he whispered.

Cate elbowed him in the stomach. He grunted but didn't loosen his hold. She tried to kick at his ankle and missed.

"Will you shut up?" he hissed against her ear. "I'm not going to hurt you."

Cate pretended to relax. She fell silent and stopped squirming. Even so, the pressure of the man's palm on her face remained the same.

"Listen. My name's Steve. I promise I'm not going to hurt you. I know you've got no reason to believe that, but unless you want us both dead, you need to stay quiet."

A fraction of the pressure on her mouth eased; Cate drew a sharp breath, readied herself and kicked backwards at the same time. Her heel connected with his shin. He embraced her in a death-grip, crotch against her backside, arm encircling her just below the neck.

"I mean it," he whispered. "Be quiet or we're both dead."

Abruptly too tired to struggle, Cate stopped pushing at him. She tried to scan the ground in search of her knife and could make out little of the pavement and road.

"Now I'm going to let go. If you scream or do anything loud, I'll run. The men out here will find you pretty quickly. You'll be in deep shit if they do. Understood?"

Cate nodded.

"Okay."

He eased away from her face and turned her around. Although most of his features were in darkness, she could make out his appraisal. Without concealing it, she did the same.

He was younger than her. Possibly early twenties. The heavy coat, scarf and gloves gave him a large presence although she had the impression not all of his size came from his layers.

"Are you going to make any noise?" he whispered.

Cate shook her head.

"What's your name?"

A lie rose to her mouth and she bit it back. "Cate."

"Steve."

"You said."

"Yeah." He let out a sigh that trembled, exposing his fear. "What are you doing here? This is dangerous."

"I'm passing through. I. . ." She shook and the memory of her anger whispered. "There was a man. I had my knife. He left me alone and I ran down here."

"Jesus. You're lucky. The guys round here are dangerous. I mean, *really* dangerous."

"Yeah. I got that idea."

Steve gazed at her, then crouched. He reached into the bushes lining the path and dug in the earth. When he rose, he held her knife.

"Yours."

She eyed the weapon, then him. "How do you know I won't hurt you?"

"I don't."

Cate took the blade and pocketed it. "Thanks."

"It's yours," he said as if it wasn't a big deal. "So, you're not from Dalry?"

"No. I came in off the parkway. Got chased from the river, then that guy. Now you." A memory of the two men in the trees and their conversation returned. Cate kept her voice as light as she could. "Is there a—" She broke off, swallowing.

"Is there a what?"

Cate studied him. As much as she wanted to trust this man, she couldn't. Not yet. "Do you live around here?"

He pointed behind. "There's a hospital about half a mile down there. I'm there. We've got a few people."

"Hospital?"

"Yeah. It's old, but warm. Not in great condition, but at least it's still standing. They were in the middle of closing it when the bombs went off. There's a newer one a couple of miles away. But when everything went down the toilet, they had to keep the place going. We use it as a base. Why?"

Have to trust him. Have to trust him.

"I ran into a couple of men by the river. I heard them say something about the hospital."

"Yeah. We've got some friends here. Same people you've met." He laughed softly, and Cate caught the bitterness in the sound. "Do you want to come with me? You can stay overnight, have something to eat. Wallace won't mind."

"Who's Wallace?" Cate said, aware she hadn't answered his question. The night pushed through her clothing, and the suggestion of somewhere warm made all other thought difficult.

"Our boss," Steve said. "She's okay."

Cate rested her hand over the shape of her knife. Steve watched her. She paused, considering, then relaxed a little.

"All right. Just tonight."

"Okay. Cool."

For no reason she knew, Cate touched her wrist. She'd lost her watch at some point a while ago and had no idea about time or date.

"What day is it, Steve?"

If he thought her question was strange, he kept his reaction hidden. "Tuesday, I think. Hard to be sure. Couldn't tell you what the date is. The twenty-third, maybe." He fell silent, waiting.

The twenty-third. Almost a month since Christmas. All the decorations in the shops and pubs should be put away for another year and everyone should be forgetting about the resolutions they made.

Cate breathed and it trembled in her mouth and throat.

"This way," Steve said.

Keeping several steps away from her, Steve led her along the road towards the hospital.

Chapter Thirteen

Nicola took the cup of coffee Tom held towards her.

"Thanks," she said and he nodded. The aroma of the drink made her want to gulp it, to taste the coffee all over her tongue. She resisted it. He'd made it with hot water—actual *hot* water—from a camping stove seconds before. The heat from the mug baked against her fingers. She didn't loosen her hold on the cup.

He selected several cans from a cupboard and set about making a meal while Nicola appraised the living room. She sat on a large brown sofa which filled most of the room. Across from her, the blank screen of the TV gazed out to the coffee table and the pictures on the fireplace. An elderly woman was in a lot of the photos. Nicola kept her focus off them. Walking through from the front of the house had been bad enough. Four frames were on a display stand close to the front door: a guy in his mid-twenties, Tom's son, presumably; and shots of two very young children. Tom hadn't mentioned them. Neither had she. No need to.

"It's going to be a bit of a mishmash," he called from the kitchen.

"Fine."

"Tinned fruit. Tinned veg. That sort of thing."

"Fine."

Tom put his can opener down. Nicola waited for him to tell her again she could trust him. Instead, he cleared his throat and picked up his can opener. Tom continued with the food and Nicola watched the candles dotted around the room. Although the light they cast flickered, they did a fair job of brightening the room. Cosy was too strong a word. Cosy or not, she'd still found some shelter.

"Chuck a bit of a wood on the fire, would you?" Tom called.

"Okay."

She crossed to the fireplace and the diminishing flame. In a bucket beside it, chunks of wood stood upright. She threw three pieces on to the fire; the flames ate into the wood happily. Smoke flew up the chimney. Worry pricked her. Despite night having come, someone might see the smoke. Someone could easily come investigating.

So what if they do? It's not like everyone left is going to be an ax-murdering nutcase, is it?

She sat again as Tom returned from the kitchen. He handed her a bowl of mixed fruit and one of carrots.

"Odd meal, I know, but it's the best I can do."

"It's great. Thank you."

"You helped me, I help you."

He went back to the kitchen and brought a loaf of bread out along with his shotgun, the barrel broken. Nicola eyed the weapon, forcing herself to not appear bothered by it. Tom had mentioned it on their walk back to his house, clearly not wanting to surprise her with the sight of it. The gun had belonged to one of his friends, a farmer now dead. Tom took it two days ago, found a box with a few shells in his friend's shed, and confessed he'd had to fiddle with it for several minutes before he'd managed to load it.

"No butter, I'm afraid. I forgot to go to the shop."

Nicola smiled dutifully, took the offered two slices and ate them with quick, hungry bites. Tom placed the shotgun beside his chair and chewed without speaking. The fire ate the wood. The room warmed. Wind blew against the living room window. Outside, the wind blew over the wide, flat fields. It scoured the roads, the ditches and spinning through the dead branches. As much as Nicola tried to banish the images, seeing the empty land surrounding them and picturing the empty roads between here and the suburbs near Stockport was all too easy.

"Something wrong?" Tom asked.

She shook her head.

"How's the food?"

"Fine. Thank you again."

"Not a problem." He chewed a slice of bread. "What happened to you? Were you at home when the bombs went off?"

"Yes." Already the memory felt as if it belonged long ago. It could have happened to her when she in her teens, not barely two weeks ago. "I was doing some work at home; the TV was on. The news. I saw it as it happened." Nicola managed a smile. "Obviously I had no idea about the Manc. It just looked like terrorists."

"It probably was, but I don't think they planned on things going as far as they have." Tom shrugged. "For all we know, they had a cure. That makes sense to me. Release a disease, and hold governments to ransom over the cure. Things went a bit quicker than they planned, though."

"Probably."

"And you've not seen many others?"

"Not really."

He nodded, not surprised. "To be expected. I heard a lot of people tried to get out of the country. Head to Europe, that sort of thing. Others went north. I imagine the wilds of Scotland seemed quite attractive."

"Do you think people got out of the country?"

"More than likely."

"Then the Manc spread."

"More than likely."

"God."

"I know it sounds trite, but we can't think about that now. We have to focus on *us*, not other countries." Tom gestured at the window. "I dread to imagine what's happening out there. No order, no government. It's been less than three weeks and everything's over. Someone will take control at some point, but for now, it's everyone for themselves. All we've got left are the cats and dogs. At least the Manc didn't kill them, too."

In the poor light, he seemed to have aged twenty years. Nicola took her eyes off him but couldn't help hearing his exhaustion when he spoke again. "What did you do before?"

"Recruitment. Sort of. Have you heard of New Steps?"

"No. Afraid not."

"Kids who'd been out of school for a while and not got a job, we got them work. That sort of thing. I was working at home when. . ."

Nicola caught him studying her left hand. She ran her thumb over her wedding ring.

"Twelve years. Scott."

Tom nodded. "Is he. . ."

"No. He was in Manchester, visiting his brother and our sister-in-law." Nicola had to stop. A piece of carrot was stuck to a tooth; she worked her tongue at it, playing for time. She said the name without meeting Tom's eye. "Julia. Our daughter. She's with Scott. I didn't get a chance to speak to her and that's. . ." Tears threatened. So did anger. "That's driving me mad. Scott managed to call me on the day it went off, but then all the phones were down and the roads were closed and then everyone got the Manc and now here we are."

She set her bowl down by her side and hugged herself.

"I'm sorry," Tom murmured.

"Thanks."

"You're going to them now?"

"That's the plan. It's a long way, but there's no way I'm staying away from them."

Tom nodded. "Understood. I'd do the same in your position." He crunched a carrot, considering. "I suppose in a way, I'm lucky. Nobody to worry about now things have gone this bad."

"Yeah," Nicola said. She was only half-listening. Inside, she talked to her husband and daughter; she told them she'd be with them soon.

"Tell me about your family. Your daughter. Her name's Julia?"

"Yes."

"That's a lovely name."

"Thanks. She's nine. Ten in February." As much as she might have expected pain at speaking of them, what she felt was closer to relief. She could keep them with her through simple words, and while the words stung, she could handle it. "I was going to go with them to Cheadle but I had some work stuff to sort out. The plan was I'd go up the day after. Have a quick visit. Scott told me I didn't need to come, but I know he wanted me to. Big on family." She smiled. "He's always been big on it which I sometimes forget. He helps me remember."

The sting inside increased and she waited until it passed before taking a few breaths.

"He sounds like a good man," Tom said.

"He is. The best. And I tell you what."

Tom kept quiet, waiting.

"I would kill to have them here with me right now. I think I would actually kill for that."

Tom considered. It was Nicola's turn to wait, curious how he would reply to such a statement. Nothing about her wanted to retract it, though.

"I'd be happy for them to be with us," he said. "Although we'd need more chairs."

Nicola barked laughter, shaking. A few tears fell. She let them, glad of the sensation.

Silence filled the room for a few moments. The image of her husband and daughter played over and over in Nicola's mind: Julia, smiling at her as she ran around the garden; Scott, standing at the barbeque, one flat palm resting on his large stomach, the other reaching for a bottle of lager.

"My wife, she was one of the first to go," Tom said. Nicola returned to their conversation, weighed down by the heavy drag of Tom's grief. "It was only a couple of days after the bombs. We were in Tesco. There's a big one a few miles away and we thought we should stock up. Things on the news were quite frightening to be honest. We drove there, and she just collapsed. Just fell straight over. She'd been ill since the night before and kept it from me. She died that night."

"I'm sorry," Nicola said.

"Then my son, he went two days later. His wife lasted until the next morning. Their children, they. . ." He broke off, shaking, weeping. Nicola remained on the sofa, grasping between her knees, waiting for Tom's tears to stop. Eventually, he cleared his throat.

"Sorry. It takes me by surprise."

"It's okay."

"Thank you."

His family is dead and you can't even get off the sofa to comfort him?

She had no argument for the voice and summoning the strength to fake one seemed like too much effort. Whoever was left now had their hurts and their grief. The world was over and what was left of it didn't care about individual pains any more than it cared about the rotting bodies filling the houses and streets.

The image of the child's body she'd passed on her way out of Stamford thudded inside her head. Nicola closed her eyes; the image remained.

Someone's child, crawling into the road, dying in the sunlight.

Go away, she told the image. *Just leave me alone.*

Out in the hallway, a door creaked. Tom rose without making a sound. He placed his bowls on the arm of the sofa and took hold of his shotgun. He placed a finger against his lips and stared towards the living room door. The creak sounded again.

That was a step.

Tom breathed to her. "Don't move."

He crossed to the living room door. He moved much more lightly than she expected given his weight. At the door, he glanced back at her and again held a finger over his lips. Nicola nodded. Tom stepped out and the shadows in the hallway swallowed him.

Realisation filled her. She was in a state of almost paralysing fear. It rooted her to the sofa, made the little food she'd eaten into a tight ball in her stomach.

From the hallway, Tom's voice rose. "Whoever's in there, you've got three seconds to get out of my house before I come in there and shoot you. I promise you I will."

Whoever caused the creak didn't reply. Nicola forced herself to rise and pull the kitchen door open. Her saliva was electric. Her heart thrummed.

"One," Tom shouted.

Nicola gripped the doorframe.

"Two."

She stepped into the black of the kitchen doorway.

"Three."

All the sounds from the front of the house seemed to happen at once. Tom kicking the door open, his deep voice bellowing, a boom of a gunshot, the quick pattering noise of something running across the floor, another booming gunshot and Tom screaming. All the sounds were a cacophony pushing at her, shoving her into the kitchen and sending her in a race to the back of the house, through the utility room and right to the back door.

To the locked back door.

Nicola slammed on the door handle. Far behind her, Tom screamed once more and in the silence that followed, cold horror filled Nicola.

The door keys were in Tom's pocket. He'd pocketed them moments after they'd arrived.

On the spot, Nicola shuffled around to face the washing room. The moonlight streaming through the window in the door made it as far as the dead tumble dryer. Beyond that was black.

The way out was back to the living room, to the front of the house and the keys in Tom's pocket. The way out was right towards whatever had killed him.

Nicola stared into the black and the black stared back.

Chapter Fourteen

They crossed an expansive roundabout, the green circle forming a junction of what Steve told her was the suburban end of Thorpe Road, the end that led to the centre of Dalry and a third road which headed to the parkway. The houses on either side of the road were all large, detached homes. Cate could have taken her pick of any one of them for a night's shelter; the idea of running from Steve and doubling back in the dark came and went, a little weaker each time it returned. She had to be honest with herself: she wanted to be around other people. She wanted flesh and light and voices. None of those would be with her if she ran away.

"The hospital's an old place. I think they built it in the sixties and opened it in the seventies," Steve said. "Probably should have been knocked down in the eighties."

"Right."

"That was a joke."

"Right."

He laughed and gestured for them to leave the road and walk back to the pavement. "You're a lot of fun."

Cate smiled. "Right."

"What did you do before? Stand-up comedy?"

Her smile fell away. Before. One little word and it held so much grief.

"Sorry. I shouldn't have asked."

"It's okay." She ducked as they passed under low hanging tree branches. "I was a university lecturer. English Lit. Nothing exciting, really. Just normal. Same as everyone else. You?"

"I worked at the hospital. I was a porter. Well, I still am. You know what I mean."

"Yes."

Steve pointed to the next road that turned off Thorpe Road. "That's Lennox Avenue. We need to be as quiet as we can once we pass that. That guy you met, he and his mates aren't far away."

"Who are they?" Cate whispered.

"Arseholes. Now listen. Keep quiet, follow me and move as quickly as you can once we get to the road, all right?"

"Yes."

They reached the junction, Steve pointed across it to a fence and they jogged. Fear had come out of nowhere to Cate. She listened to it, recognising it as the voice of instinctive survival. Cooling sweat on her back made her t-shirt stick to her skin. Fresh sweat trickled down her neck despite the cold and she promised herself as long a shower as they'd allow her once she made it into the hospital.

"This way," Steve whispered.

He led her from the pavement, over patchy grass and through an opening in the fence. They emerged on a road which ran alongside a large building and a car park. Cate caught sight of one of the signs as they ran. The building was a maternity unit. A dead maternity unit.

They jogged to hedges lining the opposite path, followed them for a moment and reached a path that cut between two squat buildings. Steve pointed down the path and Cate made out a section of what had to be the main hospital building.

"Through there," Steve breathed to her. "We'll go straight, through the car park and to the left of the main entrance, okay?"

She nodded.

He ran in front; she kept right behind him. As soon as they cleared the two buildings, the wind buffeted her, racing across the empty car park, freezing her flesh. Steve veered right. The wind brought a sound Cate hadn't heard in weeks.

A moving car.

Steve froze and crouched. Beside him, Cate did the same. The sound of the car grew louder; she scanned Thorpe Road and the houses on its opposite side. No lights glowed in any windows. Through the same instinctive survival which spoke a moment before, she knew the houses weren't empty. People were watching the road.

Her eyes darted to where the east side of the car park met the road as the vehicle appeared. Its lights were off. By the sounds of it, the windows were down and its occupants made no effort to be quiet. They shouted, swore, laughed in a noisy mix of voices breaking in the air. Cate tracked the car as it drew level with her and Steve, then passed beyond a high wall of hedges. She caught a brief sight of it as it drove beyond the car park, then Steve touched her arm and jerked a thumb to the hospital.

They ran to the path encircling the building. Two lorries blocked the main entrance. Cate couldn't be sure but many of the ground floor windows appeared to be sealed with cabinets and furniture. She peered upwards as they ran. Several of the windows on the upper floors were smashed.

"There," Steve whispered. He pointed to a jutting section of wall straight ahead—a fire exit, Cate realised. She leaned against the wall, panting and holding her side.

"Up here." Steve pointed to a patch of wall about six feet up.

"What is it?" Cate whispered.

"The way in."

Cate stared where Steve pointed. The section of the building appeared no different to any other part. "Where? I don't see it."

He jabbed a finger to the wall. "There. It's a covered hole."

Frantically, Nicola stared where Steve pointed. Then from across the car park, someone hissed in the dark. "Keep quiet, you fucking idiot."

Cate pressed herself against the front of the hospital, her heart a lurching thud in her chest. Someone else on the car park muttered in reply, their voice lost. Steve grabbed Cate, shoved her close to the wall and linked his hands in a cup. Understanding, Cate stood on one leg, shoved her foot into the cup and he lifted. She scrambled at the wall, praying the scrape of her fingers against the bricks wouldn't carry. There couldn't be more than a few seconds before the men on the car park drew close enough to see her and Steve. Blinded by dripping sweat, Cate dug her fingertips into the bricks, ran them from side to side and hit some rough material much softer than stone or brick. Desperately, she pulled at a flap and slid her arms into a disguised opening.

You've probably got about ten seconds, her mind told her.

Cate yanked herself up. The muscles in her arms felt like rocks. Fire burned in her lungs.

Up. Get up.

Her head was level with the hole. She reached blindly into total darkness and pulled herself forward.

She dropped, hit something soft and her impact was a thud in the dark. She ran her hands over the object that had caught her.

A mattress.

She rolled off it and stood. A rectangular outline of light stood on the other side of wherever she'd landed. There was no sign of Steve above. She shook and swallowed his name as it rose to her lips. Where the hell was he?

Cate backed up, hugging herself.

"Hey."

The hiss dropped to her from the little window.

"Look there."

They'd seen the opening.

Cate pulled her knife free and staggered towards the outline of light. Behind her, the men's shoes scuffled on the wall outside.

The outline was a door. The light that formed around its rectangle wavered. She found the handle and pulled.

The door remained shut.

The men's shoes kicked against the wall again. As quiet as they were trying to be, their panting breaths were still audible. Even if they struggled more than she had, they'd be through the opening in less than a minute. She was stuck.

Steve? Where are you?

There'd been no sounds of violence outside. Steve had just vanished after getting her inside.

Cate pulled on the handle again. It rattled. She resisted pulling it again. The sound was much louder than she wanted it to be.

She peered around the room. It didn't appear to be more than few feet across. A storage cupboard. Even if she could see clearly, there probably wasn't anything to use as a weapon.

"Come on," one of the men said, obviously encouraging the other.

Cate crossed the floor, her shoes crunching on small stones. She winced at the sound and the murmurs from outside stopped. Then the scuffling of shoes on the wall started again with no real effort to quieten the sound.

They were coming in.

Holding her knife, Cate crouched, grabbed one end of the mattress and pulled. It hissed as she slid it over the floor. Nothing she could do about it. Holding her breath, she lifted it and shoved it against the opening. At once, the little slice of moonlight vanished. The only illumination she had was the thin line of light beyond the door.

A thud hit the mattress. She held it. The man on the other side hit it again; it came loose for a second and she caught him telling the other there was something in his way. Cate shoved it against the opening again. She did her best to ignore the pain in her arms or the way they trembled with exertion and fear.

Nothing happened for several seconds. Then the man shoved the mattress hard. Cate's foot twisted and she hung perfectly balanced between standing and falling.

"It's gone. We can get through," the man whispered.

In the dark above, a shape appeared. Instead of thinking, Cate reacted.

The mattress slammed into the man. He let out a noise of surprise, shot backwards and Cate shoved the mattress tight against the hole. Her arms were on fire. Sweat filled her eyes. A punch hit the mattress from the other side. Then something tore. Another punch. Another tear.

They were stabbing it.

The panic of a terrified animal took her and rooted her against the wall and floor.

Punch. Tear. Punch. Tear.

The mattress shook. Tiny pieces of it rained on to her upturned face. The knife pierced the mattress again and broke through. Cate saw the wavering blade for a second. In the moonlight, the knife was a gleaming point above her head. It withdrew. Cate dropped the mattress and ran for the door. Unblocked moonlight dropped to the floor and the men's voices dropped with it.

"Quick, come on. We've got her."

The hot ball of fear sitting in her stomach had risen to her mouth. It blocked her words and blocked her thoughts.

She yanked on the handle. The door shook.

"Hello? You in there?"

She kicked at the door, ignoring the mocking whisper.

"Don't worry. We won't hurt you. We just want to talk," one of the men called to her, voice low. Behind him, the other man laughed.

They were sliding through the window while she pulled on the useless handle, sliding in while she was trapped. They were coming for her and there was no way out.

Cate gave kicked at the bottom of the door. Pain raced up her foot. It registered from faraway. From somewhere, her voice came back. *"Open the door. Jesus Christ, open the door."*

The two men laughed. One grunted. Then there was a thud. Then a second. They were both in.

"Just relax. All we want to do is talk. All we want—"

Her scream overrode him. *"Open the door."*

"Will you shut up?" one of the men shouted and he was coming at her. She whirled to face him, her knife up and ready, eager to spill his blood.

The door swung open. Light illuminated the two men inches from her. Out of the light, someone yelled to her.

"Down."

Eyes shut, Cate dropped.

Explosions roared directly above.

Chapter Fifteen

Nicola crept to the kitchen and stopped in the doorway. The door to the living room was still open. Light from the candles sent dancing shadows to the kitchen floor and over the walls.

She took another few steps and stopped at the sink. Beside it, the cutlery Tom had been using lay in a tidy pile. She took hold of a dinner knife, wished for a sharper blade, and walked to the door. On the other side of the room, the door which opened to the hallway was as Tom had left it—almost closed. Not a sound emerged from the hallway. There'd been nothing since Tom's final screams what had to be ten minutes before. She'd listened for animal noises, for barking or growling, and heard nothing at all. Even the steady breath of the wind coming in off the fields had ceased. If there was something in the front room, it was staying there instead of making its way through the house to her.

Unless it didn't know she was there. No. That made no sense. Whatever sort of animal it was, it'd had obviously been in the house the whole time she and Tom were speaking. It had only attacked when challenged.

The problem was she knew she wasn't dealing with an animal. A person had killed Tom; a person was much closer to Tom's gun than she was; a person was between her and her way out.

Momentarily, Nicola considered throwing something at the window near the TV and clambering outside. Sod the noise and the mess. At least it would mean she wouldn't have to go to the front room armed only with a knife.

She scanned the room, fully aware breaking the window wasn't going to happen. The only one of Tom's belongings anywhere near big enough to smash the glass was an armchair and she had no chance of shifting that. Gripping one of the candles, Nicola took hold of her terror and squashed it. She brought Julia's face to her mind, using it as strength and shield. Getting out mattered now. Being scared was for later.

At the door to the hallway, she held the candle high and tried to take in all the shadows at the same time. They coated the carpet at her feet and pooled towards the foot of the stairs. Anything above the third step existed in another universe. And anyone could be up there, staring down at her, faces coated in Tom's blood.

Trying to keep silent, Nicola saw Julia's face. Her daughter was calling for her. Her daughter needed her.

A white flare sparked inside Nicola's chest. Her heart shook with the need, the *imperative* to cry Julia's name as a talisman. She breathed for a moment and did her best to keep the candle steady.

"Whoever's in there, I don't care what you do when I leave. There's food in the kitchen. You're welcome to stay. All I want to do is go."

She trembled. Mad shadows formed in the flicker of candlelight.

If you don't move now, you never will.

The thought sent her forward. She crossed the hallway and eased the door to the front room open with her foot.

"Like I say, all I want to do is leave. The house is yours, okay?"

She cursed her tremors in her voice and doing so helped nothing at all.

Candlelight found Tom's feet and lower legs. He lay on the carpet, gun by his side. Nicola stared at the white carpet, now no longer fully white.

Black patches coated it. Around the patches, dots lay in random spacing. She swallowed and her throat clicked. The patches were red, not black. Red all over the carpet.

Unthinking, she nudged the door open fully and held the candle out. Shadows ran away. The only figures in the room were Tom and herself. His throat was a mess of terrible wounds. Bites or stabs. She didn't know. All that made sense was the great splashes of blood on the carpet.

They went upstairs when you were at the back. They're right behind you.

She ducked and turned and shoved her bread knife out towards the stairs. Nobody there.

Get the key. Get out.

The simple command in the words propelled her. She crouched beside Tom and, still unthinking, shoved her hand into his pocket. The keys came with a tissue and a few coins. She gripped the keys in the same hand with the knife and stood.

"I'm going now. You're welcome to stay here."

The shadows danced in the candlelight.

Nicola stepped back towards the door, stopped and turned to Tom's body. Splayed on the ground, he appeared to be reaching for the barrel of the shotgun.

Nicola grabbed the gun and did her best to not register the chilly metal. Holding gun, knife, keys and candle, she left the front room, crossed through the house and headed to the rear door. As she drew level with the washing machine, conscious thought kicked back into life. Its absence had let her do what she'd done. Now it was back and outright terror joined it.

She dropped the candle and sprinted for the door. Whispering ran through the house straight at her as she stabbed the key at the lock.

"No, please, no," she whispered and yanked on the key. It didn't budge. Wrong one.

Whispering on the front room floor.

Legs and feet running all over it.

Something awful dancing around Tom's body, feet slipping over the splashes of his blood.

Nicola pulled the key loose, shoved in the other one and turned it. The door unlocked and she threw it open as the dancing steps ran across carpet, across the kitchen floor and stopped behind her.

She wouldn't let herself turn around. Couldn't look back. *Couldn't.*

Nicola ran out of the house into the garden, legs pumping, breath a hot ache in her lungs. She jumped the remnants of the garden fence and turned back.

In the doorway, the outline of a figure stood perfectly still, watching her.

Chapter Sixteen

Cate lifted her head and peered up into the yellow light. Muffled grunts were all she could make out. The two explosions had buried her hearing. Not explosions. Gunshots.

Cate shook her head, swallowed a few times and heard a word inside the muffled grunts.

"—*up*—"

A black object waved in the yellow. A gun. Someone was waving a gun at her.

Cate kicked her legs backward, hit a solid weight and spun around. Two dead men lay on the ground. One was missing half his head, the other had a hole in his neck. Blood, bone and pieces of flesh coated the floor around them. Cate kicked away from them.

"Get up."

She faced the door and rose into a crouch. The man with the gun waved it at her, gesturing for her to stand. She did so and rested on the wall to keep herself steady.

"What's your name?" the man said.

Cate. It's Cate.

The words were lost below the gunfire and the two dead men on the ground.

"Your name," he said and lifted the gun to aim it at her chest.

"Cate. It's Cate."

"Where are you from, Cate?"

"What?"

"You with them?" He pointed to the bodies.

"No. God, no. I was trying to hide from them. They followed me in. I was with another man. He's from here. Steve."

The gun didn't drop from her chest. Naming Steve appeared to make no difference.

"You got any weapons?" the man asked.

Cate eased her hand from behind her back, realising she'd tried to hide her knife as soon as she'd dropped.

"Just this."

She closed the blade and held it up to the light.

"No guns?"

"Guns? No."

"You sure?"

Dull anger made her want to spit at him and sent a burst of pain through her head. He was amused at her. He was trying not to laugh.

"Yes, I'm sure," she shouted, and the gun lowered.

"All right, love. Calm down."

"Don't call me *love.*"

He snorted and turned away from her to running steps. "One of yours?" he said.

The runner reached the doorway. Steve. He entered the room, panting. "Are you all right?"

"Yeah. I think so. What happened to you?"

If he noticed her careful lack of concern, Steve kept it off his face. "I had to run. There wasn't time for both of us to get in that way."

"There's another way in?" Cate asked and he gave her a brief nod.

"Come on," he said.

She took a few steps after him into a corridor. The other man lowered his torch, revealing his face. He was probably no older than twenty-two. Several days of growth marked his chin and cheeks. His clothes hung loose on his frame.

"Joey. Do the honours, would you?" he said.

Movement behind her. Cate turned as a second man appeared from out of the shadows. Paying her no attention, he entered the storage room, stepped over bodies and hauled a large box from the corner. He jammed it into the window she'd crawled through, blocking it. The man then pushed a chunk of wood into place over the opening. He took two padlocks from a pocket and clicked them into place through holes at either end of the wood.

"It's basic, but it does the job," the man with the gun said.

"What do we do?" Joey asked.

The gloom inside the little room obscured his face. Even so, Cate could guess he wasn't paying her any attention let alone addressing her.

"Best take her to Wallace," the gunman said.

Cate took a few breaths. "Can one of you tell me what all this is? Who are you? Who are they?" She pointed to the two dead men.

"We're your friends. Maybe. *They* definitely weren't," the gunman replied.

"All right, Damien. It's okay," Steve said. He smiled at Cate. "This is Dalry District Hospital. Well, it was."

"Right," Cate said. It seemed like the only answer to give.

The man behind her, Joey, left the little room and joined Steve.

"Did you see anyone else out there?" he said, voice low.

"A car. They didn't see us," Steve replied.

"Shit. One of them?"

"It turned into a side road." Cate pointed towards the front of the building. "Who are these people?"

In reply, Joey yanked the door shut. The bang echoed down the corridor. He locked it with bolts at the top and bottom.

"Wallace, then?" he said.

"Wallace," Steve replied.

"Who's Wallace? What's going on here?" Cate asked.

"Wallace is in charge and you're safe. That's the important stuff. She'll fill you in on the rest."

Steve led her down the corridor. Joey and Damien walked behind her. Both men held torches. Their illumination pooled across the dirty floor and shone on cracks in the walls, on the wide split in the middle of a noticeboard and on the damaged lights above. They passed closed doors, most with piles of furnishings blocking them. After a dozen steps, Cate decided she didn't want to see any more signs of damage. She gazed at her feet as the men took her to double doors wedged open with boxes.

"This way," Steve said.

They'd come to the main entrance. Across, rubble and wrecked furniture were piled high in the foyer. Steve's torchlight passed over the blockage at the entrance. Wind blew through cracks, but that was all. Nothing solid would get through the hill of masonry sealing the entrance even if the two lorries weren't there to block the front.

"Over here," Steve said.

He'd stopped at what Cate first thought was just more rubble. She studied it in silence.

"Stairs?"

He nodded.

Stairs was probably pushing it. The steps had collapsed at some point in the last five or six weeks. Although some of the railing could be seen now that she was studying it and there was an unbroken step close to where they stood, the structure had obviously been damaged by a large explosion.

"A bomb?" she said.

"No. Not here." Steve swung his torch over the mess. "We think it was a gas leak. Brought the stairs down, blocked off a fair bit of the doors. Lucky for us. Most of the ground floor is sealed by crap like this."

"We need to get back upstairs," Damien said and pushed her forward.

"Don't touch me," Cate hissed and the light of Damien's wavering torch blinded her.

"What?" he said from somewhere inside the light.

"Don't touch me."

"All right. Let's calm down," Steve said. "This way."

She found him outside the light. He pointed to the rubble. "We go in a line. We watch each other and we tread carefully, okay?"

"Okay."

"Up, then."

Steve moved ahead of her. Damien came behind, Joey a step or two behind him. Cate kept her attention on Steve. Damien's presence close to her back sent waves of nausea through her. Telling herself there was no reason to feel that way changed nothing. His breath was grunts too close to her neck. She took a few lumbering steps closer to Steve and they ascended the wrecked stairs.

"Coming up," Steve called into the darkness. "Four of us."

"Names?" someone shouted from above.

"Steve, Joey, Damien and a new one. She's okay."

The invisible shouter didn't reply and Cate tried not to think about what might have happened if Steve hadn't vouched for her.

"Almost there," Steve said and a loose chunk of the slope broke at his feet. It hit the ground a moment later and Cate winced. Joey's torchlight swung over her to brighten the patch of the slope she was crawling up.

"Better?" he said.

"Yes. Thanks."

She gripped a jutting piece of stone and pulled. It fell. Cate grabbed another chunk which shifted but held.

"It's a lot of fun going up and down this," Steve said to her.

"There's no other way up?" she said and nobody replied.

The slope levelled out. In front, Steve's light spun around. He'd reached a flat surface and was shining his torch down to her.

"Over that last bit. See it?"

Whether by accident or on purpose, a section of the wrecked stairs rose in an uneven step a foot below where Steve now stood. If she hadn't seen it, she'd have fallen straight over it. And maybe that was the idea.

She clambered over it; Steve took her arm and pulled her upright. Shadowy figures beyond the illumination of his torch moved back but not before she'd seen the shapes of their guns.

"Are you going to Wallace?" one said.

"Yeah," Steve replied.

"Two down there," Joey said. "In the cupboard."

"They can wait until morning," Steve replied.

"Can someone tell me what all this is?" Cate replied. In the gloom, she sounded like a stranger to herself. "I've got no idea what you're talking about or what's going on."

Steve lowered his torch. "Follow me."

He led her to steps, then up. Glad to leave the other men behind, Cate studied the gloom inside the building. It appeared the remains of the steps on the ground led in opposite directions to meet on each floor, presumably for down traffic on one side and up on the other. An arrow marked UP confirmed her idea.

Where the steps curved to the next floor, Joey and Damien stood side by side, watching her ascend. She held their gaze until they were out of sight and she reached the second floor.

Steve brought her to double doors marked 2Y and pushed through them to a short corridor. A few closed doors lined both sides; the corridor opened to a ward. Beds had been removed from the first bay. Cate caught a glimpse of the space as they passed it. Armchairs and a few small tables filled the bay. Bats, pieces of wood, metal objects and what could only be several guns were piled high on the tables. Shotguns lay beside a few handguns. She spied three or four people sitting in the chairs, apparently asleep in the gloom. Windows into smaller rooms were smashed; the walls were lined with cracks and the poor light failed to illuminate every corner. The next bay contained the remnants of a small fire in a metal tin. A lone figure sat beside it, warming their hands and rocking back and forth. After that, Cate focused on Steve in front and stopped when he did.

They'd come to a half open door that appeared no different to any other. Steve knocked once and pushed it open. A middle-aged woman sat on an armchair beside a coffee table. Three candles on the table cast flickering light around the room to make dancing shadows on the sparse furniture and the woman's bulk. She was working her way through sheets of paper and glanced up when Steve entered.

"Yes?" the woman said.

"A stray."

Steve stood to the side. Cate entered the room.

"That explains the shots," the woman said.

"Two followed us. They're dead. We'll take them to the morgue in the morning."

"Thank you. Come back in a few minutes, would you?"

Steve strode past Cate and left the room. Unsure of what to do, Cate remained where she was.

"What's your name?" the woman said.

"Cate."

"I am Sister Wallace. Anne. Everyone here just calls me Wallace."

"Okay."

"So, Cate. What's your story?"

"My story? I don't. . .I'm just trying to find somewhere safe. I came in off the parkway. I met Steve out in the street."

"I meant before all that. Where are you from?"

"Does it matter?"

"Probably not other than I like to know who people are." She placed her papers on the table, being careful to keep them from the candles. The waving light shone on her face; she was easily in her mid-fifties.

"All right. Here's where we are. This is Dalry District Hospital. Or what's left of it. Out of the remaining staff, I am the most senior which means I've ended up in charge. There are another five members of staff here. Two orderlies, a member of our payroll team, a driver and a chap who worked in the chemist. After them, we have seven patients who have thankfully recovered from their illnesses and operations over the last few weeks. Then there are another nine people who have wandered in off the streets. I've yet to turn anyone away. We have plenty of food and water. We *do* have light although we prefer to keep it to a minimum. The heat's still on in certain areas although again, we like to keep it down. We have weapons which I don't like but I can see the need for." She gestured to the other end of the building. "Our A&E department is that way. It's blocked by several police cars and vans. We have a military ward up on the fifth floor and the police were doing what they could to protect it and us. In any case, we raided the vans after things went bad and the police were either killed or ran. Took guns and so forth. Not many of us actually know how to use them, but we're working on it."

Wallace fell silent. Candlelight danced over her face. Her eyes, two dark circles encircled by wrinkles and topped with a fringe of curly, grey hair, remained fixed on Cate's.

"Who are they? The people you want to keep out."

Wallace nodded. "Yes. Them. You've met some of them, I believe. We have no idea how many there are. We know they're based on the other side of Thorpe Road. There are a lot of houses that way. Plenty of land. They've been trying to get in here for the last week.

Obviously, they know we have food and medical supplies. They're trying to take them from us."

Cate frowned. "Why here? I mean, they've got this town to play with. There's got to be food in other places."

"Not as much as you might think. We send people out every few days to see what's happening elsewhere. It seems a lot of the town has been ransacked. And we are the only hospital for several miles. If they want medicine, they'll find it here."

Wallace pointed to the ceiling. It appeared relatively free from the cracks and lines that coated the walls in the corridors. "Another four floors above us. This one is where we eat and store our weapons supply. The floor below is sealed off for the most part and we always have a couple of people at the top of the first-floor stairs. We sleep on the third; fourth is the Theatres floor. Medical supplies and whatnot are up there. Our military ward on the fifth is just about stripped bare, and the sixth is closed. 6X leads to the roof. We get a fairly decent view from up there. We have people up there for a lot of the day. We've also got a load of rocks and stones up there. Sort of a last-minute defence if we need it. And binoculars. We've got two pairs, thankfully. It means we have an idea when those outside are moving about. Not that we can do much about it, mind. Down below, the ground floor is more or less impassable. We had a gas explosion. Knocked out the stairs and destroyed a lot of the rooms. We've managed to seal off windows and openings although to be honest, most of the windows were sealed with rubble. We have five Theatres. Four on the fourth floor, one on the ground floor. Obviously, that one is a write-off, but two on the fourth are operational. And that's us."

Cate shifted on the spot and asked the question that had been with her for several minutes. "You're telling me a lot, aren't you? Giving away secrets."

Wallace pursed her lips. "I suppose I am." Her right hand dropped to the side of her chair. When it reappeared, she held a small gun. The gun aimed at Cate's face remained as steady as rock. Cate made no move. The eye of the gun stared at her. From miles away, she watched this little scene play out, interested to see where it would go. With that interest, a dim fear faded in and out. The city outside had swallowed it. The run here had swallowed it. The end of the world had swallowed it.

Wallace lowered the gun and nodded as if not surprised. "You're not part of the group outside. That's obvious. Even if I thought you were, it wouldn't make sense. Why would those two men have been chasing you?"

"Or the man I met earlier," Cate whispered. A ghost of her earlier anger breathed in and out.

"Where?"

Cate gestured vaguely to the front of the building. "Out there. Before I met Steve. The man wanted to take me to others. His friends, he called them. I got away."

"Glad to hear it."

Cate chose her words as carefully as she could. "You're still taking a gamble on me, aren't you?"

"As I said, why would they have sent you?"

"To make you think I'm safe," Cate answered before she could stop herself.

Wallace lips moved into a small smile. "I suppose that's possible." She put the gun away. "But it's not true. I know how to spot a liar. You're not one."

Cate nodded, unsure of how to reply.

"Do you have a weapon?" Wallace said.

Keeping her hand away from her pocket, Cate weighed her options. Lying wasn't much of one. If Steve hadn't told Wallace yet, it could surely be just a matter of time before he did.

"A knife."

Cate pulled the switchblade free. Wallace extended a hand.

"You'll have no need for it here."

Cate gazed at the older woman, then her knife. She'd had it for a long time; she'd carried it for miles. And despite that, it was no longer a weapon. Not here. In this place, her knife was trust.

She passed it to Wallace who placed it in a drawer. "Thank you." She called Steve's name and he returned to the little room. Clearly, he hadn't gone more than a few steps from it after Wallace's dismissal.

"Find Cate a room, would you? And some food. We'll talk tomorrow morning."

"Sure," Steve said.

"Thanks," Cate said.

Wallace picked up her papers. "Welcome to the hospital, Cate."

Cate followed Steve back to the main part of the ward. A few people were in various bays and rooms. Some hammered pieces of wood against broken windows. Others looked to be fixing hospital equipment. None made eye contact with her.

"People are friendly, really," Steve said and pushed the ward doors open.

"Looks like it."

They returned to the corridor and Steve gestured for her to follow him to the undamaged stairs.

"They are. They're just not sure of you yet," he said.

They drew level with a lift Cate hadn't noticed on the way through to 2Y. Thick pieces of masking tape blocked some of the lift entrance and a line of wide, orange tape stretched from the wall to a makeshift post and back to the wall to form a clear barrier.

"I—" Cate began.

A scream raced out of the lift shaft, a single note of terrible pain sawing into Cate's head. She fell back and crashed into the wall. The noise burned into her ears, agony filling it. It faded into low sobs before vanishing completely.

"You okay?" Steve said. His torchlight struck her face. She was too dazed to shield her eyes.

"The screaming," she whispered.

"What?" He moved closer to her. "What did you say?"

The echo of the awful noise was fading out of her head. Steve's face came into focus as he lowered his torch. Concern. Confusion. No reaction to the scream.

"You didn't hear that?" she said and stared at the dark rectangle of the lift shaft.

"Hear what?"

"Screaming."

"What? No. What are you talking about?"

"I heard. . ." Cate ran to the lift shaft and skidded to a halt in front of the orange tape blocking it. Black peered out of the shaft at her. Not a sound emerged.

"You heard screaming?"

Steve was right behind her. His light pierced the shadows inside the shaft. Cables, wires and a wall were visible. Nothing else.

"It's all the stress and everything," Steve said. "The lift is knackered. It went last week. Dropped from the fifth floor and crashed down below. Thank Christ it was empty at the time. It's useless now."

I heard it.

"Yeah."

She followed him to the stairs. They ascended and she kept her eyes focused on everything but the mouth of the lift shaft.

Chapter Seventeen

Nicola swung the barrel of the gun at the branches behind her. They snapped and fell to the sloping ground.

Something cracked. She ducked and stared back the way she'd run. If there was anything there, the black of the woods hid it. She scanned the area for another moment, then stood and ran on. The stitch in her side, which had faded since she'd slowed a few moments before, returned. Pain stung deep into her. She kept running, gun outstretched to knock the skinny branches aside. The route ahead cleared, the ground sloped again and she ran from the woods to a wide grass verge beside a road. Finally stopping once on the road, Nicola looked to either end of it, then back to the trees.

"Nothing there," she whispered and had to spit. Her head thudded. Cooling sweat soaked into her t-shirt. "At least you're alive," she told herself and pictured Tom's body lying on the carpet, blood splashes all around him.

What the hell was it? What had been watching her?

She'd seen and heard nothing since running from Tom's house. The only thought in her head as she dashed over the fields was to get away, to run and run as fast as possible. Forget her bike. Just run. After around twenty minutes, she'd found the A1 again. And now she'd stopped, the questions and fear threatened to swallow her.

Panting, Nicola rubbed at the stabbing in her side and took her bottle out of her bag. She drank deeply, thinking.

The figure in the doorway hadn't been a man. They'd been too small. But then how could anyone smaller than a grown man overpower and kill someone Tom's size? And how they'd killed him? By cutting his throat? By hacking at his flesh?

None of those questions were as troubling or as pressing as the next one Nicola asked herself.

Why had the figure let her run?

Why?

She placed her bottle back in her bag, sealed it and jogged along the road. The thud of her boots unnerved her so she jogged up to the grass and ran over the softer ground. Her shadow ran beside her. Her breath pumped out in white smoke. The metal of the gun burned her fingers and she kept as tight a hold on it as she could. The road took her from the edge of the woods in a curving line to a section completely free of vehicles and what appeared to be a cluster of buildings up ahead. Without streetlights, she had no idea how many there were or what they were.

"Only one way to find out," she said and jogged towards them. As she drew closer, their outline became clearer. She was close to an industrial park. So, there was the choice: either stay on the road and follow it with only a vague idea of where she was heading after dark, or check out the buildings and see if any could be used as shelter. At the very least, she might find a light source and be able to check the notes of her route north.

"Not much of a choice, Scott," she said and clamped her mouth shut a second too late to keep her husband's name inside. Talking to Scott. Not a good idea. Thinking of him and Julia—she couldn't do anything about that, couldn't stop what she thought, but she could definitely stop what she said.

Nicola left the road, ran over an empty car park and tried to make out the names of the shops on all sides. PC World, Dreams Beds, Furniture World, Office World. She turned in a circle and hissed her joy.

Directly across from where she stood, a Tesco loomed out of the dark. Even if the place had been raided, and it probably had, there'd be *something* left there. People couldn't have emptied it while the world was ending. There hadn't been time.

"Yeah. That's something to be grateful for. Everyone dying so quickly," she said and tried to laugh. She failed when she remembered Tom mentioning the supermarket. His wife had died there. And he'd described the place as *ransacked*.

Cursing herself for letting her worry over the remaining food outweigh a man's grief, Nicola ran towards Tesco, her mind already calling up images of food and water inside, of a chair in a staffroom. Sod the cold. She would wrap herself in blankets or coats or whatever she found. Find some food, find a chair and sleep for the night.

Nicola reached the entrance and swore. Dozens of trollies blocked it. They'd been piled high on one another and formed a solid barrier of metal. She jogged alongside the building, scanning it. Many of the windows were smashed. There was still no way in. Shelving units had been wedged against the holes. Two or three men might be able to move them. She had no chance. At the corner, Nicola ran around to the side of the supermarket and skidded to a stop.

A fire exit was open ahead. She sprinted to it, already relishing the thought of resting. A question interrupted the image.

Why would the door be open and the main entrance blocked?

She managed to raise her gun an inch before someone spoke out of the darkness beyond the door.

"Drop the gun or I'll blow your head off."

Instantly, Nicola clamped her fingers around the barrel and the trigger.

"Drop it." The voice was an order with no room for argument.

She managed to loosen her hold on the gun; it dropped to the ground, clattering when it landed. Nicola winced at the noise, madly sure it would attract unwanted attention. Inside, she shrieked laughter at herself. All the unwanted attention in the world was right in front of her.

"Take two steps back. No more than that."

Nicola backed up and the man shot forward, a handgun aimed at her. Nicola's bowels clenched and she ground her teeth until the sensation passed. The man, his face obscured by a scarf, crouched, grabbed her shotgun and rose. He circled her, both weapons held loosely in her direction.

"What's your name?" he said.

"Nicola."

"Nicola? Nice to meet you." He sniggered. "Looking for something, were you?"

"Just. . ." Nicola paused for a brief a time as she dared, trying to think which would be the best answer. "Somewhere warm," she finished and hoped the reply was a better one than *shelter* or *food.*

"It's warm here," the man said. "Come on."

He took her from the fire exit, along a corridor which opened to the shop floor and told her to stand against a wall. Nicola did so.

"Hands by your side," he said and waved her gun at her as if to emphasise his point.

Nicola lowered her hands. He shook her shotgun.

"This is empty, isn't it?" he said.

She kept her mouth closed. He lifted his own gun and levelled it with her face.

"Isn't it?" he said.

"I think so. It's not mine."

"Whose is it?"

"A man. He—" She cleared her throat and kept her voice low. "He had it as a threat. Something to scare people with. He didn't have any bullets for it."

"And he just gave it to you?"

"I took it. I ran."

The man nodded. "I'll keep it if you don't mind."

Voices drew in from somewhere close. Three men. Perhaps even four. Sweat soaked Nicola's forehead and trickled down her temples. She splayed her fingers, not allowing them to pull her hands into fists. Even so, her fear was a pounding thud in her head and chest. As much as she wanted to believe the men wouldn't hurt her, that they were still decent, there was no belief here.

"Over here," the man with the scarf shouted.

The voices drew closer. Torchlight pricked the dark.

"Bob?" someone called. "What's happening?"

"We've got a visitor," Scarf Man—Bob—called behind. The other men appeared from the end of the nearest aisle. Three men, all with scarves around their mouths and noses. Two held torches. The third, the biggest of the group, carried a hunting knife. He held it like a club.

"Who's that?" one of the men said as they drew closer.

"A woman," Bob replied. Nicola caught the slight emphasis he put on the word, then the pause before his next words. "Had a gun." He passed it to the talkative man. "No bullets."

"Shit." The other man examined the shotgun, testing its weight. "We'll keep it, anyway. Might come in handy at some point." He swapped the gun with the knife and walked to Nicola.

"My name's Lee." Up close, he was older than she'd first thought. He was in his early forties, fat rather than stocky. His shaved head shone as torchlight passed over him. "What's yours?"

"Nicola." There didn't seem to be any point in stalling. If she was right about these men, then what was coming would come. All she could do was hope it was quick.

A murmur of protest spoke to her. Just because things had gone bad everywhere didn't mean the men left would all be killers and rapists. People had been good before the bombs. They'd be good now.

"Hello, Nicola. You already know Bob. That's Imran with the torch, and Christian."

Nicola had to swallow. Her throat didn't want to work. A trembling in her legs began working its way upwards.

"Please," she whispered.

"Please what?" Lee leaned towards her.

"Please don't hurt me."

"Hurt you?" He managed to sound offended and all at once, she loathed this fat man breathing against her face. "You break into our place and you're worried *we're* going to hurt *you?"*

A couple of the other men laughed. All at once, any hope the men would be like Tom vanished.

Nicola did her best to control her breathing, to keep her anger and fear from boiling out of her in shouts and sweat. Shaking spread from her stomach to her chest and arms. The world over for a matter of weeks and any sense of decency or right and wrong didn't matter at all. And in a soft explosion of light behind her eyes, Nicola found she didn't care about that as much as she cared about these men being able to do exactly what they wanted with her. Her choices, her feelings, her body were nothing to these men. She might as well be rubbish to be put in a bin. And that wasn't fair. It wasn't fucking *fair.*

"I just wanted some food," Nicola said.

"Plenty of that here. A lot was taken when everyone got sick, but there's still loads more. What were you after? A hot meal? It's cold outside, isn't it? A hot meal would warm you up. Right, boys? It's bastard cold outside."

"Very true," one of the others said. "Not nice out there at all."

"Bad people out there, too," Lee said. His mates snorted laughter. "Bad people, cold nights and a fuck load of corpses all over the shop. Nasty business, that flu. Have you got it? The Manc?"

She shook her head.

"Had it, though, haven't you? Got to be honest. You look like shit."

The others barked a huge volley of laughter.

"Funny thing, wasn't it? How some people got it and died, and others just got over it? Funny business. I tell you. Those fuckers who did it. Fucking Al-Qaeda, fucking Islamic State or whoever it was, I'm laughing my arse off now they're all dead, too. They're all dead and there's just us and our shop. *Our* shop and what we've got here."

He was breathing faster now, working himself up and all at once, Nicola saw how this would go: he was pumping himself up for attacking her, telling himself she deserved it after breaking in, after coming here to steal from them. She needed to be punished. And even if it wasn't punishment, she'd owe them for the shelter they'd give her afterwards.

Nicola saw it all. Inside, she began to shut down, to close herself into smaller and smaller compartments. His breath rolled over her cheek. Shadows moved behind him. The other men came closer. His grip on her forearm rose to her bicep and brushed the side of her breast. His other hand was a rising shape, a fist moving fast to her cheek, and the other men's howls of mocking laughter were closing in on her ears before any impact of Lee's fist.

From off in the dark of the shop floor, something creaked. Then the creak was a tremendous smash as a shelving unit fell. Torchlight played around, sending mad illumination to all angles. The collapsing unit broke into pieces as it hit freezers at the end of the aisle. Glass exploded. Cans flew over the floor. The men shouted, the tremendous crash burying their voices.

Lee's hand was no longer on her arm.

Nicola ran. She bashed into a checkout till. Despite the impact, she kept moving as fast as she could, Lee's voice chasing after her. At the end of the till, she ducked, threw herself forward and ran into the dark. Raised voices followed but no gunfire. She hit a wall, bounced off it and ran blindly through the shop. Another huge crash boomed through the supermarket. The men were screaming now, at least two of them yelling Lee's name. A blur of sounds merged into one hellish noise. Falling units, cans hitting the ground, breaking glass, the pound of her feet as she sprinted to the end of the aisle and hit a wall.

Blindly, Nicola reached to either side and held her breath. Pain sang in her hip and in her arms where she'd struck the walls. She crouched. From the direction she'd sprinted, someone approached at a frantic run. They stopped somewhere close by, panting. It was Lee. She knew it. He'd obviously lost his torch. She stared into nothing, knowing he could be inches away or feet. Either way, he'd find her if she made a sound.

The echoes of the crash from the falling units faded. A man's voice cried out. Whoever they were, they might as well have been a teenage boy.

"Lee? Jesus. Imran? Fucking *anyone?* What the fuck happened?"

The man close to her panted but didn't shout back. Nicola closed her eyes and breathed through her mouth, forcing herself to make no sound.

"Lee?" The cry was full of tears. The man was no longer an adult in the dark shop. It might as well have been a young boy. Nicola listened to him stumbling through the mess the falling shelves had made. Broken glass crunched; cans rolled over the ground. The man let out a quick, sharp cry. Then he was silent.

Ice cloaked Nicola and she fought the urge to shake. A tiny pattering, as if rain was falling inside the shop, reached her. It stopped after a few seconds. Again, Nicola flashed back to Tom's body in his front room and the splashes of blood on the carpet.

The killer from Tom's house was here.

The ice encased her entire body. Her lungs were two frozen balls in her chest.

Run. Just get up and run.

She made no move.

Close by, Lee took a few steps. He hadn't reacted to the scream.

Run, you bastard. Get out of here.

He took a few more steps. The stink of Lee's sweat filled her nostrils. She winced at the sound of her breath. He would find her head at any second, would yank her upright and then it would all be over.

He made another step. Nicola relaxed a fraction. He was moving away.

Quick steps. They were coming from the other side of the shop floor.

"I've got a gun." She was right. Lee was close to her. The others were dead, Lee had a gun and the person who'd killed the other men was coming straight towards her.

"Don't fucking move," Lee yelled.

The footsteps kept coming.

Nicola rose. Her coat rubbed against the wall, creating a sly whisper. Off to her side, Lee was still threatening the approaching person, telling them to back off or he'd shoot.

The scent of blood filled Nicola's nose and mouth. Blood was coming straight at her.

She sprinted down the aisle, heading towards the tills. There was a sense of Lee turning towards her, reaching for her. He shouted after her. She didn't hear those words, just the fury in his voice. Something hit her foot—a rolling can—and she flew forward. At the same time as she struck the hard ground, Lee had time to cry *no please don't*. Then the tearing sounds began.

Sobbing, Nicola pushed herself forward. Her body was a bright star of pain. She crawled, hit another couple of cans and lurched upright into a shuffle. Blood ran from grazes in her arms, her stomach had become a hot weight in her centre and sweat stung her eyes.

Keep going. Keep moving.

She managed to stand upright. Behind, the tearing sounds ceased. The rich, meaty smell of blood was on all sides. The salt of it stung inside her throat.

She had to ignore it. Had to run.

Nicola lurched past the checkout tills, kicked aside more cans and reached the same aisle where the men had held her. A dropped torch lay on top of a body. Its light was aimed at the feet and she thanked whatever she could that the light didn't show the face or what was left of it.

Nicola grabbed the torch, ran for the corridor, and ran for the outside.

Chapter Eighteen

At first, Cate saw nothing but dancing shadows. She blinked a few times and her eyes focused on the shapes beyond. Steps. They were built into the wall, forming a ladder lined on either side by railings. A thin line of light shone at the steps.

"Watch yourself."

Behind her, Steve turned his torch on and shone the light over the steps.

"I'll go first," he said.

He climbed the steps, pushed at a section of the ceiling resembling a trapdoor. Cate followed, keeping her eyes on the door above. Steve shoved it open; daylight coated her. Wind shoved into the building and the blue sky was right above her head. Steve climbed through the opening, clambered off the ladder and reached for her as she emerged.

"Impressive, isn't it?" he said. "Almost makes it worth it. Coming up here."

Cate let go of the ladder and moved out to the hospital roof.

"Thought you'd forgotten about me," someone called. A man approached them, crossing pipework and air vents. The sun directly behind him turned his face into a black circle. He reached her and Steve as sun slid behind a cloud.

Damien. He swung a pair of binoculars beside his leg, and his eyes were all over her.

"You know you're supposed to wait," Steve said when Damien reached them. "We're always looking, Damo. That's the plan."

"Right. Something's going to happen in the next thirty seconds before you get out there," Damien said and waved the binoculars back in the direction he'd walked. "Nothing going on." He held the binoculars to her. She took them and nodded.

"Damien's had the early shift," Steve said. "Watching the people outside."

"For the last three hours in the freezing cold," Damien said to Cate. She smiled although doing so was much more difficult than she liked. This guy, Damien, there was nothing obviously dangerous about him, but there was a layer of something unpleasant all over him, something unpleasant like old sweat.

"See anything?" Steve asked.

"Nothing much. A few of them going between houses, but they're not carrying anything. Just walking about."

"All right. Our turn. Just remember what Wallace said."

"Yeah."

Damien nodded at Cate and climbed onto the metal ladder. Cate and Steve crossed over the roof, stepping over puddles as they walked. On all sides, pipework grew from the roof. Bird crap splattered much of it and a few fat pigeons squabbled near a wide puddle.

"What did Wallace say?" Cate said.

"That we need to be looking all the time. The way it works is one person is up here for a few hours. The next person comes up to take over and they swap at the same time. Not like this with us coming up here and Damien already on his way back down. I know it's only a minute but Wallace would be the first to point out they could be doing anything in that minute."

"Who are *they?*" Cate said. "I still don't know."

"Just people. Pissed off people. They want our food, our medicine. They've been attacking us for the last fortnight. Wallace would share, I think, but they just came on the attack. Maybe she didn't like that."

He grinned and it took five years off him. She could have been up on the roof with a seventeen-year-old kid.

"I don't think they have any big plan. They want us out of here. That's pretty clear, but beyond that, we don't know anything."

"Seems a bit strange they want this place so badly, doesn't it? I mean, there's got to be other buildings they can take."

"God knows what their logic is." Steve gazed at the road and quiet houses. "I'm just concerned with staying in one piece and keeping this place together."

"They haven't tried. . ." Cate fell silent, wishing she'd thought about what she wanted to say.

"Haven't tried what?"

She studied the houses far across the car park and road. "Tried just talking to you."

Steve laughed. Thankfully, Cate heard no mocking of her question, only honest amusement.

"Talking? They're not big on that. They're more about trying to kill us, I'm afraid. They just came on the attack like we'd pissed them off. The best I can figure is we've got a permanent base. We've got food and medicine. They want us out of here." Steve pointed to the house closest to the junction of Thorpe Road and the road turning off it. "See that one? The big one with the garden?"

"Yeah."

"They come out of that one quite a bit although we don't see them go in. They probably go round the back where we can't see them. Skinny's there a lot but I'd guess the bastard doesn't stay there all the time."

"Skinny?"

"That's what we call him. If they've got a leader, Skinny's it."

"Who is he?"

"No idea. Just some skinny guy. Late thirties maybe. You'll know him if you see him. Looks like he'd blow over in the wind, but then he also looks dangerous. He's in charge of them for what it's worth."

Cate shivered.

"Cold?" Steve said.

"Yeah."

"Yeah. I would say you get used to it, but you don't." He pulled a face. "Shame the world didn't end in July, isn't it?"

"Then we'd be up here, getting soaked."

"True. We might be cold, but at least it's dry." He scanned the sky. "Not snowed lately. Not looking forward to that."

Cate shivered again as if flakes had landed on her skin, brought to life by Steve's words. The blue sky was misleading. While it could be the clear ceiling of a spring day or even summer, the temperature was no higher than five degrees.

"Come on," Steve said, leading the way across the roof. Cate followed, stepping over bird crap.

"How was your breakfast?" Steve asked. The change of subject threw her.

"What? It was fine."

"Good. You need a hot meal before you come up here."

Cate hugged herself. Out of nowhere, the memory of the awful noise from the lift shaft slapped her. She clenched her jaw and told them to go away. They'd been with her off and on throughout the night and as much as she wanted to think they'd been in her head, she knew they'd been real. Steve hadn't heard them and that didn't alter the fact she had.

"It gets dull up here, but at least it's fresh air," Steve said.

They stepped over a jutting rail and Steve pointed to the edge of the roof a short way ahead.

"What's your story, Steve?" Cate said and snapped her mouth shut as soon as the words were out. A stupid thing to say. Everyone had a story. Nobody wanted to talk about their story. At least asking the question took her mind off what had happened with the lift shaft. Sort of.

"Mine? Not much of one, really. Been working here for the last four years. It's not a bad job. I quite like it, really. When the bombs went off, I came into work and did a *long* shift. They had so many injured from Cambridge, they brought a lot of them here. I went home, slept for a bit and came back. Then a day later when everyone started getting sick, I stayed here. From what I was hearing, this was one of the safest places to be."

They reached two large units of flaking metal. Inside them, fans were motionless.

"Here's best," Steve said and they crouched beside one of the units.

Grateful to be in the open and away from the gloomy corridors below, Cate surveyed the city spread out on all sides of the hospital. Directly in front, by houses and spacious gardens bordered Thorpe Road. Beyond, green met high trees, their branches naked. She focused on the land and wondered if she could make out a thin line of train tracks far off in the distance. Behind, row after row of terraced houses ran away, the streets dotted with abandoned vehicles and signs of fire. The city centre was to her left, a mix of new buildings, a shopping centre and older buildings. Most of them had been wrecked during the rioting after the bombs. She scanned the clear signs of fire damage, the smashed windows, the looted shops and the cars jutting from the front of buildings. Ram-raiders who'd destroyed whatever they could for whatever reason they felt like.

Cate faced left and studied the rooftops and the bare trees before focusing on a parkway in the distance. A road broke off from the parkway to run alongside a great expanse of green before it reached what appeared to be a school and more houses. The school had been burned out. So had some of the houses. They'd all be dead and empty. The winter would have no problem slipping through the window frames and past the doors hanging off their hinges. In her mind's eye, she saw a door to a family home hanging from the corner of the frame, swinging back and forth in the wind. Waiting for the moment it gave up and collapsed to the ground.

Shivering, Cate realised she was looking towards the secondary school she'd passed before sheltering in the newsagents. Same building. Same destroyed wreck.

Not like the school she'd come close to her first night in Dalry. The light in the window. The sense of life in the building.

"Best to stay focused on across Thorpe Road," Steve said and she came back to herself.

"Sorry."

"No problem."

She blushed, feeling like a kid who needed to be told what to do. Cate forced away the images of the school and homes a couple of miles away and brought her binoculars back to the houses opposite the hospital.

"So, what about you?" Steve asked. "Your story."

Nausea shot up from Cate's stomach, into her chest, into her throat. She coughed; her vision fell apart and she coughed again and again, bringing up nothing. A thud hit her back: Steve slapping her.

"Are you all right?" His voice was miles away. He hit her again and her vision cleared.

"Sorry. Just had a bad moment. Thought I was going to be sick." Cate coughed a final time and cleared her throat. The nausea was passing.

"Sweet. Always enjoy a good puke. We don't get enough of that around here."

He laughed and she managed to do the same.

"Probably the porridge. You'll get used to it."

She gave him a smile and had to gaze at nothing when she answered his question. "I'm from a few miles outside Manchester. I was up there when the bomb went off. Of course, all we thought then was terrorists and explosions and that sort of thing. We had no idea about the Manc. Even when the next bombs went off."

Steve shifted closer to her and kept silent.

"I lost my friends, mainly. A few cousins. In-laws and that. My parents died a few years ago. No kids or anything so I suppose I have to be grateful for something."

"I'm sorry," Steve said.

"Thanks."

His question was on its way and there was nothing she could do to avoid it. Instead of letting Steve ask it, she answered him before he spoke. "My partner. Nigel. I lost him, too. He went quickly, so. . ."

"I'm sorry."

"Yeah."

Cate waited a moment, searching for the words. "The funny thing is I'd never even thought about this sort of thing. Life was just. . ."

"Normal?"

"Yeah. Normal. Nothing like this came into it so when it did, I had to react fast. I had to run. Now I feel sort of stripped down. Like I've left everything else behind. My job, my home, my life. I've got down to the basics, you know what I mean?"

"Survival's about as basic as it gets," Steve replied.

They sat together, neither speaking as a steady wind blew over them and raced from the roof to spread over Dalry. Again, Cate pictured the school a few miles away, its windows smashed, its classrooms wrecked, its playing fields littered with broken branches and rotting leaves. Barely a month since the bombs went off and that school would be just as empty now as it would be in a year. Or five. Or ten.

Jesus. Sweet dreams.

Cate wanted to smile to herself if only to pretend she was being melodramatic with her images of school. There was no melodrama, though, and no pretence.

Steve nudged her binoculars with his. "Have a look. Just keep your head down."

She brought the binoculars into focus. At once, the road and the large houses on the other side were right in front of her. Most of the windows appeared whole. There were no signs of fire damage as there'd been on many of the other homes she'd passed. The only clear sign of the area being different to a short time before were the cars. Five were parked end to end across the turning from Thorpe Road into—

Cate trained the binoculars over the road sign on the pavement. Primrose Avenue.

A suburban road, middle-class houses, and five cars forming a barrier into the avenue. Although it would still be possible to get in there on foot, there was no way someone would be able to drive up from the road, over the gardens and into the avenue.

"See anything?" Steve said.

"No."

"They're hiding. Plenty of them. Way more than us."

"Have they tried to make contact? In a reasonable way?"

Steve laughed through his nose. "Contact? Plenty. Plenty of throwing bags of shit and body parts at us. Plenty of shouting in the middle of night."

Cate scanned Thorpe Road. A few birds pecked at rubbish on the far pavement. She changed her focus to the bridge she'd run across the night before. Nothing moving out there, either.

"A bit of a ghost town, isn't it?" Steve said.

"Yeah. You could say that."

She squeezed the binoculars, grateful for the thin gloves she'd been given. They weren't much

125

protection against the cold up here, but they were better than nothing.

"It's about half nine now. We'll do two hours up here and then I'll show you the rest of the place. The bits we can get to," Steve said.

"Okay. Thanks."

Neither spoke for a moment. Then Steve jerked as if stung.

"Hear that?" he asked.

All at once, she did. A second before, the only sound was the steady breath of the wind. Now, something new.

"Traffic," Steve whispered.

The sound grew. The steady rumble of a vehicle.

"There. Over the bridge."

Cate followed Steve's directions. She panned her binoculars that way, focused and saw the van in the middle of the road, coming fast. It vanished from her line of sight for a moment, then reappeared as it hit a roundabout and drove straight over the green.

"I don't think that's allowed," Steve said and she gave no laugh at his small joke. The van meant trouble.

It reached the bridge over the river and picked up speed as it hit the middle, then the downward slope. At the junction of Primrose Avenue and Thorpe Road, men ran to the parked cars. Cate swung her binoculars between the approaching van and the avenue, not speaking. Fear took her words. The men ran from the houses in a steady flow. Each one sprinted to a car; engines kicked into life and the cars sped up to the gardens, crushing grass and flowers. The van slowed, swung hard and shot through into the Avenue. Seconds later, the barrier of cars was back in place. The van took a curve in the road and vanished. The men ran from the cars and headed after the van. Moments later, the wind brought the cheers up to the roof.

"That isn't good for us, is it?" Cate said.

"No."

"What is it? Guns?"

"Maybe although I don't know where they'd find any more guns. The few we've got are probably the only ones in the city."

Cate focused on the curving section of the avenue and her breath stuck in her throat.

Men ran from where the van had parked. They had rudimentary gas masks on their faces and each wore makeshift protective clothing. Each man pulled figures on leads. Each of the figures struggled and screamed as they were dragged along the ground. More came into view. A dozen. Fifteen. Twenty. Twenty-five.

"Oh, shit," Steve said in a flat voice.

The figures the men in masks were pulling were all in various stages of the Manc.

Chapter Nineteen

Nicola stood on the hard shoulder, gazing ahead to the little she could see of a village, breathing through her mouth. There was no sign of movement other than a few birds circling. Even so, she remained where she was, studying the village in the dawn light, pretending she couldn't smell it.

It was a dead place.

Denial wanted to argue against that. She wanted to offer herself *something* but had no energy to lie. Her sprint from the Tesco and the men inside had exhausted her; sweat coated her, had dried when she'd staggered to a stop a few times, then coated her again. She felt hideous.

"I would kill for a hot shower," she said to the air.

A whisper hissed behind her; Nicola whirled around to face the route she'd come. Nothing behind her but the A1 and the cars either joined in heaps of crashed metal or parked on the hard shoulder. She placed the whisper when it came again: the wind pushing through a patch of grass growing wild. If anyone had followed her from the Tesco, they weren't in sight now. During her run through the night, she'd wondered if any of it had actually happened or if she was in the middle of a nervous breakdown. Maybe there'd been no living men in the supermarket. Maybe she'd just seen bodies and her mind had given her the rest.

"Right," she whispered and faced the village. There was a B-road ahead; she joined it, sticking to the centre, and walked along Harby Road, passing empty houses on one side of the road and a wide field on the other. The village grew the further she walked; the field gave way to more houses, then a wide road presumably dissecting the village. Nicola remained on Harby Road, scanning the houses as she walked. The road brought her to a junction and the burned out remains of a post office. Moving carefully, Nicola entered the little building.

"Hello?" she called.

A bird sang somewhere.

"Anyone in?"

The place was empty.

Unsure whether to be relieved or disappointed, Nicola crossed the scorched floor and pushed at a door hanging by one hinge. Ahead, a short corridor led into darkness.

"Hello?" She whispered it, abruptly convinced the figure from Tom's house and the Tesco was straight ahead, crouched in a corner and staring back at her.

Get out of here, babe.

Nicola swallowed. *Okay, Scott.*

She backed up, not daring to take her eyes from the corridor until she reached the door and daylight. Nicola trotted back to the centre of the road and wiped sweat from her forehead.

"There was nothing in there."

Unable to truly believe her denial, she crossed to the opposite pavement and walked along the High

Street. It took her into the centre of the village with the constant stink pulsing to her on all sides. She breathed through her mouth and stopped outside a pub. The sign over the door read The Harby Arms.

"Vodka and tonic, please," Nicola murmured and entered through the smashed in door. A few Christmas decorations remained: tinsel, cards, a torn sign reading *MERRY CHRISTMAS* hanging over the bar. Pieces of broken furniture and window glass littered the floor. She crunched over them to the bar and checked for any remaining bottles in the fridges. One contained a few bottles of water.

"Thank you, God."

Nicola clambered over the bar, grabbed the bottles from the fridge and drank half of one in a few mouthfuls. Her stomach took the liquid; her throat asked for more. She had another mouthful, grabbed a few bags of crisps from a squashed box and checked the rest of the lounge for any supplies. A chunky piece of table, snapped off from the rest of the furniture, stood against the bar. Nicola eyed it, wondering if it would do as a club. She left it, found a sharp knife in a pile of cutlery and left the pub.

Two people stood on the opposite pavement. Respirators covered their faces and both wore long coats buttoned to the neck. Despite the clothing obscuring their bodies they were obviously two elderly people. A couple. The shorter one held the taller one's hand in a death grip.

Hoping the movement didn't appear at all threatening, Nicola waved. The couple stood utterly still.

"Hello," Nicola called. "I'm not dangerous."

A mad laugh threatened to burst out of her mouth and she barely managed to hold it inside. To the couple, she was probably the most dangerous person they'd seen in weeks.

"I'm just passing through." She made the mistake of taking a breath through her nose. Christ. The stink was *everywhere.* Was that why they wore respirators?

Don't be stupid. They're wearing them because of the Manc. Because you might have it.

"I'm not ill," she shouted. "I'm okay."

The woman pulled on the man's hand; they turned away and shuffled towards a narrow side street. Thin strands of white hair broke loose from the woman's mask, and Nicola realised the woman's hold on the man was due to more than fear or needing comfort. She was barely able to walk.

The man—presumably her husband—supported her as they left Nicola behind. Her stomach clenched. How were they supposed to survive here? In this wrecked village that appeared to have nothing but a ransacked pub, what the hell were they supposed to live on?

"You should have died," Nicola whispered to their backs and immediately hated herself. Even so, part of her knew she was right. Death after the Manc, or a slow death from thirst and starvation and the winter. And there wasn't a thing she could do about it. Not without staying here and letting Scott and Julia remain much further north.

The memory of Tom talking to her in his living room spoke up. Everyone for themselves. That's what he said. And Jesus, he'd been right. The world had fallen apart and while it licked its wounds, ready for whatever type of control and order came next, all she could do was keep herself alive. She could call this time anything she wanted to: a pause before things kicked back into some sort of life, the remnants of a dying society or just a hideous nightmare, but her focus had to be herself.

Something bitter laughed at her. She'd spent years focused on her career of helping young people. Her whole life had been about help and now it was all about her.

"I'm sorry," Nicola said. She left the pub and jogged further up High Street, banishing thoughts of the couple's slow death. Had to focus. Had to keep going.

Raindrops hit her hair and forehead; the sky had darkened in the last few minutes. Nicola jogged faster, passing fields that offered no shelter and the occasional house full of broken windows and holes in roofs. More rain struck her; she upped her jog to a run and saw the building ahead. A school. Despite the rain, Nicola slowed and tried to see every window, every door, checking them all for openings.

It's either this or get soaked.

Moving more from a desire to be in control of herself than a desire to remain dry, Nicola jogged across the small car park, circled the building and came to a stop at its rear. A playing field met a pathway, a high fence and more houses. A wide doorway, built into an alcove, lined the centre of the building. While it wasn't ideal, the doorway was at least dry.

Nicola eased herself against the door and stretched her legs. The relief of resting made her sigh. She flexed her toes, hoping the sting was not down to blisters although she had to admit that was likely the case. Rubbing her throbbing calves, Nicola did her best to relax. Sitting here against the school in the rain was okay. Gave her time to rest, time to let her half empty bottle fill up with rain, time to press the buttons on her phone and call Scott.

She grabbed her phone, pain in her legs close to forgotten. The screen remained as blank as it had since the morning she'd woken in her bed, covered in crap and barely strong enough to stand. No matter. She could press the numbers and imagine his mobile ringing somewhere. He'd pick it up from the floor beside the sofa. He'd call to Julia, telling her Mummy was calling, and there'd be the soft thud of her daughter's feet pounding over that same carpet as she ran from another room.

"Scott. Scott."

Nicola pressed the dead phone to her lips. The rain bounced off the playground, rose and fell again. Puddles had formed all over and the field had already become a boggy mess. Nicola let it all go and held her phone.

"I'm coming, Scott. Okay? I'm on my way. I just need some time. So, you stay where you are. You stay safe and you keep Julia safe, too. Okay? Can you do that for me?"

The dead phone said nothing at all.

"Can you?"

Out of nowhere, she wept, legs up and clasping her thin knees. Nicola pressed her forehead against her knees and took what little heat she could from her own body. Tremors shook her body and she didn't know if they came from worry and exhaustion or from sheer cold. She didn't care. Hadn't cared in days, it seemed.

The tears tapered off. She cleared her throat, loosened her hold on the phone and ran the ball of her thumb over the screen.

"Scotty, you just keep her safe. You just stay where you are. I'm on my way." She was whispering, letting her words form into tiny puffs of air. "You stay put. I'll be with you soon."

Her bottles were full. She sealed them and dropped them into her backpack. Rainwater. Still better than no water.

She let her gaze run over the playground, not stopping to study any one object or section of the ground. Probably made more sense to climb in through one of the many broken windows and find some dry shelter, but she didn't fancy that. The rooms would all be horrible messes of broken furniture and dripping water. Anything or anyone could have set up home in there. At least out here, she was able to run if need be.

"Don't lie," she whispered and a smile reached her lips. She knew it held little humour.

Definitely a lie to say she didn't want to be part of the interior because of the mess. Truth was this place was much too similar in size and shape to Julia's school. Maybe that's why she'd walked to it from the pathway across the field instead of following the pavement. Maybe she'd wanted to sit here in the rain and pretend the cold bricks at her back were the bricks of a building miles away.

"And what's so wrong with that?"

Nothing at all. Nothing if she wanted to pretend Scott and Julia were here with her and not up in Manchester, not days away from her.

Shapes flickered in and out of view on the grass, the thick sheet of rain obscuring them. Nicola stood, ignoring the protests from her leg muscles. The four or five figures were out on the grass, probably a little more than halfway between her and the pathway. She caught a flash of blue as one of them raised a hand. A blue coat against the green grass and the constant rain.

Nicola's head told her to run. Her feet remained still. When the figures on the grass began to advance, her apprehension kicked into solid fear.

They were kids. Kids on the grass and they were coming towards her. The rain continued to obscure them. All she could make out was their small height and the colour of their clothes. All she knew was her fear eating into her stomach.

"Nicola."

The voice ran over the grass, hit the playground and then hit her. All the ugly mocking imaginable held within a single word.

"Nicola."

They were calling to her, telling her they knew she saw them, delighting in her fear. And they were still coming, wispy shapes on the other side of the rain.

A child's hand touched her finger.

Nicola sprinted into the rain, veering left. She reached the side of the building, hit grass and ran to the front of the school and High Street. A few bungalows were on the other side. Almost blind, Nicola shot over the road into a garden. She followed a path to a low wall, jumped it and landed in the rear garden. Whichever way she turned, there was nowhere to hide. The sealed windows and doors of the bungalow, the wall she'd just jumped, the shed with the broken door flapping in the wind, the high fence separating the garden from the next.

Nicola ran to the fence, threw herself down to its side and crawled through mud to the back. Gloom welcomed her. An overhang from the shed roof stopped most of the rain from landing on her. Even so, water had already soaked her, making her shiver. She wiped rain from her mouth and tried to keep calm. Kids, was all. No big deal. For all she knew, they were using the school as a shelter; they'd seen her and not been impressed with someone in their space.

Which didn't explain how they'd known her name.

They said nothing, she told herself. Like the whisper behind her before she'd entered the village turning out to be the wind. She'd heard her name, panicked and run. They'd be inside the dry school now, talking about the woman who'd run from them.

Something thudded softly on the grass.

Nicola remained perfectly still. From her angle, the muddy earth, some of the wet grass and a few inches of the patio door were all that was visible.

A shadow brushed over the patio door. Something was moving on the grass. More than one thing. The shadow touched glass again. It had grown.

The kids were in the garden.

Footsteps squelched through the grass. The kids said nothing. That was somehow worse than their approach. To know they were coming to her silently was hellish.

Close your eyes, Nicola. Close them.

Scott spoke to her. She seized on his voice with simple animal gratitude and closed her eyes.

Don't look. Don't breathe. You're not here, okay? You're somewhere else. You're with me.

She was with Scott. She was with her husband and all was well.

The soggy steps drew level with the side of the shed. They stopped. Rain hit the shed roof and bounced to rise and fall down to the garden. Mud squelched under her feet. The steps moved beyond the shed and vanished.

What could have been seconds or minutes after she'd closed her eyes, Nicola opened them. Scott was gone. The warmth of his voice was somewhere else now and all she had was the cold and the rain.

She shifted position. Where the mud met grass at the back of the shed, several footprints were pressed deep into the grass. They faced the wall. There was no more walking away from it.

"Julia. Scott. You stay where you are. I'm coming, okay?" Nicola made her way back to the garden and the low wall. Mud coated her jeans up to her knees and her boots were two black balls on her feet.

"I'm coming, okay?" she whispered and climbed the wall. The village High Street looked exactly the same. On its far side, the school's windows watched her.

That didn't happen. I'm stressed. I'm seeing things.

If that was true, then all she had to do was take a few breaths of the stinking air and return to the garden. And check the muddy garden for footprints.

"The street." She gazed through the rain. "The street goes to School Lane. The lane goes back to the road."

She could be back on the A1 in fifteen minutes. Or she could go and check the garden.

Nicola walked to the road, head lowered, rain running through her hair, and the stink of the rotting village walking with her.

Chapter Twenty

Cate took the seat Steve had saved for her. The staffroom contained three battered sofas, a couple of armchairs and a few folding chairs. They were all taken. Those who hadn't found a seat stood or leaned on work surfaces. Conversation was sparse. A few people had greeted Cate but nobody had asked her name. Damien stood close to the little sink in the corner. He'd nodded at her but not spoken.

"You all right?" Steve asked her.

"Yeah." She kept her voice low, not wanting to draw any attention to herself. "Is this everyone?"

"More or less. Two up on the roof. This is everyone else."

Cate tried to study the group without being obvious. The genders were around equally split. Steve was one of the youngest in the group; the oldest, a man in his sixties. He sat in one of the armchairs, wheezing a breath and holding his chest. Nobody appeared concerned about his state. Cate forced herself to stop hearing the old guy. Too many memories inside his laboured breathing.

"What do you think their plan is outside?" Cate muttered.

"Don't know. It's not good whatever it is." Steve shook his head and scratched at his knees, seemingly unaware of his movement. "Messing with the Manc. They're nuts."

"I thought everyone who had it would be dead by now."

"They probably should be. God knows where Skinny and his mates found them."

Wallace entered the room and the murmurs of conversation fell away.

"Hello, all." Wallace gestured to Cate. "Everyone, this is Cate. Our newest member. Make her welcome, won't you?"

"Another mouth."

The mutter rumbled from behind her. A flush ran over her neck and cheeks. She kept her eyes on Wallace and spoke as clearly as she could.

"I'm another mouth but I'm also another pair of hands."

She caught Steve's grin from the corner of her eye. Wallace nodded.

"Absolutely true," she said. "And we should all remember that. So, as I say, make Cate welcome." Wallace paused, her silence acting as emphasis. The burning redness in Cate's cheeks faded, leaving her cold. "Now, news. Cate and Steve were up on the roof twenty minutes ago. They've seen movement. Steve?"

Wallace leaned against a cupboard, waiting.

"Movement. That's right." Steve rested his arms on his knees and his fingers hung limp. "We know about the cars they've got to block the avenue. Now they've got a van. A big one. Like a house moving one. They brought it in this morning. It was full of people. They've all got the Manc."

Voices rose immediately. Anger, fear, disbelief: they all flowed over Cate and didn't stop even when Wallace raised a hand to quiet the group.

"Everyone, please," Wallace called.

"What the hell are they doing?" someone shouted.

"That's what we're here to discuss," Wallace replied. The voices subsided. "Thank you, Steve."

Clearly relieved to be out of the spotlight, Steve returned to his chair. Unsure if she should, Cate squeezed his finger. His lips moved into a weak smile and she withdrew from him.

"This is obviously a new situation. And a dangerous one. But it doesn't change the fact that we're in here and they're out there *and* they can't get in. *We* can get out, though." Wallace's gaze swept the room. "I need two volunteers."

Keeping her head still, Cate studied at the people closest to her. All of them remained motionless. Most of them sat with their heads down and had been like that since Wallace entered the room. All of them kept their eyes on anything but Wallace. Without another word being spoken, Cate understood what Wallace was asking. And she understood her place in it.

"I'll go."

Everyone was looking at her. She kept her focus on Wallace's calm gaze.

"That's appreciated, Cate, but you are new here. You're not familiar with our friends across the road or the layout of the roads."

"I know. But I'll go if you want me to."

Wallace appeared to consider. Cate didn't believe she was doing so at all.

"Appreciated," Wallace said. "Anyone else? Damien? You're fast on your feet."

Cate's shoulders tensed. She'd only had a couple of encounters with Damien and didn't want another. At least not without others around.

"I'd prefer not to," Damien said and folded his arms over his chest.

Wallace nodded. "Fair enough."

Cate swallowed her surprise. Was that how it worked here? Wallace, in charge, Wallace asking people to do things and they just refused? She had to admit in the silence after Wallace's last words that she'd had no reason to assume this setup would be any different. Wallace was clearly the leader, the decision maker, but it seemed she couldn't tell anyone to do anything.

Disquiet crept up and down Cate's back. They needed structure here. They needed a sense of order. The group of patients and staff obviously wanted someone to tell them what to do. Their situation wouldn't work if they didn't play their part.

"Anyone else?" Wallace said.

"I'll go," Steve replied. "I could do with some fresh air."

"Fine. You know how it works, Steve. No risk taking. Your priority is your safety, yes?"

"Yes."

"Two AM," Wallace said. "Stick with Steve tonight, Cate. Do *exactly* as he tells you."

"I will," Cate replied.

People filed out of the staffroom, the only sound the shuffle of their feet. A few gave murmurs of good luck to Steve as they passed and Steve thanked them. Within a minute, the only people left in the room were Wallace, Steve and Cate. Damien was last out. He glanced back, face unreadable, then left them.

"I won't lie to you, Cate," Wallace said. "It's extremely dangerous out there. I can't overstate that enough, but we need to know what they're up to. Finding out won't be easy, though."

"You can trust me," Cate said.

"Glad to hear it." Wallace left them.

"So, me and you," Steve said.

Cate strode across to one of the windows. None were boarded here. They were two floors up and the room faced the rear of the building. Bright sunshine flooded the roof below.

"It's a long time until two tonight. What happens now?" Cate said.

He joined her at the window. "Now I show you around. Come on."

Cate moved ahead of him, crossing to the door and the wards. Outside the room, she looked back at him. He remained at the window. She smiled, surprised at how easily it came to her lips.

"Come on. I haven't got all day," she told him.

Returning her smile, Steve walked to her. And in the few seconds it took him to cross the floor, the scream from the lift shaft raced around and around.

Then the smell hit her.

Chapter Twenty-One

T he small hand slipped into Nicola's and she held it with as much strength as she could. Over on the other side of their garden, Scott wiped the last of the dirt from the table and used the back of his forearm to wipe the sweat from his forehead.

"You could eat off this," he called to her and pointed to the gleaming table. She laughed; he unfolded the garden chairs, spacing them around the table. Sunlight made the table surface into a dazzling sheet, and the white of the chair frames glowed. All that white on top of the green, the grass freshly mowed, the sky above utterly cloudless. The white. The green. The blue.

The hand in hers.

Nicola lifted the tray she'd placed on the stump at the edge of the patio, holding it steady so the two bottles of lager and the glass of lemonade didn't spill.

"Come on. Let's join Daddy."

All that blue and green and white. All that space of their long garden lay out before her in a smooth sheet. All the delicious scents in the air: grass cut, flowers in their beds blooming around the garden's perimeter, the roar of a lawnmower a few gardens away. All of it. All around her. Inside her. With her.

In her hand.

In her.

Nicola woke, moving from sleep to consciousness in seconds. She remained still despite the clammy sweat casing her and the ache of her dream pulsating in time with her heartbeat.

There'd been a noise. A crash.

Night surrounded her. Even so, she made no move to light a candle. She found her knife beside the chair she'd fallen asleep in. She focused on her surroundings, wishing she could focus on the memory of her dream and Julia's hand in hers.

The crash, whatever it had been, didn't happen again. Nicola pictured the house and the road it was on, seen once in the gloom of sunset. Nothing obvious in the area would have made such a loud bang, nothing *to* bang.

The back gate.

She'd noticed it as she'd approached the front of the house. Half a brick wedged the gate open. Fallen branches and other debris lay on the path from the side of the house and while she'd decided the mess was a good cover for her since it made the house look as if it was still abandoned, she'd forgotten to close the gate. Now it had banged shut.

Because someone had made it bang shut.

She mentally swore at herself. The crash might well have been the gate, but what was stopping the wind from blowing it shut?

Silently, Nicola lowered her feet to the carpet and hugged herself. Her layers weren't helping to keep her warm at whatever time in the middle of the night this was.

A tired voice spoke up. *I really have had enough of this shit.*

She stood and tried to get her bearings. This room, the main bedroom, was at the front of the house. The bathroom was behind a closed door directly across from this one; two smaller rooms were beside the bathroom. The one furthest to the left overlooked the rear of the house and the garden.

"What are you waiting for?" Nicola breathed. She walked, arms outstretched, to where she hoped the door was. Her legs hit the end of the bed. Her shins stung. She took a few breaths and moved again. Wood met her fingers. She was at the door.

You're really going to do this?

She really was. Fear was all over her, but so was anger. There was no way of knowing what had happened to Tom or the men in the supermarket. A wild animal. A crazy person following her. Right now, she didn't care.

I'll face it. I will.

The memory of the wavering figures on the school field returned and she banished it. Let the kids come if that's what was happening. She'd take them all.

Nicola gripped the knife tighter and pulled the bedroom door open. A solid wall of black filled the hallway and any of the bedroom doors were lost in nothing.

In that nothing, someone breathed. Nicola tried to throw herself backwards. Ice encased her feet and legs; her chest was a tight ball of blocked air. A few drops of urine squirted into her underwear.

A whisper flowed out of the dark. "I know you're there."

Chapter Twenty-Two

C ate eyed the handgun Steve held towards her.
"What am I supposed to do with this?" she asked.

"Point and shoot."

"You keep it. I wouldn't know how to use it."

"You'll learn." Steve's hand remained hanging in the air. Wallace's instructions from that morning echoed around Cate and she took the gun. The weapon was heavier than she expected, and the metal colder. She considered asking Steve its make or name and said nothing. Knowing either would make no difference.

"The safety's on," Steve told her. She ran a finger along the barrel, then placed the gun into her coat pocket and nodded to the ward doors.

"Now what?" she said.

"Now you see 6X."

He unlocked the padlocked doors and eased them open. His torchlight shone into the ward. Beds and chairs were heaped high in random piles on both sides of the corridor. They formed a passage that came close to making a tunnel. Cate peered in further as Steve's torch picked out more of the floor. They'd need to go single file and Steve would have to duck.

"Like it?" he said.

"It's lovely."

"A lot of people aren't happy about this. It's a weakness, if I'm honest. But we need a way out."

"It's a way in, as well," Cate said.

Steve pulled a face. "True. As long as Skinny and his mates don't work out what it is or what we're doing, we're safe."

Cate pointed to the opening of the makeshift tunnel. "So, this is what? A delay in case anyone gets in?"

"Something like that. You ready?"

She took a few breaths to calm herself. Despite keeping busy throughout the day, she'd been constantly aware of what was happening come two in the morning. Steve had shown her as much of the hospital as he could; she'd seen into rooms and wards and spoken to a few people who'd been guarded with her but not unfriendly. She'd eaten. She'd taken another watch on the roof shortly before sunset. And now here was two in the morning and a trip outside.

"Not really," she said and he smiled.

"It's easy. Just keep your head down. Don't speak unless I do. Move fast and be quiet."

"Easy," she muttered.

"One other thing?"

"Yeah?"

His eyes were white circles in the poor light and his smile had gone. "If anyone comes at us, you shoot them."

Cate pressed against the gun in her pocket. "If you say so."

"I do." Steve leaned in to her. "Listen. If they get hold of us, we're dead. They'll kill me quickly. You won't be that lucky. There aren't any rules now. You know that. You've seen what it's like out there. You know what people are capable of."

Cate thought of the scream in the lift shaft she'd heard again after the meeting, then the strong aroma that came out of nowhere before vanishing. Steve hadn't reacted to either; she'd kept a poker face and walked with him through the corridors. She'd managed to keep the memory of the sound and the smell away during the day. Being busy and focused had helped. Now, in the dark, she saw herself moving all the junk away from the lift shaft and staring down into the black, calling down into it. Smelling that smell.

"I know," she said and pulled the gun free. Steve took it from her, clicked the safety off and handed it back to her.

"Be careful with that," he said.

"I will."

"You kill anyone who comes near us."

"I will."

How easy those two words were. How easy it was to know she would kill to survive. Cate looked inside herself and felt nothing. Dismay, grief, fear were all absent at least for now. If she had to, she'd shoot the people outside to save herself and Steve.

"Let's go," Steve said.

He ducked and walked through the passage of furniture. Cate kept her eyes on his head and moved as he did. Behind them, the ward doors closed. Trapped air surrounded them. They passed the main desk, not quite visible in the poor light beyond the beds and chairs. A ghastly thought hit Cate and she spoke before she could stop herself.

"What happens if all this collapses?"

Steve snorted. "Then we'll have a headache. Keep it down."

Cate closed her mouth against a possible reply and focused on walking, not on the poles and bedframes and chairs crowding in on her.

The tunnel squeezed them in the further they walked. As they neared the end, Cate walked with bent knees and Steve shuffled forward like an old man. He waved his torch over a door.

"This is it. Remember, we're six floors up so it's windy and a long way down. Once the door's unlocked, my torch goes off. Go carefully. There's a platform straight out there. The steps are to the left. They're just like metal stairs. Try and walk as lightly as you can."

He whispered to her in the dark. His torch found her face and she nodded once. At the same time, a question came before she could stop it.

"Is this how you got in when we met?"

"Yeah. This and down below are the only two ways in. Now quiet."

Something about his words pricked at her. She let any doubt go as Steve's keys jingled. He jabbed one into a padlock. It clicked. He pocketed his key, pulled the padlock free and turned off his torch. On all sides, weighty darkness pressed on her. The fire exit opened. Night rushed in and she followed Steve out to the platform, six floors up.

Chapter Twenty-Three

T he woman placed her lit candle on the table. The little flame showed enough of her face for Nicola to be as comfortable as she could. Even so, she didn't lower her knife.

"Is this your house?" the woman said.

"No."

"Just staying here?"

"Yes."

The woman nodded and looked about herself as if the room was well-lit and not in almost total dark. "Cosy."

"What are you doing here?" Nicola said.

"Same as you. Trying to find somewhere to sleep. Maybe some food. Have you got any food?"

The woman was well into her forties although the eagerness in her voice made her sound much younger. The tightness in Nicola's stomach and the tension in her shoulders increased at the question.

"No," she said.

The woman slumped against the side of the sofa. "Doesn't surprise me. Nobody has."

"You've seen other people?" Nicola asked.

"A few. Not many since last week, I think."

"Groups?"

The woman shook her head. "No. People are keeping to themselves." She pointed to the knife. "You can put that down, you know."

Nicola made no move to do so. The woman didn't appear surprised. She sat on the sofa and let out an exhausted sigh. Nicola stared into the other end of the room. From what she'd seen of the house before going upstairs, there were patio doors at that end, the small garden beyond. The woman had said she'd got in through a downstairs toilet window. She'd tried to say her name and Nicola had cut her off by shouting at her to leave. Now here they were downstairs with barely enough illumination to see, and the woman showed no signs of leaving.

"What's your name?" the woman said. Nicola kept quiet. "Fair enough." The woman didn't appear bothered. "Going to tell me your story? What your plan is?"

"Cheadle. Hulme." It came out before she could stop it and she knew why. As much as it might be better not to tell the truth and keep a distance, she wanted to name the town, to make her family's place as real as it could be.

"God. You might as well try Manchester. Nothing that way. Nothing, anywhere." The woman slid forward. The movement caused a sly whisper. "Nothing out there and definitely not up near Manchester. That's where the first bomb went off, remember?"

"Yeah, I remember." The woman drew back at the anger in Nicola's voice. "I saw it happen. On the news." Nicola fought the urge to close her eyes, wanting to shut out the memory. "I got sick, I got better, I came here. End of story."

"Right." The woman kept her voice toneless and Nicola wanted to tell her she understood. There was no chance of a connection. They couldn't share anything. Too much fear in the way of anything good between them. Way too much shit from all the grief and horror outside the house.

That wasn't the only thing in the way, and Nicola knew pretending otherwise was a huge lie. Something had been in the house with her and Tom. Something had been in the Tesco with her and the men ready to rape and kill her. *Something*. Until she knew what the hell was happening, she couldn't make any friends. Better to stay alone on her way north. Go north; get to Scott and Julia and worry about everything else once the most important issue was dealt with.

A weak voice of doubt and fear tried to speak up, to tell her she was wasting her time because the odds were insanely high her family were gone. She stamped on it as hard as she could.

"I'm sorry." She waved her knife. "I'm just stressed. Things are. . .bad."

The woman uttered a soft laugh. "That's putting it mildly."

As much as she didn't want to, Nicola had to let her own laugh out. Things being *bad*. Jesus. How to understate it. She sniggered, free hand over her mouth to quieten the sound. Something killing everyone she met, her husband and daughter miles away, the world turned into shit, the ghosts of the children, and things were *bad*.

A great crash exploded in the rear garden. Nicola jabbed her knife into the air, close to being unable to think with any degree of coherency.

"What the fuck was that?" the woman hissed. She'd jumped to her feet and came at a run towards Nicola who threw herself backwards, twisting as she moved.

Her hip struck a bookcase and pain exploded. She fell against the wall and the woman dashed towards her.

"Back." Nicola waved the knife. The woman lurched away, looking from the patio doors to Nicola and to the doors again.

"What was that?" she whispered.

"I don't know." The hot fear eating into Nicola made thought close to impossible. "I heard something a few minutes ago. Same bang. Thought it was you."

"That's not me."

A thud struck the patio doors.

"Run," Nicola whispered and was moving before she finished speaking.

They ran for the hallway and the stairs, making no attempt to move quietly. Nicola hit the stairs a second after the woman; they raced upwards and crashed into a bedroom door. Nicola hit the foot of a bed and fell over on to the mattress. Her knife dropped and fell off a pillow.

The woman was swearing and dragging something over the carpet. Nicola turned over and found her knife. Her legs fell off the bed.

"Help me," the woman screamed.

Nicola stood and made out enough of the woman to see she was dragging a small table towards the door. She ran to her, yanked one end of the table and they shoved it against the door. Below, thuds hit glass again.

"Shit." The woman ran for the window before Nicola could stop her.

"No." Nicola after her.

The curtains shook as the woman grabbed them. Moonlight fell over the carpet and Nicola stared down to the back garden.

There was nobody there. Moonlight coated the patio area and the grass. Any green was lost in the night and while there were shadows, none were big enough to hide a person.

"What the hell's going on?" the woman whispered.

Nicola pressed her face against the glass and shook. She tried to see each part of the garden at the same time, tried to keep her eyes on the paving slabs and the rectangle of grass and the shadows coating the flowerbeds.

"Anything down there?" the woman said.

"No."

"Well, something was there." The woman said it as if accusing Nicola of something, of knowing what was happening. Nicola drew back from the window and saw the figure standing in the exact centre of the grass.

Her breath stuck in her throat. The woman was speaking, saying that someone *had* to have been there, and the figure on the grass was tilting their head back, their black clothes merging with the night so that they appeared to be made of ink or wavering smoke or anything non-flesh.

She doesn't see it. It's not there for her. It's there for you.

Nicola's breathing kicked back into life and she managed to get one word out.

"There."

Not much more than a croak.

"What?" The woman leaned against the glass and peered down. "What's there?"

She saw nothing. The figure on the grass, the figure with its head hanging back and loose as if its neck was broken was there for Nicola alone.

Her fear faded. In its place, acceptance. It had been in Tom's house and in the Tesco. Now, it had come to this house. A man wasn't following her; they weren't a crazy person. They were a thing formed from darkness, a little figure of smoke somehow alive in the cold. And this thing stalking her was for her and nobody else. She'd have to face it, but only when she was ready.

Moving smoothly, the figure lowered its head and crossed the grass to the fence at the back of the garden. It reached the shadows coating the flowerbed and vanished.

Just like the kids from the school, it had walked straight into the fence and been swallowed by it.

Still no fear and that was something. That was all she had.

"What is going on?" the woman said and Nicola pulled away from the window.

"Nothing," she said. "We'll sleep in here and leave in the morning."

"Leave? To go where?"

Nicola was already heading to the bed, knife in hand, her heart empty of fear and her head full of her husband and daughter.

Chapter Twenty-Four

Cate stood against the wall of the hospital, grateful to be on flat ground. There were three steps between the bottom of the fire escape and where she stood. Those three steps had been gloriously silent after the clang of their descent.

Steve gestured to the other side of the road. Across from them, a low border of hedges rustled in the wind. Cate secured her scarf around her face and ran alongside Steve to the hedges. She knew the route they'd take. Steve had gone through it with her earlier. They would have to follow these hedges for about a minute to a pathway. Up the path to a fence, through an opening in the fence and they'd come out to the road which encircled the maternity unit and a large car park. From there, it was a straight line down to Thorpe Road. And once there, they'd see what they could see.

As simple as that. Cate held back a smile despite nothing about this being at all funny.

They jogged beside the hedges, reached the path and Steve signalled for her to slow. They took light steps to the fence. He went through first and waved at her. Once beside him, he spoke.

"You're a natural at this."

"Yeah, I do this all the time."

He grinned. His teeth shone.

They passed the maternity unit, the silent building looming overhead. A few vehicles were dotted around the car park. There was no moon tonight and the car park was a black pool.

They stuck to the shadows cast by the hedges and fence, Cate right behind Steve. She stopped as he did, close to a point where the fence ended and a wide line of grass separated the car park from a bicycle shed.

"It's just up this way." His words were a puff of smoky air. "You know what to do if we're seen?"

She nodded. He gave no reaction.

"Yes," she said, too loudly. "Happy?"

"I will be if you keep it down." He jogged away, gun by his side like he was in a film. Cate followed. They stayed in the shadows and reached a low line of hedges bordering the pavement of Thorpe Road. Steve pulled Cate down to the earth and held a finger to his lips. She peered through the cracks in the skinny twigs of branches.

A few people were on the other side of the road. Cate counted six. All presumably men given their size. They moved without much conversation although she caught the odd word as the men passed one another. They were carrying boxes from house to vehicle or the other way around. She had no way of knowing what was in the boxes.

Guns?

The possibility was a strong one. And if that was the case, there was nothing she and the others in the hospital could do about it.

You could kill them.

A wall rose inside her and kept the thought on another side of her. If there was going to be killing, then that's what was coming.

Twenty minutes passed. Cate's legs grew numb. She shifted occasionally to keep her circulation going; the movement caused a rustling too loud in the dark. She remained still after that. Steve's attention appeared to be fully on the road and the houses. He didn't tell her to be quiet. He just watched and Cate did her best to do the same. All the same, her aching legs and stomach tight with nerves pinched at her focus. Moisture collected on her upper lip; her nose was running. Grimacing, she wiped it with a gloved hand and hugged herself. The muscles in her thighs, much stronger than they had been a few weeks before, were hot rocks inside her legs. She thought of her bed back in the hospital, back in the little office she'd been given as a room. All it contained was a mattress on the floor and a window overlooking the rear of the building, but it was hers and hers alone. Something to be said for that. She could be in there now, asleep in the dark instead of out here in middle of the night, freezing and confused.

But at least out here, she was away from the thing in the lift.

Cate's jaw snapped shut. Steve's eyes found her for the first time since they'd reached the hedge. She pretended she hadn't noticed his glance. He looked back to the road. Cate tried to make her stomach relax. The screaming thing, whatever it'd been, was behind her. She was out here and she could only deal with that at the moment.

Away from the lift. Away from the smell. The good, clean smell.

Something in her head shrieked, shoving up another wall in attempt to block off the name of the smell.

Shampoo.
I didn't smell it. I smelled nothing.

But she could. And more than that, she saw the bottle sitting on the side of the bath, bubbles and moisture running down from the cap, obscuring the name on the label, a trickle of foam running over the little picture on the label.

This isn't the time or the place. You need to focus on being out here and the people out here. Anything else will get you killed.

"Black coat and the hat," Steve whispered.

"What?"

He pointed to two men who appeared to be leading the others. "Two of Skinny's mates. Only ever see them in that hat and that black coat."

Cate peered, trying to give the figures more identity other than their clothing. In the dark and with her vision obscured by the twiggy branches of the shrubbery, their features were lost as was the colour of the man's coat. The other guy wore a baseball cap, the rim pulled low over his forehead. The bulkiness of both of them radiated intimidation despite the poor light and the distance over the road. They led a few of the men with the boxes to a car and signalled for them to put the boxes in the back seat. The men did so, then took a piece of paper from the guy in the hat and studied it. Someone laughed and a snatch of their conversation drifted over the road.

"A school? Stupid fuckers."

Cate shivered. The few words were full of mocking, of contempt. Whoever they were talking about, they had no respect for them. Cate shifted forward, fingers digging through earth. While she knew Steve was still right beside her, was staring at her, she—

Shifts forward, pushing through the prickly hedge to roll over the pavement and road. A ball of air invisible to everyone. A rock skimming over the ground. A mote with only one sense left: hearing. And hear is what she does.

"How many are we going for?" The man holding the paper keeps his voice low as if afraid of who's listening in the middle of the night.

Black Coat snorts as if the man's question is stupid. "As many as you can. We want as many as you can."

It's more than the threat of danger or violence in his voice. It's a deep note of need. Black Coat wants and that's all he knows. Anyone getting in the way of what he wants doesn't come into it.

"We can fit twenty in the van."

It's The Hat's turn to speak and he does without seeming to pay any attention to the men. "Make it thirty."

"Thirty? You think they'll fit in there?" The man waves at a white van.

"I couldn't give a fuck. Just get them. Now get the fuck away from me."

Black Coat and The Hat cross grass, push through a side gate and vanish into a dead family's garden. The two men beside the car call to a few others. Figures jog to another car and the van and—

Cate slumped towards Steve. He caught her in a clumsy embrace. Her mouth worked but no sound emerged. Car engines kicked into life.

"You okay?" Steve whispered.

Her mouth struggled to form words. She managed to lift her head, convinced headlights would spear her and Steve seconds before gunfire would find them. The cars' lights were off; two of the vehicles turned out of the

Avenue into Thorpe Road. The van followed and it seemed to be a long time before the noise faded.

"They're going," Steve breathed.

Cate blinked a few times to focus. She could do nothing about her thudding heart or the nausea in her stomach.

Out on Primrose Avenue, the last of the men were heading to one of the houses. The parked vehicles were all silent. A light passed a window. Candle light. It went out.

"What the hell happened to you?" Steve murmured.

"Nothing. I just felt odd. Sick. I'm okay."

"Sure?"

"Yeah."

Steve shook his head. "No idea what they're doing now. On a mission for something."

Cate stabbed her fingers into the soil. How the hell had she heard what they were saying? Their voices hadn't carried all the way over the road.

They hadn't needed to. She'd been right beside them. She'd listened to every word.

No, you didn't. You didn't move from here. No voices. No noise in the lift. No smell.

Cate exhaled slowly and it burned in her throat. "Now what?"

"We wait."

They crouched in the hedges. Another ten minutes passed. Cate's ears thudded with the heavy silence. She closed her eyes for a moment and nebulous shapes danced in front of her.

"Going to talk to me, then?" Steve said. Her eyes opened and his face was close to hers.

"What?" she whispered.

"Come on. You've been with us for a day and a night and we know nothing about you."

"Did Wallace tell you to talk to me?"

"No, but she won't mind if I find anything out about you."

They spoke in whispers that weren't much than air. She considered reminding him of what he'd said back at the steps about keeping silent. She said nothing. There was nobody anywhere near them.

"Not much to say. I lost my partner to the Manc. Nigel. I didn't get sick. I just hid. Then I had to run. People were coming through the streets. They were going to each house, looking for others or food or whatever. I don't know. I ran out the back and I kept running. I went from town to town, hiding, sleeping wherever I could, eating whenever I found food. There were a few people about, but everyone kept to themselves. Nobody offered anyone anything which was fair. Nobody had anything to offer. Anyway, I kept on the move. Now here I am."

He sniffed. "That's it?"

"That's about as much as you told me," she said.

"True. Maybe we should get to know each other. And that is not a crap chat up line. I promise."

"Are you sure?"

"Sure that I promise or sure that it's not a crap line?"

Cate let out a laugh, no louder than his had been. It seemed warmer in the hedge than a few moments before. While the cold was still poking through the holes all around them, she could pretend they were doing something less dangerous.

Relax. You can run. You're good at that.

"Run," she whispered.

"Eh?"

She stared at him. "You ran, right? When I was going through the hole in the wall."

"What are you talking about?"

Cate forced herself to speak calmly. "Yesterday. I went through the hole with those two men after me and you ran."

He nodded. "Yeah. Why?"

"You got in through the door on the sixth floor. How did you do it so quickly?"

Steve sniggered. "Trust me. We all know how to run fast when we need to. I'm a nifty mover."

He sniggered again and she wanted to believe him. Given the distance from the front of the hospital to the steps and then all the way down to the same room she'd entered through, she couldn't. He couldn't have moved that fast.

From nowhere, fear touched her. Her eyes were still on Steve's, still seeing him, and animal fear had claimed her. Lights fell over her face, all spinning, all dancing, flickering in and out of her vision. Her arms flew up, hands two shoving pistons. The ground below her was a spinning wheel, pushing her over and over to send the sky down, the ground up and the sides to all corners.

A scream grew. She went with it, a mote pierced by moonlight. Fresh moonlight. The moon glaring down at her. A face of rage, of judgement, and her cry boiling over to answer it.

Then she was back to her body, still in the hedge with Steve as he slapped a hand down on hers.

The thin branches in front of her face had been pulled apart. At the junction of Thorpe Road and Primrose Avenue, a figure stood slouching, head down, one hand rising, one finger pointing.

Luke Walker

Vision and sound skipped. Cate stood on the road behind them, already turning back towards the hospital, aware of Steve launching himself out of the hedge and coming to her. Aware of him and not caring any more than she cared about being silent.

Cate sprinted up the road towards the shadows of the maternity unit. Behind her, the pound of Steve's feet filled the air.

He called her name and any answer she could give was lost below the mocking shouts of the men from Thorpe Road.

Steve smacked into her. She spun and hit the wall that formed the side of the maternity unit. Winded, she collapsed. Steve yanked her arm and pulled her to the back of an industrial waste bin.

"Quiet," he hissed at her.

She sobbed, trying to swallow the tears back. The people from the other side of the road drew level with the bin. They giggled and told each other to be quiet, making no attempt to do so.

"Are you coming out or what?" one called and the others laughed.

Steve's hand shook and the gun came close to hitting the side of the bin. She grabbed his wrist and stared at him. He nodded; she let go and he was steady. Cate flexed the muscles in her legs, readying herself to rise and start shooting.

Chapter Twenty-Five

Nicola went from sleeping to conscious with no pause. She faced the wall; the covers were up to her neck, and the stink of her fully clothed body in her nose.

She shifted and something wet trickled down her neck.

At once, Nicola froze. The bedroom was silent. Light fell through the gap in the curtains. Goosebumps spread on her arms, shoulders and legs.

"Are you awake?" she said, forcing herself to speak at a normal volume. The woman gave no reply.

Ask her name.

No. She would not. The woman was just *the woman* and that's how she would stay.

Nicola shifted again, brought her knees up and pulled one of her arms free. She touched more moisture and there was no way she could remain still. Rolling over, she saw the woman beside her.

Her head had been severed from her neck. It lay on the pillow, a few inches above the neck. Blood coated pillow, duvet, wall. The woman's mouth was wide open. Her tongue was a curled-up piece of meat.

Each one of Nicola's senses skipped as if momentarily switching off, then back on. In the time it took her to breathe or to pass a day, they all returned and she stood close to the bedroom door, facing the carnage in the bed. Her senses, gone for that moment, brought everything to her: the rich stink of all the blood, the harsh, steady pant of her breath, the garishly bright red on the pillow and splashed up the wall. She saw, smelled, heard it all. She was all of it down to the last drop of blood, down to the drying saliva on the dead meat of the woman's tongue.

Nicola backed up until she hit the door. Body freezing, she found the handle and shoved. The door didn't open. She needed to move forward to open it. Forward, closer to the body and the blood.

"You can do this. You can."

She boosted herself forward, unable to take her eyes off the mess. The door opened; she backed up again and slammed the door shut on the image.

"It's playing with me."

It. Not he or she or them. *It.* That decided the matter. Whatever the little figure was, it wasn't human. And it was playing with her. Outside in the garden last night. Outside, where it could bang and wake her up, where it could tap on the patio window, where it could be invisible one minute and stand in the middle of the garden the next before walking into nothing and disappearing.

Where it could come back in silence and kill the woman beside her in bed.

"Playing with me."

Nicola screamed. And when she ran out of breath and fell silent, her fury was a pulsing beat behind her eyes.

Play with her? Torture her like this? Let it come, then. Fuck it, whatever the hell it was. Let it show itself and she'd tear it apart.

Anger breathed and that was a wonderful feeling in her head, better than fear or confusion of grief, better than anything in the world. She was fury and she would hold it with both hands.

"Julia," Nicola croaked. "Scott."

Two names. Faces. Family. They were all she had. This mad business wasn't hers. *They* were.

Think about it. What are the chances they're still here? Jesus Christ, why would they be? Just because you want them to be? Get real.

There was no snide cast to the voice or question. All it held was honesty. No denial here. No way around the question.

"They have to be," she told it. "Okay? They just have to be and that's all I've got so shut up."

She gripped the doorknob and held the metal without turning it. Her bag was in the room, but she didn't want it, anymore. Not with the stink of blood all over it. Better to find something else.

Leaving the bedroom door shut, Nicola went downstairs to the garage. Nothing in there she could use. Same in the cupboard under the stairs. The owners hadn't taken much when they'd left to hide or find safety or to die, but there was still some left for her.

Ignoring the ache in her stomach that demanded food as easily as she ignored the outrage in her head wanting to know how she could be hungry after the bedroom, Nicola headed to the conservatory. There, on the sofa.

It was a child's schoolbag, zipped closed. Moving with little conscious thought, Nicola unzipped the bag and tipped the contents to the floor. A few books, a calculator, a mobile, some magazines. They fell in a careless pile and she paid them little attention. The child who owned them was gone. She was here and she needed their bag.

In the kitchen, Nicola filled the bag with tins of food and a few bags of crisps. She took a tin opener and a couple of knives from a drawer, then raided the entrance hall for a winter coat and gloves. No scarf. She'd have to live without one.

"I've lived with worse."

The words made her laugh. The sound was too shrill in the hallway and she snapped her mouth shut to cut it off.

"Julia. I'm coming, baby. All right? You stay safe."

Her mobile was upstairs. She'd left it in her bag before collapsing into unconscious. It would still be up there, asleep in her bag.

Shit.

"You don't need it," she told herself and stared at her hand. It was halfway to the door, stuck there when she'd remembered her phone. Her pale skin and thin fingers looked like they belonged to someone else. "It's dead. It doesn't work. It—"

Light exploded silently behind her eyes, turning the magnolia walls and white door into a trembling black. Inside the black, she roared at herself.

The phone's useless. Leave it and get moving. They can't call you. You can't call them so just leave it.

She took a few breaths, gripped the chair she'd shoved against the front door the night before and slid it over the carpet. With the door open, she felt slightly better.

You can't leave your phone here.

She could. She would. Her phone was no good to her now. All that mattered was finding Scott and Julia. Even the little figure didn't matter when compared to them.

Nicola left the house and headed towards the main street, tracing the route she'd taken the evening before through the village. She stopped after a few moments and consulted her scribbled notes. She could join the A60 in about an hour and a half as long as she could get through any blockages in the road. And at some point soon, she had to find a new bike. Walking was taking too long.

Nicola moved on, squinting when the sun moved out from behind thin clouds. "Cold today," she told Scott. "I need a scarf."

Scott said nothing.

"I need a clothes shop. A shopping centre, maybe. Fresh clothes. *Definitely* fresh underwear. I stink." She laughed at herself and Scott said nothing.

Nicola turned into Catfoot Lane, passed a derelict primary school and kept her head down. No need to see the remains of the building or listen to the steady breath of the wind blowing through a shattered window beside the entrance. The lane took her alongside clear fields. The wind blew straight off them at her, causing her to stumble and making her gag. Nicola studied the grass and realised the fields weren't clear after all. A few rotting cows lay dotted around, the animals nothing but stinking meat. They'd survived the winter and the Manc but they hadn't survived a lack of fresh food.

"Now I *really* need a scarf, Scott."

Nicola held her breath until she'd moved beyond the dead animals. The lane curved. She stayed on it.

A60 ahead. The A1 and north somewhere miles in the distance.

"I need a bike, too. I need. . ." She trailed off, afraid to speak. What she needed was to increase her speed, to get to her family. Nicola told herself to relax. She'd find a bike on the way. After all, there had to be hundreds lying around now.

After a moment's silent walk, a thought spoke in a soft, sad voice. *You didn't find out her name.*

So what? she replied to herself. *She's dead. Like Tom. Like those men. Like everyone. They're all dead. The world's dead.*

And maybe the worst thing was that was true. The world was over. The ghosts of the children she'd seen at the school proved it. The world was a dead place now.

Nicola kept walking.

Chapter Twenty-Six

The pain in her legs was too much. Time to make it go away. Time to—

Steve touched her back. He shook his head and held a finger to his lips. Cate listened and understood.

The men moved past them. All of them spoke at the same time, the sound an ugly noise containing the odd word she understood. *Flush them out*. That came clearly. So did their laughter and utter lack of fear. They could have been searching for a couple of children.

The group headed further up the road. It would take them another thirty seconds to reach the opening in the fence which then led to the fire escape. There was no way of knowing how far they'd head up the road. Any potential threat from those inside the hospital didn't appear to be an issue for them.

Steve touched her back again, signalling for her to follow. They crept around the side of the bin, the thin line of their shadows behind them. Remaining in a crouch, Steve peered around the side of the bin for a moment. He slid back towards Cate and whispered to her.

"They're going right up the road. I don't think they'll go to the end, though. We have to move now."

She nodded and his eyes remained on hers.

"We'll talk about this later," he murmured and turned away from her. Everything he wasn't saying came clear in the dark.

We'll talk if we get back inside. And he'll ask me what I saw.

Cate kept her eyes off Thorpe Road. She wouldn't let herself see it or the figure raising a hand, extending a pointing figure. She *wouldn't.*

"Come on," Steve whispered.

He ran out into the road, keeping his head low. She ran after him. They reached the opposite hedges and crouched there. Steve checked both ends of the road, head whipping back and forth as the men laughed way off in the dark. Watching Steve, Cate understood their problem. Ahead meant running towards the men even as it meant running to the hole in the fence. Running the other way meant a much longer route back to safety. It also meant heading straight towards the figure and its pointing finger.

She pushed past Steve and jogged towards the fence. Behind, Steve's hissed breath chased after her. *"Cate, stop."*

She turned back to him, still moving, and hit something solid. Something with claws grabbing her.

Her scream was no more than a breathless whisper. The man who'd been hiding in the shadows held her forearms and pulled her close. He stank of dirt and sweat.

"Hello. Pleased to meet you." He didn't shout, didn't attract the attention of the others. She had that much to be grateful for.

The man pulled her again, smiling. "My name's Brian. What's yours?"

The question was a cajoling whisper, one friend to another. In the moonlight, she saw his face.

The man who'd attacked her. The man she'd met her first night in Dalry.

He stared at her as she stared at him.

"You," he said.

He looked over her shoulder and spun her around, twisting her arms, pulling her against his chest as Steve sprinted straight at them. Cate had no time to process the sight let alone react. Steve crashed into her and Brian, sending all three of them to the ground. Yelling, Brian tried to keep his hold on her. Her elbow found his stomach and hit him as she registered the pain all over her body from Steve's impact. Brian's hold weakened a fraction. She kicked both feet and twisted herself around. The shrieking instruction to stand was the only thought in her head. Inches behind her, Brian was swearing, calling her a bitch, shouting for the other men. A huge explosion blew away all other sound for Cate. Wetness hit her neck, head, hands. Heat in the wetness. Sticky.

Brian's blood.

He fell, dropping at exactly the right speed for her to complete her turn towards him and see the hole in his head.

Steve stood over her, gun in hand. Even in the poor light, she saw how pale his face was, how he shook.

A clamour sounded from the far end of the road. Cate threw herself at Steve, clambered up his body and grabbed his arm.

"Run," she said and didn't recognise the coldness in her voice.

They dashed past Brian's body, ran through the gap in the fence and sprinted towards the fire exit steps. Behind, the shouts closed in. They stopped for a few seconds. The men had found Brian's body. Then Steve shoved her in front to the steps. Her feet were two clanging beats on the steps and the men were baying at them.

Cate ran. The wind was a howling beast out of nowhere, pushing and playing with her.

"Faster," Steve yelled.

She upped her speed to its maximum. Below, one of the men fired, the gunshot momentarily drowning out their yells and the crash of them on the steps. Another gunshot. Steve fired back even though there was no chance of hitting anyone on the move and in the dark. The men returned fire and something buzzed past Cate, and Steve pushed her on her back. His howls to run, to move, were swallowed by the wind and she knew nothing but pain and fear and the door to the fire exit rushing towards her in a terribly black hole.

Cate hit it; someone grabbed her and threw her forward. She struck the ground, skinned her elbows and crawled forward. Behind, the world was a storm of voices and Steve coming down on top of her and three men crouching behind an overturned table. Her gun was useless metal stuck to her fingers.

Then the men from outside were in the doorway, swinging their guns around even as the men behind the table opened fire.

Bullets found chests and faces and heads. Blood and bone rained. The top half of a man's head hit the door. He dropped, death spasm in his finger squeezing the trigger. The bullet struck the floor. Then he was gone, falling backwards. Holes in their bodies, teeth blown out, the stink of blood and shit and the guns firing over and over and her eyes seeing all of it in its horrible sights and sounds.

The last man dropped to his knees, face a hole, chest seemingly one giant opening of falling blood. He pitched forward. The shooting stopped.

Steve grabbed Cate's shoulders. He yelled into her face and it didn't matter. All she heard was the echo of the gunfire.

Chapter Twenty-Seven

Nicola shuffled through the long grass, ignoring the moisture soaking into the legs of her jeans. The aroma of smoke and the murmur of the voices grew stronger the further she moved. So did another smell. Meat. *Cooking* meat.

Her stomach growled; Nicola held a hand over it as if that would quieten the noise. She knew her mouth was watering, but it felt as if it was happening to someone else. Someone who wasn't making their slow way through wet grass beside a dead road.

One of the people ahead spoke and she caught a complete sentence. "Is it ready yet?"

"Almost."

That was a man answering a woman and Nicola suspected the third person was another woman. Two women and one guy. Much better than the other way around. Safer.

Not every bloke is a rapist.

True, but she couldn't take any risks. And she couldn't spend any time with them. Not after what happened to Tom, the men in the supermarket and the woman in the bed.

Nicola's stomach clenched as her mind brought up the image of the woman's severed head, of all the splatters of blood sinking into sheets and mattress. No good could come of thinking of it. Had to let it go. Had to keep moving.

Nicola shuffled forward, parted grass and made them out. Three people sitting at the side of the road, a small fire burning through chunks of wood twigs. And meat cooking. Real, solid *meat.*

Her stomach demanded food; her mouth was a wet hole. She had to eat.

She took a quick look behind. The bike she'd found a few miles back at the side of the parkway remained where she'd left it. Making sure she moved slowly, Nicola rose. One of the women saw her first. Her mouth dropped open. The man whirled around, stood and reached for a long knife strapped to his leg. His fingers rested on the handle but didn't pull it loose. A sling kept his other arm strapped to his chest. The second woman stood and nodded a greeting.

"Hello," she called. A slight accent tinged the word.

Nicola found her voice. It seemed weeks had passed since she last spoke. "Hi."

"Are you okay?"

"Yeah."

Apparently convinced she wasn't dangerous, the man relaxed. "Are you alone?"

"Yeah."

The second woman staggered to her feet. Her loose hair flapped around her face, obscuring her features until she brushed the strands behind her ears. She was a few years younger than the other woman, and in a quick look, Nicola knew they were related.

"Come on," the woman shouted. "Join us."

Nicola checked the faces of the man and other woman. Neither seemed as welcoming as the younger woman, but then neither argued against the welcome.

"Come on," the woman called again and the man nodded.

"You best come and have something to eat," he said.

Nicola crossed through the grass, the wet earth sucking at her boots. The three people on the road backed up as she approached. They appraised her, making no effort to hide their scrutiny. She returned it, taking in as much of them as possible.

The man looked about twenty-five. He hadn't shaved in weeks. Although his face was lined and tired, alertness lit his eyes and he kept his free hand close to his knife. The first woman appeared to be around the same age. Dirt coated her jeans and coat. She'd tied her hair back in a tight pony-tail which did little to help the tightness in her cheeks. The second woman was no older than twenty. She offered Nicola a weak smile and hugged herself.

"What's your name?" the man said.

"Nicola."

"I'm Alan." He pointed to the woman beside him. "Marie. My wife. And that's my sister-in-law Pat."

Nicola licked her lips and realised a second later what she was doing. "Hello."

"Where are you from?" Alan said.

"Stamford."

He frowned. "That's miles away."

"Yeah?" Nicola shrugged.

Alan nodded after a moment. "Yeah. We're from London."

"Enough talking," Pat said. "Food. I need to eat."

She crouched beside the fire and jiggled a stick over the flames. They'd made a makeshift kebab, Nicola saw. Her stomach growled again and Marie laughed.

"That sounds familiar," she said. Nicola placed her accent as French.

"It's been a while since I ate," she said. "I've had to raid a lot of corner shops and—" She stopped herself.

"Houses?" Alan asked.

Nicola nodded.

"Understandable. We have to take what we can."

Marie pulled paper plates from a backpack. "We found this chicken earlier in a hotel. The freezers were still working so the meat is okay." She held a plate towards Nicola.

"Are you sure?" Nicola said. "I mean, food's pretty scarce at the moment."

"Take it," Alan said. "We need to help each other out."

"Thanks," Nicola whispered. She took the plate.

Pat turned the chicken over. The flames licked the meat and Nicola forced herself to look at something else despite how much her mouth watered.

Three bikes lay in a pile, backpacks around them. She focused on them. Anything to take her mind off the meat.

"You've biked all the way from London?" she asked.

"No. We were in a car for a bit." Alan replied. "Ran out of petrol. Had no chance of finding any so we went on foot. Found the bikes in a shop in Peterborough."

"Not far from me," Nicola said.

"There wasn't much left of it," Pat said.

"Anyway, we've been on the move since. Thought about getting out of the country."

"Getting back to France," Marie said.

"Back to France," Alan echoed.

"Aren't you going the wrong way?" Nicola said.

"A lot of people went south when Manchester and York were bombed. Then when London and Cambridge went, it all got messy. There are more dead people down south than north." Alan spoke with little emotion. Nicola wished for something other than the flatness to fill his tone. He drew a semi-circle in the air. "We're going in a loop. It'll take time, but it's safer. North, then west. Then we try and get down to the coast."

"You can join us," Pat said, face and voice as eager as a child's.

"Thanks." Nicola gazed at the chicken on the fire. "But I have to go north. My family."

She sensed them exchanging looks and understood. "They're together, my husband and daughter. Near Stockport. I have to get to them."

"Nicola." Marie slipped a gentle hand over Nicola's. "Stockport isn't far from Manchester. The chances are. . ."

"I know what the chances are." She wanted to tear free from Marie's, but the sensation of simple human touch was much too welcome and her anger was too far away. "But I have to get to them."

"It's not safe to be alone." Marie gave Nicola's hand a weak squeeze and Nicola tried to smile.

"It's not like every man is a threat," she muttered.

"Have you seen others on the road?" Alan said.

"A few."

Tom, torn apart. The men in the gloom of the supermarket, inky blood staining the floor. The nameless woman minus her head. And behind all of them, the little figure in the garden walking into a wall and disappearing.

Nicola let the cold sink into her bones and muscles, too weak to fight it. Even if the little figure had come running through the grass behind her, she was too tired to run, too tired to think.

"Anyone you met got any news?" Alan said.

"No."

"Shit."

"Yeah," Nicola said and surprised herself by laughing. Alan did the same.

"How long have you been on the go?" Marie said.

"I—" Nicola broke off, trying to think. Time had become a single unbroken event. "Three days, I think. Hard to be sure."

"What about before?" Marie leaned forward, hugging her knees. She looked like a curious child. "What did you do?"

"I worked with kids. Helped them into education or work. That sort of thing." The words tasted foreign, the idea she'd been something before right now was close to alien. Nicola laughed again. They looked at her, waiting for an explanation.

"Sorry. Just seems strange to think about what I used to do. All I've thought about since I got over the Manc is my family. Everything else has gone out of the window."

"Understandable," Pat said.

"Maybe."

"Enough. We're eating," Alan said.

Pat pulled the chicken free from the fire. Juice ran from the meat. Nicola's memory tried to force an image of the blood-stained pillow in front of her. She ignored it. This was time to eat. Time to be with people.

If only for a few minutes.

Chapter Twenty-Eight

Cate leaned against the wall beside the doors to 6X. If she tried hard, she found she could block out at least some of the voices on all sides as people argued and nobody made sense. Straight in front of her, three people parted. Steve pushed his way through them. Cate pressed herself against the wall and wished she hadn't volunteered for the scouting mission. She wished, for a brief, miserable second, that she hadn't come anywhere near Dalry District Hospital.

"We'll talk later." Steve leaned towards her and spoke fast. "For now, you don't know anything."

"What?"

"Quiet, please." The shout came from the stairs. Wallace was on her way up.

Silence fell and people parted to let Wallace through. She emerged through the crowd, flanked by two men with torches. Immediately, she found Steve and Cate.

"I would like to speak with you two." She pointed to three men. Cate made out Joey's face as the torch found him. She didn't know the others. "You three.

By the doors in there." Wallace pointed to 6X. "Make sure they're locked."

"What about the bodies?" Joey said.

"Just get them out of the way. We'll take them to the morgue in the morning." The torchlight found Cate's face. "You two. With me, please. Everyone else, back to your beds."

Laughter bubbled up from Cate's stomach. She held it inside although doing so was hard. Wallace was like a teacher admonishing unruly children, not a nurse in charge of a random group of survivors. Even so, they obeyed. Muttering, people headed to the stairs. Within a few minutes, Cate was left with Steve, Wallace and Wallace's torch-bearers. The nurse took one of the torches.

"Thank you," she said. The men left. Wallace waited until the clatter of the steps faded before she drew closer to Steve and Cate.

"What happened?" she asked.

"We were attacked. They saw us when we were down at the end."

At the clear sound of Steve's tiredness, Cate wondered if she had ever been so exhausted. "Down in the bushes next to Thorpe Road. They saw us. We ran; they followed and. . ." Steve sighed. "You saw the rest."

"I did," Wallace said. "You're not injured, are you?"

"No."

Wallace's light ran up and down Cate's body. "Cate?"

"No, I'm fine. Just shaken up."

"Understandable. Here." Wallace pulled a rag from a pocket and held it to Cate. It had once been a tea towel, Cate saw. She took it and did her best to wipe drying blood off her neck and hands. Doing such a thing sent ghastly fingers crawling all over her skin. A hot shower. That's what she needed.

"You did the right thing. If you'd stayed out there or hidden, they would have found you and killed you. Or taken you with them." Wallace's voice was clipped, dry as sand. "I know plenty of others will say letting them follow you was a bad idea, but we were ready. It was the only thing you could have done."

Steve made an odd sound. Cate glanced at him. It'd been somewhere between a sigh and a laugh.

"To be honest, I wasn't thinking of that. We just ran," he said.

Wallace nodded. "I understand. Now, did you see anything of value?"

"Something although I'm not sure what. Two of the men, the one in the baseball cap and another guy in a big, black coat, they sent a couple of guys out in a van after sticking some boxes in the boot. They said something about a school. I didn't get any more than that."

"Cate?" Wallace said.

"Yes?"

"Did you see anything?"

The fingers were back, crawling up and down her spine while cold sank deep into her flesh. She saw herself back out on Thorpe Road, emerging from the bushes to the men and hearing every word they said. And how the hell was that possible?

It wasn't. She'd heard nothing.

You answer her right now.

Cate held the bloody tea towel in a death grip. "No," she said.

"Are you sure?"

"Yes. Why?" The belligerence flew out of her mouth and she cursed herself for coming across like a stroppy teenager.

"Two sets of eyes are better than one." Wallace shone her light on the ward doors. "Best get some sleep. I'll be after volunteers to help move the bodies in the morning," she said to Steve. Cate cleared her throat and Wallace's torch found her.

"I'll help," Cate said. "I'd. . .like to."

The light hid Wallace's face. Beside her, Steve gave no reaction. She might as well have not spoken.

"Fair enough," Wallace said eventually. "I'll send someone for you. Now bed."

She waved her torch to the stairs. Steve went first, Cate followed. The light led them down to the next floor. A few candles acted as beacons on the black corridor. There was nobody in sight. The others were listening, though. Probably had been the whole time. Exhausted, Cate rubbed at her eyes without thinking and inhaled the stink of the blood of the man Steve shot on the road. Her stomach recoiled and she forced herself not to gag.

"I'll get you some hot water," Steve said without turning. She stared at his back, wondering in a rational, calm way if he could read her mind.

"Thanks," she muttered.

Wallace's torchlight landed on Cate's door and remained there while Cate opened the door.

"I will see you in the morning," Wallace said.

"Okay."

The torchlight danced and Wallace was somewhere beyond it. "You did well tonight, Cate."

"Thanks."

Wallace left her. Steve was an outline in the doorway.

"Wait here," he said.

He headed the opposite way to Wallace. His footsteps faded after a few moments. Cate rested on her makeshift bed. In her silent room, pictures came to life in her head.

The figure across the road extending a pointing figure. The face turned away just enough to be obscured by the night. All that horror and fear running over the road and pavement to eat her alive.

"And don't forget the screaming in the lift," Cate whispered and hugged herself. All at once, she wanted nothing more than to run down to the next floor, fall down the slope of the wrecked stairs, find a broken window and escape the hospital. Even if meant running through the night, running from the people across the road and running until her lungs burst, she could do it. At least she'd be away from the things wrong with this place. And there *were* things wrong here. She'd heard screaming in the lift shaft. It had been as real as her own flesh. And the thing out there tonight.

The inhuman thing.

Cate groaned.

Something was after her. Something awful. And the only way she could avoid it was to run.

No. You stay here. You stay with people.

There was no comfort in the thought, only an unemotional instruction. The words might as well have come from a machine, not her frightened heart.

Again, she smelled the good, clean scents of the shampoo. Again, she saw the bottle on the side of the bath, foam working its way down the side of the bottle, coating it to cover the label. Her hands were wet with bathwater; bubbles buried the rings on her fingers and her ears were alive with the sound of laughter.

"Go away," she whispered to the sights, smells and sounds. They went, promising to return.

Black moved in the doorway, a looming shape closing in on her. She pulled back.

"It's me," Steve said. He held a bowl of water and a towel. "Best I can do."

Cate forced herself to stand and took the bowl and towel. "Thanks." She placed both on a small desk and didn't turn back to Steve.

"All right. Everyone is gone. This is between us."

"What is?" she said and knew.

"What the hell happened? What made you run?"

"I don't know. Nerves."

"Nerves? Bollocks. You were scared."

"Why wouldn't I be?" She faced him and wished she could see his face instead of the shape of him. Electric light seemed very far away.

"We're all scared when we go out there, but you ran from something. And we almost died." He took a step towards her. She took one back and hit the desk.

"I told you." Cate spoke with as much calm as she could manage. "I was scared. I ran. I. . .the guy you shot. He was the man who attacked me before I met you. The same guy."

"You ran before you saw him. That's not what scared you."

Cate closed her mouth. Seconds pulsed in the space between them. Everything was pregnant around them and she waited for whatever was coming in her little room.

"Okay." He backed away. "Don't tell me." His shape reached the door. "I'll see you in the morning."

He left her. His anger remained.

Outside, on the road. The man in the hat and the other in his black coat telling the men what they wanted. And the figure pointing to her.

The school. They're going to a school.

The light in the window and night all around her as she'd stared across the grass to the squat building.

Was that what the men meant? Where they going to the school she'd seen that first night?

Cate undressed. Her dirty clothes dropped in a pile at her feet. Thought dropped with her clothes and that was a good thing. That was the best thing.

Staring into the dark, Cate washed a dead man's blood from her hands and neck and hair.

Chapter Twenty-Nine

A few minutes after leaving them, Nicola turned back to check for Alan, Marie and Pat. They were where she'd left them: in the middle of the road, each holding their bike while the remnants of the fire were no more than wispy lines of smoke. Nicola waved and one of the women, presumably Pat, returned the gesture.

Come with us. We can get out of the country. We'll be safe together.

Pat's words repeated around Nicola's head and she made no effort to silence them. Better to hear them and take all the comfort she could out of them.

"You could have gone with them," she muttered. Yes, she could have. All it would have taken was accepting her family were dead.

"As easy as that."

Right. As easy as that. As easy as accepting Pat, Marie and Alan would be dead like everyone else she'd met if she'd stayed with them.

Nicola mounted her bike, gave the group a final wave and faced the other way. Ahead, the carriageway was a straight line, lined with dead trees and the occasional abandoned car. She didn't want to look at the trees. Dead all around her. Dead and rotting.

Without thinking, she inhaled and tried to pretend the smell had lessened over the last mile. It hadn't. If anything, it had grown stronger.

The bodies were out of sight. Their stink was all around her, though. The bodies were in the houses beyond the grass and skinny trees. They were in their gardens. They were dumped and fallen and forgotten. They were as dead as the trees and she could smell them.

"Get a fucking grip." She swallowed a few mouthfuls of water, then swilled some around her mouth before spitting it to the road. The splat made her stomach wince but at least it gave her another taste to put against the stink of all the rotting bodies.

Nicola sealed the bottle and pulled her notes from her pocket. Another three days to Cheadle Hulme. Maybe two if she was lucky.

"Julia," she muttered.

Nicola closed her eyes tightly, squeezed them shut until purple and green spots swam in front of her. She opened them, touched her notes one more time and folded the paper closed.

As she pedalled, the wind blew to gently buffet her back. The time felt to be early afternoon. Sunset would be on her in about two and a half hours. She'd need to find shelter in two hours at the latest.

Nicola closed in on the curve in the road, picturing the house she'd slept in the night before. A nice place. Roomy. Big gardens. A place to have a family and not worry about crime or bad drivers. A place she could have used as shelter with Julia and Scott.

"Right. Then what happens when that thing comes after you?"

A horrified sob escaped from her mouth. The words belonged to someone else, the awfulness they contained was out of a bad dream. And yet, she had to admit they were true. Whatever the little figure was, it kept coming to her whenever someone else was with her. Why wouldn't it come when she found her husband and daughter?

"You hurt them and I'll kill you," Nicola whispered, pedalling faster. "I'll tear your fucking head off." She knew her legs were two pumping pistons, she knew she was moving too fast and kept going. "You fucking try it. I dare you. I—"

She hit the curve and saw the mess ahead. Squeezing the brakes, she skidded to a stop about a foot from the crash.

Dozens of vehicles were jammed together in a horrible, *welded* manner as if someone had found a way of joining cars with vans and buses and bikes but not cared how they did it. Her eyes tracked over the accident, unable to stop.

The back of a transit van was wedged in the roof of a Mini. The spilled glass from the two vehicles coated the twisted remains of a motorbike. Half a car, the model impossible to see, had rear-ended a bus. Nicola let out a shaking giggle. What she thought was half a car was a normal vehicle. It had crunched like an accordion when it hit the bus. Her mind brought up an image of the people inside the car and how they would look now. She groaned, nauseated.

Beyond the car and bus, broken glass and twisted pieces of metal led to five cars jammed together in a pile. Around that pile, three loose wheels were overturned. And all around, bloodstains coated the road. Splashes. Dots. Streaks. The stains of dry puddles. Blood everywhere.

"Jesus Christ," Nicola whispered.

Where are the bodies?

Frowning, Nicola steered her bike to the hard shoulder, trying to watch for glass and trying not to take her eyes off the accident.

No bodies. Unless they were buried in the cars at the bottom of the piled wrecks. But that made no sense. People had been in all of the vehicles, not just those under others. So, where the hell were they now?

"It doesn't matter. Just get moving."

Nicola listened to herself. She pushed her bike forward and kept her gaze on the road. None of the glass appeared to have spread this far. She walked and she spoke to her daughter while the cold pricked at her.

"I hope you haven't had to see anything like this, Julia. I hope you didn't see any of it. You don't need to see it. But don't worry if you did. I'll keep you safe, okay? I'll make sure you're all right now."

Heat was on her cheeks. She blinked tears and their warmth coated her cheeks again.

"You'll be fine, Julia. Daddy has you, doesn't he? And I'm coming. I'm sorry it's taken me so long but I'll be there soon, all right? Is that okay? Is that—"

Nicola's words fell apart as she sobbed.

"It's okay, Julia. I'll be with you soon."

She walked. She pushed her bike. Julia spoke to her. Nicola replied. She laughed. She walked. The wind ate at her exposed flesh. She laughed. Julia laughed.

Her front wheel struck a fallen branch. Nicola stopped. The road at her side was clear. The mess of the accident was behind her now.

"All right. Time to get moving again," she whispered and steered her bike to the centre of the road. She mounted and took a last look at the accident.

Moving like a blown shadow, the little figure was a jerking black pool darting from vehicle to vehicle. It touched each one, caressed the smashed metal and spun around to dance over glass.

"I see you," Nicola whispered and the little figure froze. It might have been facing her. It might have been facing the curve. Nicola saw no features. She knew nothing but shrieking terror. Inside that terror, anger breathed.

"Come on. Come and get me."

It shifted and she knew which side was its face: the side it presented to her.

"You come and get me now because if you wait until I find them and come anywhere near me then, I will kill you."

The head section rolled. An arm rose, a finger was pooling out of the black. Cold sweat landed in Nicola's eye. She wiped it away, then froze.

The figure was gone. The wrecks remained, but the figure had vanished.

Something new registered.

A car.

Coming fast.

Coming straight towards her.

Chapter Thirty

C ate stood at the top of the ruined stairs, looking down despite Joey telling her a moment before she shouldn't. The angle and drop to the ground floor exposed from the lack of steps sent vertigo through her head. Even so, she kept her gaze level with the floor below. Better to keep her focus on it than meet anyone's eye. Especially Steve's.

He was talking to three other men. She saw him from the corner of her eye, though. He was looking straight at her.

She shifted on the spot as Joey tried to get her attention. He was pointing to the stairs going up. Three men were coming, man-handling a wrapped corpse down the stairs. The last of the shot men from the night before.

The murmurs of conversation fell apart. The only sounds were the grunts of the men, the tread of their steps and the thud as one end of the corpse hit the wall.

The men dropped the body onto the pile of others and stood away from it. All of them were sweating.

None made any move to wipe their faces or foreheads. Cate knew why. No desire to get blood or the stink of the bodies onto their flesh.

She backed up with the others when Wallace approached from the doors to 2Y. People filed against the wall, waiting.

Wallace glanced at their bodies. "They need taking to the morgue. Volunteers?"

"Count me in."

Cate knew without turning Steve had spoken just as she knew his immediate reply didn't give her any choice. She raised a hand and nodded when Wallace met her gaze.

"Two. I need another four. Two per body."

"Yeah, suppose so," Joey said and shuffled to stand beside Steve. Damien did the same. Cate kept her eyes on the bodies while other people offered themselves. She didn't know their names, didn't want to although she did feel a vague gratitude that one of the volunteers was a woman. If luck was on her side, she'd be teamed with the woman.

"I want you there and back within fifteen minutes. Keep conversation to a minimum." Wallace handed keys to Joey. He jingled them and made a fist when Wallace stabbed him with a look.

"You're the boss," he said and took hold of one end of a body. Damien took the other.

"How are we going to get them downstairs?" Cate said. Everyone looked at her or so it felt.

"How do you think?" Damien said. He and Joey carted the body to the slope and dropped it. The body tipped over, shifted loose rubble and fell. It created a deeply unpleasant whispering noise as it skidded through the rubble, turning end over end before dropping the last few feet and crashing to the floor. Two others took hold of a body.

I can't hear that four times.

But she could. She'd have to.

Two of the other bodies went the same way as the first. Any hope Cate had of being teamed with the other woman had disappeared a moment before. That woman had stepped forward with another volunteer, leaving Cate with Steve. He brushed her shoulder as he moved forward.

"We're up," he said.

He yanked the last body by what was probably the shoulders. Steeling herself and pretending all the others weren't watching, Cate took hold of the other end. The bodies had been wrapped in sheets; their shape was almost lost inside the material. She felt it, though. This had once been a person who walked and talked and ate and drank and was now a pile of bones and bloody meat wrapped in hospital sheets.

She was holding a pile of waste filled with holes.

Dizziness blurred her vision. She blinked rapidly and focus returned.

"All right?" Steve said.

"Yes."

"Good. Bend your legs, not your back. We'll lift on three. One, two, three."

They lifted the body. At once, the muscles in Cate's arms, shoulders and lower back protested. Straining, she shifted around and carted the body to the slope.

"Down we go," Steve said. "Drop it."

She did. The body went the same way as the others to crash on the ground floor.

"Fifteen minutes," Wallace said. "Everyone else back to work."

The group dispersed, people heading back to their rooms to prepare food or wash clothes or do anything that didn't involve carting bodies around. Cate joined the small group heading to the top of the wrecked stairs. Steve drew close behind her.

"How did you sleep?"

"Fine. You?"

"Not great. A lot to think about."

She nodded, keeping her face still. Joey and the woman were in front of her. Using the light that made its way through cracks and gaps in the fortified entrance, she saw where they stepped. She did the same as the group headed down.

"Why did you volunteer for this?" Steve said, too loudly.

Joey glanced back. "She didn't have any choice. It's down to both of you that we've got these four to deal with," he said. He didn't appear angry. His reply was delivered in a matter of fact manner that chilled Cate.

"We didn't want them to follow us," she said and Joey's gaze made it clear he wasn't concerned with anything she said.

The group reached level ground. Joey spoke directly to Cate. "It's through those doors and then a straight line to the right, okay? We'll pass a lot of doors, but they're all shut. We go right to the end."

"Fine," Cate replied.

Everybody took hold of an end of a body. Resigning herself to being stuck with Steve, Cate gripped dead ankles and lifted when Steve did. She kept her eyes off him. Focus had to be on the body, had to be anywhere but Steve's face and his questions.

They turned into a corridor and walked in a line. Within seconds, the aches in Cate's muscles had become solid pain. She clenched her jaw and ignored it. A mark on the sheet caught her eye. It grew as she watched and there was no surprise when she realised blood was soaking through the sheets. It formed an uneven patch, red colouring the blue around where the man's stomach would be. Steve didn't appear to have noticed it, or if he had, he was pretending not to. Something niggled at her, something wrong with their situation. Moments passed. She told herself the worry was purely down to nerves. She would do the same as Steve.

"Almost there," Joey murmured, his voice strangely hollow. No normal hospital sounds to compete with it, to amplify it or muffle it. All they had was the hot tang of breath, of aching arms and hands, and shuffling trainers and boots over a dirty floor. Joey's torchlight swung backwards, pooling on each body and each person carrying the bodies.

"We all right?" he said.

"Fine," Steve replied. "Just keep the light in front, will you?"

The torchlight skipped over cracks in the walls and a broken window in a door before illuminating the remainder of the corridor. It ended at double doors, both shut. They were padlocked. Moving fast, Joey unlocked them, swung them open to reveal a small alcove and a large single door at the other end. That, too, was padlocked.

"In here," he said. "Quick."

He jogged ahead, the group followed and Joey unlocked the morgue entrance.

At once, the stink hit Cate. She tried to breathe through her mouth and tried not to picture the rotting flesh ahead. No power in the morgue. No freezers to store bodies. Just a room they could seal the dead inside. The morgue was nothing more than a big storage cupboard.

"Best idea is to take a few breaths now and hold it when we're in there," Steve told her.

She followed his advice, wincing at the taste it brought into her mouth. Ahead, the first two were taking their body into the morgue. Others followed while Joey lit the way and some of the area beyond the door.

"Our turn," Steve said.

Chest burning for fresh air, Cate backed up into the morgue and Joey brought his torch around to show the other bodies stacked against the wall.

"Just there," he said.

They dropped the final body on top of the others. Cate could no longer hold her breath. She let it out and took a huge one in, not caring for a moment about the stink. It coated her tongue and nostrils like glue. She breathed again, coughing away as much of the taste as possible. Spots danced in front of her eyes; she coughed again and leaned on a table for support. Light pulsed for a moment as if a bulb was on its way out. Then the light was a rapidly shrinking line, a dot, winking as it pulled away from her.

The morgue door was closing and she was still leaning against the table.

Cate staggered off the table, reaching for the diminishing light, calling Steve's name. The light shrank to a pencil-thin line, the door closed and the line vanished.

She stood in utter black, stink assaulting her on all sides. For a spinning moment, all Cate knew was a steady howl of horror. Then she was running to the door, hammering on it, screeching Steve's name. Pain filled her fists from the impact of bashing them on the door;

her screams echoed around the morgue, bouncing off the walls to hit her ears and run away again.

Sobbing, Cate croaked Steve's name. This was his idea. Punishment for the night before. Punishment for being scared and alone and trapped. And now she really was trapped. Stuck in the void of the stinking morgue.

She reached forward and took a moment to find the handle. Moving the freezing metal was like trying to move rock.

Lighter.

Yes. The lighter. Eagerly, Cate slapped a hand against her jeans pocket and the shape of her lighter. The little object wasn't a way out, but it was still something other than the impenetrable nothing weighing on her eyes and ears.

She fished the lighter out, clicked it. It sparked. She clicked it again and the small flame burst to life. Cate held it to the handle as if that would unlock the door.

"Think," she whispered. *"Think."*

There had to be another door or a window somewhere. This was a morgue, not a bank vault. All she had to do was have a look around and get the hell out.

Out of nowhere, she knew what the niggle from a few minutes before had been.

Bodies don't bleed.

Forget it. She had to get out.

Cate whirled around, psyching herself up for moving through the morgue. She saw them immediately.

The four bodies, still wrapped in their bloody sheets, stood upright, swaying in the rolling shadows cast by her lighter.

Chapter Thirty-One

Nicola slid down the grass. The rustle of her clothes rubbing against the ground made her stop. Sound carried in the wind.

From the road, voices were audible. She'd seen a couple of them a moment before. A man and woman. It sounded as if there was a second man with them. Briefly, she'd hoped she'd made a mistake and the people on the road were Alan, Pat and Marie come to help her travel north. No chance of that, though. They'd be miles behind by now, and here she was in the grass, feet away from strangers.

Go away. Get back in your car and go away.

They didn't. They'd come to a stop on the other side of the road after making their slow way past the accident and debris. Nicola heard the woman say the word *bike* and cursed herself for simply dropping her bike and not shoving it into the broken vehicles. Instead of her bike being part of the accident, it was clearly unmarked and undamaged by what had happened here.

One of them shifted metal aside and Nicola caught the little scrape as her bike frame rolled over the ground.

"Looks brand new." The woman was speaking and Nicola did her best to name the emotions in the three words. She wanted to hear concern but caught only basic interest. There'd be no help here. But then she couldn't rely on help in any case. Every person she met ended up dead.

She dug her fingers into the grass. The cold was back, caressing her skin, dancing over the fine hairs on her neck and arms.

Nicola shifted to look behind herself. The slope of grass met a wide field. The grass out there was already unkempt and messy. Standing on it probably a quarter of a mile from where Nicola lay, the little figure was a black smudge over the green.

"No," Nicola whispered. "Go away. Leave me alone."

It came toward her as if it was on wheels.

On the road, one of the men said: "We need to get moving. Come on."

"We should have a look around." The speaker was the other man. He sounded younger than the first. "Might be something we can take with us."

"We haven't got time. They're not that far behind us."

"Relax. They're miles away."

The voice of a young man impatient with an older one. Nicola chewed her lower lip and wished for the younger man to listen to the other guy.

Run, you idiots. Get out of here.

"John's right," the woman said. "I don't want them finding us here. Not after yesterday."

The shadow behind Nicola was still advancing over the green, still too far away for her to make out its face.

"We need food. We need water," the younger man shouted. "Just give me a minute."

"We won't find anything here, Danny. It's a mess. Come on."

"Just give me a fucking minute," Danny said. He shifted aside chunks of vehicle, swearing softly as he presumably found nothing but splatters of blood and no bodies.

Get out of here, she thought at them. *Please, just run.*

Behind her, the little figure was closing in as if blown by the wind. Its arms were rising in two spindly lines and hands grew from the lines. Hands to reach and grip and claw and tear.

"Danny," the woman said. "Please. Let's go."

A moment of total silence dripped on to Nicola. She clawed at the grass and wished for them to run away far away.

"Where are the bodies?" All at once, Danny sounded even younger than he was. Nicola tasted his fear. Cloying and thick. "There are no bodies," he said.

That's right. No bodies. And you know why? Because it took them. It's keeping them.

Nicola shook. How long before the little figure's hands closed over her throat and tore her head from her neck?

Then pulled her body from the grass to its pile of bodies somewhere off in the dark?

"We're leaving," John said. "Now."

There was no argument from Danny. Nicola listened to their running steps, then the car engine kicking into life. Wheels crunched over gravel and the car was moving past her, leaving her with the cold and the traffic accident.

Behind, again. Nothing but untouched grass. The little figure had left her alone because she was alone.

"I'll beat you. Trust me. I will."

If there was any reply, it was the steady breath of wind blowing over the grass.

Nicola waited another three minutes. She counted the seconds and eased herself off the slope when she reached one hundred and eighty. Her bike had been moved from where she'd dropped it. That and the fact that some of the wrecks had been disturbed were the only signs anyone else had been there.

Exhausted, Nicola crossed the road to her bike, stood it upright and shifted her bag over her shoulder. The daylight was clearly growing thin. Gloom had closed in on the road from the grass and trees as the grey sky darkened. She needed shelter now. She needed rest.

Nicola mounted her bike and froze. A car was coming. Fast. Scott spoke to her.

That woman was scared. Even with two men with her, she was scared of the men behind them. Hide, Nicola. Hide right now.

Nicola found the pedals. She began moving away from the smashed cars and everything was much too slow, everything was weighed down.

She knew without looking back that the speeding car had reached the curve behind her.

Chapter Thirty-Two

The dumb thunder of the door unlocking, her steady shrieks, the shuffle behind of the approaching bodies.

Cate fell as the door swung open. Arms caught her; she kept moving forward, pushed the arms away, hit someone's chest and crashed to the floor.

Voices above. "What the fuck's going on?"

Joey, Damien and Steve looked down, frowning. Steve held a hand to her, clearly ready to help her up. She slapped it away, boosted herself forward and made it to her feet. They shook; her legs shook. Everything was a trembling mess.

"Cate?" Steve said. "You okay?"

She made it one step towards the morgue doors. That was all she could manage. The light from the men's torches penetrated a short way into the room. Enough to see the bodies they'd piled on the floor. None had moved.

Speaking was an effort, but she made it. "Why did you lock me in there?"

"What?" Joey's torchlight ran over her body and landed on her face. "We didn't. You were with us."

The complete solidity of the lie took any reply. Cate held on to the urge to smack the torch away from him. "No. You did it. You left me in there. You locked me in there."

"Cate." Steve moved closer to her and shone his torch towards the floor. "We didn't. We really didn't. You were with us. You were near the back with me. *I* saw you. We got to the stairs and you weren't there. You just weren't."

"Fuck off," she said and spun around.

They chased after her as she ran up the corridor towards the main entrance. Steve caught her by the shoulders as she reached the mess of the stairs.

"Listen," he said. "I'm not lying. We saw you. Then you weren't there. I'm telling you the truth."

Joey and Damien jogged from the corridor and both stopped several steps away as if afraid they might catch something off her.

Steve leaned closer to her. "What did you see? What happened?" he whispered.

A dull heat of anger flamed between her breasts. As much as she wanted to aim it at Steve and the others, she couldn't do so. They were telling the truth. She could smell it off them, taste it, see it.

"I need to speak to Wallace," she said.

Steve nodded. "Probably a good idea." He glanced at the other men. "You two go first."

"I'll go last," Cate said before he could suggest she follow Joey and Damien. Steve shrugged and followed the men up the slope.

Cate counted to five and headed up, forcing her eyes to see nothing but the torchlight as her mind played back the darkness in the morgue and the shuffle of the bodies as they'd come closer and closer.

They reached level ground. A few people were dotted around the corridor. Most appeared to be in rooms and wards.

"Do me a favour, Damien. Tell Wallace we need to speak to her," Steve said.

"Sure."

Damien entered 2Y, the doors easing shut behind him.

"Have a look up on the roof," Steve told Joey and the small group around him. "And keep quiet."

Joey and a couple of the other men headed to the stairs, all staring at Cate with unconcealed dislike and suspicion. Without speaking to Cate, Steve headed down the corridor. Cate followed. They passed open doors. People were talking together, mending furniture, cleaning pots, loading guns, nailing broken pieces of wood over windows. They were all nothing to do with the horrible dark in the morgue. Whatever had been in there had been for her alone just like the scream in the lift shaft had been for her.

I need to leave. Tonight.

And what chance was there of that? She'd be lucky to make it out of the hospital grounds before someone saw her. Saw her, killed her. Or worse.

Steve stopped outside Wallace's door which was ajar. He tapped on it and stood aside.

"You're not coming in?" Cate said.

"No."

She eyed him, making no move to enter Wallace's room. "You think I'm mad, don't you? Or causing trouble?"

"Would you be surprised if I did?"

Cate laughed. Doing so here and now felt wrong and it felt wonderful. It made the terror of the black morgue and the upright bodies go away if only for a moment. "Not really."

"Then change my mind," he said. "Talk to me later."

Any anger or disbelief had left his face. All that remained was a weak confusion and hope she would do as he asked.

"Are you coming in?" Wallace called.

Steve walked away. Cate counted to five, listening to him go. She entered Wallace's room which was much the same as it had been during her only other visit. Damien was nowhere in sight. Presumably, he'd told Wallace what had happened and was lurking nearby, hoping to hear their conversation.

"Have a seat," Wallace said.

Cate took an old chair against the wall, grateful she wasn't on one side of the table with Wallace on the other.

"So, can you tell me what happened?" Wallace said.

"You mean can I tell you how the others saw me with them while I was locked in a morgue?"

"Yes."

"No."

Wallace tapped her nails against a glass. "For what it's worth, Cate, I believe you were still in the morgue. The others say you were with them until they reached the stairs. Damien says you were beside him at the back. He looked away and you were gone. There's no way you could have made it back to the morgue before they went back there. In any case, the doors were locked."

"So, you believe they saw what? A ghost?"

Wallace smiled although it struck Cate as more of a grimace. "I don't believe in ghosts, but then I don't believe you're lying and there's no reason for the others to lie."

"Someone is," Cate said.

She wanted nothing more to get away from Wallace and her questions, Wallace and her calm eyes and her soft voice. She wanted to be outside it all, away from it all.

Get away. Get out tonight.

Cate ignored the thought.

"My bigger concern is you," Wallace said. "I want. . .I need to know you're all right."

"Why wouldn't I be?"

Wallace struck the desk. Pens rolled off and fell to the floor. The thud of her fist on the desk was hollow in the little room. Her face had flushed. "Don't treat me like I'm stupid. I know you've been through some horrible things out there. Everyone has. I respected your privacy when you arrived and I respect it now, but don't pretend we're in a normal situation or that how we act and what we do isn't important. I need to know you're not dangerous to yourself or to anyone else."

Wallace didn't raise her voice. Cate wondered if doing so would help.

"I'm not dangerous. Never have been."

Wallace nodded. "All right. Next question. What did you see in the morgue?"

Cate's tongue was a thick slab in her mouth. "See?" she said.

"What made you scream?"

What wanted to be genuine anger took hold of Cate. She welcomed it. "Who says I had to see something? I was locked in a pitch-black morgue, for Christ's sake."

Wallace remained silent. Her face said she could stay silent for a long time.

Cate took a breath. "I didn't see anything. I *couldn't* see anything."

The blood pooling on the sheet, the body bleeding as they carried it to the morgue. The ghastly sight of the corpses standing behind her. The line of light in the crack of the door growing smaller and smaller.

"Cate?" Wallace said.

Cate punctuated each of her words as precisely as she could. "I didn't see anything, Wallace."

Outside in the corridor, a volley of noise rose from nothing. At once, Wallace was up and running to the door. Cate followed, the cold enveloping her again.

They're out. They got out of the morgue and they're coming.

"What is it?" Wallace shouted and Steve bellowed his reply.

"They're coming. Outside. They're coming in."

Chapter Thirty-Three

Nicola shoved a hand out at the last second, hit the hanging branch and shoved it away from her face. She dashed past the tree; the branch swung backwards. Whoops and cheers closed in and as much as she tried to run silently, her panting breath and the crunch of her boots on the dead leaves betrayed her.

She ran through a small clearing, ducked below more branches and reached a shadowy patch of the wood. Bark scrapped against her and she bit back a gasp of pain. Blood ran in trickles down to her fingers. She wiped her hand on her coat and crouched beside a dead log. The mossy stink of it filled her nose and she did her best to breathe without making a sound.

The men were coming.

One of them shouted to the others. She didn't catch the words, only the tone of a question.

"No. Not yet," one yelled back.

They were close. The tread of their feet, the constant mutter of their voices as they made no attempts to be quiet, the rustle of the grass as they crossed it—all of it hit her, the mass of sounds doing their best to make thought close to impossible.

The road was diagonally right from where she sat, probably a mile away. Even if it was right in front of her, she had no chance of getting to it and her bike. Travel on the road and they would come after her in their car. At least here, they were on foot as she was. Here, she was able to hide.

The last several minutes were a blur of shouts chasing her, of ditching her bike and running from the road into the grass and woods. There'd been a few seconds when she'd first started pedalling away from the wreck that she'd thought she had a chance. That vanished at the first ugly sound of jeering.

Now they beat their way through the woods, smashing branches down, hacking at the long grass with kitchen knives. She'd got a momentary glimpse of them in the horrible seconds on the road as she'd run and they'd followed, cat-calling and whistling at her. Four or five men, all big, lumbering figures with knives and bats. Not that long before, they were probably family men, probably men who went to the pub with their mates, probably men who were all right. Now things had changed.

Nicola rose, straining to hear. Their voices moved away. She crept from the dead log, rounded a curve of the path and felt her way along wet tree trunks. She had no idea which way she was heading. The road was no option and all that left for her was to keep moving.

Branches snapped behind. Nicola froze. She would keep fighting when they came for her, go for their eyes, give them no choice but to kill her. Better a quick death than anything else.

"She's here somewhere," one of the men said from much too close to her. The leaves rustled and more branches snapped over to her right. Moving with light steps, Nicola crept to her left, eyes ahead, fingers like claws. The path took her between tall trees; the branches hung over her like arms. She passed below them, the land sloped and she stumbled down it. Her boot hit a loose pile of twigs and stone and the impact was a thundercrack in the cool quiet.

"She's here."

Nicola ran. She skidded through the wet grass, bounced off a wide trunk and sprinted deeper into the woods. Shouts chased after her, the thunder of the men's feet, the eager call of their voices, mocking her, telling her to stop, telling her they wouldn't hurt her. She upped her speed to its maximum, shot between spongy bushes and jumped at the last second over a log.

She crashed into a wide clearing, stumbled and made it to her feet.

Four women were tied together in the middle of the clearing, bound at the wrist and foot. Tatty pieces of cloth covered their mouths. Tear-filled eyes stared at her. One, the oldest, frantically jerked her head to the other side of the clearing.

Horror-struck to the point of not thinking, Nicola ran. She hit a prickly bush, fell through it and landed on the wet floor. Blood ran from a dozen tiny scratches on her wrists, arms and legs. Nicola pulled herself into a ball and rested against a tree trunk. Her mouth was a trembling muscle; a hot line of tears worked their way down her dirty cheeks.

The women. Tied up. In the woods. The women.

Nicola held her legs. Anger exploded from close behind.

"Where the fuck did she go?"

"You were supposed to be following her, you cunt."

"Fuck off."

Sounds of shoving, of shouting, of threats. Then a calmer voice.

"Leave it. Leave it. Look for her."

The arguing descended into mutters. Nicola listened to them shoving branches and twigs aside, their knives hissing as they swung them, then the blades hacking through grass.

Following her. She'd been herded this way. Nicola closed her eyes for a moment. Herded to the clearing to join the other women. As soon as they found her, she'd be taken to the others and tied with them.

Outrage filled her and she snapped her mouth shut to keep her furious bellow inside. The world finished, everything destroyed and all for nothing wasn't enough. These bastards wanted to take it further and ruin the little that was left.

Nicola lowered her hand and squeezed it into a fist. The pain of her nails cutting into her palm was wonderful. She wanted to take that pain, make it grow into a fiery ball and give it to the men behind her. She wanted to hear them screaming.

"Where did she go?" one shouted. A thud followed it and sobs followed the thud.

He was beating one of the women. Nicola closed her eyes again.

"You see her? Huh? Did you see her?"

More thuds in between each question. More weak sobs.

"Gary, leave her alone," another man said. The first man mumbled a reply. Then a tremendous thumping filled the trees. It sounded as if he had struck the ground with a huge branch. The women let out heart-breaking wails, the noise muffled behind their gags.

"I said, leave her alone for fuck's sake."

"Piss off."

They were moving away from her side of the clearing; the women pleaded to be left alone. Picturing them took no effort and Nicola could do nothing but silently sob.

Something snapped close by. Nicola whirled around, already trying to stand.

Crouched right beside her, a man smiled.

"Hello," he whispered and lifted his hand. A switchblade. In his other hand, he held a small gun. "What's your name?"

Chapter Thirty-Four

C ate sprinted ahead of Wallace. A man stepping out of a door at her side missed her by inches. He shouted at her as she ran on.

Out of nowhere, someone grabbed her forearm and spun her around before she could come to a halt. Steve held her.

"Get to the roof."

He shoved her away into the jostling people. Someone's elbow hit her side; she shoved through the milling people and saw Steve running the way she'd come. Wallace was running from her office. Cate pushed through the people and grabbed for Steve as he reached Wallace.

"What's happening?" she yelled over the noise.

"They're coming in. Fifty of them, at least. Doesn't look like they're armed," Steve said to Wallace.

Wallace nodded once and didn't appear at all surprised. "Okay. Ten at the top of the stairs, Steve. Everyone else to the next floor. Cate, get to the roof."

"The roof? Why me?"

"For God's sake, Cate. Just do it."

Wallace and Steve dashed up the corridor, both barking commands to the crowd. Unsure, Cate followed them. Glass exploded from somewhere below. Shouts followed it, then gunfire cracked out.

That decided her. She sprinted towards the stairs, hit a blockage of people and fought her way through them. Most of the people were shoving their way up to the next floor. Hands pressed into Cate's breasts by accident; she pushed at someone's back, stumbled forward and fell against a man. Damien.

"What are you doing here? Get upstairs."

He pulled her with him as he hid behind a jutting section of wall and lifted his gun. Glass cracked below again and Cate peered around the side of the wall.

She'd made it close to the entrance to the corridor from the stairs. Figures crouched there, sheltering behind overturned tables and beds. Steve stood beside Joey, both men armed with shotguns. Three others were reaching into piles of debris, of rocks and broken bricks. Two women were soaking rags with a clear fluid and stuffing them into bottles.

"You need to get upstairs," Joey told her.

"Give me a gun."

"You're having a fucking laugh, love. Get upstairs. Get to the roof."

"Give me a gun. I want to stay."

He shoved her away. "Run, you stupid bitch. Upstairs."

Three or four people hit her and ran on to the stairs. Winded, Cate fell and fought for breath. Her chest and throat burned. Struggling, she managed to stand. Joey was still hiding behind the wall, crouched now, gun ready. To him, she might as well have not been there. A few others jostled past her. A woman whose name she didn't know called for her to follow. At the shout, Steve turned back and frantically waved at her to go upstairs. She ran towards him and slowed. He was already facing front again, dismissing her. Below, more glass broke. The people outside jeered and called to those inside.

The roof.

Cate sprinted for the stairs.

Chapter Thirty-Five

The man pressed his knife against Nicola's wrist. He was still smiling. His mouth might as well have been frozen in place.

"Don't make a sound," he whispered.

The women in the clearing were still sobbing. The other men were close by although Nicola thought they might be creeping away.

"You're very pretty." Sweat ran from his temples to trickle through the wiry hair on his cheeks. Nicola inhaled and wished she hadn't. The man's stink was a mix of old sweat, dirt and something else. Excitement. The rottenness of it pressed into her nose.

"Me and you will go that way." He jerked his head to the left. "Just for a few minutes. Then you can join the other ladies. You'll fit in. They're good fun."

Fun? Did he say fun?

Black spots danced in front of her eyes. Nicola blinked them away and the throbbing anger in the centre of her head breathed in and out. She wanted it to grow. She wanted it in her hands.

The man held the blade of his kitchen knife on her skin while he looked through the prickly bush to the clearing, waiting. As soon as the other men were faraway enough for him, he'd move. He'd make her stand and he'd lead her away from the clearing into a more secluded place.

The spots danced in front of her again, moving as if music was playing somewhere close. The cold of the woods sank into her skin, into her bones. The freezing touch was as welcome as the beat of rage in her head.

Nicola's right hand flew off the ground, her left swung up and shoved the knife off her skin. Then the knife was a falling light; the barrel of the man's gun pushed towards her face and she shoved herself off the tree trunk.

Nicola's fingers found his face, his eyes. He let out a groan, the gun hit her arm and the pain was nothing. She pushed him backwards, grabbed the knife and swung herself in a half-circle.

She hit something as solid as rock. The rock grunted.

She'd stabbed him in the throat. The blade plugged the wound and only a little blood seeped out. He raised his open hands, fingers squeezing air. His eyes were unblinking and fully aware even as the blood trickled out of his neck.

The black spots danced, her rage sang and she yanked the knife free. Blood sprayed. The hot liquid hit her face, her hair. She pushed the man backwards, grabbed his gun and stood. Her vision was a misty red and that red sang with her anger.

She slammed the knife deep into the man's stomach. His scream emerged as a hiss through the tear in his throat. Nicola yanked the bloody knife free from the wound and ran.

The ground sloped in a dirty trail of old leaves. She stumbled, managed to right herself and sprinted. There was no way she could avoid making noise and didn't focus on it. Ahead was the important thing. Running ahead.

Nicola skidded over a small area of wet grass and registered the change in daylight somewhere off to her left. Brighter that way.

She shoved through the low branches, breath boiling in her mouth, a stitch pounding at her side as she ran faster. Nobody chasing behind yet. No running feet. Yet.

Her route took to a pile of overturned trees. Nicola launched herself up and forward and cleared them before landing awkwardly. Pain danced through her ankles and shins as she landed, then pitched forward.

Gasping, Nicola rolled. The daylight shifted and shook all around her. She seized on it as if it was a solid object and stood. Still no shouts from behind, but it could only be a matter of seconds before the others found the man she'd stabbed. Her fingers twitched and the knife was hot metal on her skin.

Run.

Nicola staggered forward and broke into a run which became a sprint. Thin branches poked her face and drew blood on her arms in thin lines. She ran on, sobbing for breath, smashed through branches and saw the road straight ahead at the same time as she registered the woman sprinting straight at her.

Chapter Thirty-Six

C ate slammed the door open and shielded her eyes against the harsh daylight. She ran, skidded on a frozen puddle and saw six others close to the roof's edge. They piled rocks in fast, fluid movements. She ran towards them, shouting. One of the women glanced at her.

"Come to help?" she asked as Cate reached them.

Cate nodded, too winded to speak. Her dash from the second floor had been powered by adrenaline and she was now slightly queasy.

"I'm Alice," the woman said. "Get stuck in."

"What's the plan?" Cate said.

The only man in the group answered her. "Rocks. Stones." He was the old guy who'd been struggling for breath in the meeting. He'd be no good downstairs. "We'll drop them on those bastards."

"Guns?" Cate said. There were two handguns on top of a set of pipes.

"From up here? You won't hit a thing."

"Rod's right," Alice said. "We need to drop stones on them. It's all we can do."

Cate joined the others in sorting through the rubble to find decent sized rocks. Within a few moments, they'd made ten piles and exhausted the supply of stones that would do any damage.

"It's not enough," Cate said and scanned the roof. If they had some way of pulling sections free, they'd have some serious weight to throw over the side. There was no time for that, though, and certainly no tools for it.

"It's all we've got," Rod said to her.

"Look," one of the women said and pointed to the car park.

A removal van slid over Thorpe Road, apparently driven by someone who didn't know what they were doing. It spun around, the rear hitting the pavement and mounting it. It hit a bench, smashed it and jerked to a stop. The back doors flew open and bodies fell out.

"Oh, my God," Cate said.

The bodies moved. It would have been better for them if they were already dead, but they moved. They crawled. They managed to stand. They advanced towards the hospital entrance.

Children.

And every single one of them was sick with the Manc.

They advanced on the car park, some attempting to support others, some pulling themselves along the ground. As much as she wanted to look away, she had to see each of them, had to force herself to be part of their pain.

All were dressed in torn clothing; all were desperately thin. The youngest, perhaps six; the oldest, no more than fifteen. Children. Dying children coming for the hospital, the Manc steaming off them like a filthy smell.

"Dear God," Rod whispered.

His words broke Cate's paralysis. She ran to the roof steps, the few people at the edge calling after her. None followed, which didn't surprise her. She was on her own.

Shadows below loomed up as she clambered down. She dropped the last few feet and sprinted to the ward doors and smashed through them, already calling Steve's name.

A few people were grouped at the far end of the corridor, blocking the doors to the stairs.

"Move." Cate sprinted to them. "They're coming in. The sick."

She knew her words wouldn't make any sense to them. No time to stop and explain. She hit the doors a moment after the small group moved aside, ran out to the corridor and skidded to a halt at the stairs. From below, people desperately yelled to each other. There was no order in the noise, no control.

"Steve."

Cate leaned over the railing of the stairs and tried to make Steve out of the throng of bodies below. If he was there, he was just a part of the milling flesh.

"Steve."

Someone on the third floor looked straight up and saw her. Joey.

"Get Steve," she screamed. *"Up here now."*

Joey disappeared again as someone shoved into him. Swearing, Cate ran for the stairs, bounced off the railings and called Steve's name. Below, another gunshot roared and a window exploded. Cate shoved through the people on the third floor and ran down to the second. Several people noticed her and she screamed Steve's name again. He appeared, standing close to the railings below.

"The roof," he yelled at her.

Desperately, she waved at him to come to her. He made no move to do so. Cate stabbed her finger towards the barricaded front. "Kids. They're coming in. They've sent the sick. The Manc. It's coming here."

He heard her. She saw it on his face.

He pushed his way through the bodies, turning back and calling for Joey. At once, Joey followed. The men made it free of the crowd and ran up to her.

"They're sending in a load of kids." Cate struggled for breath. "Across the car park now. I saw them from the roof. That's what they meant about a school. They've got a load of infected kids."

On the floor below, the thin control Joey and Steve had managed to generate was slipping into nothing. Steve raised his gun and fired once into the wrecked stairs. More than a dozen pairs of eyes focused on him and the noise began to die.

"Everyone into the wards now," Steve shouted. "Damien, Billy. You stay here. If anyone else stays here, I will shoot you. Go."

Without giving anyone chance to reply, Steve pushed Cate back to the rising stairs. They ran to the third floor and Steve pointed to the right end of the corridor. "Third office," he said to Joey who sprinted up the corridor.

"What are we doing?" Cate said and Steve passed her a handgun.

"Point and shoot," he said.

Cate took the gun. She ran with Steve to a small office that overlooked the front of the building and clambered over fallen furniture with him. He stood on one side of the window and gestured for her to stand at the other.

Steve crouched and peered outside. "Fuck," he whispered. "There's loads of them."

Cate looked. Thirty or forty children were crossing the car park. They might as well have been walking corpses.

"We can't let them get any further," Steve said. "Can't run the risk of reinfection." He smashed out the glass of the window with his gun. "Keep your head down. If they can hit the windows below, they can hit us."

"Jesus Christ," Cate whispered.

Gunshots exploded from somewhere close. Joey was shooting.

A car window blew in as one of his shots went wild. His next hit a boy in the stomach. He collapsed and pulled himself along, leaving a wide line of blood. A girl, no older than thirteen, fell as Joey's shot hit her in the neck. Blood sprayed behind her. A second shot took off most of her head.

Steve shoved his gun out of the wrecked window and fired. The explosion deafened Cate. A little boy, his face a swollen mess of weeping buboes, dropped to his knees. Blood coated his chest. He tipped forward, managed to crawl another few inches and a bullet struck him in the back.

The sick were still advancing despite the gunfire, despite the falling rocks from the roof. They passed the final line of cars and began crossing the flowerbeds in a shuffle. Now they were closer, Cate made out their faces. Each one was splattered with blood; each mouth was open in a wide circle and each child was crying out a wordless noise, a beseeching cry. A bullet hit a kid in the centre of his face; his falling body hit the girl at his side and brought her down. And the others were still coming forward. There could be no more than another twenty feet to the barricaded front of the building.

Steve grabbed Cate. "Shoot. Shoot them. If they get any closer, we're dead."

"We can't. Jesus Christ. We can't."

"Shoot."

Steve fired outside again. The room was thunder. Cate winced with each shot.

Fifteen feet to the barricade.

Children dropped. Blood rained. Children shuffled over the flowerbeds, over the carpark. They were dead and they were still coming. They were the Manc coming for her again.

Black dropped over Cate's sight.

Thunder filled her ears. Explosion after explosion roared up out of her fingers and she knew nothing but the explosion of her gunfire from somewhere at the other end of the nothing closing in from all sides.

Chapter Thirty-Seven

"I'm sorry. I'm so sorry."

The woman lowered her arm and backed away. Nicola forced her hand to drop. The knife jutted from her fist. The woman hit a tree and pressed herself against it, her eyes darting from the knife to Nicola's face.

"I almost killed you," Nicola said.

"I'm so sorry."

"Forget it."

Nicola moved forward, painfully aware of the ache in her stomach and legs. Even though she'd made it to a road, she didn't have the strength to keep running.

"I'm coming with you," the woman said.

Nicola whirled around, knife rising. "No, you're not. It's not safe."

"I have to come with you." The woman shook. Nicola's dispassionate eye took in her torn clothes, her skinny frame, the bruises under her eyes and the blood around her mouth. "They'll kill me."

"I'm on my own," Nicola said. She ran for the road, pretending she didn't care about the ache in the muscles of her calves or about the self-disgust inside her head. She closed in on the road and the woman ran after her, her movement much too loud on the ground.

"Please."

"Jesus Christ," Nicola whispered and reached the road. She ran on before staggering to a stop. The heavy slap of the woman's trainers on the ground followed her. Nicola turned as the woman reached her, already opening her mouth to tell the woman she couldn't come, and the leaves at the side of the road were trembling green dots.

She swung herself around the woman and bashed against her. The hand holding the gun jerked out of the bushes, the gun rising as Nicola brought it around to bear on it.

"Don't fucking move. I'll shoot. Come out now."

Leaves and branches shook as the man emerged. He was dressed in much the same way as the man she'd stabbed, all torn jeans and a filthy coat. Rainwater ran from his unkempt hair. He grinned.

"Two of you. Result."

"I'm leaving and you're staying here," Nicola said.

He laughed. "You can fuck off. I'll have her back, though."

"Please," the woman whispered. Her trembling body vibrated against Nicola's back and legs. Her head felt like it was about to explode. She couldn't take any of this, couldn't take any more.

"Julia," she said and the man with the gun was raising the weapon. He was still smiling. Nicola saw that as clear as the trees and bushes lining the road.

She pulled the trigger. Nicola's vision slowed as if she was under water. Earth and grass close to the man's feet jumped out of the ground as her bullets flew. Mouth open, the man twisted as if he'd been hit, earth pattered on to his shoes and the road, and his gun was a black snake bearing around on her.

Nicola's vision stammered as if caught, then hit a normal speed.

She fired and the man's chest exploded in a shower of red. He flew backwards into the bushes, his own blood following him down to the wet grass.

Behind Nicola, the woman let out an animal howl.

Chapter Thirty-Eight

The car park was a sea of bodies.

Cate tried to see the figures as individuals, as people. There was no way of doing that. They were just twisted shapes, some close together, others lying alone on the red ground.

The splatters of blood had formed puddles which in turn became wide pools. If she forced her eyes to pass at speed over the surface, the car park could have been haphazardly coated in red paint. Better to think that than to admit all the red was blood. Or to admit all the bodies were full of bullet holes. Or even that they were sick children sent to advance on the hospital for Christ knows why.

Steve placed a gentle touch on her wrist and she lowered the gun. He was speaking and his words were lost in the muffling weight on her ears. Cate swallowed several times and shook her head. Her hearing returned a little although she wondered if she'd be able to hear normally at any point soon.

"What the hell was that?" he said.

She held the gun towards him. Eventually, he took it.

"I shot them," she said.

"No shit. Been practising?"

She shook and crossed her arms below her breasts. Still, her eyes remained fixed to the bodies. She hadn't made every shot. Far from it. But she had hit enough of them for Steve to wonder about her. And for her to wonder about herself.

"Steve." The shout rang out in the corridor. A moment later, Joey appeared in the doorway. "You okay?" he said.

"Yeah." Steve pushed Cate towards the doorway. "Everyone else all right?"

"Looks like it. Wallace is asking for both of you."

"Shit."

Cate strode forward before Steve could lead her out of the office. The corridor was mostly deserted. Most of the noise had subsided; people were moving about on the floor below, it seemed, and the hammering of wood over windows had already started.

Steve pointed down the corridor. "She's at the stairs. I think she's sorting out burning the bodies outside."

"Nice job for someone," Steve muttered and glanced at Cate. "Come on. Best not keep her waiting."

They walked down the corridor, not talking despite Steve's clear desire to do so. He pocketed both guns and sped up as they neared the stairs. Cate followed and there was no surprise at the naked interest with which Wallace studied her. The few men around Wallace did the same.

"You were supposed to be on the roof," Wallace said.

"I came down when I saw the children coming towards us."

Wallace nodded at Steve. "Join the others, would you? Check the barricade."

Without a word, Steve and the other men slid down the rubble to the ground floor.

"This way," Wallace said to Cate.

They sat on uncomfortable benches outside the doors to one of the wards. Already, the gunfire seemed distant. Voices and hammering had replaced it, and the sounds could almost be called normal.

"A spot of shooting, then?" Wallace said and Cate's fingers burned.

She nodded.

"Are you any good?" Wallace asked.

"I don't know. Not much experience, really."

Cate studied her nails, each one dirty and broken, and wished she didn't feel like a petulant teenager whenever she was around Wallace.

"You don't like being told what to do, do you?" Wallace said. A hot flush of anger boiled in Cate's stomach and chest.

"What did you want me to do? Stay up on the roof when I see who they're sending towards us or come down and warn people? What would have happened if the sick had got any closer to us? Do you want the Manc in here?" Wallace was trying to speak; Cate wouldn't let her. Without warning, tears exploded from her eyes. "Children, Wallace. They were just children. They were.
. ." Words left her. All she had was a terrible burning deep in the centre of her chest and the images of the bullets striking the dying children.

Wallace embraced her, thick arms encasing Cate's thin body. She wept against Wallace's warm neck. The echoes of the gunshots sang in her head. She saw them all falling again and again, holes in their chests and faces, coughs of blood following them down to the ground.

Coughing, Cate wiped her nose on her sleeve. "Why the hell were they coming towards us? Why not just drop down dead when they were set free? I saw them. Most of them could barely stand up so what the hell kept them coming?"

The hot anger vanished. Deep freeze took its place and she knew it was all over her face.

"What is it?" Wallace said, pulling away to study her face.

"Nothing." Cate moved along the bench.

"Don't lie to me, Cate. What is it?"

The scream from the lift shaft was bouncing off her ears, hitting the wall and racing back to her.

The thing she'd seen out on Thorpe Road.

The risen bodies in the morgue.

They were all around her, all back to stay with her.

No, you don't. Leave me alone.

"What kept those kids coming?" she said. The older woman stared at her. "They could have tried to run when those people let them out of the vans. They didn't have to come towards us. What kept them coming?"

"I. . ." Wallace licked her lips and said nothing else. Cate spoke and her voice was somebody else's.

"They were dying anyway. Someone made them come. Someone who made them more frightened of not coming to us than they were of dying."

"I'm more interested in where they came from. And how the hell Skinny and his friends found them."

Cate kept her reply locked away. She knew the answer. It was obvious. She'd seen the light in the window those few days ago, she'd walked away from the building and she'd heard the plan spoken out on the street with Steve by her side. And now all those children were dead.

"Cate? Something to tell me?"

"No."

Wallace licked her upper lip and stood. "Cate." She licked her lip again and Cate understood the action didn't come from nerves. This was all about a calm preparation. "I need to ask you something. A favour. Sort of."

"What is it?"

She knew, though. The only surprise was that it had taken Wallace this long to bring it up, and the only comfort was knowing this moment had been coming since she'd first entered the hospital.

Wallace licked her lip again and kept her eyes on Cate's. "I won't tell you to leave, but I will ask you to think about doing so."

Wallace rose and walked away, heading back along the corridor, leaving Cate to stare after her and tremble.

Chapter Thirty-Nine

Nicola bent double, gun and knife held close to her knees as she panted, inhaled and spat. Her body was a ball of burning pain and exhaustion, and the thought of crawling into the long grass beside the pathway kept prodding at her.

She spat again and stood upright. The woman was a few steps away, eyeing her and the gun.

"Helen," the woman said.

Inwardly, Nicola groaned. The last thing she wanted to know was the woman's name. Acting as if the woman hadn't spoken, she peered over the grass to the carriageway. No sign of the men or a car. The body and all the blood had to be a mile behind by now. Far enough for them to stop and catch a breath. Not far away enough to keep the men from giving chase on foot. At least there was no way of getting a car over the muddy grass to this road.

"We're all right. We made it," the woman said.

"Listen. You have to get away from me. I'm not safe," Nicola replied and walked as fast as she could. No thought of which way she was going. No thought of a plan. Only the need to move.

"Wait." The woman jogged after her and Nicola whirled around, bringing her gun up.

The woman backed away, hands up, cringing.

"Shit." Nicola lowered it. "Look. I don't mean anything. I just. . .I just want to go on alone, all right? It's better for both of us if I do. Trust me."

The woman's mouth opened, closed and opened again. "I'll come with you just for tonight," she said. "We can split up in the morning."

She shook and Nicola had no idea if that was due to the cold or fear or reaction.

What might have been a car engine roared in the distance. Nicola ducked. The woman did the same.

You can't leave her here, Scott told her.

Like she'd left the other women in the woods.

"Just for tonight," Nicola said.

"Yes," the woman said and Nicola wondered if she would be able to hear such meekness again without screaming.

"Come on, then."

They followed the path at not quite a jog. Beyond the grass, the road was as empty as it'd been for weeks.

"Helen," the woman said, panting.

"Yeah. You said."

"What's your name?"

"Be quiet."

Nicola crouched and pulled her notes and map from her back pockets.

"Do you know where we are?" she said without looking from her papers.

"Near Mansfield, I think. I heard the men mention it the day before yesterday."

"Mansfield?" Nicola ran a fingertip over her map. If she had it right, the road they'd run from was the A617. "Shit," she whispered.

"What is it?"

Nicola traced the lines of the roads, willing them to be wrong. They weren't.

"Nothing. Come on."

They jogged in silence for several minutes. The grass beside them rose and fell in small peaks and dips before shrinking in size. The road twisted; they passed a few abandoned cars and fallen tree branches. As they reached a flat pavement, Helen staggered to a stop. She held her side, gasping.

"Can't run. Sorry."

"It's all right."

Struggling to keep calm, Nicola crossed to the pavement and took deep breaths.

"What's wrong with the map?" Helen said.

"Nothing's wrong with it. I'm just not where I want to be."

"Where's that?"

Nicola closed her mouth, then opened it again. What harm was there in telling the woman? She'd leave her as soon as she could. No need for another death to haunt her journey north.

"The M1."

Helen frowned. "Why?"

"I'm going north."

Helen gazed behind them to the quiet road, then checked ahead. "How far is it?"

"Further than I'd like. Let's go."

They moved at a fast walk, the cold rolling in off the fields and the constant breeze drying the sweat all over Nicola's body. She caught a whiff of herself and grimaced. Her body and clothes stunk of sweat, blood and fear. She wanted to tear her coat off and run and run. Attempting to distract herself, she took a few breaths. At once, she smelled something other than her body.

Nicola stopped, held the hand with the knife up to her mouth and tried to cover her face. The blade, inches from her lips, made her flinch. Too easy to think about the hands which had held the knife before her.

"Here," she said and jabbed the knife towards Helen.

Helen took the knife and wrapped her fingers around the handle.

"Thanks."

Nicola nodded. Helen took a rag from her jeans pocket and pressed it over her mouth and nose.

"You'd think all the bodies would be frozen, wouldn't you?" she said.

Nicola breathed against her skin for another moment, then lowered. "We need to keep going. Find a house or building. Somewhere warm."

She dropped her gaze as she spoke and desperately wished for the woman, for Helen, to not notice it.

You lying bitch.

She knew lying would keep the woman safe and she still hated having to do so. Walking with someone, having someone physically close. . .God.

They walked on into the lengthening shadows. Minutes passed and Nicola waited. She knew it was coming. Helen's question was a breathing thing between them.

"So, what happened to you?" Helen said and Nicola almost smiled.

"The usual. Probably the same as happened to you."

"Your husband killed in a riot, was he?"

Nicola pursed her lips and shook her head. "No. He's. . .Christ." She shook and hunched her shoulders in an effort to keep warm. "He's in a place called Cheadle Hulme with our daughter. Near Manchester. They were up there when it happened. The first bomb. Visiting his brother and our sister-in-law. A weekend away. They were going to come back the next day but when they stopped all the trains and people started getting ill, he—" She broke off. Letting it all out was oddly pleasant, like scratching a healed scar.

"Right," Helen said. "Sorry."

"Sorry about your husband," Nicola said.

"Thanks. At least it was quick for him. He didn't have to see all this." Helen wiped at one eye. "Only ten days ago which just feels mad. We were in Nottingham, trapped in the city. There weren't many people left, but those who were left, they had guns. They had cars. They were just treating the city like a playground, you know what I mean?"

Nicola nodded.

"We were trying to get out of the city. Me, Dave, a couple of others. Turned out some of the army were left. Maybe they got stuck there when all the others ran. Anyway, they were in a supermarket, using it as a base. There wasn't much left there. Even I could see that. But the others, the people with the guns, they wanted to get in. Dave. He got shot. Right in front of me as we ran the other way. He got shot as we ran the other way." Helen coughed hard, wiped at her eyes and shook. "The others I was with, they dragged me away. We made it to the road and ran. Two days later, they got us. The men. In the woods."

Nicola waited. They walked. Shadows drew in closer.

"There were six of them. They already had three women. I think they wanted as many as they could. Two of them came out of the woods when we were on the road. They shot the men and the older woman I was with. They took me."

"I'm sorry," Nicola said. It seemed to be the only thing to say.

"Thanks. And thanks for killing that one. Gary."

"I got another one in the trees. Stabbed him."

"Good."

Nicola shook again and found herself wishing she felt guilt or horror or *anything* at murdering the two men. The most she could manage was a weak sense of relief and a deep tiredness. There was no happiness at what she'd done, but then nor was there any regret. The men had needed to die for her to live. And they needed to die for what they'd done. Simple. Brutal. True.

She twitched at the memory of shoving the knife into the man, at the kick of the gun exploding, at the flying blood. She'd liked it and there was no getting away from that. Just like there was no getting away from the blood on her skin and in her hair.

Helen was talking again. Her husband. The Manc. Words after words after words. Nicola nodded, not hearing it. Instead, she saw.

All the roads led from the town, all the roads slipped away from Cheadle Hulme out to the green and the rivers, out to the quiet places where people knew their neighbours, where they talked and drank together.

Nicola saw the roads taking her out of Cheadle Hulme, taking her to the narrow lanes and hedges lining those lanes. Scott's father lived out there; he lived with his dog and his little house; he had his local pub and he had his chair at the bar, that one at the end. He sat there with the dog at his feet and he drank from his glass and he talked to his friends who'd be there with him in the rain or in the sun. He knew the little pub as well as he knew his own house and she knew it through his eyes. She knew the lines at the side of his mouth when he smiled at Julia. She knew the weight of his big arms when he hugged her and she listened to the rasp of his beard on her cheek as he kissed her.

All of it there in the little pub and the narrow lanes and the green and the rivers. All of it in the roads leading away from Cheadle Hulme and the rotten stink of a city of bodies all frozen in the December wind.

Chapter Forty

"Up on the roof," Cate said not quite under her breath.

Steve zipped his coat up to the neck and hugged himself. "Are you going to start singing?"

Cate shook her head, wishing she could give him the laugh he wanted. Forcing a smile let alone a laugh was out of the question. Nothing had been funny in days or weeks or God knows how long.

Steve shifted closer to the air conditioning unit they were sitting beside and scanned the ground with his binoculars.

"About fifty by my count," he said.

"Are we going to burn them?"

"Yeah. No choice."

Cate sighed, the breath full of tears. "Tonight? After dark?"

Steve said nothing. He was still looking through the binoculars and now faced towards the curve of Thorpe Road that led into Dalry's suburbs.

"Vans. Four of them."

Cate lifted her own binoculars and studied the roads. The vans drove into view. Four of them as Steve had said. Each one was spattered with mud as if they'd been driven across fields or along country lanes. At least two were missing their windscreens. The one coming up at the rear appeared to be driven by someone who didn't know what they were doing; the van careered from one lane to the other and repeatedly came within inches of crashing into another van.

They disappeared out of shot. The rumble of their engines burned in the air. Cate shifted her position so she had a better view of the road. Steve joined her. The heaviness of his arm wrapped in a thick coat was comforting but she made no move to slide closer to him.

"What are those bastards doing now?" Steve murmured.

"More of the sick?" Cate said.

"They can't. I mean. . ." Steve sucked his teeth. "How the hell are they finding these people? Everyone's dead. And how the hell are they getting them to come at us? Why don't they just lie down and die?"

"Same thing I asked Wallace before. . ."

He lowered his binoculars for a few seconds to study her. She'd pulled hers from her face a fraction and made sure she met his eye. "Before she sent us up here. I asked her what made those kids keep coming even when we shot them."

"What did she say?"

Before she asked me to leave. Before that, Steve.

"She didn't."

Steve brought his binoculars back to his eyes and swore. Cate refocused on the road and immediately understood.

The vans were gone. No sight or sound of them at all.

"Where'd they go?" Steve pointed to Thorpe Road. "This is the only way along here."

"Maybe they took another turning."

"Maybe."

Cate spied movement at a front door. Steve named the figure as she focused on them.

"Hello, Skinny. How are you today, you bastard?"

Skinny crossed a garden, heading to the road and looking no more dangerous than any guy taking a walk. He stopped in the centre of the road, faced towards the hospital and stood, eyes shielded, as if was staring back at them.

"Fuck you," Steve murmured.

"Who is he? Who are any of them?"

"Just people. They want to get in here and they want us out. They can piss off and die."

Skinny carried on appearing to appraise them. His steady gaze infuriated and chilled her in equal measure. How great it would be to stand and shove her fingers up at him. Show him she wasn't scared.

A big lie. Several hundred feet away and up from the figure facing her, she was scared shitless.

Skinny glanced at a nearby house as if someone had called his name. He gestured to someone out of Cate's shot; a moment later, the man in his familiar black coat walked from a rear garden and joined Skinny. Both men stood side by side, facing the hospital.

"Cheeky fuckers," Steve whispered.

"They can't see us, can they?"

"No chance. They're just pissing about."

Cate kept her mouth shut. If the two men were simply attempting to frighten anyone who might be facing them, their timing was a huge coincidence. Standing there now suggested they knew someone was looking their way.

"Maybe they know we watch from up here. Maybe they've got binoculars, as well," she said.

"Maybe," Steve replied.

She lowered her binoculars as he did the same. Grinning, Steve jabbed his middle finger into the air. His grin faded as two men abruptly walked to a house and vanished.

"Arseholes," Steve said and a lot of the humour had left his voice.

Behind them, a hollow clang rang out as the door swung open and bounced off metal railings. At the steps leading down to the top floor, Damien waved and jogged to them.

"Steve." He shouted it as he ran. "You best get down here."

"What is it?" Steve stood and extended an absent hand to Cate. Not caring how it looked, she took it and rose.

"The bodies down there." Damien took a breath, held it and let it go in a puff. The air had turned his nose and cheeks bright red. "Me and Joey. We were at the windows, checking them out. You know. How many and that. One of them. It's got something stuck to it."

He spat.

"What is it?" Cate said and Damien paid her no attention. Instead, he spoke directly to Steve.

"It's a note."

Chapter Forty-One

Nicola kicked at the remnants of the broken glass in the door. It collapsed inwards. Gingerly, she reached through the hole and found the handle. The post office door swung open, crunching over the broken glass.

Directly ahead, piles of overturned furniture lay in heaps. Shards of glass covered the dirty carpet; food wrappers, empty crisp packets and flattened drink cans had either blown in from the street or been dumped by people. There were signs of small fires dotted around. It appeared bits of chairs had been smashed into pieces and burned in little piles. Nicola scanned the interior, not surprised that the glass over the counter had been destroyed. Whoever had wanted access to the area beyond the counter had only needed to throw a chair or a metal pipe or anything they damn well liked through the glass and the post office had been theirs. All she could do was hope they were long gone.

"Are we going in? It's getting cold," Helen said.

"Yeah."

Nicola crunched over the glass and ignored the air coming in through the broken door and windows. She considered telling Helen they should find somewhere else. No point to that, though. They'd passed several buildings after coming off the B-road. Just about all of them were in a worse condition than the post office. The shops had been raided for food; the businesses had been set alight. At least here, they should be able to find a staffroom probably untouched. And at least here, they didn't have to deal with the people who'd died in their homes.

Nicola wandered through the mess on the floor, hugging herself. Helen stayed close behind her. The post office was thick with a strange mix of scents. Nicola inhaled and caught the aromas at the back of her mouth. Stale air. Freezing cold. Food rotting somewhere. And.

And.

Decaying flesh.

"Shit."

She'd reached the counter and there it was. The body on the floor of the other side.

Helen let out a single sob.

At least we know how he died.

Nicola closed her eyes momentarily. It didn't help to lose the image of the jagged chair leg jutting out of the man's back.

"We should go," Helen whispered.

Nicola studied the blood on the man's coat and the floor around him. Her eyes kept returning to his left hand splayed on the carpet like a dead spider. His sleeve had ridden up to expose a skinny forearm.

"He's been dead for ages." Nicola breathed through her mouth. "The smell. His colour. The blood. This is old."

"I don't care," Helen hissed. "We should go."

"Where?" Nicola said lightly. She clambered on to the counter and swung her legs around so she could drop to the other side. More glass crunched below her boots. A thin blanket lay on the far side of the narrow area, the blanket thrown over a chair. Not much, but it would do.

Nicola yanked the blanket off the chair and dropped it over the man's head and upper back. There was no way of hiding the murder weapon. Not without making a ghastly tent of chair leg and blanket.

Nicola had to close her eyes again, nauseated by the image. "Are you coming?" she said and listened to Helen's grunts as she boosted herself up and over the counter.

The women made their way to a door wedged open with a pile of folders, and followed a short corridor filled with chaotic piles of office furniture clearly meant to be barricades. The corridor took them to a few storage cupboards, past more broken windows and to a small kitchen. A terrible stink emanated from the grey water filling the sink. Smashed plates and cups covered the work surface beside the sink. The scene suggested someone had methodically broken as many plates and cups as they could find for whatever reason.

"Why would they need a reason?" Nicola whispered and only realised she'd spoken aloud when Helen asked what she'd said. "Nothing," Nicola said and left the kitchen.

The door opposite the kitchen opened to a staffroom. A dozen chairs were lined against a wall and there were a few low tables piled with old magazines. Smiling faces were on the magazine covers. Dead celebrities.

Nicola took two cans from her bag. Both baked beans. "This or nothing," she said. "Which do you fancy?"

"This," Helen replied. Nicola had to steel herself against the meekness in Helen's reply. It hurt her stomach to hear it.

"Enjoy," she said and handed Helen a dirty fork.

They ate the beans without speaking. Food. That was all it was about. Get the food into her mouth, chew, swallow, repeat. She could forget about the terrible aches in her legs and back while she ate. No blisters. No cramps in her calves threatening to make her weep at any moment. Just food.

They finished the cans at the same time. Helen pushed two of the chairs together and lay on them.

"You don't talk much, do you?" she said.

Nicola stayed quiet.

"Is that a joke?" Helen said eventually and Nicola managed a smile.

"Almost," she replied.

Silent minutes passed. Dusk weighed on the windows. Using the light from one of her few remaining candles, Nicola pushed a few pieces of wood into a pile and tore up three of the gossip magazines. She lit the pile. Warmth spread out to fill the room.

"It won't last, but at least it's warm now," she said.

Helen had fallen asleep. Her slow breathing and still body gave it away. While there was a chance she was faking it to avoid conversation, Nicola didn't believe that. The silence of the dead country was one thing. Creating that silence between two survivors was another.

Nicola warmed her hands on the fire for a few minutes, then used her candle to guide her to the other end of the staffroom. Nothing down there but a few more chairs and a table. Dancing toys, box sets of books, ornamental presents lay in untidy piles on the table. She held her light over the objects, wondering when anyone would pick them up or box them away. Tomorrow? Next week? Next month?

Nicola headed towards the door. Helen was still asleep. Her deep breaths occasionally rose into snores. Nicola listened for another moment, then crept out to the corridor.

Are you going to leave her? Scott asked her and Nicola shook her head.

Not right now. Later.

Maybe you can stay with her. Maybe it'll leave you alone.

Nicola shook her head again. *No. It's too much of a risk.*

Scott was silent at that although she sensed his dislike of her plan.

Holding her breath, Nicola tried a few of the doors. They were all locked. She walked on, still holding her breath, watching the shadows dance in front of her candle. The corridor ended at a locked door and she had no way of knowing what was beyond the door. She let her breath out in a hiss.

Go back to her. Don't leave her.

Scott, again. His voice was implacable. Even so, Nicola found an argument in herself.

I stay and she dies. That's what happened with everyone else.

A breath brushed her neck.

It was behind her. The little figure was right behind her.

The shadows on the door and wall shook and danced. Her arm was a shaking stick sending the shadows mad.

A breath again.

Nicola closed her eyes and found her inner voice. *I will face you when I am ready. Understand? Until then, leave me alone.*

The thing behind her breathed a soft laugh and the sensation on her neck was like a trailing spiderweb.

Nicola opened her eyes. It had gone. Nothing behind her but the still corridor.

As much as she wanted to complete the movement inch by inch, Nicola forced herself to turn around fast, letting her candlelight flicker over the floor and walls. Nothing there.

It's killing Helen. While you stand here, it's ripping her head off.

Nicola trotted back up the corridor to the staffroom. Helen lay on the two chairs in exactly the same position she'd fallen asleep in. She didn't appear to have moved at all in the few minutes Nicola had been away.

Abruptly exhausted, Nicola sat. She placed her candle on one of the tables and watched the fire gradually die.

She slept. There were no dreams or if there were, she didn't know they were dreams.

And when morning light landed on her eyelids, Nicola knew without making a move that she was alone.

Chapter Forty-Two

Steve reached the office door first, Damien pushed past him and Cate ran forward. She knocked into Damien and shoved past him as he swore. Unlike most of the others, the window in this office was unblocked. Knowing she needed to keep her head down, Cate leaned out of it and stared down to the ground.

"Get your head back in, for fuck's sake." Damien pulled her. She kicked out at him and he swore again.

"Stop it," Steve said and stood beside Cate. "Where?" he asked Damien.

"Down and to the left. Near the flowers."

Cate saw the dead boy immediately. He'd fallen on his back and most of his head was missing. A white sheet was stuck to the blood blanketing his chest. One of his hands rested on it as if wanting to keep it there.

"His hand is in the way. Even with binoculars, I couldn't make it out," Damien said.

"It's definitely a note." Steve pulled himself back into the room.

Cate shifted away from the window and tried to ignore the dislike radiating out of Damien's face towards her.

"Have you told Wallace?" Steve said.

"Not yet."

Steve drummed a rhythm on a table. "We need that note, but we can't get it in daylight. Not without getting our heads blown off."

"They'll let you get it," Cate murmured. She faced the window and the houses beyond Thorpe Road. She had no way of knowing how many of the windows in the houses were acting as eyes, no way of knowing if anyone was looking back at her right now. For a moment, she was too tired to care.

"What?" Damien said.

Cate turned away from the window, oddly glad to no longer see the sky. All that white made her feel much too small.

"They want us to read it. They'll let us get it."

"Yeah, right." Damien laughed. "Someone goes out there, gets the note, reads it and they shoot the poor fucker. Count me out."

"If they shoot whoever gets the note, then how would anyone else know what it says?"

Damien's clear dislike of her shone. His unblinking eyes, his mouth closed in a fine line, his hate pulsing off him: Cate took all of it and didn't give a shit.

"Think about it," she said. "They want us to read it."

Steve pulled his gun free. "Get Wallace," he said to Steve. "We'll be upstairs. Meet us outside the ward doors."

Damien's unblinking eyes landed on Cate for another few seconds before he turned and left the office.

"He doesn't like me, does he?" Cate said.

"Not much, no. Come on."

They jogged along the corridor to the stairs and headed up. Cate resisted the urge to speak until they stood outside the doors to 6X. Steve gestured for the two men guarding the doors to move aside. They wandered over to the opposite ward doors and stood close together.

"I could be wrong," Cate murmured.

Steve smiled without any humour. "You're not, though, are you?"

"I don't think so."

He laughed at that, the sound close to genuine amusement as if she'd told him a joke.

"Good enough for me," he said.

Footsteps approached from the stairs. Cate took a few breaths to calm herself and faced the doors as they swung open and Wallace and Damien advanced.

"Damien's told me," Wallace said. "I don't like this."

"Neither do I, but it does make sense." Steve tapped the ward doors. "I'll go and get the note and be back up in a minute."

"And what happens if they see where you come back into the building?" Wallace asked.

"They won't. You can't see it from across the road."

"It's not a great idea, but we need to find out what's on the note," Damien said.

"Cate? Your thoughts?" Wallace said.

Cate met Damien's eyes. "Damien's right. We need to get the note."

Be careful with him. He's dangerous.

Cate ignored the interior warning and gave Damien a wide smile that she knew held no warmth.

"Jesus." Wallace rubbed her mouth and nodded. "I want five men up here," she said to Damien. "All armed. If anyone does come after Steve, we kill them. Get another four on the second floor at the windows. Get them there in the next two minutes."

"Right." Damien ran down the stairs, shouting to the people below. The two men who'd been guarding were joined by others. Each man held either a handgun or a shotgun. For the first time, the disquieting thought of how many bullets they had left hit Cate. She ignored it and faced Steve.

"You don't have to do this," she said.

"Yeah, but I like being the tough guy."

She laughed, knowing he needed to hear it.

"Unlock it," Wallace said.

One of the men undid the padlock on the doors and pulled them open. Again, Cate saw the mess of overturned chairs and beds filling the ward. If it was possible, the linked chunks of metal seemed more chaotic than during her one other visit up here.

"Ready?" Wallace said and Steve nodded.

"I'll do the other doors," Cate said and pointed to the fire exit.

Wallace and Steve exchanged a look.

"You need someone there, right?" Cate said.

"True." Wallace took the key from the man who'd unlocked the ward doors. "I'm coming with you."

Fully aware this wasn't the time to argue, Cate nodded. She, Wallace and Steve made their slow way through the tunnel of chairs. Wallace turned back to the corridor when they reached the fire exit.

"Tell them to be ready in the next minute. At the windows," she called. Her message was passed on in a relay to three floors below; Wallace unlocked the fire exit and rested one of her big hands on the frame.

"Are you sure, Steve?"

"Yeah."

"Go quickly."

Wallace shoved the door open. The wind hit Cate as it had before although it now flowed in with bright sunlight instead of the two in the morning dark.

"Keep it shut and give me three minutes," Steve said.

He was gone before Wallace or Cate could speak—a darting figure running down the steps. Wallace pulled the door closed and kept her hand on it as if relishing the icy metal on hot flesh.

Cate swallowed. The silence was thick, as if she would be able to taste it if she opened her mouth. Wallace paid her no attention. She stared at her watch, marking seconds.

"Going to ask me to leave again, then?" Cate said and cursed herself. This wasn't even close to the time or place.

"No. I'm going to hope and pray Steve makes it back in one piece."

If there was an admonishment in the few words, Wallace managed to hide it well. She might as well have said she was going to have a sit down and wait for Steve to wander back in.

"Right."

All of the armed men in the corridor stood ready with their guns as if they would start firing at any second.

I don't know any of their names. For some reason, the thought made her cold and brought back the image of the standing body bags in the morgue. Easy to place that image over the faces of the men in the corridor.

I need to leave here. I need to be on my own. I'm better on my own.

And what the hell did that mean? On her own? Christ, nothing could be worse given the state of the world outside the hospital. At least in here, she didn't have to run through empty streets or over fields or hide. At least here, there was flesh and blood all around her.

Steve gets the note, he comes back in and everything's all right. I'll make a fresh start here. Apologise to people for being off with them. Find out their names. Talk to them. It'll be okay.

She licked her moist lips and froze when a peculiar sound rose from somewhere in the distance. Whatever it was, it held a muffled, distorted note she didn't like. Any association she could make with it was a feeling of apprehension rather than an image.

"What the hell was that?" she said. Her answer came from one of the men in the corridor.

"They've got a megaphone. Across the road. They just yelled something at Steve."

Wallace grasped the bar on the fire exit. "Any shots?"

"Nothing," the man shouted.

There was another crackle, then the muffled sound broke through the air again. No mistaking it. Laughter.

"They're playing with him," Wallace said.

"They're playing with *us*," Cate replied.

Thumps hit the steps outside.

"Steve," Wallace said and tensed her grip on the bar. Cate backed away. "Get down," Wallace ordered and Cate dropped, understanding. Any shooting and she'd be in the middle of it.

The thumps on the steps crashed to a stop and Steve's voice, full of gasping breath, was right outside the door.

"It's me. I got it."

Wallace pulled the door open and caught Steve as he threw himself in. She slammed it shut and Cate stood. Shaking and sweating, Steve leaned against Wallace and handed her a crumpled sheet of paper. Blood had smeared over it in irregular patches.

"Nothing," Steve said, panting.

"What?" Cate said.

Wallace unfolded the paper. The blood smears were the only marks on it.

"Bastards," Wallace whispered.

"They've got a megaphone." Steve swallowed. "The Hat, I think. He shouted at me when I got it. Told me they hoped I liked it. Then he laughed."

"Those bastards," Wallace spat.

She strode away from Cate and Steve, shoving her way through the barricade to the corridor. Not speaking, Steve and Cate followed. Wordlessly, Cate passed the keys to one of the men and walked with Steve down to the next floor. A few people called to Steve from various rooms and he said nothing. They reached an empty section of the corridor and he abruptly pointed to a door further ahead.

"In there. Don't speak," he hissed.

Cate closed her mouth and followed Steve to the door of a male toilet. He opened it and pulled her into the gloom. Silently, he pointed to the wall opposite the urinals. She stood there while he checked the four cubicles.

"It's all right. They're empty," he said.

"What the hell is going on?"

In response, he strode to her and pulled something from his back pocket.

A sheet of paper. Blood was smeared all over it.

"Read it," he said.

Cate opened the sheet of paper and read the words printed in the middle.

WE JUST WANT HER.

Chapter Forty-Three

N icola pushed the loose hair from her forehead; the wind caught the strands and played through them. She leaned against the stone of the bridge and gazed at the water below. It lapped at its edges and the few houseboats still tethered, creating a pleasant sound. Calming. Made it easier to think.

"Yeah," she muttered and unfolded the note Helen had left on the table. The words scribbled on the paper at some point while she slept:

NICOLA. I'M SORRY. I DON'T TRUST YOU. I HAVE TO GO. BE SAFE. MERRY CHRISTMAS.

"Merry Christmas," Nicola said and let out a soft laugh. Without Helen's note, she'd have had no idea about the day. The minutes and hours and days were merging into one exhausted constant. All she knew was her tiredness and the need to move.

Nicola dropped the paper, paying no attention to where it landed on the water. It would fall and sink. Didn't matter to her any more than where Helen had gone.

She wheeled her bike from the pavement to the road and zipped her coat up to her neck. She'd checked her map before setting out half an hour ago. Her route would take her another couple of miles from the bridge to the parkway, then north. Cheadle Hulme was no more than sixty miles away. If the roads were as empty as they'd been lately, she would make good time. Be with Julia and Scott within a couple of days at the most.

"Julia," she whispered and let her daughter's face fill her eyes. She relished the image, bathed in it.

Get moving, love. Christmas dinner soon.

She sniggered. "Okay, Scott. On my way."

Nicola cycled to the slope of the bridge, followed it and saw the man and the woman sitting on a low wall outside a house as they saw her.

Shocked, she squeezed both brakes and skidded before stopping. The woman stood. The wind played in her unkempt hair. A few flakes fell.

"Hello." The woman raised her voice as if Nicola was much more than fifteen feet from her.

"Hi." Nicola eyed them both and made no effort to disguise her appraisal. The man hadn't risen yet and that could only be a good thing. He studied her with the same naked curiosity she gave him.

"What's your name?" the woman called. Her voice wavered. Nicola eased her right foot off the ground and placed it on a pedal.

"Vic," Nicola said. "Yours?"

"Sue. This is Trevor."

The man stood. Nicola tightened her hold on the handlebars.

"What's in the bag?" Trevor asked and moved towards her.

"Why don't you stay there?" Nicola kept her voice level.

"Why?"

In the back of her head, Nicola wished she'd taken another route to the parkway. The carriageway she'd passed would have taken her to it in a little longer than this route, but at least she would have been able to see anyone coming.

"Because I'd like you to stay there."

Trevor took another step. Nicola unzipped her coat and took her gun out. Trevor's eyes became wide holes in his face. He licked his lips and moved backwards.

"No need for that," he said.

"Not if you stay there."

"Please." Sue began to cry. "We're hungry. We're cold. Just a bit of food, please. In your bag. Your bag. Food, please. We're starving."

"Shut up," Nicola said. Julia's face filled her eyes again and she blinked the sight away. Needed to focus on the two people here. Needed to keep it together.

"Please," Sue whispered.

"You can spare a bit, can't you?" Trevor said.

"Sorry," Nicola said. More small snowflakes fell. She swallowed. The taste in her mouth was thick, electric. Water. She needed fresh, cold water to fill her mouth and dissolve the electricity all over the tongue and gums and teeth.

Sue's sobbing became heavier. Trevor placed his arm around her and pulled her close. Sue's arm dropped over his back and Scott spoke to Nicola.

Here it comes, babe. Do what you have to.

Trevor shuffled forwards; Sue's arm flew from him, gun in her hand.

Nicola fired.

Sue dropped, red filling the green of her jacket, reaching for her chest, horrible gurgling noises coming from her mouth. She squeezed the trigger of the small gun she'd taken from Trevor and the bullet flew into the ground.

"Bitch."

Trevor sprinted towards Nicola before he'd finished yelling his one word.

She fired and shot him in the neck. Blood coated his face as he fell. Nicola kept her aim on Trevor; he didn't move. Sue continued to gurgle. Nicola wheeled her bike closer to Trevor and studied his gore-streaked face.

He was dead.

Sue squirmed on the ground, mouth opening and closing as she searched in vain for the gun. She tracked Nicola as she approached.

"I'm sorry," Nicola said. "I told you to stay where you were."

Sue opened her mouth, freeing blood. She was choking on it.

"Julia," Nicola said. She said the name again and again. She howled it to the grey sky and the soft snow. Flakes landed on her head and in her eyes. Sue managed to groan, the sound full of liquid.

Nicola shot her in the head. The bubbling groan and the gurgling stopped.

"Julia," Nicola whispered.

More flakes fell, pattering on the ground around her and around the two bodies. The two people she'd killed.

"I did what I had to do."

Scott agreed. Scott told her she'd had no choice. Kill or be killed on this little bit of a road in a part of the country she didn't know at all.

"So fast."

Scott agreed with that, too. How mad to think two minutes ago she'd been on the bridge, chucking Helen's note down to the water and now here she was, standing next to two people she'd killed. Surely something so huge couldn't have happened in such a short space of time. Surely not.

But it had. No time for questions or debate or thought. Just time for reaction.

Nicola pocketed her gun, zipped her coat and steered her bike to the centre of the road. Ahead, the road was empty. The snowflakes died away again although the day tasted of them.

She could have helped the people. She knew it. Could have handed over a few cans. Could have asked them to come with her. Could have told them the little figure might let them live if they had. Could have told them they'd be dead within hours if they joined her.

"Maybe I've pleased it," she whispered. Maybe she had. Maybe even now it was watching her, happy she'd murdered two people so it didn't have to.

Her bike dropped from below her; she tried to yank the handlebars around to keep herself upright and failed. She fell, striking her arm hard on the ground. The impact knocked the breath out of her. Spots flew in front of her eyes; nausea spun in her stomach and she managed to turn her head at the last second.

Nicola vomited a thin stream and spat out the remnants.

Jesus Christ. I killed them. I really killed them.

She really had. And there was no getting away from that.

Nicola closed her eyes, spat until her mouth was clear and eased herself upright. She shook and focused on the trembling and not the terrible urge to turn around to see the bodies and all their wounds.

"No choice," she said, wiped her mouth and faced the road ahead.

The scent of snow followed her but no more fell.

Chapter Forty-Four

Cate pressed her face against the dirty glass and peered out to the little of the car park and Thorpe Road visible through the window. Nothing moved on the road; bodies littered the car park. With a bit of luck, rain would soon fall and help to wash the blood away.

She closed her eyes, still seeing the children falling, their bodies ruptured by bullets. *Kids*. They'd sent *kids* to die.

"You bastards."

It did no good. The children were still dead; she'd still killed to protect herself and the others, and nobody else here appeared to give a shit.

Cate opened her eyes. Her breath had fogged on the glass. She ran a finger over it, thinking. Dozens of dead children. An attack on the hospital. Proof that Skinny and his people would do anything to get in here. And nobody was acting as if any of this was unusual. Despite the horrors everyone had experienced since the bombs went off and the sickness was released, not caring now wasn't right. It wasn't normal.

This is how it is now. Things have changed.

She shook. The man who'd attacked her before she found Steve had said something similar, and she could not accept that. The world had gone to shit but that didn't mean they as the survivors had to go with it. They needed to still care what happened, what they did to survive. There had to be more important issues than the basic fact of their continued existence.

Cate took a breath and smelled the shampoo, faint but unmistakeable. At the same time, a hand slipped over her fingers. She squeezed her eyes shut and a deep, savage ache filled her chest, her throat, her head.

Not here. I'm not here.

The scent faded. The touch in her hand dropped away. She was left with the window and the terrible sights below.

"I need to leave," she whispered. "They'll throw me out if I don't."

And if she didn't leave soon, all she had to do was wait for someone to find out about the note. Once word spread about what it said, she could probably count her time left here in minutes. As much as Cate wanted to believe Steve wouldn't let the others chuck her out, she knew he wouldn't be able to stand against the group. She didn't belong here, and if Wallace wanted her to go or if whoever the people outside were wanted to get to her, there'd be plenty of others happy to show her the door.

"Damien."

Yeah. That fat bastard would be the first to shove her out, doubtless with a meaty hand all over her body as he did it. Unwillingly, Cate clenched her hands into fists.

Try it. I dare you.

Her eyes returned to the littered bodies and again she asked herself why they'd kept coming when they'd barely had the strength to stand. What had made them move? Had Skinny and his friends promised to let them go if they advanced on the hospital? Surely they'd known that was a lie. But maybe they hadn't cared. Maybe they'd been too far gone to care.

"Nobody else cared so why should they?" Cate whispered.

She breathed on the window, deliberately fogging it. Better that way. Made it harder to see. Resting her palm against the glass, Cate pressed, wondering how much pressure it would take to break the glass. And why not do it? All the other windows were broken holes.

Not all. Most.

Discomfort prodded her for some reason. Most. *Most* of the windows were broken. Why should that bother her?

Because it was too—

"Neat."

Something like that. Too neat, too *fitting.* Her mind flashed back to her first sight of the hospital's corridors, that gloomy walk from the ground floor to the wreck of the stairs and up to the cracked walls and broken windows of the second floor. As much as she'd been trying to work out what was happening, the sights of the ruined building had still stuck to her, still slipped to the back of her mind to ferment.

The figure rocking back and forth beside a small fire.

Cate replayed the image, tracing her eyes over the shifting flames, over the skinny frame, over the suggestion of the face lost behind shadows.

Too fitting. Too. . .

"Forced."

She shook, unsure what was frightening her, ordering herself to focus on the present, on the danger the note might present to her. Even so, a whisper worked its way up from far below. A single word.

Staged.

An explosion created a hollow thud from somewhere in the distance. Cate staggered, fell against the window and scanned the exterior. Nothing. A jangle of confused and panicked voices was already coming from outside her room.

She ran to the corridor, sprinted to the other side and to an office. In the suburbs at the rear of the hospital, what had once been homes were now flaming torches. Three of them were lit. Two of the roofs had been blown out; the street was awash with bricks and glass and the few remaining windows on the homes opposite those on fire were now broken holes.

Gunfire cracked and Cate ducked. A mix of revving car engines and mad laughter followed her down. More gunfire roared.

Steve appeared in the doorway.

"You okay?" he shouted over the noise and she nodded, not trusting herself to speak, happy to lose the strange fear troubling her a moment before.

"They've changed their plans. Going round the back. Come with me, quick."

She ran to the corridor. On all sides, people were running shapes. Most appeared to be heading to the steps at the side of the building. Joey stood at the entrance to the main stairs, calling to others as they joined him, guns ready.

"Everyone's going up to the sixth floor," Steve told her. "Some are on the roof. They come anywhere near us and we'll shoot the fuckers."

"I'll come—"

Cate got no further before Steve interrupted her.

"Go up to Four." He jammed his mouth against her ear. "The changing rooms in the theatres." He stabbed a finger upwards. "You get in there and keep your head down."

"Why?"

He laughed. The breath was warm on her ear. "You know why. Wallace doesn't know what they really want. Go."

He pushed her and ran to the main stairs. Torn, Cate followed. Someone barrelled into her and she lost sight of Steve. His last words echoed in her head and she ran for the theatres. More people coming the other way jostled her; none shouted at her to follow them and she saw no faces she knew. Without checking for anyone noticing her, Cate smashed open the doors to the theatres and sprinted to the changing rooms.

Inside, she sat on a low bench and hugged herself. The noise from outside penetrated the walls despite the distance. Cate rocked back and forth. In the dark, she tried to keep calm, keep focused. The chaos so close made it impossible. Cate stood and felt her way back to the door. Someone sprinted past and she withdrew her shaking hand from the door. Someone else screamed, their gender lost in the high-pitched wail. Cate hugged herself again. She could run. She could make it to the side stairs and get down to the ground floor without anyone really noticing. She'd be seen, yes, but she could still do it without being challenged.

Get downstairs and get to the secret hole in the cupboard.

"Then what?" she whispered.

Run out to Thorpe Road? She'd be dead in less than a minute, probably. Same if she ran the other way and followed the road to Dalry's streets.

She was trapped.

Cate blinked back frustrated tears and touched the vague shape of the door.

Behind, a foot slid over the ground.

Don't turn around. Don't look at it.

She grabbed the door handle, pulled it and jumped forward. As she flew out of the doorway, the footstep came again right behind her.

Cate smacked into the opposite wall, landed heavily and struggled to rise before eventually making it into a crouch.

The changing room door was closed. Even through her fright, she knew the door shouldn't have been more than half closed. She hadn't pulled it with her as she jumped.

The same voice that told her not to turn around boomed again in her head. *Run. Run now.*

Groaning, Cate stood and held her bruised shoulder. The handle of the door jerked downwards. The door eased open.

Cate sprinted for the main doors, not caring about her bruised body or keeping out of sight. She bashed into the doors and bounced off them. They remained shut.

A sigh blew against her back and neck. It was out. Whatever it was, it had come out of the changing rooms. Unable to think, Cate pulled on the doors; they opened and she ran out to the corridor. There was nobody in sight at either end although the maelstrom of gunfire and shouts was as loud as ever.

Moving between a stagger and a run, Cate headed towards the main stairs, sobbing as she moved.

Don't look back. Don't see it.

She wouldn't. It would be the last thing she'd do.

Another breath ran over the skin of her neck and Cate shrieked. Her vision shook. Greens and blues and reds filled her eyes, burying the cracks in the walls and the doors and the dirty floor. Everything in the swimming colours shook, and behind those colours, empty roads and fields of unkempt grass all below a grey sky unbroken by starlight or sunshine.

Outraged shouts broke through the vision. Cate's vision returned. Her feet carried her through the open doors to the foyer above the rubble of the ground floor. At once, she saw.

Men and women, all no more than staggering bodies, were pooling from the ground floor corridor. Blood had burst from their noses as membranes ruptured; their eyes were slits in their faces, blinded by pustules.

They walked. Despite their sickness, they walked and reached the bottom of the slope. Voicing their revulsion, the three men opened fire.

Bodies below blew apart, scattering blood and flesh to the ground, to the other advancing men and women. The air was a spinning red mist as the sick crashed into one another or fell, dead before they landed on the floor. Deafened by the clatter of gunfire, Cate could do nothing but watch, horror-struck, as more people flowed out of the corridor even as those at the front collapsed, holes opening in their faces, chests, heads. And in the thunder of guns, she understood.

They'd slid through the opening in the cupboard and broken through the locked door. While almost everyone was upstairs or on the roof, Skinny and his people had sent the Manc to the opening. The explosions and the gunfire at the back were a diversion to get the sick into the hospital. And it had worked perfectly.

The bodies had fallen together in the rubble, forming a small hill. Those who could still move stumbled through the corpses. The first of the Manc began to crawl up the slope at the same time as one of the three men ran out of bullets.

The woman leading the sick lifted her head and extended a shaking hand as if wanting to point. Gunfire took off her fingers. Blood and flesh splattered her narrow chest. Then bullets hit her in the face.

Her body dropped and those behind crawled over it.

The second man's gun ran empty.

Blackness dropped over Cate's eyes. She welcomed it. It took everything away, everything but the crash of her feet as she ran, as she kicked open a door somewhere, as she found two heavy canisters.

Darkness over her eyes. Welcome. Cooling. Safe. No worries here. No fear or regrets. Just familiarity.

The thud of her feet running again.

The slosh of liquid in the canisters as she sprinted back to the stairs.

The darkness she could live inside and know nothing else.

Nothing else.

Nothing.

Light exploded all around, and Cate was left with her dancing hands, the three men reaching for her. She kicked out, hit one in the stomach and the others grabbed for her.

Cate ducked and threw one of the canisters. It flew, spinning end over end to crash on the slope just above the advancing sick.

"What the fuck are you doing?"

She ignored the shout beside her head, dropped and tore the lid from the canister.

Petrol spilled to the rubble and ran down to the second canister.

"Burn them." Her words belonged to the darkness no longer over her eyes. It swam there, chasing itself end to end.

One of the men crouched, yanked a lighter from his pocket and flicked it. He dropped it to the running liquid and a trail of flame raced downwards.

Behind the flames, the people dying of the Manc burned and Cate watched from the darkness she lived inside.

Chapter Forty-Five

Nicola wheeled her bike to the side of the carriageway and took a long swallow of stale water. Her throat and mouth ached for more, but she held back. Although she had another full bottle, the one she was using only had a few mouthfuls left.

"I can fill it up somewhere," she told herself, not believing it.

She'd drawn level with a suburban area of whatever town she was passing. Dusk was descending. Time to find a house. Time to get some sleep.

Her body ached at the thought. She'd been cycling for what felt like weeks. While it had been a few days, the unused muscles in her legs and back needed a break. They needed sleep.

"House, food, sofa, sleep. In that order."

She giggled and steered her bike towards the town. As tired as she was, she'd be lucky to do anything before sleep.

"Could do with a wash, as well."

That was a joke. She laughed aloud. It had been days since she'd managed anything approaching a shower, and if there was a plus side to the ever-present stink of a dead country, it was that the stink covered her own rank aroma.

"Rank," she croaked and cleared her throat, wincing at the sting it caused. And if she was honest with herself, a tightness in her chest had been with her for a few miles.

"I'll pick up some Lemsip later," she whispered.

Moving on, Nicola passed a sign telling her she'd come to a village, not a town. Duckmanton. Fumbling with her map, she placed herself. Not far from Chesterfield. She pocketed the map and studied the area. It appeared that a lot of the buildings had escaped much of the damage she'd seen on her journey. Few of the windows were broken and there was no fire damage. As good a place as any to stop.

She moved on, passing a wild field, bus stops, and followed the pavement to a point level with the closest houses.

"Which one do you think, Jules?"

Julia didn't answer. She probably didn't care or was just too tired to answer.

"Scott? What about you? This look okay?"

He didn't answer either. She glared at him, irritated by being forced to make the decision without his help or support. She blinked. Scott was gone.

"He was never there," Nicola whispered and blinked away tears. Scott wasn't there. Neither was Julia. She was on her own miles away from her family. Talking to them made no difference. After all the miles she'd come and all the torture of her journey, she was still much too far from them.

"I could keep going tonight," she whispered. How easy it would be swing her leg over her bike, turn around and cycle back to the M1. Twenty miles through the night. Maybe thirty. Easy. Well, perhaps not *easy,* but possible. Had to be about four o'clock now. Dawn was another twelve or thirteen hours away. She could cover a lot of those thirty miles in that time.

Cycling in the dark. Moving through the dead and silent country with no illumination other than moonlight.

"It's left you alone so far."

True although Nicola knew the little figure and whatever it meant for her wasn't her only danger. Plenty of people out there like the men in the woods. Plenty of people who'd hurt her simply because they could. People like Trevor and Sue, ready to hurt her because they were hungry and frightened.

"There aren't any rules now, Scotty."

Nicola chose the house on the left. She wheeled her bike over its gravel path and tested the door at the side of the building. Locked. She went around the back. The window in the back door had been smashed. Jagged pieces of glass grew at odd angles in the frame. Gingerly, Nicola reached through, found the handle and pushed. The door opened.

"Home, sweet home."

She left her bike against the wall and entered the house. The door opened to a small utility room complete with washing machine leaking in drips, a lawn mower and various boxes. All the boxes were full of clothes. It looked as if someone had been planning on making a move, and Nicola wondered idly what had changed their mind.

"Maybe they died."

Mentally, she swore at herself. Yes, that was possible, but so was the chance they'd run from their home and left everything behind. She herself had done more or less the same.

Nicola crossed to the opposite door and eased it open to expose the hallway. The kitchen was off to one side and what was probably a living room was a bit further down. She took a few steps, saw the stairs at the front of the house and froze at the whisper of her name.

It was here. The little figure.

No. Something else. The thing had never spoken to her. Even so, she knew the word hadn't come from it. There was something new in the house.

Nicola backed up until she reached the doorway of the utility room. Four or five running steps to outside and her bike. Ten seconds to the pavement at the front of the house. She could be away from it before it reached her.

Anger spoke up. *No. Stop running. Face it. Right here. You're so close to Scott and Julia. Face it here.*

Shaking, she eased one of her feet over the carpet. Then the other.

Face it, she screamed at herself.

Rage kicked inside her mouth. She raced down the hallway, hit the living room door and booted it open, shrieking.

"Leave me the fuck alone. Fucking leave me—"

Her mouth snapped shut and she stared at the bodies in the living room.

Trevor.

Sue.

Helen.

The two men from the woods.

The nameless woman.

Lee from the supermarket.

Tom.

They'd been torn into pieces; their bodies were nothing but wounds and holes. Blood coated the two sofas and armchair, painted the walls, soaked deep into the carpet. The room was an abattoir, a stinking pit of slaughter.

Gagging, Nicola stumbled backwards and rested against the wall. Her mind made no attempt to process the sight or to force it into any kind of sense. It simply reported what she was looking at. A horror show. A massacre. A hell.

Each face was unmarked other than with sprays of blood and a few bits of torn flesh. Even from several feet away, Helen's face was as clear as it'd been two days before. There were no tears or scratches on her cheeks or around her mouth. The others' faces were red with their blood but no wounds ate their skin. The thing that had done this had torn them open, had cut the nameless woman's head from her neck and had torn poor Tom from his neck to his crotch, but it had left their faces. Left them for her to see them, to know them.

Each body opened its eyes.

The corpses looked at her.

Nicola shrieked once, the sound lasting no more than two seconds before she lost her voice. It dropped into a breath, a whisper.

They were looking at her. All apart from the woman without a head, her mind shouted. Looking at her. *Seeing her.*

She'd turned around somehow. Was facing the door at the other end of the hallway.

It had closed.

Nicola ran for it and dropped immediately into the soaked carpet. Blood splashed into her face and eyes and mouth. Trying not to swallow, Nicola fell forward and sent more blood splashing to soak the walls and her face.

From behind, footsteps squelched.

They're coming, babe. Run as fast as you can.

"Scott." Her word was a weak whisper. She could manage no more.

Steps squelched again. Nicola dragged herself over the sodden carpet, hit the wall, then a radiator. She pulled herself up and forward, then ran for the closed door, howling. And the howling hit a terrible pitch when the door opened and the little figure stood before her.

Its arms were open as if to embrace her and Scott was a shouting command, bellowing at her to run right through it, to come to him and Julia, to *run.*

Nicola ran.

There was the briefest sensation of sharp air blasting from a freezer, a crackling in her ears not unlike burning wood on a bonfire, the crisp scent of a winter morning. She ran through it all and hit fresh air. She found her bike, sprinted with it to the pavement and ran for the road. Sobbing, she tripped, fell to the ground, her bike spinning ahead of her. She stared back the way she'd run. Thick shadows grew in from all sides. The house was almost in darkness. Red stained her hands. The same on her arms, her legs, her clothes, her hair.

"Julia, you stay with Daddy, okay? I'll be with you soon. Be with you soon."

Still weeping, Nicola pushed her bike to the centre of the road, a black line reaching back to the M1.

"Outside Chesterfield already." She cleared her throat and tried not to shake. "Not too bad. Could be worse."

Tears tracked through the blood on her cheeks. She let them fall, too cold to take her hands off her bike and wipe her face and too frightened to touch the blood.

She walked on the carriageway as fast as her aching muscles would let her, looking back at the slightest noise, looking ahead and talking to her daughter as she drew closer to her family.

Chapter Forty-Six

Cate ran for the same office she'd taken the petrol from and shoved the window up. Fresh air filled her mouth and helped to take away the stink from out in the corridor. She took deep breaths, swallowed, breathed again.

"Cate."

Her name from the corridor, turned her around. Joey ran past the door, saw her and backtracked. He held his gun limply at his side.

"What?" she croaked.

"They're dead but the bodies are still burning. Come on."

She took a last breath, relishing the taste and returned to the corridor. Smoke filled it. So did a ghastly stink of burned flesh, of ruptured bodies, of the Manc.

Eight or nine of the men were throwing mop buckets of water down on to the remains on the rubble below. Cooked flesh crackled and steamed and Cate failed to miss a body falling down the slope, torso separated from its legs. Innards chased down after it: lumps seared black.

"Christ," Cate whispered.

People descended the stairs, a few calling out questions of what had happened, what was the stink. Someone saw below. Someone started screaming.

Joey waved his gun and bellowed to the people above even as several others followed them down. *"Everyone shut the fuck up. Anyone panics and I'll beat the shit out of you."*

The screams subsided; two women had pressed their hands over the mouth of a struggling teenage girl.

"We've got a problem and we'll deal with it," Joey shouted. "Where's Wallace?"

The cry of Wallace's name ran up the stairs as people relayed it in a human chain. They pushed themselves against the walls and railings, parting as Wallace's voice dropped from above.

"I'm coming."

She appeared at the curve of the stairs, moving fast. Damien ran down after her, a few steps behind. She saw the bodies on the ground floor; she winced and that was all. She reached level ground and scanned Cate.

"What happened?"

Joey answered Wallace. "They got in. Must have been through the cupboard which means those fuckers know about it." He jabbed his gun towards the front of the building as if the weapon was a knife. "Christ knows why they haven't used it before."

"You can only fit one person at a time through," Wallace replied, studying the bodies, making no attempt to shield her mouth or nose despite the stink.

"What drove them?" she whispered. Cate kept her face motionless. Even if she and Joey had been the only two to hear Wallace, she had no urge to be part of the conversation.

Wallace lifted her gaze and spoke rapidly. "We'll need a dozen men. This needs to be cleared. You'll need full protective clothing and it needs to be done now. We'll also need two men on the cupboard door at all times." She faced the assembled people above and silence fell. Wallace addressed them. "I know how bad this is. Believe me, I know. We fell for a trick and they exploited that. We won't fall for it again. I need everyone back upstairs now. Stay on the fifth floor."

Murmurs rained from the stairway. Some of them managed to sound convinced by Wallace. Others just sounded terrified. People began moving back up and Cate watched dozens of wet eyes staring down at the plague-ridden bodies who'd broken into the building.

We really fell for their trick, Wallace.

Wallace glanced at her as if she'd heard the thought. Cate backed up.

"You burned them?" Wallace said.

"Yes."

"How did you know about the petrol?"

Cate stuttered a reply, any sense in her words lost below her fear.

She hadn't known about the petrol. She'd just run. Just like she'd started shooting earlier.

"In any case, it was a good plan," Wallace said.

Cate managed to whisper a reply. "Thanks."

"Genius trick." Wallace rubbed her mouth. "Distract us like that and then exploit our weakest spot. Genius."

"Did you see anything up there?" Joey said.

"No. Just the fires. They were shooting but it was random. Designed to confuse us. It worked very well."

"Yeah," Joey said and spat over the edge of the stairs.

"We need this cleared, Joey. And make sure everyone is protected."

"Yeah," Joey said again and headed towards the stairs.

Wallace called after him. "Where's Steve?"

Joey glanced back. "Upstairs, wasn't he?"

"No. I thought he was down here with you."

Light fingers brushed Cate's neck.

"Cate? Have you seen him?"

Cate tried to answer Wallace. Her voice was frozen.

"Cate?"

She managed a croak and that was all. Joey returned from the stairs, frowning as he approached.

"What's going on?" he said.

"Cate?" Wallace murmured. "Are you all right?"

The light fingers on Cate's neck didn't touch her again; they had no need to. They'd done their work.

Inside, she shrieked. She wept and howled Steve's name, and inside, she knew it made no difference.

Someone screamed in the corridor behind her. Joey shoved past and ran through the doors. Wallace grabbed Cate by the arm and they dashed into the corridor. Joey had already reached the woman who'd screamed. She'd shoved herself against the wall and was pointing to a bundle of clothes on the floor close to the opposite wall. Red was smeared all around it. Joey crouched beside the bundle and pulled at it. Cate's stomach clenched like a fist and a soft flower of colours exploded behind her eyes.

She knew she was falling just as she knew the bundle of clothes was Steve's body minus its head.

She knew both and had no way of changing either.

Chapter Forty-Seven

N icola saw the layer of broken glass a second before her front wheel would have run over it. She pulled on the brakes and twisted the handlebars at the same time. Her feet flew off the pedals and she slapped them down on the concrete, heart thudding.

Her bike light shone on the glass and the smashed wine bottles, which had rolled towards a bench. There was no way of knowing how long the glass had been on the ground or who had smashed the bottles. No way of knowing if they were anywhere near her. Watching her.

"Calm down," she told herself and backed up for a few seconds. There was little to see in the gloom. She'd come off the M1 a short while before and cycled south. Following a particular road which cut between houses and fields into a gradually more built up area, she'd looked for possible shelter and found nothing that appeared welcoming. And as much as she wanted to avoid people, there was a fatalistic itch that wanted to know who was around, if anyone. As the minutes and miles passed, she felt more like she was living a bizarre nightmare. The country had been emptied of anyone normal. Alan, Pat and Marie had been oddities. They were no more part of the world now than she was.

"Shut up," Nicola said and slapped her forehead. Focus. She needed focus not this bullshit.

Shivering, she pressed her lips against her scarf. She had no idea about the name of the town; it was probably on her map but after cycling through most of the night and the day, she had no energy to unfold it and attempt to place it. Better to find some shelter and turn off her bike light.

She'd stopped on a wide road which opened further ahead to a green roundabout. One road from the roundabout would take her to a Holiday Inn; the road straight over passed a destroyed KFC. She crossed the roundabout. Marching down towards her, dozens of shops and businesses stood in silence. Some were empty units and they'd been left alone during all the riots. Others had been torn apart in all the unrest. No shelter there.

Nicola steered her bike closer to the buildings and made her way towards what was left of a branch of Barclays. The moon, risen for the last hour, shone on the quiet town and cast enough illumination for her to be able to turn off her bike light.

"Need some sleep, Scott. Need a drink, too."

He agreed that was a good idea and told her to keep going. Nicola reached a wide space, roads spreading from it, buildings encircling it. Wherever she was, this appeared to be the centre of town. Across from her, silent hulks rose in the poor light and it took her several seconds to work out she was looking at JCBs and a few removal lorries. Work had been taking place on whatever the building was on the other side of the road.

Scaffolding covered it, and it appeared a green square had been developed over the paving. Given a few weeks, it might have been pleasant. As it was, she was next to a dead building site.

Nicola headed towards it, passed through the vehicles and saw the church beyond the old building. It appeared the building was to be torn down, freeing up space around the church.

"Work may be delayed," she whispered.

At the church doors, she came off her bike, pulled it over the steps and placed a gentle hand on the doors. They eased open, surprising her. There was no light inside the church. She might as well have been staring into oil.

"In here or out on the street," Nicola said. Decision made, she entered the building, stopped after a few seconds and clicked her bike light on. It cut through the dark ahead, illuminating pews and stone floor and little else.

"This'll do." And it would. Half of her expected the church to stink of the rotting dead or for the bodies of the people she'd met to be here as they'd been in the house. Other than the ever-present winter, the building was free of any scents and there was no sight of bodies. If people in this town had congregated anywhere to die, it'd been somewhere else. Using the light as a guide, Nicola made her way towards the pulpit. She laid her bike flat and pulled the light off the frame. Her light picked out the altar and some of the images on the windows. The glass appeared to be whole. That had to be worth something.

She sat, emptied her bag and ate a can of spaghetti hoops. The sauce stuck to her lips and teeth; she licked them clean and ate more. She had half a packet of chocolate digestives left and ate three. Chunks of biscuit stuck to her tongue and she remained still, relishing the melting chocolate, before crunching the chunks with satisfied bites.

Nicola allowed herself four swallows of water from one of her remaining bottles, then placed her empty can at arm's reach. She unpacked her sleeping bag and crawled into it, fully dressed. No chance she was taking her hat or gloves off let alone her big coat or boots. The stink of her unwashed body no longer bothered her. It barely registered. Neither did the cold. Both were sensations she knew existed; nothing more than that.

Sleep crept in. She turned off her light and closed her eyes against the oily black. Sleep came in closer. She dozed and dreamed or thought or saw.

Someone was outside the church. Someone touched the closed doors with a small hand. Someone wanted to come in.

Go away, she told them in her sleep or thought or sight. *This is my place. It's not yours, so go away.*

Someone lowered their hand and gazed at the old doors as if unsure of what they were. Someone was as dark as the night all around them. Someone was a flickering shadow, dancing over the stone steps, the cracks in the paving slabs and in and out of the silent vehicles. Someone touched the frozen metal of the machines with colder fingers and whispered to the winter air of their name.

And the winter air took the name up and up to the sub-zero currents in the empty sky, held it in their palm before dropping it like a falling bomb down to the church roof.

Where it exploded without making the slightest sound.

Where it trickled through the cracks in the old roof and ran down in blood-red streams.

Where it steamed to swim in the air.

Where it descended on to Nicola's head and body, slipping through the strands of hair poking out of her hat, twisting to curve its way into her nostrils and creep through the tiny gap of her parted lips.

Where it set up home in her head and in her heart.

Outside, someone left the church doors untouched.

Chapter Forty-Eight

"**D**o you have a minute?"

Cate remained looking out over the edge of the roof. Wallace had approached without making an effort to be quiet and Cate gave no reaction. The others watching from the roof had tried to get her into their conversation but they hadn't tried hard and that was fine with her. Let them talk about the plague bodies and about Steve. She had nothing to say about either.

"Cate?" Wallace stood beside Cate and rested on the railings. "Got a minute?"

"For what?"

"For talking."

The others had fallen silent and made no attempt to hide the fact they were listening. Wallace and spoke as if she was addressing the air.

"Come with me, Cate. This way."

She headed to the left side of the roof, stepping nimbly over pipework and loose stones. Moving on something close to autopilot, Cate followed. They stopped at the far left of the roof. Below, shadows were growing thick over the pavement and road. Cate stuck her bare hands under her armpits and blew fog from her mouth.

"What are we talking about, Wallace?"

"About you."

"What about me?"

Wallace ran her gloved fingers over the metal railing as if stroking it. Cate let the smooth movement lull her.

"About you leaving," Wallace said. Cate jerked back as if she'd been dozing and a loud bang had woken her.

"What?" The word was a weak pretence. She'd known as soon as Wallace said her name what was coming.

"We need to talk about you leaving." Wallace faced her. Her face and eyes didn't hold any anger or judgement, only a deep tiredness and fear. Cate had no reason to believe the fear was aimed at her. Wallace had all the power here, after all. No, this fear was something outside their little conversation.

"Why? What have I done now?" Cate said.

"Nothing. As far as I know, but I can't deny that things have become more difficult here since you arrived."

"And that's *my* fault? How, exactly? All I've done is what I've been asked to. I've helped out; I've tried to get to know people. For Christ's sake, if it wasn't for me, those people down there would have got up the stairs, and then where would we be?"

She was close to raging, unable to lower her volume, and the knowledge that the others on the far side of the roof could hear her only angered her more.

"I know all that." Wallace leaned in close. "So, I want to give you a choice. I'm happy to."

Cate forced herself to calm down. "What sort of choice?"

"The choice to talk to me. Or to leave. I don't like unpleasantness and I definitely don't like threats, but I have to think of the bigger picture here."

Cate gripped the railing they were leaning against and relished the sting of it on her fingers.

"Okay," she said.

"Let's start with a few days ago. Nights, specifically."

A cold that had nothing to do with being up on the roof or the winter slid across every inch of Cate's skin. It was like a hundred icy fingertips tracing their way over her body.

"Nights," she said.

"You and Steve go out there; you come back on the run. I know you saw something that made you run. I heard Steve."

What made you run?

Steve's few words. His question. She hadn't answered it. Hadn't dared to.

And Wallace had heard him. Wallace, looking fat and slow while being clever and quick and secret. All the things that made her the woman in charge here. She'd heard it and she'd kept it until she needed to use it.

"I've seen things," Cate said. "Here. In the morgue. The bodies." She squeezed the railings and stared down to the dark street. Anything could be down there. Anything could be staring back at her as she looked at it.

"They stood up. Before the others came back for me. The bodies stood up right behind me. What would have happened if the others hadn't let me out. . .I don't know." She gave Wallace a weak smile. "I don't want to know."

A brief gust of wind blew between them and skidded off over the roof. Cate studied the gravel coating the roof and imagined a bird's eye view from the other side of the roof to swim over the empty houses and the quiet roads. It would head out to the suburbs and sit on the homes and paths and pavements where people no longer walked or lived. It would touch a dead town, then the county, then the country. All the roads, houses, shops, fields, woods, ponds and rivers and hills and mountains; all the green and all the tiny lanes and all the narrow streets: the wind up here on the roof would blow through the dead places and nobody would know it had passed over her on its way out to the sleeping country.

"I've heard things." She closed her eyes for a moment. "Well, *thing.* Screaming. From the lift shaft. My first day. Steve was walking me through the building, telling me what was what and I heard a scream come straight up the shaft. Steve didn't hear a thing. He didn't react, didn't ask me what was wrong, didn't know it was there, but I heard it." Cate met Wallace's eyes for the first time during their talk. "I heard it."

"What do you think it was?" Wallace murmured.

"No idea. Could have been a woman or a child." Cate shrugged. "Could have been a man for all I know. There was no word in it. Just the noise." She hugged herself. "And I keep smelling. . .shampoo. Like really strong. And no, I don't know why."

"Cate?"

"Yes?"

"Who did you lose?"

Cate's arms dropped. "What?"

"We all lost someone. Lots of someones in many cases. I need to know who you lost."

"Why?"

Cate hugged herself again. She hadn't told Wallace about the phantom hand slipping into hers. And she wouldn't. Never.

"You're obviously under a great deal of stress. Most of us are. I just need to know you're dealing with it." Wallace placed a gentle touch on Cate's elbow. "Talk to me."

Cate's throat worked. She swallowed too much saliva. "Nobody. My parents died years ago. No brothers or sisters. Not married. Lucky in a way, I suppose."

"Friends? A boyfriend?"

"Friends? Everyone lost friends, Wallace. No boyfriend."

Wallace nodded and her next question was as calm as Cate knew it would be. "What did you see, Cate? That night with Steve?"

"Nothing."

Wallace pursed her lips. "All right. What happened to Steve?"

"How the hell should I know? I was busy with the sick people. Busy trying to stop them get up here if you remember."

Shouting, again. And again, she couldn't stop it.

"I remember it and I appreciate it. If you hadn't done it, then God knows what would have happened." Wallace looked like she might vomit. "All those children. My God. What was making them move?" She searched Cate's face and Cate gave her nothing. "Those children, those people, they were so close to dead, they might as well have been bodies, so what was pushing them forward?"

"I don't know," Cate whispered.

Running with Steve. Running back to the hospital in the middle of the night and desperate not to think of what was behind her.

Not think of it.

Not see it.

"The kids," Cate said. She gestured towards the front of the hospital. "We killed them, Wallace."

"I know."

"Do you?" Cate searched the older woman's face. "We murdered children and everyone's acting like it's no big deal."

"You really think that?" Wallace had paled. Her lips were two bright red slashes in her mouth. "You honestly think we don't care about killing children? Jesus Christ." She spat her final few words, obviously disgusted. "Get over yourself, Cate. Don't make the mistake of thinking you're different to us, that you're better than us. You're *exactly* like us and if I can remind you, *you* were the one who shot most of them. And *you* were the one who burned the people on the stairs. *You* did that. We all do what it takes to survive now. Don't forget that and don't ever think you do anything different to the rest of us."

Cate kept her mouth shut, afraid if she spoke, the trembling in her body would fall out of her mouth.

"People are talking, Cate. I can't stop them. I *can* stop what they do. For now. So, tell me what happened to you out there that night with Steve and I can stop people from throwing you out of here."

Cate licked her lips. They were frozen. She said nothing.

"Do you not know what's happening here? Steve is dead. Someone murdered him, Cate. I don't think it was you for a minute, but people are scared. When they're scared, they look for answers. If there are none, they make their own, so talk to me."

Cate said nothing.

"Okay." Wallace stepped away from the railings. "Think about it, Cate. Talk to me or I will ask you to leave. By tomorrow morning."

Wallace moved away and Cate spoke a second after she realised she was going to. "This place, Wallace."

Wallace turned back to her, face neutral.

"It doesn't add up." All at once, Cate's doubts and strange, niggling fears were a torrent falling from her. "Things don't make sense. I mean, look down there. We've got a load of extra buildings down there." She pointed to the five or six buildings surrounding the car park. "What's stopping anyone outside from getting in there? And why the hell are they so desperate to get in *here*? It doesn't add up. All they've got to do is go a few miles and there's another hospital, right? So why this one?"

Wallace simply stared at her.

"And what about the guns? You've got probably the only guns in the city. Just because the police were here? And Steve. First night. He ran." Cate had to swallow. "I got in through the opening, he ran and the men outside didn't see him. How is that possible? It's like he vanished."

"I—" Wallace began and Cate spoke her over.

"This doesn't feel real, Wallace. I think I might be nuts. How about that?"

There. She'd said it, the word she'd thought a few times in the dark and silence of her room when sleep was moments away. And maybe it was true. Maybe the end of everything had driven her mad.

"This is real, Cate. You need to accept that. All of it."

Wallace left her. Cate stood alone against the railings and stared down into the streets, heavy with shadows.

Steve's destroyed body.

The children, too sick to move, somehow propelled towards the hospital to spread their infection.

The staggering people falling onto the slope of the stairs, the petrol racing towards them and the fire streaking down to burn them away.

Running from Thorpe Road and the horror on the other side of it.

Cate closed her eyes. It did no good. She still saw everything.

Chapter Forty-Nine

Nicola woke when weak daylight broke through the nearest window and landed on her eyelids. Rolling over, she groaned. Everything ached. Everything was a pulled muscle or an exposed bone.

"You're almost there. Get up."

Groaning again, she pulled her legs up and pulled herself out of the sleeping bag. The air hit in a steady flow and she turned in a circle, searching for the source.

The church doors were open a fraction. Nicola stared at them, unable to pretend the chill she felt was purely down to the morning entering the old building.

It had come to her in the night. It had been here while she slept. She remembered her strange dream from last night—something outside, something she'd told to leave her alone.

"That was a dream. I was asleep."

The maddening thing was that felt to be completely true. She'd fallen asleep in seconds, knocked unconscious through exhaustion. The image of something outside the church had been a jumbled dream.

"So, it can come in dreams and when you're awake. Wonderful."

Nicola packed her bag, wheeled her bike through the church to the doors and stepped out to the morning. Her breath frosted in the air. She exhaled deeply, pushing the fog outwards, tasting the day on her tongue and teeth. Bracing. Refreshing.

More of the town centre was visible in the bright sun. Not as many of the buildings had been damaged during the riots as she'd expected. Maybe, while the country was tearing itself apart, the population of this town had tried to keep things together. Or maybe they'd been too busy dying.

"Jesus."

Furious with herself, Nicola thumped her leg. There was a chance there was some good left here. There had to be. It didn't need her automatically assuming the worst.

She pushed her bike forward and jerked to a stop.

Two marks stood out from the concrete at the foot of the steps. Nicola crouched. They were only a few inches long and perhaps two inches wide, both side by side, both seemingly etched into the paving. There was every chance they'd been there the night before; she wouldn't have had any chance of seeing them in the dark. They stood out now, though: deep black against the fresh white of the paving. They stood out too much. As if they wanted to be noticed.

You're overthinking it, love, Scott said to her. *You always do.*

"Probably," Nicola replied. She stood and ran the toes of her boots over the marks, hoping to smudge them. At once, heat raced up from her toes to her shin, to her knee, then streaked high up into her chest. Her flesh was burning; her throat had closed to a pinhole. She tried to breathe through it and only managed a weak gasp. The heat faded. She blinked tears away and knew what the marks were.

"They're footprints, aren't they?"

The wind picked up for a few seconds. Food wrappers and a few empty cans of Coke on the other side of the street rolled out of a shop doorway and clattered and rustled their way to the road.

Footprints. It was playing with her. It was telling her it had been with her in the night and marked the ground. Marked it like some sort of. . . what? Demon? Some monster refused access to the church, unable to step onto hallowed ground?

"Fuck you." The words helped. She said them again and again. "I don't believe you. This is just a game." She slapped a foot over the marks and her toes remained frozen. "You want me, then come and get me. Stop bullshitting me with this crap."

One of the drinks cans rolled into the middle of the road. There was no wind. The can flipped upright and stood in the precise centre of the road.

"Is that the best you can do?" Nicola muttered.

Everything around her remained utterly still, holding its breath.

"Come and get me now or leave me alone. I have had enough."

A held breath. An unblinking eye.

Nicola wheeled her bike to the middle of the road, eyed the can for a moment, then kicked it as hard as she could. It flew to the window of a bakers, smacked into the cracked glass and dropped to the pavement. The echo ran up and down the street.

"There are fifty miles between me and my family," she told the air. "If you come between me and them now, I will kill you."

Nicola mounted her bike and left the church and the marks burned into the ground.

Chapter Fifty

"**T**en steps."

Cate flinched. She hadn't known she was going to speak. Probably didn't matter, though. She'd seen nobody in the last fifteen minutes and the nearest voices sounded as if they were coming from three or four doors away.

Ten steps to the lift shaft. Ten steps between her and the opening like a mouth into the framework of the building. All she had to do was take those ten steps, pull aside the orange tape and the masking tape and take a look straight down.

As easy as that.

She let out a soft snigger, not at all amused. If anything about this was easy, she wouldn't be standing here now. She'd be with Wallace and all the others. She wouldn't be an outsider.

Cate checked both ends of the corridor. Empty. Other than murmuring voices and some sporadic hammering, she could have been alone.

"You *are* alone."

She swore at herself. Not the time to be thinking that even if it was true. No Steve. No friend here.

What happened to Steve? What killed him, Cate?

Wallace's words came back to her and she closed her eyes, banishing them. Opening her eye, she jerked backwards. She'd moved without realising it, and now stood inches away from the lift shaft. She stared at the black inside it and the black stared back.

Leave it alone.

No. She wouldn't. Something was happening here. Something *wrong,* and it was that something that was pushing her away from the others.

Cate hissed, welcoming her anger. Better to be angry than scared all the time. Better anger than confusion.

She craned her neck and peered over the jumble of chairs as far as she could. From her angle, she was only able to make out a few feet down the shaft.

"Hello?" She whispered it, conscious of her voice carrying to the others. "Talk to me. It's okay."

Nothing.

"Are you there?"

Something was down there. She knew it, could picture eyes staring up, desperate to see her, to let her see them. "Talk to me. Please. I want to help. I want—"

The scream raced up out of the shaft and hammered at her. Cate threw herself backwards, skidded and dropped. The din ran on and on. No person could have enough oxygen in their lungs to power such a noise. The pitch and volume remained constant; the clamour was a shriek of fear and hurt and it held no gender or age. Cate slapped her hands over her ears and kicked to push herself over the floor. Her back hit the wall and the noise faded into weak sobs. They lasted a few seconds before falling silent.

Cate stood and tried not to shake. A horrible tightness had clamped over her stomach, threatening to loosen her bowels.

Nobody else had heard the screams or the sobs. If they had, they'd have come running. As it was, they were still talking quietly in the ward, and the sporadic hammering hadn't changed. Just like before, the scream had been for her alone.

Cate wiped her mouth and tried to think. She had to find out what or who was making such a terrible noise. *Had* to. And the only way she could do that was to go down to the ground floor and search through the rubble and the wrecked rooms.

She shook. Going down to the ground floor meant passing through the mess left from the remnants of the burned bodies. It also meant getting close to the morgue. There was a possibility there were other stairs going down, but she didn't know where they were and couldn't find out without arousing suspicion. She'd have to take the stairs down into the main reception.

"Shit," she whispered and walked a few paces towards the lift shaft. Fear made her stop. Couldn't hear the scream again. Couldn't hear it and know she was the only person who heard it.

"Maybe I *am* nuts."

Maybe. Maybe not. Maybe all this was something bigger than her state of mind. Or maybe she should just run.

No. Not yet.

Cate strode towards the ward doors, eager to be around people even if those people didn't like her. From the stairs, the noise of running people was immediately followed by shouts. Cate pressed herself against the wall as two men made their way up the slope of the stairs.

Both moved fast, the one in the lead calling to the one behind.

"Need to tell Wallace now. Need to tell her."

He was out of breath, his face a red, sweating circle. Both men reached the top of the stairs and a third followed them. Damien. He saw Cate and looked away without acknowledging her.

"What is it? What's happening?" she yelled as all three men passed her. The two at the front slammed the ward doors open and ran on. Damien jogged after them; she dashed to him and grabbed him by the shoulder.

"What's happening?"

"Problems," he said and shook her arm free. He ran ahead and Cate followed him into the ward. People emerged from the offices, some shouting. The two men Damien had appeared behind were at the far end of the ward, one calling for Wallace. The people parted. Wallace was there as solid and implacable as ever. Powered by a nasty fear she was unable to name, Cate ran to two men and Wallace and caught one word.

Bus.

Anything else the man was saying was lost below the chaos on all sides. Wallace raised her hands, saw Cate, and spoke over the noise. "Please. We need quiet. Please calm down, everyone."

The shouts subsided. Wallace kept her focus on Cate for another few seconds, then shifted it to Damien and the two men. "What is it?"

"They've got a bus," one of the men said. He was still gasping for breath. "About a mile away. We were out for supplies. Saw them. It's full."

Damien spoke. "It's full of the Manc. Loads of them."

Utter silence filled the ward. Cate had time for one rushing thought—*you need to get out of here right now*—that sped through her mind like a bullet. Then someone's fist crashed into the side of her face.

A white flare went off in her head. She turned, feet twisting together. Cate dropped. Above, a high voice screeched.

"It's her. She's doing all this."

A dozen voices rained on all sides. She tried to stand. Her legs might as well have been boneless. Her face throbbed. Someone lifted her arm and pulled. It was Wallace.

"With me, quickly."

Wallace yanked her to the closest bed and shoved her on to it. The woman who'd hit Cate broke out of the group and rushed towards Wallace. Joey grabbed her, swung her around and pushed her back into the group. She bounced off a man and someone held her even as she screamed it was all Cate's fault. Behind the woman, a maelstrom of noise rose. Any sense in the raging voices was lost and Cate wanted nothing more than to crawl over the bed and pull the covers over her body.

"Silence, please," Wallace bellowed. She repeated it and much of the noise began to die. The woman who'd punched Cate continued to rage. The man holding her tightened his grip. Wallace pointed at another man. "You. Go with him. Get her out of here."

"Where to?"

"I don't care. Just get her out of here."

The two men took the struggling woman to the other end of the ward. Her voice raging against Cate echoed back to the group.

"Anyone else have a problem?" Joey shouted.

Nobody made a sound.

"Good," Joey said and a man at the back of the group shoved his way to the front.

"Jenny was right. She's what this is about."

"Shut the fuck up," Joey said and moved to push the man away. Cate rolled off the bed and stood beside Wallace. Tears fell.

"What have I done? Why is this my fault? I haven't done anything. I just wanted somewhere to stay when I came here." She coughed, still weeping. "I'll go. I'll leave now."

Wallace stepped closer to her. "No, Cate. You don't need to."

Cate wiped at her eyes, understanding the words Wallace had left out.

Not right now.

"Yeah, I think I do." She cleared her throat and faced the people. A dozen hungry eyes stared at her. "Who wants me to leave? Go on. Put your hand up. Let's all tell the truth. We're friends, right?" She was shouting and not able to stop it any more than she could halt her sarcasm. "Let's be honest with each other. Who wants me to go?"

Silence, again, but this one was a thin line ready to spill her one way or the other.

The man who'd come forward lifted a wavering hand and lowered his eyes. Beside him, a woman lifted her hand. At the back, two men raised theirs.

"Any more for anymore?" Cate whispered.

Three more hands rose.

"Fine. I'll go tonight, Wallace. After dark."

"Cate, I. . ."

It didn't matter what Wallace wanted to say. Cate was already shoving her way through the group, hot tears in her eyes, running for the stairs and the roof.

Chapter Fifty-One

A few flakes flew against Nicola's face. She brushed at her nose and mouth, the bike wobbling as she steered it one-handed. More snow hit her face. She stopped, yanked a bottle from her coat and drank the too cold water. The brief flurry appeared to have stopped although the sky promised more.

"Not here. Please."

She swallowed, a stab pricking her throat. A harsh cough broke out of her mouth. Thumping herself in the chest helped to dislodge mucous. She spat.

"No snow. Not here."

Her pleas made no difference to the darkening sky. While she estimated the time to be late morning, the gloom suggested night was coming soon. And that was just about the worst thing she could face with the route ahead.

Nicola unfolded her map and stared at it, willing another route to present itself. No luck. The A628 would take her from South Yorkshire towards Greater Manchester. There were other ways to go but none were as direct as this way. All she had to do was cut through the Pennines and she'd be more or less there.

"Shit."

Nicola coughed again and pocketed her map. Beside her, Scott asked what she was afraid of, what was so daunting about cycling through the Pennines. She had no single answer. As much she'd wanted to avoid towns and cities on her journey north, she had to admit there'd been some odd comfort to be taken from the sights of buildings and homes. Made it easier to imagine the country was asleep, not dead. Easier to deal with being stuck in the middle of nowhere when she could use shops and houses as landmarks. Out here, though, there was nothing but the road, the massive fields, the wind blowing at her, and the growing gloom living in the cracks and valleys of the Pennines.

"It's not just that, Scotty," Nicola said, voice cracking.

Scott wanted to know what else it was. She told him

"Anything could be out here."

There. She'd said it. Given the horrendous idea flesh simply by speaking.

Beside her, Scott laughed. Nicola stared at him, unblinking. The wind made his hair flap and dance.

He told her she'd come this far; she'd survived everything to get here. And whatever the thing was following her and killing anyone she met, it hadn't left her alone just because she'd stuck to the roads. Why would it be any different out here?

"That's not very comforting."

Scott said it wasn't meant to be. All he was saying was she needed to move *now*, and screw the little thing following her. She had stuff to do, places to go, right? So do them.

Nicola gripped her handlebars. Shaking, she cycled between a few car wrecks, steered her way pass broken glass and looked back. Scott was gone.

He was never there.

Nicola tightened her hold, cycled and tried to ignore the pattering snow. After twenty minutes of cycling and peering ahead to the long road, she could no longer pretend. As much as she needed to keep moving, biking through what was going to turn into nasty weather was asking for trouble.

"No. Fuck you."

She pedalled faster, harder, panting for breath. Her bike wobbled. She rounded three cars joined into one a mess of broken metal. There was a building ahead. A pub.

Snow hit Nicola directly in the eyes. Swearing and briefly blinded, she rubbed at her face and stopped outside the pub. Although the flakes weren't overly thick, the snowfall had noticeably increased. Nicola took a last look straight ahead along the road and wheeled her bike to the pub car park. There were no cars in it and no signs of life in any of the pub windows. Nicola tried the main doors. Locked. For all she knew, the owners had barricaded themselves inside or they'd legged it.

The wind changed direction, pushing at her from behind. She made her way along the building, stepping over a few smashed garden tables and crossed a path to the rear of the pub. Wide doors led to the restaurant side of the building. They were also locked. Nicola pressed her face against the glass doors, cleared her throat and spoke as loudly as she could.

"Hello?"

She smacked a fist against the doors. They shook but didn't move.

Nicola swore under her breath. Thicker flakes fell on her. They were beginning to coat the ground and grass. She hammered at the doors again and Scott spoke close to her ear.

They're gone. They're all gone. You need shelter so what are you waiting for?

Nicola jogged back to the front of the building and the stone wall that formed its barrier with the neighbouring field. Way over the grass, a few white shapes lay dotted on the green. Thankfully, the aroma of the rotting sheep was lost in the wind. Nicola shoved at the rocks lining the wall, scraping her knuckles, working a rock loose. It clattered to the ground. She grabbed it, held it tight to her stomach and ran back to the rear.

"One last time," she shouted at the doors. "Anyone there?"

All she got in reply was a gust of wind.

Nicola threw the rock at the doors.

The centre exploded inwards, scattering shards of glass down to a stone floor. Wind blew white into the building. Nicola kicked at the glass around the hole, forming a wider hole. Behind her, Scott wanted to know what she was waiting for.

"You're not far away," she told him. "I could keep going. I could be with you soon if I keep going."

Freezing snow hit her eyes. Resigned to it, Nicola kicked the last of the glass away and eased her way through the hole into the pub. Turning around to check the force of the snowfall, her mouth fell open.

Dozens of figures were advancing on the pub from across the fields.

Chapter Fifty-Two

"Fuck them."

Cate tasted the words and wished they'd helped. She still felt as horrendous up here on the roof as she had down below with all the eyes judging her, all the raised hands telling her to leave, telling her she was an outsider.

At least she'd stopped crying. Hard to do anything while crying. Now she was free to think. Now she was able to plan her route away from this hospital and out of this town. Why stay here, anyway? The country was open. She could go anywhere as long as she was sensible and stayed away from most of the cities. Plenty of open space. Plenty of market towns and villages and hamlets with houses to choose from. Christ, if things got bad, there were thousands of farms and barns she could set up home in.

"Yeah. Just get the dead cows to move over and I get my own piece of hay."

Cate snorted and wiped her upper lip. Movement below caught her eye. Two men, both toy figures given the distance, ran from one of the houses on Thorpe Road to the cars blocking the avenue. They started two of the vehicles and drove them to the pavement, mounting it and not stopping until they'd crushed grass. The men exited the vehicles. One adjusted their hat.

"The Hat," Cate whispered. "Where's your friend? Where's Black Coat?" Cate ducked and kept her eyes on the two men as they ran back to the remaining cars and drove them to the side of the road.

"Something coming, gents?"

In reply, an engine rumbled. The bus.

It drove into view beyond the bridge, moving fast. The single decker passed over the roundabout, hit the bridge and barrelled down on Thorpe Road. At the last possible second, it braked and turned into the avenue. Skidding to a stop, it came close to smashing into dead trees. The men who'd moved the cars drove them back into place and jumped out of the vehicles. One of the men stopped in the middle of the road and faced the hospital. Even with the distance, Cate could make out enough of his features to name him.

"Skinny."

He waved to her.

"Fuck you."

Skinny waved again as if in reaction to her whispered words. He ran after the first man and disappeared from view. Cate strained to see any other movement. Nothing down there. Nothing she could see, anyway.

"What are you doing with that bus, you bastards? *What?"*

The most obvious answer was to use it as transport. And maybe that was true. Perhaps their plan was simply to pile everybody in the group into the bus, take whatever supplies and get out of the city. They had someone who could drive it; they had fuel. Maybe after their attempts at a siege having failed, they were calling it a day.

Do you really believe that?

No. She did not. Way too easy. Way too much of a happy ending for her and the others in the hospital. Happy endings had nothing to do with this business here. None of this had been about happy endings since the moment the first bomb exploded in Manchester.

She groaned, held a hand against her forehead until the dizziness eased and blinked a few tears away.

Movement below. The bus was backing up from the curve of the avenue, the driver clumsily manoeuvring it to a side road, crushing a kid's bike, grass, braking and then coming back out to the avenue so the front of the vehicle faced Thorpe Road. It backed up several feet and Cate caught the faint sound of the engine dying. She ducked, kept her head level with the bottom of the railings and shifted along the roof until she had a better view. While she had no way of seeing the interior of the bus, she could at least make out the shapes close to its windows. People. Lots. The doors opened and the driver emerged. Three other men, all armed with bats and clubs, sprinted from one of the houses and crowded around him. All were shouting and gesturing for those inside to exit.

They did. All of them, men and women, old and young, were sick. She could have been looking at dead people brought back to a sort of life, and despite the distance, she saw enough of their condition to know they were all in the advanced stages of the Manc. The swollen faces and necks, the weeping pus, the figures bent double as they coughed up blood, the staggering, shuffling older people, the soft horror of their moans rising on the breeze. All of it was as clear as it could be for her. All of it just like the country had been weeks ago when—

Vertigo flowed through her head. She slumped and held herself until the sensation eased.

"Focus," she croaked and rose into a crouch. The infected people were gone, presumably led into one of the spacious houses lining the avenue. The bus remained in the same place.

"What are you doing with it?" she whispered.

The men emerged from the house on the right of the bus, the one closest to it. They jogged from a side path which led to the rear garden. They were working in groups of two, either man holding the end of large metal cylinders. They crossed the grass to the bus; Cate raised her binoculars and focused on the cylinders.

Twelve of them. All appeared to be older than the ones Steve had shown her on her first day during her tour of the hospital. The cylinders down on the fourth floor were green and the ones the people beyond the road held were a dirty orange. Not oxygen cylinders like she'd seen with Steve, then. Something else.

Unable to speak, Cate could do nothing as the men finished loading the cylinders into the bus and closed its doors after the last man emerged. She scanned their faces. All were talking, laughing. They headed back to the house, looking like men who worked together or were on their way for an afternoon drink. Her stomach turned over and she let out a weak sigh.

The final two men stopped close to a tree in the garden. One gestured for the other to go ahead; he did so. In a leisurely movement, the first man walked a few steps from the tree so he was completely exposed.

Skinny had smiled at her a moment before. He was no longer smiling.

Cate kept her binoculars levelled on him and cursed him, a man she didn't know at all.

Sunlight blazed over the man's face as if a mammoth spotlight had kicked into life. It lit every line, every centimetre of pale skin, every black hair of his stubble. Wind, blowing from nowhere, made his loose hair flap, and when his mouth broke open in a toothy smile, his teeth were perfect white squares.

Now tinged with red.

Now blood-stained fangs.

Skinny threw his head back and howled her name. It roared up from the avenue and the road, pinning her to the hospital roof and smashing through every window to the ears of the people below. And now they'd heard it, they'd come for her and throw her out where Skinny could get to her, where the one behind Skinny would finally be able to bury her alive in its wavering smoke.

And oh God, she knew him. She knew his face.

Outrage went off in an explosion inside Cate's head. She fought against it, bringing herself back to her body and the cold of the roof.

No blood-stained teeth. No howl of her name. And nobody far below but the man she didn't know and who didn't know her.

"Get a grip," she muttered. "You've got enough to deal with."

Cate refocused on the area below and Skinny eventually followed the other men, leaving the avenue empty. Cate lowered her binoculars and stared at the bus.

The bus that definitely wasn't for transport.

Cate was nothing but arms and legs. She sprinted over the hospital roof, kicking up tiny pieces of gravel into the harsh sunlight.

Chapter Fifty-Three

Nicola staggered backwards, crunching over glass. The figures out on the fields kept coming, a shuffling mass of bodies. Most were too far away for her to make out their faces and no sound of their steps reached her. She hit a wall, followed it to a door and fell into the restaurant. Gasping, she ran through the restaurant, found another door and emerged in a short corridor. One door led to the bar, another led to the front of the pub. She ran for the front doors and bounced off them. Locked.

She wiped at her eyes with a gloved hand, ran to the bar and came within inches of tripping over overturned tables. Resting on the counter and panting, she tried desperately to think. Forget the snow. She had to get out before the figures reached her.

And go where?

That was all her, not Scott. He'd vanished. She was on her own.

Go back to the M1. Get away from here.

And what good would that do? She'd still be stuck outside.

Nicola ran back to the corridor, shoved a door open and passed a couple of staff entrances. Briefly, she considered hiding in a room or finding a way into the cellar. She dismissed both plans. She needed to run, not hide.

Back to the rear door and the smashed glass. Back to the approaching figures.

They'd drawn much closer. Nicola stared outside. While her eyes were exhausted, she couldn't close them let alone blink as she struggled to make sense of what she was seeing.

The figures were clearly people, not the ghastly smoke of the little figure following her since Stamford. Men, women and children walked over the fields. Hundreds of them. Some moved by themselves; others walked in groups of six or more. And others came as couples. People of all ages and races and backgrounds crossed the grass towards the pub and road, all moving at the same steady speed, all—

"They're dead."

Nicola tried to back up again. The dead advanced on her and she flashed back to the school in the rain days before. The dead children. The dead children following her into the garden and disappearing at the wall. She'd asked herself if the world was full of ghosts now, if the world was a dead place. And here was her answer.

Without seeming to move, Nicola stood at the wrecked door, mouth open, watching through the falling white.

The centre group of the ghosts reached the far end of the beer garden while those who lined either end of the main section moved from wild grass towards the road. They made no sound at all. Nicola could have been looking at smoke wafting towards her. Except the fog had faces and bodies. The fog was a country's dead.

They parted to skirt around the pub. Nicola crept forward, pushed at the doors. They opened silently. She moved out to the beer garden, weeping. Nobody saw her. *She* could have been the ghost. The dead kept coming, kept parting to flow around either side of the building. Nicola walked with them, between them. Her voice came and went to tell them any noises of comfort she could find. If they heard, they paid her no attention. They walked. She walked with them. They took her to the road in the snow, drawing ahead, black shapes in the falling white. Nicola walked behind them, her bike a memory in the pub behind her. The road took her on; the dead led her. And for the silent miles walking through the Pennines, she knew nothing but the black shapes floating through the falling white.

Chapter Fifty-Four

C ate dropped down the steps from the roof, sprinted through the ward and barged her way out to the corridor. Deserted. Voices below.

She ran for the main stairs and dashed down, drawing breath to warn the others. At the last second, she snapped her mouth shut and jerked to a stop on the fifth floor.

If she ran into the group, yelling about a bus made into a bomb, all hell would break loose. She'd cause a riot. And she'd definitely do herself no favours. Everyone here already thought she was bad news. *Giving* them bad news would be the worst thing she could do.

Trying to walk at a normal pace despite the fierce need to run, Cate descended to the second floor, entered the long corridor connecting the two wards and headed right. A few small groups were dotted around, some people talking, others making beds and others involved in the general maintenance. Still wanting to run, Cate walked at a quick pace to the end of the ward and knocked on Wallace's door.

"Yes?"

Cate pushed the door open. Damien and Wallace were at the open window, facing outside. Wallace glanced back.

"Cate? Are you all right?"

"I need to speak to you."

Speaking slowly was an effort. Her heartrate thundered and now she'd stopped, Cate was fully aware of the sweat all over her.

"Okay."

Wallace left the window and gestured for Cate to sit. Cate remained where she was and glanced at Damien.

"Alone," she said.

"I'm not a big fan of secrets, Cate."

Damien gave no reaction. She might as well have been talking about someone completely different.

She means it, a voice told her. The voice offered no room for argument here.

"Outside." Cate had to stop. She coughed. All at once, her mouth was much too dry. "I was up on the roof. I saw them and their bus. They're turning it into a bomb."

"What the fuck?" Damien said. He strode from the window and Wallace reached her arm, blocking him. He stopped.

"How is it a bomb, Cate?" Wallace said.

"Cylinders. Lots of them. Oxygen, maybe. Gas. I don't know what. I watched them load the bus after they got the sick people off it." Cate indicated the window. "You'll be able to see it from here. It's facing us now."

"Acetylene cylinders," Wallace said.

"What?" Cate tried to think. All she wanted to do was curl up and go to sleep.

"We saw it. We've been watching. Luckily, everyone else has been on the other side of the building for the last twenty minutes." Wallace jerked her thumb to the window. "They wanted us all to see. I have no doubt of it. As it is, I'd imagine you were the only person other than Damien and I who saw it."

This was all wrong. No urgency or commands for everyone to gather. Cate backed up.

"Damien," Wallace said lightly.

In two paces, he was upon Cate, closing a hand over her mouth and his other arm encircling her to pin her body against his. Cate shoved backwards. Damien rocked on his feet but didn't loosen his hold. She squirmed and his grip tightened.

"Cate, please," Wallace said. She drew closer. "We need to talk."

Cate tried to level her foot with one of Damien's. She stamped and hit the ground. His left arm rose and pressed slightly against her neck. Understanding at once, she stopped moving and glared at Wallace.

"You won't be hurt. Don't think you will. I just need you to calm down." Wallace gazed at her and Cate wished the older woman dead.

"Can you listen for a moment?" Wallace said. She nodded. "Yes. You can. Good. Damien?"

"Are you sure?" he asked.

"Yes."

He let go of Cate. She whirled around, fists and nails aimed at his face. He sidestepped and pushed her back easily.

"You fucking bastards," Cate hissed and went for him again. Wallace grabbed her by both shoulders and spun her around. Cate swung, losing her sense of direction. Blindly, she threw a fist and it hit Wallace in the corner of her mouth. Pain from the impact made her want to groan. She held it inside, happy for a second to see Wallace bleeding. Presence loomed behind her. Damien, coming for her.

"Leave it," Wallace said. She touched her lower lip and winced. "Good punch."

"Fuck off," Cate said. She shook and hated herself for it.

"Listen. Just for a minute, stop reacting and *listen.*" Wallace dabbed at her mouth with a tissue. "We have a big problem and since you've seen it, *you* have a big problem. I need you to work with us."

"What are you talking about?" Cate wanted to slump into a chair. The adrenaline was fading, leaving her sick and shaky.

"We can't last here. We've got no chance." Wallace dabbed at her mouth again and wadded the tissue into a ball. "We always knew they'd do something like this. So, we've been preparing. There isn't a lot, but we have managed to get some supplies out of the building. Food, some water, some medical supplies. We've got them in a community centre about a mile away. Not enough to last all of us for long. It's enough to get us out of here, though."

Cate took a single step towards Wallace and Damien moved with her exactly as she'd known he would.

"You knew? You saw them with these cylinders?"

"Yes. To be honest, I suspected something like this to happen any day. They've obviously raided the cylinders from somewhere. And why not? Everything is just left lying around now. Anything and everything can be picked up for free so why the hell not?"

She let out a sob, then gathered herself.

"So why aren't you telling people now?" Cate said.

"Because as soon as I do, they'll panic. We need to keep people together. I need to keep people calm. I'll tell them later today. After dark."

"You're not going to say anything now?"

Wallace shook her head. "I need you to do the same. Can you?"

Cate pursed her lips. "You're the boss."

"That's not what I asked."

"All right. Okay. If you think it's a good idea, I'll keep quiet on one condition."

"Which is?"

Cate turned to face Damien. She moved fast; he blinked, obviously surprised by her speed.

"That this fucking arsehole doesn't touch me again."

"Agreed, but please understand, you were never going to be hurt," Wallace said.

"I don't care. He never touches me again."

"Fair enough."

Cate kept her eyes on Damien's, glad when he lowered his gaze.

"They're really going to do it. They're really going to blow us up, aren't they?" she murmured.

"They're certainly going to try." Wallace stood beside her. "Like I said, I knew they would at some point which is half the reason we've been stashing supplies outside of here. It just means we have to leave before we have enough to really keep us going."

"What time are we getting out?"

"After dark."

"Good."

Nothing else needed to be said: the people outside with their bus would attack soon after dark. All the better for chaos. All the better for them since the people inside wouldn't be able to see what was happening. A big bang, a building falling apart, and then to finish them off, an influx of walking corpses. The Manc come to visit Dalry District Hospital.

"Tell her," Damien said. He smiled and Cate wanted to punch him in the mouth.

Wallace sighed. "Yes. I should. Cate." She crossed her arms over her breasts. "Our earlier conversation."

"The one where you told me to leave."

"Yes." If Wallace was embarrassed or uncomfortable, she was hiding it. "It's still the case. The people here, they'll be scared and confused at first. But once we're away and once things are a bit calmer, they'll feel the same about you as they do now." Wallace tried a smile. "I'm afraid you got off on the wrong foot and haven't been able to improve things since."

"Right. Okay. You're telling me I can come with you before we all die, but I have to leave once we're outside?"

Inside, she saw the bloody note Steve held. *We just want her.* As awful as those words were and as frightened as she'd been of someone other than Steve knowing about them, they meant nothing now. Those outside were going to come in; those inside had to run and she had to run with them, only to be abandoned once they were somewhere else.

"Not immediately." Wallace closed her mouth as if realising how weak her reply was when it came to sounding supportive.

"Not a problem." Cate fixed a wild grin to her face and wished she was anywhere but Wallace's office. "That was the plan, anyway."

Wallace nodded, eyes down.

Cate passed Damien and stared at him. "Don't," she said and he smiled in a secret way.

Outside in the corridor, Cate hurried past all the half-open doors and the little groups, past all the eyes furtively watching her. The anger was coming up and so were the tears. Hurt. Fury. Fear. All three wanted to boil out of her. She had to keep them all inside. At least until she was alone.

Moving faster, Cate reached the stairs, ascended to the third floor and stopped outside her room. She took a few breaths, placed a hand on the door and her tears flowed, finally free now she was back in her room. Sobbing, Cate shoved her door open and registered everything a second too late.

The mess of her overturned mattress and discarded clothing, the little light making it through the covered window, and the arms pulling her into the room.

Chapter Fifty-Five

"Tintwistle."

Nicola tasted the word, wondering if it made sense somewhere else. Here, it was nonsense.

"Tintwistle."

Still nonsense. Still—

You need to get inside.

"Scott?" she whispered and bent double, coughing. Spots danced in front of her eyes. She blinked them away and returned to herself.

Inside. Needed to get inside.

The dead.

Nicola stood upright. The dead had gone. Ghosts, memories, whatever the hell she'd seen and followed through the Pennines for the last ten hours were gone. All she had was the pain in her throat and chest, the snow blown by the gusting wind and a deep exhaustion.

She staggered on, lurching from the centre of the road to a pavement. Up it. Forward. Squat houses lining her way. A church ahead.

"Another church. It can't come into churches."

Nicola made it to the church doors and fell against them. They were locked.

"No."

Not here. Not now. She was no more than fifteen miles from Cheadle Hulme, too tired to move any further, too sick to think straight and these fucking doors were locked.

Howling, Nicola smashed her fists against the old doors. They remained locked.

"Bastards." She coughed the word and stumbled back to the pavement. Had to keep moving. Shelter. Needed shelter.

No fresh snow had fallen in the last few hours; the wind shoved through the layer coating the ground, sending flakes up into her face and eyes. Almost blind, Nicola walked on, talking to Julia, telling her she loved her and would be with her soon, they'd all be together soon and be safe together.

An open door.

Swaying, Nicola stared through the swirls of whites and made out the shape of an open door.

A faraway fear whispered to her. *It's in there.*

"Good. Then I can kill it."

Laughing, Nicola crossed to the front door, shoved it open fully and entered the little house. The wind entered with her. Too weak and confused to care about any danger, she shut the door and made her way through the gloom of the hallway to a living room. There were no signs of life. She went through to the kitchen, wincing at the stink of rotting food, then found the stairs.

"Up we go."

Couldn't do it. Too much effort.

Nicola?

Scott stood at the top of the stairs, gazing down at her.

"Scotty?"

Come on. You need to sleep.

Weeping, Nicola pulled herself up step by step. Scott wavered through her tears. He spoke to her, told her to keep coming. She made it halfway and fell, pitching forward as lightly as a feather.

Large hands caught her, carried her, stripped her soaked clothes. They took her through the dark of the second floor, placed her with gentle care on a bed and slid the covers over her.

Large hands smoothed the covers and lips placed a kiss on her hot cheek.

And then something as light as air wept in the silent bedroom.

Chapter Fifty-Six

S omeone shoved Cate forward. She hit a wall, bounced off it and tried to let out her pain and anger and fear. The noise, muffled by the gag around her mouth, emerged as nothing louder than her voice.

She was grabbed the by the shoulders, spun around and shoved down. She landed heavily, jarring her legs. A second later, a fist thudded into her stomach.

Hands yanked her by the ankles, straightening her legs, shoving her feet together. Something wrapped around her feet, binding them together. Still trying to breathe through the pain radiating throughout her body, Cate struggled to pull her legs up. The material holding them together kept them secure. Her assailant bound her wrists. She coughed; it burned in her throat. She coughed again, a deep, hacking breath.

Someone whispered against her ear. "I'll take this off your head for now. You make a sound and it goes back on. Okay?"

The speaker pulled the cover off her head. She panted against the wrap on her mouth and flinched when the light sparked into life close to her face.

A lighter. A narrow hand and long fingers.

Joey.

"All right, Cate. Time to listen. I know what's happening outside. You know, too. We don't have much time. We'll all either be dead or out of here in the next few hours. Wallace will be looking for you before long and it's a pain in the arse people are all over the place. I was going to take you downstairs, but there's no way of doing that, so we're stuck here. Me and you."

He fell silent and her mind raced, desperately attempting to work out what the hell he was talking about. His lighter clicked off and gripped her thigh.

Outrage exploded inside. He was still talking and the words belonged somewhere behind her repulsion. To have come through all this shit, to have survived a hell and end up here at the hands of this bastard. No. It would not be. It would not.

He stretched his fingers higher, the movement almost absent, splaying over her thigh, the tips close to her crotch. He leaned closer to her and she came back to his words.

"Not much time, Cate. We'll have to be quick. Wallace will want to know where you are before we get out of here. She likes you. *I* like you. You like me, too, don't you? Yeah, you do. All we need to do is get this out of the way and we can carry on with getting out of here and getting somewhere safe because those people outside, Skinny and his mates, they won't leave us alone, but I'll keep you safe. Don't worry about them. We have to look out for each other and that's what I'll do for you, okay?"

His breath was a hot whisper on her mouth and nose, his hand a horrible weight on her leg. It shifted and pressed on her crotch. She could do nothing but focus on the worst thing of all: he was pressing his hand on her tenderly as if he was her lover and they would make love in the dark and in the secret.

It won't be rape. Not to him. It'll be an opportunity.

"I know about the note. I know what it said."

The note. Jesus Christ.

"I saw it. Steve didn't know I did. He thought he could keep it secret." Joey giggled like a kid. "Pretty clever of him to cover it up and tell Wallace it was blank, but I saw it. We just want her. That's what it said, Cate. So, you tell me. Who the hell are they and why do they want you? Why the fuck did they start attacking us, huh? *I* know. Because they knew you were coming. That's why. We've had their shit for days. They've been after us and this place for ages. Do you not get that? They wanted you before you even got here so you tell me why. What's so special about you?"

Cate's breath was frozen in her mouth and nose. Joey leaned closer to her.

"Okay. We'll try it another way. What's it worth for me to keep quiet about it? I do you a favour and you do me one."

Her knife. Given to Wallace days before. Locked away in a drawer.

Her bound ankles and tied hands were useless. Another snatch of hot breath on her face, another twist of hand on her crotch and things inside her began to shut down. She was a machine going to sleep. She was the blank screen, the flat battery, the off switch. Inside the growing darkness, a far-off voice mocked her. All the time here, she'd been worried about Damien's attention, and now here was Joey ready to hurt her. Here she was, closing off, going into the dark and undone by everything she'd seen, everything, *everything*—

"Cate," he whispered.

Then he was gone.

Cate remained with the darkness even though her eyes were open. She walked over nothing but black and ran her fingers though tendrils of thin fog. She could live here. She could be happy inside the black, away from all people, away from all the horror and the blood.

She opened her eyes and stared into the solid shadows filling her room. Joey's invading hand and breath weren't on her, anymore. There was no sensation of him being anywhere near her.

He's gone.

That made no sense. Where the hell could he have gone without making a sound?

Fear came in closer with each passing second and she wished for the anger of moments before to return. It wouldn't. She was left with simple fear.

Locked in a dark room. Locked inside with Joey except Joey was gone.

Silently, Cate tried to bring her feet up. She managed to move a few inches off the wall but that was as far as she was able to go.

Get up, she shouted at herself. *He's gone so get up and get out of here.*

Get up. That was a laugh.

Then stay here and die.

Fuck off, she replied to the interior voice and it fell silent.

Cate took a few calming breaths through her nose and tipped herself over. She hit the floor and bit back a groan. Moving like a worm, she crawled forward and twisted around so her feet were against the wall. Bending her knees, she boosted herself off the wall and forward a few inches. The door. Had to be ahead. Her room was small. Get to the door. Kick at it until someone heard her and let her out.

Cate shifted forward again. Sweat coated her; strands of her hair were stuck to her cheeks. Ignoring both, she managed another inch over the floor and rested, panting behind the gag.

Something wet squelched on her cheek when she lowered it to the floor.

A coppery smell hit her nose.

Trying to shriek, Cate kicked away from the blood on the floor and rolled over. She rolled again and hit the wall. Gasping for breath, she stared upwards as a whispering chuckle came from somewhere in the black of her room.

Horror closed in. So did the darkness.

Chapter Fifty-Seven

Nicola woke, screaming. She twisted under the bedcovers, trapped by their weight.

In bed. She was in a bed somewhere not too far from Cheadle Hulme.

Everything hit her in one silent explosion. The snow, the exhausting walk through the Pennines as she followed the dead before taking the road into a tiny village.

Tintwistle.

That's where she was. While she slept in a dead person's bed.

Groaning, Nicola pulled her legs free, pain from overused muscles howling at her. She flashed back to the morning she'd woken in her own bed, body caked in filth, too weak to stand after suffering with the Manc. Wincing from the stabs eating into her ankles and calves, Nicola rested against a wardrobe. A weak laugh escaped her. So close to the end of her journey and she might as well be standing in her own bedroom more than a hundred miles away, weak and confused and cold.

She gazed at her skinny body and placed a gentle hand on her ribs. Naked. She was naked.

Her clothes lay in a stinking pile beside the bed.

"Who undressed me?"

For that matter, who put her to bed? Her last memory was of staggering up the stairs. There was no way she'd had it in her to undress.

Large hands pulling her clothes free.

"Jesus."

It had *not* been Scott. Absolutely not. Mad things were happening all around her; there was no problem with admitting that. The country was a dead place and that was fine. She could deal with that. But any idea Scott had come to put her to bed was insane. Hadn't happened.

Trying to convince herself she remembered undressing, Nicola rummaged through the wardrobe and dressed in the owner's clothes of a heavy sweater, thick socks and jeans. She grabbed her boots, went downstairs and gazed at the street.

The snow had stopped falling and the wind appeared to have died. Drifts were heaped on the pavements and on top of a few cars. A couple of birds squabbled over rubbish from an overturned bin. Black marks coated the crisp white in the middle of the road.

Already knowing what she would see, Nicola crossed to the window. Footprints ran from the front of the house to the middle of the road. They went nowhere else.

"Shit," Nicola whispered.

Ignoring the aches filling her body, she walked to the front door. A few damp patches coated the carpet and mat. Outside, the prints marched through the small garden and met the marks on the road.

"Why are you playing with me?"

If there was an answer, it was silent. Not allowing herself the luxury of fear, Nicola returned to the centre of the house, found her bag, pulled a woolly hat over her head and marched outside. Each step sent bolts of pain up from her ankles to thighs, her ribs and to her chest.

"So what? This is almost over."

Sticking to the pavement, Nicola walked, the glorious white of the snow dazzling her. The road brought her to a small junction; she checked her map and took the road on her left. Several minutes later, she passed a sign, read it, said it aloud if only to prove to herself the words were real.

"Manchester Road."

She had easily another fifteen miles to go. And there was no way around her route taking her through towns, through streets and roads while all she wanted to do was head to the fields and keep to the green, secret places.

"It doesn't matter. I'm not stopping, Scott. You keep hold of Jules, okay? I'm not stopping. Here I come."

Fully aware something was watching her, Nicola walked and made sure she kept her eyes focused on the road taking her towards her family.

Chapter Fifty-Eight

C ate groaned around her gag. The sound of her muffled voice shocked her into consciousness. She moved sharply and hit her shoulder and arm against the wall.

Everything came back, bringing savage terror. She kicked at nothing, forced herself upwards and pulled her legs in as far as she could.

The room stank of blood and sweat. She had to ignore the stench. Had to get out.

Grunting and trying not to, Cate squatted and rocked back and forth on her heels. Her hands clasped, she rested on her knuckles, took a breath and rocked backwards. Her back hit the wall, enabling her to take the pressure off her hands although the muscles in her calves were like stone. Using the wall as a guide and support, Cate pushed herself up it. She blinked away sweat and shuffled along the wall at a crawling pace. Her bound ankles protested; she kept going, not letting herself try to move any faster. Do that and she'd fall.

Several minutes after waking up, she reached the door, turned so her back was to it and fumbled for the handle. She swore behind her gag.

The door was locked.

Hammer on it.

She considered it but only briefly. Banging on the door might attract someone's attention. *Might.* But she needed her voice. Needed to get this fucking gag out of her mouth. And that meant she needed to free her hands.

Cate shuffled past the door, reached the corner of the room and followed the wall until she hit the table she used as a makeshift desk. She trailed her fingers over it as she followed its shape around to the other side and back to the wall.

Almost there. Just a bit further.

Her shoe squelched on something and she swallowed her groan. Another step. Her trainer squelched in liquid again. Closing her eyes, Cate followed the wall to the next corner, then hopped the last few feet to the window.

The next bit would be almost impossible.

You think that and you might as well just sit here until you're all dead.

Cate faced the centre of the room, banished all thought of the blood on the floor and her face, and leaned forward. At the same time, she strained her hands up, fingers dancing.

Come on. Fucking come on.

Material brushed her fingertips, then fell away. Cate squeezed her eyes shut, blocking out the sweat rolling off her forehead, and reached again.

She found the curtains, gripped the hem and pulled. They parted a fraction and light broke through between the boards blocking the glass.

Come on. Just a bit more. Just a little bit more.

She pulled again, twisted her head around and pulled. The curtain dropped away from the other one and beams of sunlight broke through the gaps in the woods on to her face, her body.

She let go of the curtains and stood straight. A mess that had been Joey lay on the floor.

His head hung on his neck by a few scraps of flesh. Blood lay around him in a wide circle. Trickles of it ran to all corners of her room. Joey's mouth was wide open as if he had died screaming. Blood coated his teeth and his tongue; specks of it dotted his cheeks.

His eyes were missing. Cate stared at the two holes left in his face and wondered from faraway how she would appear to him since his head at such a funny angle.

Her stomach twisted and she fought the urge to vomit. She wouldn't choke to death here. Absolutely would *not.*

The threat passed. She forced herself to focus. Whatever had happened here wasn't her concern. Not right now. Getting out of here *was* her concern. To do that, she needed Joey's key.

As simple as that.

If she'd been able to laugh, she would. She pictured herself squatting beside Joey, facing away from him and attempting to dig through his pockets with her tied hands. No chance of that. She had to free herself first.

Cate leaned on the curtain and used her shoulder to drag it further. More light streamed in. Turning again, she bent and searched blindly, eventually finding the edge of wood. She dug her fingertips into the top of one of the chunks of wood and pulled as hard as she could. The wood creaked. Cate pulled again, muscles and tendons in her wrists straining. A piece of wood, small by the feel, broke free. In her shock, she dropped it, grabbed the edge again and hissed as a splinter stabbed her flesh.

Get a hold on it. Get it off right now.

Cate pulled. More splinters pricked her. She pulled again. The wood snapped in half.

Resisting the urge to believe she might actually get free, Cate faced the window. She'd snapped off a piece of wood about four inches long and maybe two inches wide. Not enough for what she had in mind but at least it helped to let more light in.

Fighting claustrophobia from the taste of the gag, she studied the room. Nothing she could easily pick up with her secured hands. Nothing that she could use as a weapon or a weight.

Fuck you, Joey, you bastard. Fuck you. I'm glad you're dead. I'm glad. And guess what. I've got no idea why Skinny and his mates want me. And guess what else. I don't care.

Abruptly raging, she wished for her feet to be free if only so she could kick him. Attempting to keep calm, she ran her eye over the room and its meagre furniture again. Bed. Desk. Chair. Clothes.

Chair.

Cate shuffled to it, faced away and awkwardly dragged it out from under the table. Its legs scraped across the floor and she wished for someone close by to hear the noise. They wouldn't, though, and she knew it. She was on her own.

Not for much longer.

She stood as close to Joey's body as she dared, bent and gripped the top of the chair. Leg, back and arm muscles howled; she ignored them.

You've got one chance.

Cate bent forward, pulling the chair with her so it rested on her back, the legs jutting from her body. She hopped towards the window and shoved up and forward at the same time.

The legs hit the glass and the crack of the breaking window made her want to cry out her joy.

She dropped the chair, and in the clatter of the metal and wood hitting the floor, she heard it.

The child screaming below.

Chapter Fifty-Nine

Nicola walked along Marshall Street and kept her eyes on each of the houses. What was left of them.

Fire had torn through the terraced buildings, leaving none of them untouched. Much of the damage appeared fresh as if the flames had been extinguished only a few hours before. Nicola paused outside the last house in the row. A wide square of green now coloured white separated it from the next section. Blinking, hands squirming together and her mouth trembling, Nicola had to take a moment to work out what was wrong with the house.

The exterior wall was almost completely gone. It had collapsed inwards, spilling some of the roof straight down. She tried to make sense of the remnants of normality still visible inside the house. The sofa, the TV miraculously unmarked by falling stone and brick, the radiator still attached to the wall: little parts of a normal home now sitting beside burned shells of houses.

Nicola walked on. She passed the square, walked alongside the next row of houses, these ones slightly less damaged by fire. After a few minutes, the road turned into Allen Avenue. Bare trees lined it. Snow coated branches. A few cars remained outside the semi-detached and detached houses although not many.

An abrupt squawking from behind made her turn, fists clenched. Three birds were fighting over something buried by a hedge. Something that looked like a man's leg.

Nicola closed her eyes, took a few breaths and lowered her head. She opened her eyes. The snow, thinner here than miles behind, was clear apart from her footprints. She traced her route back to the point where the prints vanished from sight. All those steps, mile after mile through the two towns and countless buildings she'd passed.

She walked, still resisting the urge to run. No running allowed. No fear in her mouth and in her heart.

"Shut up," Nicola whispered. She walked in the middle of the road. Better to do that than stick to the pavements and be too close to any of the empty houses.

As much as she wanted to keep her eyes straight ahead, she kept casting furtive glances at the homes on either side. Despite the low temperatures, several of the front gardens were clearly growing unkempt. A few branches had either fallen or been broken from a big oak tree, and a wide flowerbed outside number thirty-nine was a boggy mess of melting slush.

"Focus," she said and did so. Eyes ahead. Feet on the ground. Breath coming faster, crunch of her boots louder, dead homes on either side running past, dashing past her, running, running, running, she was running as fast as she could, sprinting over the road and not giving a shit about the burning in her chest and throat or the shrieks in her shins and feet. Had to run. Had to *move.*

Nicola sprinted, shadow long and thin beside her, aware of nothing but her tearing breath and the fire in her feet and legs and the need to move.

She changed course, hit long grass bordering the pavement and she squelched through dirty puddles before she crashed over the pavement, rounded the curve and jerked to a stop at the corner of Lenton Road.

Fire had eaten the houses on both sides of the road.

She managed to whisper one word. "No."

Standing was too much of an effort. She dropped to the pavement and welcomed the solid ground on her bottom and legs. Easier to think about that than anything else.

"You can't do that, love."

Scott rested beside her and stretched his legs. He wore his old trainers. The dirty white ones he kept by the back door. He trailed his heels through the gravel, making thin lines.

"You really can't do that."

"Why not?"

"Because you're so close to us. We want you with us. And what's the point of coming all this way, taking all this time to get here and not go a bit further?"

His grubby trainers traced lines in the gravel. The sound scratched at the air.

"Look at that." She pointed over the grass to the fire-damaged buildings.

"I see it." He was as calm as ever. "But so what? A few damaged homes aren't the end of the world, sweetheart. Come on. Up."

Nicola remained where she was. Easier to do that.

Scott's shadow brushed her legs, then her stomach as he shifted to stand directly in front of her.

"Please, Nicola. Please." He was crying now, trying to speak through the tears. "We want you with us. Julia wants you. She misses you."

Finally, Nicola looked at her husband. Much of his face was hidden in shadow since the sun was behind him. She shielded her eyes and reached for him, as he wept. Nicola took his hand and her heart sang at his skin on hers. She let him pull her up and into him and he held her, his comforting shape against her.

Scott held her and all was right.

"Come with us, Nicola. Please come with us."

He breathed against her neck and ear, his breath a hot tickle, his tears dampening her skin. Nicola closed her eyes and held her husband in a death grip.

Scott, growing cooler. Growing thinner than he'd been in years.

"No. Please," she said, not opening her eyes.

Cooler and cooler. Cold, now. Thin, now. Faint.

"Please, Scott." She could only whisper it.

Cold. Air.

He was gone.

Nicola opened her eyes and dropped her arms from the nothing she held.

She ran. She left the ruins of the houses, ran for the dead grass and ran between the burned shells of houses, not stopping until she saw it.

Her in-laws house was built a little way back from the road. And at first glance, it might have been as it was before the end of everything.

At first glance.

Nicola walked towards it, taking slow, hurting steps.

The front door was missing. Slush, dead leaves and food wrappers had gathered in the entrance hall. Nicola crunched over the leaves and McDonalds wrappers and crisp packets. The wind entered with her as if eager to explore the house. She stopped for a moment, knowing that if she didn't pause right here, she was going to scream. Yes, she would scream and scream and all of it would be over.

You need to get a grip, love.

"Okay, Scott."

The hallway opened to the living room on her left, the kitchen on her right and the curving stairs ahead. Nicola went left.

The living room furniture was as she remembered it: long, leather sofas, coffee table, big TV mounted to the wall, patio doors letting in weak sunlight. Nicola gripped the arm of one of the sofas and told herself Scott had sat there with Julia in his arms.

She crossed her arms over her chest and returned to the hallway.

"Scott? Julia?"

Most of the kitchen cupboard doors were wide open, the food shelves ransacked. She ran her eyes over the remaining food—packets of pasta, a jar of peanut butter, coffee, tea bags, herbs.

"No cans," she murmured and squashed the little voice of hope that wanted to speak.

Nicola tried the back door. Locked. There were four keys on a loop beside the microwave. She left them where they were and headed back to the hallway.

No cans.

"Shut up."

No cans didn't mean a thing. Neither did the emptied cupboards. She needed more than that before she could or should start thinking anything.

Nicola went upstairs, her steps light and careful. All four doors to the three bedrooms and bathroom were wide open. Daylight emerged from the two rooms which faced the front of the house. Holding her breath, unable to think, Nicola entered the closest room, the one her in-laws used as a spare room.

The bed was made, the room tidy. She'd expected a chaos of clothes thrown all over the place and wrecked furniture.

Nicola scanned the room, searching for any signs of her husband and daughter. Nothing at all. She might as well have been in a complete stranger's house.

The next room was the same. She stood outside it, breathing slowly, holding on to the door frame, and watched a few branches wave on a tree in the front garden.

"Where are you?"

In here.

Scott's whisper emerged from the third room. Nicola eased the door open fully.

The chaos she'd expected in the first two rooms filled the third bedroom. On top of the two mattresses on the floor, piles of clothes lay in messy heaps. The window was shut and the room stank of mustiness and dirt. Nicola inhaled deeply, telling herself she was smelling her family. She entered the room and pressed the toe of her boot against one of the mattresses, convinced this one was the one her husband and daughter had slept in.

"Julia," Nicola said and wanted to sink into the mattress. She remained standing and took slow, deep breaths.

A few toys and books lay in a pile below the window and a pair of man's boots she didn't recognise had been tossed beside them. One sock poked out of a boot.

They'd all slept in here, crammed into one bedroom instead of using the other rooms. Safety in numbers.

"Comfort in numbers."

Sobbing, Nicola returned to the stairs and went down. Blindly, she returned to the kitchen and fell into a chair at the table.

Her family were gone. They'd left her. After all the time spent coming to them, after nothing but days of exhaustion and fear, they were gone.

And soon, it would come for her. Come and finish the job it had been threatening to do since Tom took her into his house outside Stamford.

"Come on, then. Do it." Nicola gazed around the kitchen as if expecting the little figure to appear out of thin air. And why should that feel like such a mad idea? It had done so before.

Grimacing, Nicola studied her hands. The remains of the blood from the other house still marked her fingers.

"Are you here? Do you want to kill me now? You might as well."

She spoke to the silent house and heard nothing in return.

Her eyes landed on the fridge. A scrap of paper was stuck to it, held in place by two magnets.

All at once, her legs didn't want to work. Neither did her lungs. Breathing was an impossibility.

Nicola threw herself up and crossed the kitchen in four large steps. The note was in her hand before she registered she was reaching for it.

Two scribbled lines covered it. Loops and swirls etched deep into the paper.

NICOLA I HOPE YOU FIND THIS ONE DAY. CATE AND NIGEL ARE DEAD. WE'RE GOING TO DAD'S HOUSE. I'LL FIND YOU. CAN'T

STAY HERE. SOMETHING IS AFTER US. LOVE YOU.

Panting, Nicola leaned against the sink and read the note again.

Dad's house.

Can't stay.

Something.

It had been here as well as with her. Tormenting her. Tormenting her family.

"No. No, you don't fucking dare. I'll fucking kill you. I'll tear you in half."

If anything else was in the house with her, it remained silent.

Dad's house. He meant out in Denshaw, a village maybe twenty or twenty-five miles away. Out there with its lanes and fields and pub, they'd be safe. They'd be together.

Nicola ran for the door and for the street.

They were alive. Scott and Julia were alive and she would find them.

Nicola ran and the dead house fell behind her.

Chapter Sixty

Cate knew what she had to do.

She placed her hands over the slivers of broken glass and eased them down to a jutting piece. Smaller pieces stabbed into her wrist. Pain hit at the same time as the sensation of her flowing blood.

No time for bleeding.

No. That wasn't right. A film. She'd seen it. With someone. Watched it. No time for bleeding.

Fire ate her skin. She was cutting as much flesh as she was the binding.

No time for bleeding.

Who said that?

She cut. She sawed into the binding and she sawed into her skin. Blood. She smelled it like she smelled her sweat and the stink of Joey there on the floor.

Ain't got time to bleed. Light flashed in front of her eyes as if someone had taken her photo.

Didn't matter who said it any more than it mattered who she'd been watching the film with. Whatever it was.

She bared her teeth, wanting to frighten something away.

Her wrists were on fire. The muscles in her forearms and shoulders were rocks twisting against one another.

There was a loud snap behind her as the cloth broke.

Her free hands fell to her side, the left scraping against glass as it fell. Cate dropped to her knees and stared at the ruined mess of her fingers. They looked as if she'd dipped them in red paint. From her elbows down, her arms were two slabs of dead meat.

Ignoring the pain, Cate pulled at the gag around her mouth. Blood pattered to her legs and the floor; the rich smell stuck to her nose. She held her breath, pulled at the cloth and it came free. Gasping, Cate undid the binding around her ankles. She was trying to stand straight even as she pulled the cloth loose. Standing upright was out of the question so she crawled to Joey's body and grabbed his front pocket. Nothing in it.

"Shit."

Cate wiped at her eye to dislodge sweat. Blood smeared at her face. She bit her lip to keep the shout inside and shoved herself against her mattress. Still desperate to bellow her pain, she shoved a pair of her underwear on to her left wrist, squeezed a piece of the material into her fist and held it against her stomach.

Back to Joey. To his other pocket. It was as empty as the first.

"Where's the key, Joey? Where's the fucking key?"

She stood and furiously kicked his head. It swung on the flap of flesh and his sightless eyes were two holes.

"Where's the fucking key?"

Fuck the key. She'd got the gag off. She'd scream herself hoarse to get out of here.

Cate staggered to the door, drawing breath to call for help. The breath ran out of her in a weak gasp.

The key was in the lock.

"What?" Cate whispered.

She ran a trembling finger over it. Metal.

"No."

Absolutely no. She'd seen Joey pocket it. How the hell had it got back into the door and. . .

And all she'd done to free herself had been pointless. The key was in the lock the whole time. Someone had put it there. Someone was now laughing at her.

The scream was rising, rising. She had to swallow it. If she let it loose, she'd go nuts. Totally fucking bananas.

"Good joke." She tried to smile, eager to show she appreciated a laugh.

Behind her, something giggled.

Cate turned the key, listened to the bolts moving and pushed the door open. The shafts of light behind her pushed into the corridor.

Whoever giggled didn't repeat it. Cate entered the corridor and listened to the voice inside.

Get out of here. Right now. Don't talk to anyone. Don't stop for anyone. Run.

Run. She could do that. Running was easy. She was good at running away.

Cate jogged to the end of the corridor, followed the junction and gazed ahead.

Nobody in sight.

If she was quick, she could get to the stairs and down within two minutes. If she saw anyone. . .

"If," she whispered.

Blood dribbled from the wounds on her hands and rained on the floor as she ran.

Chapter Sixty-One

Nicola skirted around a wreck of four or five cars and clambered over a low wall bordering the road with the fields and hills. Damp grass soaked into her jeans; wet earth sucked at her boots. She kicked dirty sludge loose and climbed back over the road when the road cleared. She staggered on, gazing at the fields which sloped towards the roofs of a few houses, then grew towards the hills. Buildings in the distance, this narrow road beside the grass and nothing but the breeze around her.

She walked a few paces and hissed. Pain in the soles of her feet stabbed through her. They wanted to stop, to make her sit down. She wasn't having any of it. Not this close to getting what she wanted.

"Just a bit further."

She made her way through the remains of a collapsed phone pole and its coils of wires, reached a curve in the road and looked back.

Smoke rose from the direction of Manchester as whatever was left of the city burned. Let it burn. Let it sleep just like Stamford now slept. She'd given it a lot of thought over the last few hours. She'd find her family;

they'd have a home by the sea and they'd listen to the waves rolling on to the beach. Maybe they'd walk on the sand on sunny days. Maybe they'd get a football and Scott could kick it to Julia and she could kick it back, her thin legs shining in the sun.

"I like the sound of that," Nicola said except it was more of a croak. She was almost out of water. Hadn't drunk any in hours.

She swallowed a small mouthful and ignored the fire in her throat that wanted to drink the rest. Needed to make it last. At least until she knew what sort of supplies Scott had managed to put together.

Nicola left the road, stepped over a wide dip that ran along the edge of the field and walked through the long, wet grass. She heard children.

They were playing somewhere close. Running over the grass. Laughing. Shouting.

Nicola froze and tried to see everywhere at once. Nothing but her and the waving grass. And the laughter of children.

"No." She whispered it, not daring to speak any louder. "No. They're not here."

A little girl giggled beside her. Then the laughter faded away, the breeze blowing it over the grass.

"Julia," Nicola murmured. The name was an incantation. Her magic spell. She said the name again and began walking. The sound of children returned. Now, they were screaming.

Nicola did the same, unable to stop herself. Dozens of boys and girls were crying all around her. She broke into a lurching jog that became a sprint. Wet grass slapped against her shins and knees and she skidded. Nicola whirled around, stumbled before righting herself and running again. Still, the shrieking children ran with her, right beside her eye and just out of sight. Skittering shapes to the left and right kept pace with her, formless things with howling mouths and sobbing voices that didn't quite make it to words.

Directly ahead, the familiar black shape grew from the grass. Perhaps fifty or sixty feet over the field, the little figure gazed at her, eyes lost behind its undefined face. Nicola skidded to a stop. The sobs faded but didn't totally vanish. The children were waiting to see what she would do.

"Go away. Leave me alone."

The figure extended an arm and pointed a skinny line of smoke that might have been a finger.

To the houses beyond the fields.

"No. Not now. You wouldn't fucking dare."

It lowered its hand and stood motionless. Waiting.

Weeping, Nicola sprinted towards it, her fingers becoming claws. The shape grew no more distinct the closer she came to it. It made no move. Nicola bore down on it and the only word she made out through her screams was her daughter's name.

She skidded on a patch of wet grass and dropped to one knee. She made it upright before the pain registered and she had to stop. Ahead, the little figure moved further away, drifting lazily.

Nicola tried to shout, to curse it.

I will kill you, she thought at the shape and it shifted as if about to face her. It could have been smoke blowing in the wind.

"Look at me," Nicola whispered, infuriated. "Don't you dare ignore me."

Smoke blowing over the grass. Nothing more than that.

Nicola broke into a run again. Fierce stabbing radiated from her knee and her run became a lurch.

Mummy.

The voice on all sides, around, above and below. It was the air and the grass. Sobbing, Nicola stopped again and hugged herself.

Mummy. Where are you?

Nicola tried to speak and her words were lost in her tears and the boiling agony of her fear and hurt.

Hurry up, Mummy. We miss you.

The words danced through the wet grass and the wind would take them up, up and away where they would be blown from cloud to cloud, always out of her reach.

"Julia," Nicola said and she screamed when her daughter shrieked right beside her ear. The horrible noise cut off after a moment as if someone had muted Julia. It didn't return. Grey wavered in front of Nicola's eyes. How soft the grass would be when she fell on to it. How wet with rain. How soft.

Stinging blossomed in her lower lip: she chewed through it. Blood filled her mouth. She spat; the grey fell away and she ran again, pounding over the field. And she was finally coming close to the little figure, bearing down on its formless shape with the village so close to her but so much closer to the shadowy thing.

Nicola ran over the field, a soundless fury coming for her daughter, her husband and the little figure was thirty feet away, twenty, ten, turning towards her and all the denial in the world rose in front of Nicola, blinding her.

She couldn't see it. Couldn't. *Couldn't.*

Her course changed, veering her to a sharp right as a gust of glacial air blasted straight towards her, turning the grass to blades of ice and the land to a dead waste.

Nicola rounded the little figure in a wide curve, conscious of nothing but the need to not see it. The ground levelled out. She raced over it and something speeding right behind her hissed.

From the corner of her eye, she saw it.

The little figure was coming with her into the village, almost matching her frantic pace.

Nicola ran faster. So did the terrible thing behind her. Nicola bolted over the green, shot through grass growing up to her knees and hit the road.

The hissing was still right behind her.

There was no more weeping. No energy for it. She ran in the centre of the road, winter sunlight running with her and the thing at her back. Part of her begged it to leave her alone; the rest of her was concerned only with getting into the village before it could.

She rounded a curve and raced towards a level crossing, sending a prayer of thanks that the barriers were up. On the other side of the crossing, the road sloped towards the main part of the village and nothing moved out there but the few leaves on the trees.

Already close to exhaustion, Nicola ran on and drew closer to the crossing. Soundlessly, the lights flashed. Her mouth dropped open but she didn't stop.

Impossibly, the barriers were coming down.

A mental shriek exploded inside her and she refused to voice it. She increased her speed and raced towards the descending barriers and the train tracks. Behind, the little figure kept up with her, always slightly out of sight.

You won't beat me, Nicola thought and flew towards the barriers, the silent flashing lights, the tracks lined with overgrown weeds beyond. With just a few feet to spare, she threw herself down and rolled under the barrier. Gravel stripped skin from her forearms and the pain sang. Ignoring it, Nicola kept moving, hit train tracks and stood.

The barrier on the other side was closing in on the ground. Nicola shot towards it, ducked and the bottom of it brushed her back. A second later, there was a solid thud as it locked into place. She was already running and looking back from the corner of her eye to see if the little figure was with her.

Nicola voiced a wounded groan of shock.

The barriers at the tracks were up. Just as they'd doubtless been for weeks.

I saw it. I fucking saw it.

Nicola ran on, aware in a loose way that she was close to coming undone. She had no more to give. Even now, so close to the village, she was slowing down, too tired to keep up her desperate pace.

Fingers hot like smoke brushed her hair and she ran, eyes unable to blink.

It was still with her, still coming into the village.

Nicola staggered down the sloping road and entered Denshaw.

Chapter Sixty-Two

C ate stood motionless at the top of the sloping stairs, staring down.

Other than the pieces of rubble and bits of debris, the floor was unmarked. No fire damage. No remnants of the bodies.

"Hello?"

It was the second time she'd called the word in the last few minutes. The first, shouted in the corridor between wards behind her, had brought back nothing. As much as she'd wanted to get out without attracting any attention, something was wrong.

"Everyone's gone," she whispered and wanted to laugh. Unless she'd been stuck in her room for at least an hour, there hadn't been time to get everybody organised and out of the building. In any case, she would have heard them.

Sure about that? You were unconscious. Then you were making a lot of noise.

Cate banished the voice and its questions. She took a final look behind herself to the empty corridor and made her careful way down the sloping stairs. Doing so took longer than she'd expected due to her injured hands.

Much of the blood had stopped dripping but the agony had grown into a burning weight deep inside her skin. She pressed the hand wrapped in the sodden underwear beneath her armpit and lurched the last few steps to the ground.

There'd been no fire here. Nothing at all.

"Hello?" she whispered.

Light bloomed behind her in a silent explosion.

Cate whirled around. The barricade blocking the main entrance was gone. Whole windows had taken its place. Open-mouthed, she tried to make sense of what she was seeing. The entire front of the entrance was now glass. From left to right, four huge panes marched across while there were another six vertical windows. In the centre, wide glass doors let in the sunlight. It flashed over the design in the centre of the floor.

"This is not real."

She moved one step towards the doors, then froze. God knows what would happen if she touched them. She had to get out the same way she'd come in.

Cate turned back to the foyer with the lifts and jogged to it, then the long corridor. She had to run to the storage cupboard, out through the secret opening, then away from this insane place. Wherever she ended up had to be better than here.

Cate crossed a short way through the corridor and then someone spoke behind her.

"Cate?"

She spun around, fists up, knees bent.

Skinny had come for her. He'd come to kill her because, because, because—

Nobody there.

You're hearing things. Just get out.

Yes, she was hearing things. A man's voice saying her name as a question, as a word full of longing, and her messed up head deciding it was the man from outside, a man she didn't know.

"Get the fuck out of here," she whispered at herself. Instead of running to the cupboard, she moved hesitantly the other way. Within a few steps, she realised she was heading towards the lift shaft.

The lift shaft and Theatre Five.

Steve had told her about it during the walk around on her first day. The TOP Theatre, he'd said, and she'd tried to guess what TOP stood for. He'd told her and his words echoed.

Termination of pregnancy.

Fear told her to run away. Anger overrode it. Someone had spoken to her. Someone had screamed inside the shaft and she was not crazy.

Time to see. Time to end this.

Cate moved closer towards the shaft. As she passed the second opening to the main foyer and the wide pool of sunshine falling through the windows, a noise bellowed from outside.

The noise of a bus starting up.

Chapter Sixty-Three

B odies littered the road. Nicola kept her speed up, desperately attempting to pay the corpses no mind. She altered her course slightly, veered past three rotting bodies and jumped over a fallen bike. Her landing was heavy and the last of her burning breath exploded out of her lungs. Gasping, she ran to the side of a building and used its long length as support for her to stumble forward. The ground dipped; she stumbled again and reached blindly. She found an open window and she pulled herself up and forward.

A pub. She was alongside the pub. She was alongside her father-in-law's local and the road was full of dead people.

Nicola ran through them. No choice. She skidded on loose clothing and reached the opposite pavement. The hissing behind, absent for the last few moments, returned.

Inside, she raged at the thing coming with her and it did no good. Still with her. Always with her.

She cut through a thin path between houses, a high brick wall on one side and a smashed fence on the other. Objects hit her peripheral vision: overturned garden furniture, a man's bike, a shed door wide open, and she was past the wall and fence and out on to Parson's Lane. Out on to the unmarked houses and the few cars still parked on their drives, windows gleaming.

The lane was unlike all the other places. It wasn't destroyed. And her family were here.

She.

Had.

Made.

It.

Nicola drew a breath and howled Julia's name. It tore in her throat and she didn't care. She howled it again, only slightly aware she was no longer running but moving no faster than a crawl up to the pavement, staggering over the wide curve of someone's lawn and flowerbed and stumbling through the damp hedge to the driveway of number nineteen Parson's Lane.

Another noise whispered from behind. Not a hiss this time. A whisper of her name.

No longer running, no longer with any need to run, Nicola walked towards the door, lifting a hand to push it open, eyes widening to see as much as possible in the poor light of the hallway, the stairs, and nostrils attempting to close when the smell from upstairs registered.

Chapter Sixty-Four

Cate mounted the rubble filling the width of the corridor and staggered up to the top, bending at the waist to make it over to the other side. The loose brick and stone below her shifted with each step but held for the most part. Rational thought spoke to her with every step, ordering her to turn around and raise the alarm before the bus crashed through the entrance. She ignored it and did so easily. This was her answer. It was all around her in the quiet debris and the cracks lining the walls and in the wrecked lift doors.

She stood before them, not daring to move closer. Steve had told her the truth. The lift had dropped from at least two or three floors above and crashed down here. The doors bulged out in irregular peaks as if someone inside had smashed giant fists against the door.

"Hello?"

There'd been no more whispers of her name and nothing replied to her word.

You're in there, aren't you? I heard you screaming and you were screaming to me. *Who are you?*

Inside the lift, a mechanical voice spoke, the sound muffled by the doors, corrupted by the damaged circuits.

"Ground. . .floor. Theatre. . .Five. . .Exit."

The lift doors opened as smoothly as they would have once upon a time when everything was as it should be.

The smells. They were first.

Good, clean scents. Shampoo. It coated her nostrils, all the aromas of bath time, all the laughter and the splashing. Then meat. Cooking meat. Burgers and sausages cooking on a barbecue. Juices from the meat spitting into the flames. Crisp tang of salad in a bowl. A splash and a hiss as Diet Coke was poured into a plastic cup, then a clink as a bottle opener met a bottle of lager, and the distinct scent of the lager reached her.

Shampoo in bath time.

A garden alive with the aroma of a barbecue and the freshly cut grass cooking in the heat.

All those scents falling out of the lift.

And more.

A voice. A child saying a lone word that she couldn't hear. Couldn't hear at all.

Then the last.

A hand grasping hers. A small hand, the flesh warm.

Cate opened her mouth and said silent words. Her lips and tongue worked. She was mute.

The scents eased away, replaced the familiar smells of the building. The land left her and any words she could say were as lost as the single word given to her from the lift.

Cate backed up a step and the figure emerged from the shaft, stumbling out, hands reaching and gripping nothing.

A woman. A woman groaning her pain, her sickness. She'd brought up blood; the red stained her chin and neck. The figure shuffled further out, still groaning, struggling to lift their head, to pull the hair away from their face. And Cate knew. She was looking at someone lost in the far stages of the Manc. She was looking at herself.

The figure managed to raise their head. They shrieked a name and blew apart into nothing.

"I didn't see that," Cate said to the air. "I didn't."

In complete silence, figures emerged from the shaft. Horrendous injures cut through their flesh, exposing bone and torn sinew of shredded flesh. Men, women, children shuffled further out from the shaft, drawing closer to her, still making no sound. Blood ran from dozens of wounds, from the stumps where arms had been severed. Within seconds, the floor was a coated mess of red and feet tracking through it. A man drew a few steps ahead of the others. Half a steering wheel protruded from a massive wound in his chest like a bizarre growth. One of his eyes had been replaced by a shard of glass. Windscreen glass, Cate knew. She was looking at the victims of a terrible car accident. God knows how many vehicles had collided to kill this many people.

Wind gusted from the shaft, bringing the scents of a freezing day, of open fields and bare trees. Winter had broken in to the hospital, winter from miles distant. And with it, a thought spoke.

Now I know where the bodies went.

Cate doubled over, vomiting before she'd completed the movement. It pattered to the floor. She spat, trying to groan. More vomit fell. She spat again and again, able to think of nothing but the sensation.

371

Any wind there might have been faded to leave the ground floor still and empty.

There were no bodies around her, no victims of any accident.

Walking as if on stilts, Cate made her way over the rubble to the junction and stared down its short length. On one side, a smashed window formed a clear opening into the building. She could walk to the car park at the side of A&E in seconds.

Cate crunched over pieces of glass and rubble towards the remains of the window. Polar air and sunshine coated her and she hugged herself. Nothing about this made any sense. The hospital wasn't impenetrable at all. Even if the people outside hadn't known about this hole, it wouldn't have taken them long to find it.

Cate moved closer to the hole, step by step bringing her to the car park and the dead town. Something screamed at her from faraway, screamed her name over and over, demanding she stop, demanding she open her eyes and see.

The theatre doors opened. Nothing held them in place and still, they stayed open.

Two figures stood in the doorway, facing her.

Skinny stood beside a shifting ball of smoke, glaring at her. She could do nothing as his mouth opened in a smile, no warmth in it at all. His teeth were razor sharp fangs, shining and polished.

Cate.

The word dropped from the ceiling, rose from the floor and shoved at her from both sides. The skin and flesh of Skinny's face split as he'd been unzipped. It fell in to halves, exposing the muscle and sinew below, dropping further to take off his neck, his chest and arms. Cate could make no sound. All the breath in the world had left her. Skinny's flesh continued to peel away, sliding off him like a peeling banana. It dropped below his waist, reached his knees and fell to the ground with a soft thud. Exposed, he was a raw piece of meat, tendons and cords of muscles lining his form. And beside him, the buzzing smoke-form shifted, two slits opening in it that might have been eyes. Seeing her.

Light pulsed over both figures.

Complete silence filled Cate's ears and her head. She was at the far end of the universe, lost beyond everything and all she had was the image of the man and the girl facing her. The man, now not skinny at all, but as big as he'd always been; flesh and blood and a body she knew as well as her own. The girl named a moment before by the thing from the lift.

Words formed and they meant nothing. The man opened his mouth and whispered her name and that meant something. That meant—

Cate finally managed to scream and landed back in herself.

Have to warn them.

Yes. That's what she had to do. Warn the others in the hospital. The bus revved its engine, throwing the sound into the day as the people outside prepared to smash down the barrier at the front of the building and kill them all.

Cate ran from the exit and the theatre, bellowing Wallace's name. At the same time, two other names echoed around inside her, coming closer and closer the faster she ran.

Chapter Sixty-Five

Nicola stood in the bedroom door exactly as she had in her in-laws' house, one hand resting on the frame, the other a twisting animal by her side.

"Julia?"

She heard the word and knew she hadn't spoken it. Not possible for such a sound to come out of her mouth. Had to be someone else here.

Her hand twisted and rolled and danced.

Nicola sank to her knees and shuffled forward across the dirty carpet. Its stink and the stink emanating from her body and clothes belonged to someone else now. All she had was the whisper of her tired knees on the carpet and extending her dancing hand for the shapes on the mattress.

"Julia."

The smallest shape turned over and opened its eyes. Two white holes for eyes glared at her.

Nicola blinked and the shapes on the mattress were as they'd been for the last few minutes or hours or however long she'd been with them. Both motionless. One splashed with blood.

An itch crawled over the top of her head. It grew to form a distinct line from her forehead, across the middle of her skull and down towards her spine. Wasn't uncomfortable. Almost pleasant.

"Scott. You were. . ."

She trailed off, unsure what Scott had been or what she wanted to say. Scott was supposed to do something. She knew that. The image floated just out of reach.

He was supposed.

To.

Keep.

Supposed to keep her.

Safe.

Keep Julia safe.

Yes.

"You were supposed to keep her safe." Grief and a terrible rage flew out of her with the words. Nicola bent double, hugging herself and trying to breathe through her tears. She threw her head back, screaming silently, her vision lost behind her sobs and the itch in her head trickling downwards to cross her face and extending its reach all the way down her spine. She let it prick at her. If all it would take to scratch the itch was simply moving a hand, she'd just stay still and the itch would spread through her, widening into an opening.

Even in death, the buboes coating her husband's throat and face remained. While they'd faded, they were still all too clear. Big bubbles full of blood and pus. Big bubbles growing on his neck, eager to cut off his breathing and leave him choking. Her eyes danced to take in the rest of the small room. Like the downstairs, the furniture had been smashed into pieces; it littered the carpet, and in the spaces where the carpet actually showed, splashes of blood stood out. Dark red on white.

Nicola pushed herself to the bed, pulled the covers back from her daughter's waist and stared at her lower half.

Her eye twitched. She felt it just like she felt the constant wind sliding in through the open window. Twitch. Twitch. Twitch. In time with her heartbeat. In time with Julia's heartbeat, she'd often thought but never said. Not even to Scott.

Her mouth formed her daughter's name but no sound emerged. She was mute. Mute at the sight of the blood and the unmarked skin around Julia's throat. No Manc for her little girl. No plague. Just.

Just.

People.

Nicola's hands moved without her telling them to do a thing. Scott's note, in front of her again and the scribbled words shaking between her fingers.

Someone. Not something.

She'd misread. No little figure here to torment her family. Just people. Just bad people who'd had no need to kill Scott. He had the Manc. He was already dead. Julia. She didn't have it. And maybe the worst thing in the world was that it would have been better for Julia if she'd had the Manc.

Nicola rose. Black spots swam in front of her. She waited until they faded, bent and gripped Julia's body. Her flesh was much too hard, much too cold. A far-off voice told Julia it would be okay, she just needed to be cleaned, then she could sleep.

Nicola held her daughter tightly against herself. She rocked back and forth. She smoothed Julia's matted hair. The same far off voice told Julia it was bath time.

Nicola carried Julia from the bedroom across the hall to the bathroom. In the doorway, she stood, staring at the bath, trying to think. A creaking murmur inside her head spoke up.

No water.

Tightening her hold on Julia, Nicola picked up a bar of soap, pocketed it and gripped the bottle of shampoo.

Down the stairs. Through the house. To the kitchen. To the stink in the dead fridge and the small bottle of water on the shelf.

Nicola carried Julia outside and eased her down to the patio. The sun had broken free from the low clouds while she'd been in the house. While it held no warmth, it managed to brighten the day. Shadows from the two trees at the end of the garden and from the hedges bordering the next garden coated the ground. Overhead, birds flew. And all around, there was a steady throb of silence.

"Going to wash you now, Jules, okay?"

Her skin burned; muscles in her legs and back trembled, threatening to spill her to the ground. Ignoring all of it, Nicola stripped Julia, poured water on to her hands and rubbed her fingers deep into the bar of soap. As gently as she could, she washed the blood from Julia's body, rubbing it out to leave the skin white and unmarked. The terrible bite of the air sank teeth into her flesh; she kept washing and rubbing, splashing more liquid on to Julia's body. Rivulets of water trickled from the child's chest and stomach. Nicola dropped the snow, wet her hands and squeezed a few drops of shampoo into Julia's hair.

"Almost done," she whispered and washed her daughter's hair. She smelled the shampoo; she inhaled it as deeply as she could and she told herself to never let go of the clean, comforting smell.

With the last of the water, she rinsed Julia's hair, picked her up and cradled her.

"Time for bed."

Nicola returned to the house and stairs. Growing shadows walked with her.

Up. The hall. The bedroom. Through the door to the quiet and peace of the bed ready for her baby, her sweet Jules.

Nicola eased Julia down to the bed, kissed the child's lips and stood.

Something whispered at her back.

It had joined her in the bedroom and why shouldn't it? It had been with her all the way here. It had killed for her. It had stalked her across the country and now here it was at the end of her journey.

Here in the dead room.

Nicola wiped her eyes and kept her focus on the bodies of her husband and daughter.

"One chance," she whispered. "Leave now or I will kill you."

It whispered and the sound might have been a word. Might have been her name.

Nicola touched her nose. The itch pulsed and again, the sensation was pleasant. Felt like—

I'm breaking. I'm coming apart and I like it.

Her throbbing feet whispering over the carpet as she moved, Nicola began to turn around.

Chapter Sixty-Six

C ate sprinted along the corridor, trying to call for the others. She didn't have the breath so she ran, praying they would hear her. At the doors that opened to the main entrance, she skidded to a stop and ran through them into darkness.

Night had replaced the sunlight. It pressed in on the windows and doors of the entrance, and moonlight illuminated the road and footpath which led to the car park and then to Thorpe Road.

Banishing her confusion, Cate ran past the quiet lifts and clambered up the slope of the stairs, panting and trying to call for Wallace. She slipped halfway up, landed on her hands and slid down. Swearing, Cate staggered back and caught sight of her fingers in the poor light. Dirt coated the digits but at least she hadn't injured them in the fall.

She lurched up the last section of the stairs, fell flat on the ground and crawled forward to the corridor doors. Upright, she banged them open and gazed up and down the shadows between the wards. A few of the office doors were open. They let in some of the moonlight but not much. Both sets of doors to the wards were closed. Through the frosted glass, nobody was visible.

Where the hell is everyone?

Limping, close to collapse, Cate headed towards 2X. She passed the second set of doors to the landing and heard the sound she'd been dreading: the bus. She faced the wide windows overlooking the front of the grounds. Two headlights bloomed into life on the other side of the car park, nailing her.

They were coming and they were coming *now.*

"No," she whispered and ran for the ward doors.

The ward doors easing open to reveal the man and the girl.

The man saying a word.

Nicola.

Cate howled. Her head was coming apart. She was a breaking thing, a splitting hole and all the light of a summer day broke out of her to blind her.

And her feet and legs carried her forward, her arms coming up and all the pain in the world sitting on her chest, all the pain in the world for her.

Cate ran to them. She ran to her husband and her daughter as the headlights broke through the windows and the bus was a roar speeding across the car park.

It crashed through the glass of the main entrance, filling the building with shattering thunder. She fell against the warmth of her family, fell deep into it and welcomed what it meant.

Lost at the end of everything.

The cylinders in the bus exploded. Pressure pummelled into her; the deafening roar of fire consuming brick, stone and her all at once and she fell, dropping through the raining rubble of the dead hospital, dropping away from her family and the name on her husband's lips.

Nicola.

Chapter Sixty-Seven

With the sunshine at her back, Nicola completed her turn and stood motionless. Fear had been cut out of her. All she had left was her sight and the alternating warmth of the sunlight and the breeze blowing through the window.

Between her and the bedroom door, the little figure floated a foot off the carpet. Its form shimmered like hot air. Its face, such as it was, wavered and two holes that could have been eyes found hers.

"Last chance." Nicola's voice was a weak croak and she didn't care. "Leave me alone or I'll kill you."

The figure shook. It coalesced into a more defined shape; the face fell out of the dancing smoke; the eyes grew wider. The mouth opened.

It shrieked. The terrible sound exploded through the bedroom, sent pieces of window scattering down to the front garden and split chunks out of the wall. Nicola's eyes had closed the second the thing in front of her began its noise; she rocked back and forth, refusing to fall before it. The barrage of horror and pain and rage pummelled at her. She took it all; she welcomed the ever-growing itch in her head.

She opened.

The shriek cut off. She opened her eyes and the form before her was Julia. Whole. Unmarked. Alive.

Julia.

"Why?" Nicola managed to speak the lone word although it took all of her strength. Further speech out of the question, she could only think.

Why? Why hurt me? I'm sorry, baby. I'm so sorry. I should have been here. I should have got to you sooner. I should have. . .

The thought decayed into so much dirt, then blew away. She'd failed her child and the punishment had been with her every step of the way from Stamford. In every lonely minute, every gust of the ever-present wind and almost every person she'd met being a threat. Fate or luck hadn't directed her to anyone free to help without being torn apart. Instead, the punishment for failing Julia and letting her die at the hands of monsters in the shape of men had sent Nicola towards the same sort of men again and again.

Nicola walked forward into her daughter. Smoke consumed her. She swallowed it deep down; she bathed in her daughter's scent and in the good weight of her skin and body and bones.

And her blood.

The blood on Julia's hands, etched deep into the tiny grooves in her fingertips. All the blood of all the people Nicola had met on her way here. Blood that had to be spilled from the moment she left Stamford, the moment she'd passed the body of the child on the road, the moment she'd lost her daughter.

The itch in her head was an opening. *She* was opening.

Nicola split. It rent her in two. And she welcomed it.

Darkness flowed through her. She welcomed that, too.

Black above and below. A tremendous rushing in her ears as if she stood below a waterfall. A howling gale streaming into her from across vast, empty plains of ice and barren land.

She welcomed it all. She inhaled the ice and the waterfall and it tore her in half.

Ahead, the front door. She'd descended without knowing anything and that was perfectly fine. She left the house, crossed the unkempt garden and an idea gleamed. It sparked.

She walked around the side of the house to the back garden and kicked at the shed door until the wood snapped and her foot was a hot ball. Neither mattered.

Inside the shed. Top shelf.

She walked back to the house, can of petrol swinging by her side.

To the stairs.

Petrol thrown over the carpet. The stink of it soaking into the carpet and the wall beside the stairs. A trail leading to the living room and the last of the liquid splashing into the sofa.

Outside, again. She stood before the house, head cocked and mouth trying to work.

She was unable to make sounds. Sounds belonged to someone else. They belonged to Nicola. She was—

not Nicola, not now.

There was no Nicola left. She could be anyone else. She could be.

They're all gone and I'm going with them. Going away now. Going all the way.

Flames appeared in the living room window. Thick, rolling smoke immediately followed. The little voice far below asking what had lit the petrol was no bother.

Questions. Always questions. They should leave her alone.

The smoke pressed itself against the window and blew out of the open door. Wind caught it, parted it and exposed of the stairs. They were alight. Although the petrol only reached halfway up, the flames would grow. They'd make their way upstairs into the bedroom and the bodies.

She turned away. Heat pressed against her back.

She walked, head still cocked and mouth still attempting to work. At the pavement, she looked back once. A wavering line of smoke blew out of the front door and rose with the wind.

Going away now.

She didn't wait to see where the wind took the smoke.

Chapter Sixty-Eight

She landed on rubble and knew nothing but the thunder of the fire on all sides. The ground shifted; she rolled over, dropped down a few feet and stood.

Nothing hurt. Nothing was on fire. She'd dropped through flames and falling stone to land on unmarked floor.

She'd landed in the middle of the main foyer, facing the steps which sloped upwards to the first floor. Hands took hers on either side. She closed her eyes and her daughter's voice floated up from the ground.

Mummy? Are you here, Mummy?

"I'm here." She was smiling even as she wept. In her other hand, Scott held her with his warmth and his strength. He held her in love as he always had.

Are you coming with us, Mummy?

Agony tore through her. To have them so close. To have them back. To know she couldn't go with them.

Light blazed over her eyelids, then winked out. She opened her eyes and gazed at the silent hospital. Behind her, sunshine broke through the gaps in the barricade and shone on the dirty floor and chunks of rubble all around her.

Her hands were empty. Wind traced its way over her palms. Her head was empty and that was fine. Gradually, light trickled into it and a name flowed in with the light. Her name.

"I'm sorry," she said and didn't know to whom she was apologising. Nobody around her. Nobody close. "I'm so sorry I wasn't there with you. I. . ."

Her words and apology dried up into silence. She licked her lips, tasted sweat and dirt and lifted her hands to her face.

Streaks of mud coated them. She'd crawled through gardens and fields and woods to get here. To get somewhere safe. Somewhere she could use as shelter. Somewhere she could find people and have friends. Somewhere people were as much flesh and blood as the life she'd left behind.

Had to get some sleep. Had to rest.

She staggered to the slope of rubble, dug her fingers deep into the loose stones and pulled herself upwards. Her movement was labourious; sweat blinded her and she shook her head to dislodge it. Muscles aching, body full of tight, burning pains, she lay sprawled on the mess and panted for breath.

Almost there. Almost in a safe place away from the darkness below.

Groaning, she pushed herself forward further, reached blindly for something to grip.

Two hands closed over hers.

Blindly, she stared upwards into gloom. Faces formed behind the shadows, moved closer to her and the hands pulled. She rose into light, swayed and someone slid a palm around her back to support her.

"Are you all right?"

She tried to find her voice, tried to know what words were let alone what words she should say.

Others joined the person who held her upright. Faces swam in and out of focus. Concern reached her and she seized on it. Safety here. Comfort. Shelter. She had to keep hold of it. Had to.

Live here. I have to live here.

"What's your name?"

A woman strode through the others. A large woman, control and order radiating out of her. She extended a hand. Her fingers and grip were solid. Meaty. The man beside her, the one who held her, shifted to the side and sunshine exposed his face, revealing him to be younger than she expected.

"I'm Steve," he said. "Are you okay?"

Still, she was unable to speak. Words were lost below where there'd been fire and pain and bitterly cold wind blowing in through. . .

Through what? She didn't know. Nor did she know what the image of the man and the girl meant to her, the man's mouth forming a word.

"What's your name, my love?" the woman said. "I'm Sister Wallace. Well, just Wallace these days."

Name. *Her* name.

She knew it. She owned it. She spoke it.

"Julia. It's Julia."

Wallace and Steve and all the people with their friendly faces and open arms walked her from the stairs to the corridor and the sunshine falling through the open windows.

They held her and they told her she was safe and she welcomed the words as if they were old friends.

Epilogue

F ood wrappers and cans roll against the kerb of Thorpe Road, the cans clattering when they strike each other. Wind pushes them along; plays with them before blowing away to the middle of the road, then up and out to the city.

Stillness.

Dalry sleeps.

On the front garden of an abandoned house, a little figure with unblinking slits for eyes gazes over the road to the car park and the derelict building beyond the car park. It sees through the walls to the woman walking along the second-floor corridor. She is talking. She has found shelter. She is not alone and that is what matters for her.

Wind blows through the shape with the eyes. Dusk falls down around it, coming to coat the still road and the silent houses and the hospital. Shadows grow together and the wind hums through the bare tree branches. The shape watches the woman walk in the hospital. She enters one of the wards, talking and happy now she has good people around her, now she has shelter from what is left of the world outside. The little figure sees the woman pushing open damaged doors as she speaks to shapes with no more substance than smoke, as she's led through the ruined hospital which will now be her home.

Then the gathering dusk carries the little figure as if it is smoke blowing over the ground.

Carries it towards the hospital.

And towards its mother.

About Your Author

Luke Walker has been writing dark fiction for most of his life after getting hold of paperbacks belonging to his dad and brother and reading Poe, King, Herbert and Lovecraft when he was far too young. His books include the horrors The Unredeemed, Hometown and The Mirror Of The Nameless as well as the dark fantasy Dead Sun. Several of his short stories have been published online and in magazines and books.

When not writing, he can found watching bad films or reading good books. He has novels and short stories to be published soon and is currently working on new fiction.

Luke welcomes comments at his blog which can be read at www.lukewalkerwriter.com and his Twitter page is @lukewalkerbooks. Sign up to his newsletter at www.tinyletter.com/LukeWalkerWriter.

He is forty-one and lives in England with his wife.

Other HellBound Books Titles
Available at: www.hellboundbookspublishing.com

The Unredeemed

Four hundred years ago, Benjamin Harwood butchered whoever he saw fit to kill, knowing that sacrificing his murder victims to a demon would keep him safe from eternal punishment.

But now, their agreement has been torn in half and the demon is coming for Harwood's soul, coming to set him to burn.

Preparing for war, Harwood gathers the worst of the worst, the monsters and murderers he calls friends.

With this group of damned killers, Harwood must return to the crimes of his past and seek help from his most recent prey: a teenage girl whose family he destroyed, a girl with more reason to loathe him than anyone in his life or death.

Only then he can try for a redemption that may be impossible or face a universe of suffering.

But Harwood doesn't know there is a hole in the floor of the world. And something much worse than the dead is down there…

Ascent

When terrorists target an American air force base with a nuclear bomb, Kelly Wells races to find her sister in a nearby office block, desperate for them to be together in their final moments.

At the same time, a handful of others fight their way through a panicked city to reach the building-frantic to make it to loved ones before the device ignites less than fifty miles away. In the frozen instant of the detonation, Kelly, her sister and three strangers are locked in that moment and trapped in the offices.

But they are not alone. An ancient god from the deepest pits in the earth has woken and knows their most private secrets and guilt.

Now, horror takes the form of their darkest dreams to draw sustenance from their terror, and the beast stalking them will dine well.

Because everybody is afraid of something.

Them

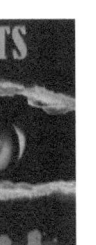

Ray Sanders returns home from Florida to bury his mother.

Soon, the supernatural evidence behind his mother's demise begins to surface in the form of dreams and mysterious happenings.

During all of the madness, Sanders must face his destiny and vanquish the generations-old evil that has plagued his family since the 1800's...

In 1854, Louis Sanders, with the help of Elias Atkins, dug a well to provide water to the family farm. What they did not anticipate was the water to be infested with Odomulites - ancient sins. These malevolent beings - were trapped in our world on their way to the spirit world - formed a pact of protection with both Sanders and Atkins; the families would serve as guardians of the Odomulite nests and in return, a blind eye would be cast when the Odomulites took host bodies to inhabit and feed upon. It was this pact, which in 2016 would propel Sanders and Julie Fontaine - a young woman with a special connection to the Spirit World - into the heart of the last active nest to rid the town of its insidious Odomulite population.

Southern House

"Move over Slenderman, there's a whole new reason to be afraid of the dark!"

There are some places that lie where the barrier between worlds is thin and growing thinner. These corridors are as old as the Earth itself, hidden in dark and forgotten places, waiting to be found. There is a being who stalks these places and travels between those worlds. He was given the name Mr. Shift by generations of children and madmen. Just as Hickory Grimble hits rock bottom, he inherits his grandparents' farm and believes his luck is changing. He soon finds he inherited more than money and land. Haunted by his own inner demons, now he has new problems. He begins to see strange creatures on the dark, sprawling acreage, animals that have no business living in middle Tennessee. He also discovers a decrepit, abandoned house in the forest that never seems to be in the same place twice. Balanced on a razor's edge between, addiction and fate, Hick is now face to face with an ancient evil that has returned once more to claim more of the town's children.

Worship Me

Something is listening to the prayers of St. Paul's United Church, but it's not the god they asked for; it's something much, much older.

A quiet Sunday service turns into a living hell when this ancient entity descends upon the house of worship and claims the congregation for its own. The terrified churchgoers must now prove their loyalty to their new god by giving it one of their children or in two days time it will return and destroy them all.

As fear rips the congregation apart, it becomes clear that if they're to survive this untold horror, the faithful must become the faithless and enter into a battle against God itself.

But as time runs out, they discover that true monsters come not from heaven or hell...
...they come from within.

Schlock! Horror!

An anthology of short stories based upon/inspired by and in loving homage to all of those great gorefest movies and books of the 1980's - that golden age when horror well and truly came kicking, screaming and spraying blood, gore & body parts out from the shadows...

It was the decade that brought us everything in the cinema and on VHS from the Italian 'nasties' to *Elm Street, The Lost Boys, Hellraiser, The Thing, Day of the Dead, Reanimator, Return of the Living Dead, My Bloody Valentine, Henry: Portrait of a Serial Killer, Cannibal Holocaust*....and superlative directors such as David Cronenburg, John Waters, Roger Corman and - of course - Clive Barker.

All of this was, naturally, reflected in the books we devoured - Guy N Smith, Clive Barker's *Books of Blood*, James Herbert, Jack Ketchum, Gary Brandner and Richard Laymon, to name but a mere handful.

This 80's themed/inspired tales of terror is compiled by one Mr. **Bret McCormick**, himself a writer, producer and director of many a schlock classic, including *Bio-Tech Warrior, Time Tracers, The Abomination, Ozone: The Attack of the Redneck Mutants* and the inimitable *Repligator*.

Luke Walker

**A HellBound Books LLC
Publication**

http://www.hellboundbookspublishing.com

Printed in the United States of America